JANE

An Intimate Biography
of Jane Fonda

JANE

AN INTIMATE BIOGRAPHY OF JANE FONDA

by THOMAS KIERNAN

G. P. PUTNAM'S SONS, New York

795

SBN: 399-11207-3
Library of Congress Catalog Card Number: 73-78589

For A. C. P.
   . . . *a friend*

Contents

Foreword

I KNEW Jane Fonda briefly about fourteen years ago when she was first studying to be an actress in the New York classes of Lee Strasberg. Since that time I have seen her infrequently but have managed to keep track of her career and personal fortunes through mutual acquaintances. The last time I saw her was one late night in the fall of 1970, when I unexpectedly ran into her in a New York restaurant. We had a brief reunion and an interesting chat about her intensifying social and political activism.

Shortly afterward Jane was arrested in Cleveland for allegedly smuggling drugs into the United States and assaulting two officials who detained her at the Cleveland airport. You might recall the story. It made headlines throughout the country for a week or so, then disappeared from the front pages and in no time at all was forgotten. I encountered the story again last year while doing research for a book I intended to write on the history of the American antiwar movement. When I learned of the outcome of her arrest, I thought it might make interesting reading—especially in view of the fact that almost everyone I knew blithely assumed, because of the way the incident was handled by the press, that Jane must have been guilty of the charges.

What started, then, as a desire to make the story of Jane Fonda's Cleveland adventure part of my history of the antiwar movement has evolved into the present book. At the time the suggestion was made to me that I endeavor to persuade Jane to collaborate in a separate book on her life. I put the question to her by telegram in May and June, 1972. I received no direct answer, but word eventually drifted back through the grapevine of mutual friends that she would not be interested in collaborating. It was then suggested that I write a straight biography of Jane, without her collaboration or authorization. During the fall of 1972 I tried on several occasions—in vain—to reach her by telephone and by mail with a view, still, to enlisting at least her cooperation, if not collaboration. I talked to her acting agent, her press agent, her secretary, several of her close friends—all to no avail. Indeed, in the course of these conversations I learned that Jane would look unkindly on a book about herself. I also learned that she had by then contracted with a large New York publisher to produce an autobiography. Since there was still interest on the part of other publishers in an unauthorized biography, I agreed to proceed with this volume.

Strange things happen when you write a book about a living person, especially when that person possesses a considerable degree of celebrity. It was not long before I began to receive letters from lawyers representing Jane; they claimed all sorts of subterfuge and bad intentions on my part and threatened lawsuits. Several people who had agreed to talk to me about their participation in various phases of Jane's life suddenly grew surly and uncommunicative. Others demanded extravagant sums of money in exchange for juicy tidbits of information. But that was just the beginning.

I hadn't even started the manuscript before I was the recipient of a series of curious phone calls—some from two different individuals who claimed to represent an agency of the government, others from people who identified themselves as friends and protectors of Jane. (One caller said, "Never mind my name, just know that I'm a friend of Jane's." His subsequent calls, four of them in all, opened with "This is you-know-who. . . ." Of course, I knew-not-who, but I had a lot of fun guessing.) The irony of the phone calls amused me mainly because it seemed an appropriate metaphor of the larger ironies of Jane's life. And with both her friends and her enemies trying to dissuade me from writing about her, I began to feel like a shuttlecock in a badminton game.

Jane Fonda has become a household name—in more ways than anyone might have anticipated when she first burst upon the show-business and motion-picture scene back in the late fifties. As a result of her recent years of social and political activism, she has transformed herself from a mere film star into a national *cause célèbre.* Yet in spite of the emotions her statements and deeds have incited in the American soul, probably less is known about her—and about what motivates her—than about any other highly visible individual in our society who aspires to moral leadership in social and political matters.

A biography of Jane Fonda is not just the story of a movie star's life. It is the story of a life of our time. It reflects, I believe—on a more heightened and intense level than the life of an average thirty-five-year-old woman—all the confusions, uncertainties and rapidly changing attitudes and values that have bedeviled so many Americans during the past decade. As a life it is in many ways a clearly focusable microcosm of the polarization of the American spirit that has taken place in recent years.

Of more immediate interest, however, is the life of Jane Fonda the woman—the mercurial, enigmatic, chameleonlike, often contradictory, always impassioned and driven woman. Who is she? What is she really like? What has made her the way she is today—to some a heroic fighter for peace and justice, to others a naïve, irritating and intensely unwelcome fool? And where does she go from here?

A biographer would himself be a fool to suppose that he could provide complete answers to such questions. My intention in this book is not to provide answers but simply to try to shed as much light as possible on some of the factors that have contributed to the creation of Jane Fonda today. What emerges, I hope, is a portrait of a modern, intense and iconoclastic woman, larger than life and overflowing with a basic humaneness, compassion and decency that are possibly sometimes mischanneled in their expression—a brave, lonely, often compulsive human being with contradictory appetites and a singular purpose. The life of Jane Fonda is, after all, an intensely American life.

There are scores of people I should thank by name for their help in contributing to this portrait, but they know who they are. Since more than a few of them have, for one reason or another, requested anonymity, I shall forgo the usual acknowledgments. I have also decided to forgo the custom of larding the text with footnotes identifying and documenting my sources of quotation and other information. I have done this principally to keep the text free of typographical clutter, but also because I believe that although Jane Fonda's life is worthy of popular inspection, it has not yet reached the stature of footnote treatment. Suffice it to say that all the quotations I include, from Jane and others, have appeared elsewhere in other contexts or are verbatim extracts from taped interviews I have conducted with the individuals quoted. With regard to the straight-narrative aspects of the book, for these too I possess a plenitude of taped and documentary research material to support their accuracy.

T. K.

Sundown, New York

Prologue

IN the warm twilight of the evening of April 10, 1972, nearly a thousand notables of the motion-picture industry gathered in Los Angeles' Dorothy Chandler Music Center for the forty-fourth annual Academy Award ceremonies. The atmosphere of anticipation was thicker than usual for an Oscar night. Although the event had lost much of its glamor in recent years—for many it had become a tiresome ritual in self-congratulation—tonight's festivities had an extraordinary suspense.

Jane Fonda was one of the nominees for an Oscar as best actress of 1971 for her performance as the cynical call girl Bree Daniel in the film *Klute*. If Jane Fonda had been an ordinary movie star, the evening would have been nothing more than the highly emotional moment of truth all stars are said to at once pray for and dread. But Jane Fonda was no ordinary movie star. She was a maverick—in the eyes of millions of Americans a treasonous one at that. Over the period of two years she had become the outspoken representative of a political point of view and life-style that even in the traditionally liberal circles of Hollywood were hard to swallow.

Thanks to television, the Academy Awards are America's great annual collective going-to-church night. The event is our most convenient form of communal worship and our most direct link to the true heroes and heroines of our culture. We worship our movie stars because they are the surrogates of the dreams and aspirations we are too timid to reach for except in our fantasies. Their potential is the model for all of us, their decadence the logical extension, yet exact reverse, of the reality to which we are chained. Oscar night, like some daintily civilized revival meeting, liberates us. And when it finally bores us with its orchestrated banality, it helps us perceive the ironies and contradictions of the American dream.

If feelings about Jane Fonda ran high throughout the satin-and-sequined assemblage in Santa Monica, they were positively bouncing off the ionosphere of outrage across the country. Naturally, the question in everyone's mind was: Would she win? The more pressing question, though, was: Should she win? It was common knowledge within the film community that when Jane was nominated two years earlier for her performance in *They Shoot Horses, Don't They?* she was voted down because of her increasing political activism. In 1970 Jane Fonda had already begun to infuriate America with her incessant diatribes against this, that and the next thing; and two years later contempt for her had mushroomed.

Everything America held dear, she was in the process of throwing away. She had loudly and blatantly transformed herself from saccharine all-American sex-kitten movie star to militant raggedy-Ann anti-American shock troop of the radical movement. The public watched with the squeamish and untrusting fascination of schoolchildren observing a silkworm emerge from its cocoon. Some were convinced she was merely playing the comedy of disobedience—such a fashion among those who have everything and still want to be accepted by those who have nothing and a natural consequence of Jane's career-long rebelliousness. Others, more cynical, dismissed her increasing involvement in demonstrations— first for Indians, then for Black Panthers, then for Chicanos, then for GI's—as mere opportunism, gutsy but transparent publicity stunts. Still others, more cynical yet, attributed her self-proclaimed radicalization to darker motives, all verging on the psychoneurotic.

She was a drug freak, went one explanation—a theory that had been reinforced in the public mind when she had been arrested five months before at Cleveland and charged with smuggling drugs into the country from Canada.

Or her behavior was a Freudian acting-out of the inner rage that had been smoldering for years as the result of some unresolved father fixation.

Or it was due to pure and simple decadence—the result of her long liaison with a publicly hedonistic, amoral Frenchman.

Or it was her reaction to the decadence she had experienced and shared, which had climaxed in the brutal murder of her friend Sharon Tate by the Charles Manson slaughter squad.

Or it was her late-in-life realization that she had been an exploited woman and her guilt-adorned reaction to her complicity in that exploitation.

Theories abounded, but Jane Fonda was moving so fast they could not keep up with her. Only a few years before a harmless, unthreatening movie star, a caretaker of America's fantasies whose public pronouncements were as innocuous and transparent as the costumes she wore, she had grown almost overnight into a stiff, shrill, iron-hard presence. Wealth, privilege, humor, beauty, the traditional modest grace of womanhood—she had thrown all these away without the requisite request for permission. She had turned the American dream inside out.

America has always distrusted the self-appointed altruist. And in a choice between rage and admiration, life in the United States during the past decade had made the former easiest. By Oscar night, 1972, Jane Fonda had brought a nationwide hammer of rage down on herself. What was worse, she had swallowed America's contempt and defiantly spit it back in the face of its sponsors. Her voice, once fey and redolent of Park Avenue drawing rooms, had become a strident drone in the ears of an already high-strung, divided nation. Her glance, trained by hundreds of publicity photographers to be coy and fetching, was now a hot stare of dangerous challenge. Her manner, once vaguely aloof and self-consciously protective in the ages-old style of the narcissist, had grown uncompromisingly aggressive, grating the sensibilities of all who believe there is a time and place for everything.

A time and place for everything—it was precisely this notion that had the Academy Awards gathering, along with the millions who were expectantly tuning their television sets, taut with anticipation. For here was the second question in everyone's mind: If she did win the Oscar, would Jane Fonda turn her acceptance speech into another of her insolent political gestures?

Two months before she had won the Foreign Press' Golden Globe Award. To the Golden Globe dinner, another big event on the Hollywood award circuit, she sent a Vietnam veteran to accept her prize. He showed up wearing blue jeans, boots, and an oversized Army tunic bedecked with mock medals. Everyone there agreed that his acceptance speech on Jane's behalf cast a tasteless political pall over an otherwise pleasant evening. There was, after all, a time and place for everything! His speech was greeted by boos and hoots of derision.

At first, no one was even sure Jane would appear at the Academy Awards. When her nomination had been announced, she was quoted by a reporter as saying, "I don't care about the Oscar. I make movies to support the causes I believe in, not for any honors. I couldn't care less whether I win an Oscar or not."

But wait—there she was. A buzz of excitement spread through the auditorium as Jane made her way down the aisle. Dressed in a plain black-knit turtleneck sweater-and-pants outfit, devoid of jewelry and makeup, she looked fragile and nervous as she smiled wanly at the occasional sympathetic acquaintance who greeted her. Every eye in the house was on her as she took her seat next to Donald Sutherland, her co-star in *Klute* and her constant companion for the past two years. Photographers swarmed around her like bees.

It was as if the extravaganza had been timed to start with her arrival. No sooner was she seated than the houselights dimmed, the orchestra struck up the overture, and the show was under way. The intent furrow on Jane's brow as the auditorium darkened suggested to everyone that she was hastily running her acceptance speech over in her mind. And from the way she was dressed her intentions could only be political. Many were delighted by these deductions. They couldn't wait for Jane to win. They were all looking forward to watching her make a fool of herself.

We've seen it countless times—the celebrities at the podium reeling off the names of the nominees . . . the television cameras picking each actress out of the audience and framing her in a close-up of lip-biting anxiety . . . the envelope please . . . the deliberate fumbling with the flap . . . more quick shots of the nominees shrinking into their seats in terror . . . and the winner is . . . a disingenuous pause as the presenter coyly looks out at the audience . . . then the name . . . a sudden collective exhalation of breath . . . a shot of the winner in stunned disbelief . . . a thunderclap of cheers, shouts, applause . . . reaction shots of the losers gamely smiling, their hands fluttering reflexively into applause . . . the winner rushing, tripping, stumbling toward the stage . . . the tears . . . the speechlessness . . . then the soppy, rambling litany of thanks. . . .

When Jane Fonda's name was announced, an ever-so-brief silence fell over the auditorium. For a moment one was not quite sure what was going to happen. Then, before anyone realized it, Jane was halfway down the aisle. A loud sigh escaped from the throng, then trailed into uncertain applause. A few shouts of praise could be heard as Jane walked resolutely toward the stage, and an occasional boo as well. As she hit the steps the applause intensified, but it was still restrained, anticipatory. Jane strode to the podium, accepted the gold-plated statuette and calmly turned to the audience. Her cool, unadorned dignity stood out in striking contrast with the bejeweled opulence of the largely hostile crowd she faced.

She hesitated for a second, and in that moment her face reflected a troubled thought. Through the glare of the lights, with a professional's second nature, she picked out the tiny red spot of the television camera that was trained on her. It might have been as though she felt the invisible beam from the camera's lens boring into her with the insistence of a bad conscience. Her brow creased in the frown of someone caught in a dilemma of divided loyalties.

She knew the audience was waiting to pounce on her. She knew also that thousands of her radical friends and comrades all over the country expected her to exploit this rare opportunity for national coverage for all it was worth; if she failed to, she would lose much of her hard-won credibility among them. She didn't need much prodding—her passions were afire with the evils she perceived in America, even tonight.

Yet she had made a promise to her father only a few hours before, and she knew he was watching her. She looked down at the Oscar in her hands, testing its weight, looking highly charged but strangely sad. She raised her head again. Contempt, defiance, pride—they all seemed to flow from her like energy from a cyclotron. When she spoke, her voice thrummed with barely controlled emotion.

"There's a lot I could say tonight," she said, bending slightly to catch the microphone. "But this isn't the time or the place." She held the audience in her gaze a moment longer, then spoke again. "So I'll just say—thank you."

There was a short, dumbfounded silence as she quickly walked offstage and disappeared into the wings. The audience sagged back into their seats in a combination of wonder, disappointment and relief as the orchestra hesitantly drifted into music.

The meaning behind Jane's brief, bland utterance was clear. She had seized the drama and tension of the moment and turned them around on the audience, indeed, on the country. It was an exquisitely underplayed performance straight out of her celebrated father's book. Its effect was infinitely more memorable than the five-minute political peroration she had been tempted to give. For perhaps the first time in her public life Jane had acknowledged her father's philosophy—less is more, in life as well as art.

For Jane, the moment was a quintessential turning point in a life full of turning points. For Hollywood and for the country at large, it represented another chapter in the continuing and rapidly changing mystery of Jane Fonda.

Part I

Lady Jane/1937–1958

1. The Fonda-Seymour Inheritance

Acting is putting on a mask. The worst torture that can happen to me is not having a mask to get in back of.

—Henry Fonda

THE name Fonda is Italian in origin. The Marchese de Fonda was the head of a branch of a noble family that lived in the Apennine Valley near Genoa during the middle Ages. A political activist and family maverick, the Marchese is said to have fought against the church for the establishment of a republic in northern Italy. He lost and was forced to flee to Holland in the late 1300's. The exiled Fondas became established in Holland over the next three centuries. Then, in 1642, a Dutch descendant of the Marchese, one Jellis Douwse Fonda, crossed the ocean to the New World. He and his family were among the first Dutch settlers of what is now upper New York State.

Jellis Douwse Fonda settled his family at Fort Orange, later to became Albany. As the family grew through the next two generations, it branched west to Schenectady and achieved a measure of wealth. In 1700 Douw Fonda was born, and to him fell the task of expanding the Fonda landholdings. By 1735 he had explored the wilderness of Mohawk Valley west of Schenectady and found desirable lands near an old Indian settlement called Caughnawaga, on the north bank of the Mohawk River. Fonda claimed the lands and soon established a settlement there.

Despite running arguments with the Indians over the Fondas' rights to the land, by 1750 the settlement was a thriving one. Douw Fonda was by then the patriarch of the family and had persuaded most of his relatives in Albany and Schenectady to pack up their belongings, livestock, and

1

slaves and move west. The settlement came to be known as Fonda, New York, and it grew to hamlet to village to prosperous mill and river town over the next 200 years.

In 1766 Douw's second wife gave birth to a son, whom they named Henry. Douw Fonda made it clear when the Revolution broke out that he was on the side of the colonists and even sent two older sons off to fight against the British. In 1780, with the Revolution at the height of its fury in upstate New York, the Fonda settlement was attacked by a band of vengeful Indians. Much of the settlement was burned, and the hated Douw Fonda was scalped and died.

The family fled back to the safety of Albany. At the conclusion of the War of Independence, with most of the hostile Indians swept from the Mohawk Valley, the Fondas resettled their lands. Henry Fonda, the slain Douw's youngest son, left home to fight in the War of 1812 and returned a brigadier general. He then became an innkeeper.

By the mid-1800's at least a dozen branches of the founding family had evolved, but not all stayed in Fonda, New York. Several members of the family, no doubt motivated by the Fonda penchant for traveling westward, joined the great migratory tide of the 1850's seeking fortune beyond the Mississippi.

William Brace Fonda, whose parents had been born and reared in Fonda, New York, himself grew up in Nebraska. The offspring of a family with an Italian background so remote as to have lost its Latin volatility, William Fonda was a stern, rock-ribbed Midwesterner of modest abilities and extravagant dreams. By 1900 he had established himself, however uncertainly, as the owner and operator of his own printing business. With his leonine, faintly Mediterranean good looks and earnest manner he won the heart of a bright and wistfully beauteous Nebraska girl, Herberta Jaynes. Their marriage produced three children, the first of whom was a son, born on May 16, 1905, in Grand Island, Nebraska. The firstborn was christened Henry Jaynes Fonda, and he was followed in short order by two sisters—Harriet and Jayne.

Young Henry Fonda grew up in and around Omaha. He recalls that he started out in life wanting to be a writer. When he was nine, his grammar-school teacher wrote the usual note to the effect that "while Henry's daily lessons are very good I regret to report that his conduct is very annoying and unsatisfactory." This would seem to have made him eminently qualified for the writing trade. At ten he wrote a story called "The Mouse," a tale told from a rodent's point of view. At the time he and his family were living in the Omaha suburb of Dundee, and the story was published to great acclaim in the local newspaper. His maternal grandfather, to whom Henry was very close, predicted that he would be a journalist, and his mother encouraged his interest in writing. At twelve he came up with another literary effort, this time a two-chapter novel for which he made the prefatory claim "In this story the author brings out vividly the boyhood of youth."

When Henry was thirteen, the family moved into a big clapboard house in a pleasant residential section of Omaha. By now he was a fairly serious young man with an independent streak and a stubborn nature—not unlike his father. His conduct at Omaha Central High School evidently improved over that of his grammar-school days, for by the time he was seventeen he had won eighteen merit badges as a Boy Scout, passed his YMCA Bible Study Examination with a grade of 90, and demonstrated that he was competent in basketball, incompetent and self-conscious in romance.

At eighteen he went to the University of Minnesota to study journalism. There he worked at off-campus jobs to supplement his $10-a-week allowance from home, for which he had to return a weekly accounting. "I had a picture in my mind of what college meant," he has said, "and it didn't mean going to classes from nine to two, then slogging back to Unity House, where I was a settlement worker, to labor from three to ten. It was always eleven before I could get back to my room, and I'd fall asleep over my homework."

In 1925, miserable after four months of his second year at Minnesota, Fonda decided to quit college and return home to face the music of his father's displeasure. Weathering that, he set himself to look for a job.

It is typical of Henry Fonda's untheatrical approach to the theater that he never entertained the usual incandescent yearnings for it. The idea of becoming an actor had not occurred to him. Although he was a safely handsome twenty-year-old, his taciturn nature and unaggressive manner qualified him more for the accounting profession than the theater. And for a while during the months after he quit college it appeared that accounting was to be his destiny.

Hanging around Omaha during the summer of 1925, restless, looking for a career job at the prodding of his father but unable to come up with anything to his liking, Henry Fonda was at loose ends. Dorothy Brando, an amateur actress and close friend of Henry's mother (and at the time nursing a child named Marlon), heard about his plight and suggested he drop around to the Omaha Community Playhouse, where his age and type might make him right for a part the director was trying to cast.

Henry showed up at the studio of Gregory Foley, the director. Foley, a short redheaded Irishman who was Omaha's resident bohemian, thrust a script at the bewildered Fonda—it was a published version of *You and I* by Philip Barry—and asked him to read the part of Ricky, the juvenile lead.

"I didn't even understand the typographical layout of the dialogue," Fonda later recalled. "I'd never even participated in high school dramatics. But they were hard up for somebody to play the part, and they offered it to me. I thought, 'Why not?' Actually, I was too embarrassed about the whole thing to get out of it."

Having mustered insufficient push to escape show business, young Fonda haunted its periphery for the next nine years, enacting in real life the personality many of his later characterizations were to make famous—the lank shamble-along who gropes and trips, but who has a stubbornness in him that knows exactly toward what he is meandering. And meander he did, from walk-ons in Midwestern variety houses to bit parts on Broadway to scenery paintership in summer theaters along the East Coast. It meant living on high hopes and cold sandwiches, the diet that keeps young actors slim.

Once he realized what he had done in accepting the juvenile lead in the Barry play, "I was sure I didn't want to go through with it. At rehearsals I found myself in another world. It was a nightmare. I didn't dare look up. I was the kind of guy who thought everybody was looking at *him*. I was very reluctant. I still had no ambition to be an actor. But it was summer, and I had nothing else to do, so I joined the company."

It was not that Fonda was so very good in his interpretation of young Ricky in *You and I*. In fact, he was terrible. About the only emotion he projected was his own fright. But he had a quality onstage which shone through the terror and caught the eye of everyone at the Playhouse.

He stayed at the Playhouse for two nine-month seasons and played four principal roles. He practically lived at the theater. He helped construct sets, painted scenery and learned to love the smell of greasepaint and cold cream. Most important of all, he became addicted to the power of performance and soaked in the sweet bath of self-discovery. When his parents discovered they had an incipient actor on their hands, they were not pleased.

In order to appease them, he took a job as a trainee with a retail credit company in the summer of 1926. He was just learning the system—filing and cross-filing—when Foley asked him to play the title role in George S. Kaufman and Marc Connelly's *Merton of the Movies*, a play that had been a hit on Broadway. Henry, by now having lost his ambivalence about the theater, immediately accepted, but when he arrived home with the news, he was roundly castigated by his father.

William Brace Fonda had been growing increasingly impatient with his son's failure to settle on a respectable career. When Henry announced that in order to play Merton he would have to give up his job at the credit company, words flew, threats were made, then icy silence prevailed. Henry was no different from most young men who spend their youth seeking the praise and approbation of preoccupied, incommunicative fathers. He was frustrated, angry, bitter. He thought of leaving home, of making his way in a world of his own choosing.

"The upshot of the argument was that I did both. I went to work at Retail Credit at seven in the morning and rehearsed for the play at night and on Sundays. On opening night I got my first feeling of what acting was all about. I liked the whole idea of getting up there and being Merton."

That wasn't all he liked. *Merton of the Movies* was the first play in which he acted the lead role. He was the focus of everyone's attention, not only during rehearsals, but in performance as well. When it was time for curtain calls, Henry Fonda received a standing ovation.

For the next two years his life revolved almost totally about the Playhouse. In 1927 he was given the job of assistant director at a salary of $500. He played the male lead opposite Dorothy Brando in Eugene O'Neill's *Beyond the Horizon* and was beginning to think there was such a thing as making a living in the theater. A brief trip to New York, where he saw nine plays in less than a week, reinforced that feeling. Then came the clincher.

George Billings, an actor who traveled about the country giving one-man performances of his famous impersonation of Abraham Lincoln, came to Omaha in the spring of 1927 and let it be known that he was planning to expand his act. Fonda dashed off a sketch which had a part in it for himself and submitted it to Billings. The veteran actor hired Henry at a salary of $100 a week to tour the vaudeville houses of Iowa and Illinois that summer, assisting him in his act. It was that tour which convinced Henry that the theater was the only thing in life worth pursuing.

In the summer of 1928 he made his move. Armed with a little more than $100 he had managed to save, and with the grudging approval of his parents, Henry set out for New York to see if he could make a go of it in the theater. He failed to realize that summer was the low point of the

New York theater season. His meager finances wouldn't last more than a couple of months at best, so he headed straight for Cape Cod, where he heard there were some summer theaters.

His first stop was Provincetown. "I was apple-cheeked and looked like a farm boy. . . . I walked into the theater, was told they had nothing and walked out."

He caught a train to Dennis and walked into the Cape Playhouse, where he found the company in the middle of a rehearsal. He stood around for a while, too frightened to ask anyone anything, then left and went to a nearby boardinghouse to arrange to spend the night. As it turned out, most of the leading players of the Dennis company were staying at the same boardinghouse. That night he timidly introduced himself to some of them and was taken on as third assistant stage manager, at no salary. So much for the notion of high-paying professional theater in the East. He was probably "hired" more out of compassion for his Midwestern reticence than out of any conviction that he could make a contribution to thespianism.

"Practically everything that has ever happened to me," Henry Fonda has said, "has been the result of the long arm of coincidence. It's been a matter of getting the lucky break, of being in the right place at the right time." Although his wallet was practically empty of money that summer, it was filled with luck.

The Dennis Players, compelled by the same compassion that had moved them to take him on in the first place, gave him a bit part in a play called *The Barker*. "I was as unprofessional as possible—stood in a corner learning my lines while the others were rehearsing. The mark of an amateur. I was really a naïve guy."

But soon the actor who was rehearsing the juvenile lead dropped out, and the next thing the greenhorn from Nebraska knew the part had been offered to him—this time not out of compassion, but because the Playhouse was running out of actors. He acquitted himself, if not memorably, at least competently enough for an Omaha friend who had come to see the play to suggest he pay a visit to another summer theater company that was forming in nearby Falmouth.

Calling themselves the University Players, a group of young Princeton and Harvard undergraduates had leased a small theater in Falmouth with the idea of giving themselves and other theatrically inclined students a chance to practice their careers professionally before graduation. Its members, almost without exception, would eventually achieve stature in the theater and motion-picture field. They included Joshua

Logan, Bretaigne Windust and Norris Houghton, practicing to be directors, and actors Kent Smith, Mildred Natwick, Myron McCormick, James Stewart, John Swope, Charles Arnt, Margaret Sullavan and Charles Leatherbee.

Though not a college student, Fonda went to see the University Players. It was mutual love at first sight. Fonda liked their ideas, liked their enthusiasm, liked them and accepted their invitation to leave Dennis to join them. They for their part were intrigued with his lean honesty and his dry, spare way of expressing himself. When they asked him what he had done, there was none of the usual hyperbole young actors, anxious to impress, indulge in. Instead, they received a mild and unadorned recitation of his acting credits, the naïve simplicity of which made them the more believable. Perhaps the fact that Fonda had spent the previous summer on tour, earning $100 a week, impressed the youthful Easterners more than they knew.

The members of the University Players affected a high Ivy League sophistication. Among them Fonda appeared like a tall blade of Nebraska grass in a riot of hothouse flowers. But there in Falmouth began an association that would last for three years and would eventually effect just about everything Henry Fonda accomplished in his later career.

Joshua Logan recalls meeting Fonda for the first time backstage at the Falmouth Playhouse. "I had no idea who this strange, shy, lanky youth could be. He stood there in sad, skinny white linen knickerbockers. It was the late twenties, the days of the plus fours, and this Fonda guy was wearing minus twos. His golf socks and sweater were black, which was either superb taste or Midwestern ignorance. His chest was so caved in and his head and pelvis so pushed forward that I wasn't sure whether he was tall or short. But still there was that beautiful male face."

The University Players were rehearsing a Florentine costume drama called *The Jest* when Fonda arrived on the scene. Because of the scarcity of actors, several players were required to play two and sometimes three different roles in the play. They were so glad to see Fonda that they immediately gave him one of the parts—that of an aging Italian nobleman. According to Logan, he was disastrous. "His Nebraska drawl in that Florentine setting made the poetic Italianate speeches sound like conversations around a cracker barrel."

During that initial summer with the University Players Henry Fonda played his first lead role as a professional actor. The play was a minor confection called *Is Zat So?*, and the young actor gave such a poor performance that the play's director suggested that he be dropped from the company. Fonda was too well liked for that to happen, however, so he was relegated to such offstage duties as tending the box office, ushering and scenery painting. In fact, it was his skill in scenery painting that was to help him through the lean years to come.

At the end of the summer, with everyone in the company going back to college, Henry Fonda went to New York. In spite of the criticisms he had received as an actor on Cape Cod, he was irrepressibly optimistic about his possibilities. "It never occurred to me to be discouraged. I wasn't terribly smart. If I'd been smart, I would have given up and gone home."

Bretaigne Windust, the director, had suggested to him at the end of the summer that he would never have any success as an actor but that he had a talent with stage paints and ought to concentrate on becoming a scenery designer. But Henry Fonda, a stubborn young man who remembered those standing ovations in Omaha, would not be denied. If he couldn't be an actor, he'd be nothing.

From the winter of 1928 until he achieved his first measure of stardom six years later, Henry Fonda had a rough time of it. He alternated summer stock seasons (three more at Falmouth), where room and board were at least guaranteed, with winter seasons when he seldom had money for his next meal. In six years he got walk-on parts in three Broadway flops and aroused some mild interest as a comedian in a revue entitled *New Faces*. He also played in winter stock in various towns and cities of the East.

It was while he was in Baltimore at the beginning of the 1930's that, at the age of twenty-five and still practically penniless, Fonda married for the first time. He had met Margaret Sullavan, a bright, intense, brittle young actress from Norfolk, Virginia, two summers before when she joined the University Players in Falmouth. He immediately fell in love and spent the next two years playing opposite her, courting her as well. They both shared the same birthday—May 16.

It was by all accounts a bravura courtship. According to one eyewitness, "They fought and they made up. They wouldn't be speaking to each other in the wings, but they couldn't wait to get onstage for their love scenes. It wasn't a placid romance. Maggie likely as not would toss a pudding in his face, storm out of our dining room, cross the sands to the ocean and go plunging in, fully clothed. And Hank would grope after her, wiping pudding from his eyes, to rescue her from her watery grave. This went on and on. You had to admire their stamina."

It went on and on through two sunny summers and two bleak Depression winters. Then, on a Christmas Day, while the University Players were in Baltimore for a winter stock engagement, Hank Fonda and Maggie Sullavan were married. The ceremony took place in the dining room of the Kernan Hotel. Bretaigne Windust played the wedding music, and the entire company was on hand.

The couple left on their wedding trip, one story has it, in an ancient, rusty Stutz Bearcat which Fonda had gallantly bought with just about all his meager savings—$75. After four blocks the Bearcat collapsed and died, never to move under its own power again. Undaunted, the newlyweds returned to the hotel. Mrs. Fonda bought a geranium plant for their room, while Hank painted a placard to read OUR HOME and hung it on the door. They loafed for a week, then returned to their acting.

From a marital point of view this was a mistake, for soon thereafter Margaret Sullavan was winning critical acclaim on Broadway and Henry Fonda was growing more bitter with the disappointment of his repeated failures.

The barometer of Henry's quiescent career yielded its lowest reading in the summer of 1932. Already on shaky ground with his wife, whose star was continuing to rise, and without the prospect of any work on the stage for himself, he took a last-gasp job as handyman and chauffeur at the Surry Playhouse in Surry, Maine. For five weeks he wielded a broom and drove a station wagon. Then the company's scene designer quit. Fonda had spent some of his spare time sketching the actors in rehearsal, and his portraits were hung in the theater's lobby. They were evidence that he could at least draw, a talent he had discovered in kindergarten but never had much interest in cultivating. He was promoted overnight from the janitor's broom to the scene designer's brush. For the rest of that summer he was a bit more content and a lot more occupied in the work of the theater, even if it was only in designing sets.

He returned to New York in the fall of 1932 pleased with the job he had done. But paradoxically, the reputation he was earning as a scene designer—although it appeared to be fulfilling Bretaigne Windust's prophecy of four years' earlier—deepened his despair of ever making an acting career.

His days that fall were further dimmed by his inability to find work and by the chatty, incandescent happiness of his wife over the way her career was taking off. She was succeeding a little too fast for the comfort of Henry Fonda's ego.

By Thanksgiving Day they were no longer on speaking terms. Henry tucked their turkey under his arm, found a policeman who knew of a poor family with hungry kids, and that was that—they were on their way to divorce. Margaret Sullavan immediately went off to fame and fortune in Hollywood, though she would reappear again in Henry's life.

Many fans of film and theater imagine to this day that Henry Fonda sprang full-blown onto the show business scene from the brow of some Venus-like goddess of stardom. That this was not the case was certainly not unusual; what was unusual was that the longer Fonda stayed in New York, the farther away his goal seemed to appear. One might wonder why, in the face of all the discouragement he received, he continued to persevere. After all, he had a loving, if by now extremely anxious, family waiting to welcome him back to Omaha. And he could have returned without too much loss of face—it was no disgrace to have tried and failed. He might have settled comfortably into Omaha working as a credit manager or junior accountant and indulging his love for acting on the boards of the Omaha Playhouse, where he would have been received with open arms. But such was not to be. Although he was nearing thirty and had little to show for his six years in New York but a broken marriage, Henry Fonda was thoroughly addicted to acting.

As so often happens with men of lofty ambition, the farther Fonda's dream seemed to recede, the closer he was to its realization. Luck, however reluctant, still clung to him. It would soon conspire with his basic integrity and innocence to reward his tenacity.

He started the next summer again as a scenery designer, this time at the Westchester Playhouse in Mount Kisco, New York. He was not too happy about it, but at least he was still in the theater. Then—another stroke of luck, compounded by Fonda's expanding sense of wile. Midway through the season Day Tuttle, the director of the playhouse, told Fonda that the coming week's guest star had taken ill. They needed to find an easy-to-stage play as a quick substitute, or the theater would be dark for a week. Fonda thought fast. There was a play called *It's a Wise Child* which he had once performed with the University Players. It all took place in a living room, so that no elaborate scenery was required. It had only four principal parts, plus one important bit part—an Irish iceman who appears briefly after the opening curtain and again near the end.

"I know just the play," Fonda told Tuttle. "You'll only need two men and two women. There's another little bit part, but I know it so well that

I can play it. It'll save you from having to pay an extra actor." Tuttle agreed. What Fonda had not told him was that the part of the iceman, though a bit part, was the feature of the play. The iceman had all the best lines; he was the one character who convulsed the audience every time the play was shown.

The play went on, and Fonda convulsed the audience. In fact, he managed to steal the show with a performance that led Tuttle to invite him back to Mount Kisco the following summer as an actor. The Mount Kisco iceman was the first semifast one Fonda had pulled in his career. He was losing some of his Nebraska innocence.

He returned to New York in the fall with a certain reputation for onstage drollery. He had gotten over his disastrous marriage and was feeling more positive about things. His optimism got a boost when he appeared in Leonard Sillman's *New Faces* on Broadway in the spring of 1934, doing skits with Imogene Coca. Leland Hayward, who was just beginning a career as an agent, saw him in the show and offered to become his manager-agent. That summer Fonda went back to Mount Kisco and was soon playing leading roles. He knew then that the door was about to open. He could smell it coming.

In midsummer Hayward wired Fonda from Hollywood that he had a film deal in the works and urged him to fly to the Coast immediately. At first Fonda declined interest—his dream was Broadway, and he had yet to conquer it. But Hayward was insistent, so Fonda went.

When he arrived in Hollywood, he found that Hayward had arranged for him to sign a motion-picture contract with well-known producer Walter Wanger. Fonda, still not interested in being a movie actor, thought he would scotch the deal by asking for the astronomical salary of $1,000 a week. Wanger agreed, and the astonished Nebraskan signed a contract to do two pictures a year.

There was no picture ready for him, however, so he immediately returned to Mount Kisco and the role of the Tutor in Ferenc Molnar's *The Swan*. The actor Gregory Kerr played the Prince, and Kerr's wife, actress June Walker, was so impressed with Fonda that she suggested him for the title role in her forthcoming Broadway play, Marc Connelly's *The Farmer Takes a Wife*.

Max Gordon, producer of the play, arranged to borrow Fonda from Wanger and gave the long-frustrated actor the part. It delayed Fonda's debut in motion pictures, but he couldn't have been happier. The play opened in the fall of 1934 to enthusiastic reviews. The critics were especially impressed by Fonda. Brooks Atkinson wrote in the New York *Times* of his "manly, modest performance in a style of captivating simplicity." From as restrained an observer as Atkinson this was high praise indeed. Other notices were equally laudatory. One described Fonda as "a believable Dan Harrow, strong and sweet and silent as a Dan Harrow should be." Another declared that "Henry Fonda is perfect. It is an extraordinarily simple and lustrous characterization."

In the role of the farmer Fonda finally put the indelible imprint of his character on the dream he had pursued for so long. This was the part that made him. Now, like his Dutch-Italian ancestors before him and bearing the psychic scars of his long struggle, he headed West.

Roughly about the time the early Fonda settlers were populating their lands in the Mohawk Valley, other colonial families were establishing themselves more prominently in Philadelphia, New York and New England. The Biddles were already on their way to becoming the first family of Philadelphia. The Pells, Stuyvesants, Howlands, Stoutenburghs, Anthons, Fords and Fishes were some of the leading families in and about New York. The Adamses had installed themselves in Boston, and the Seymours, who traced their family line from English royalty, practically owned Connecticut. Intermarriage among these families became common over the span of the next two centuries as a way of preserving class boundaries and extending family dynasties.

Out of this elite mix on April 4, 1908, appeared Frances Ford Seymour, the daughter of Mr. and Mrs. Eugene Ford Seymour of New York and Canadian society. Frances Seymour grew up with several brothers and sisters in the insulated world of town houses, finishing schools, yacht clubs and debutante parties. By the time she was graduated from the Gibbs School in Boston she was a pretty, vivacious, fair-haired young woman highly schooled in the skills of social intercourse. Reared by her parents to become a good wife to the qualified man who sought her hand, she was imbued with a healthy sense of household organization, pride in her surroundings and taste. Notions of dignity, even-temperedness and honesty were impressed on her, and she was reminded almost daily by word and example not to take lightly her privileged position in an imperfect world.

On January 10, 1931, Frances Seymour, then twenty-two, in what was the great marital surprise of the social season, was wed in New York to fifty-two-year-old George T. Brokaw, wealthy retired lawyer, noted

sportsman and former member of Congress. The Brokaws set up house
in the Brokaw family mansion on Fifth Avenue and proceeded to live in
understated eighteenth-century elegance. Almost directly across Central
Park on West Sixty-third Street was the miserable two-room flat which
Henry Fonda had been sharing with James Stewart, Joshua Logan and
Myron McCormick. They called it Casa Gangrene after the malodorous
smells that clung to its walls.

Frances and George Brokaw led an active life of entertaining and
being entertained, although in honor of the Depression it was done on a
simpler, less conspicuous scale than might have been the case otherwise.
Frances became pregnant soon after the wedding and nine months later
gave birth to a daughter, whom the happy parents named Frances
deVillers Brokaw.

George Brokaw had previously been married to Clare Booth, the
writer. After their divorce he was in constant legal conflict with her over
matters pertaining to the support of the daughter of their union. Except
for the pall this cast on her marriage, life breezed along satisfyingly for
Frances Seymour Brokaw during the first three years of her stay in the
Brokaw mansion, while on the other side of town the young actor from
Omaha, of whose existence she had no inkling, struggled with a fractured
marriage, a bruised ego, a deflated dream and poverty. Then, just when
Henry Fonda's fortunes were turning for the better, Frances Brokaw's
changed for the worse. Indeed, the worst—for George Brokaw suddenly
died of a heart attack in May, 1935.

It took a year for Frances to get through the traditional mourning
period, deal with the transfer of her late husband's enormous estate,
settle the continuing dispute with his former wife, put her own affairs in
order and reorganize her life as a widow. These tasks completed and her
young daughter safely entrusted to the care of her parents and a
governess, she embarked with her friend Fay Devereaux Keith, who was
engaged to marry one of Frances' brothers, on a get-away-from-it-all
tour of Europe and Britain. It was the summer of 1936.

Having finally made his mark on Broadway a year and a half before,
Henry Fonda had gone to Hollywood. By 1936 he had played in six
motion pictures. These included the film version of *The Farmer Takes a
Wife*, his first picture, and a movie called *The Moon's Our Home*, a frothy
comedy in which he played opposite Margaret Sullavan, his ex-wife.
Fonda was now making his mark as a motion-picture leading man and
had become a film star practically overnight. He had overcome his

indifference to movie acting and with characteristic intensity absorbed himself in it, hardly finishing one film before he began another. He shared several rented houses with his old roommates from New York, James Stewart and Joshua Logan, and was thoroughly enjoying the Hollywood way of life.

Fonda had also starred in Hollywood's first outdoor Technicolor picture, *The Trail of the Lonesome Pine*. When it opened early in 1936, people flocked to see it. It was his fourth picture, and if his stardom had been on the rise as a result of his first three, it was secured by *Lonesome Pine*—he was magnetic as the hot-tempered, yet romantic, idealistic mountaineer, Dave Tolliver.

Now it was England's turn to make a Technicolor film. Because Fonda had come across so well in *Lonesome Pine*, the English producers insisted on him for their picture. More because he had not been abroad before than because he was interested in the leading role, Fonda accepted and sailed for England.

Although Fonda had acquired a bit more sophistication over the past few years—he was already gaining a reputation as a tough, temperamental actor, critical, sometimes moody, always demanding of perfection—he was still basically Henry Fonda from Omaha, Nebraska. The same values were operating as when he had left home nine years before, only more intensely. He now had the power and confidence to assert his will and beliefs. His natural and rigorous honesty in dealing with other people, though often strained, usually prevailed. True, his ego was large, his power was growing, his often stubborn convictions about things were becoming even more fixed than before, and in the bargain he was learning what it was like to be a movie star. But what temperament he evinced came from a genuine artistic impulse, not from the process of "going Hollywood." Fonda never went Hollywood; in spite of a forgivable minor affectation here and there—for after all he was not without a sense of wonder about it all—he consistently hewed the line of simplicity and directness.

In June, 1936, while he was in London completing the filming of *Wings of the Morning*, Britain's first Technicolor production, Fonda was introduced to the vacationing widow from New York, Frances Seymour Brokaw. By then Frances Brokaw had heard of Henry Fonda and had probably even seen one or two of his films. They were immediately attracted to each other. But widowed for little more than a year, the rich, youthful and attractive Mrs. Brokaw was at first hesitant when the thirty-one-year-old actor expressed an interest in seeing her again. She was puzzled by the strong attraction she felt toward the lean, gentle-eyed, soft-spoken Fonda. She momentarily fought against it, then yielded and agreed to his request.

Henry Fonda's attraction was even stronger. At first drawn by Frances' soft beige hair, glittering smile and the direct way she had of looking at him, he was also beguiled by the seductive grace of her speech and the obvious intelligence that shone from her eyes. He had been married to a lovely but insecure and highly excitable actress, who had left him slightly wounded. He had been in close contact with dozens of other career-minded actresses—all beauties in their own way, but women he was unable to relate to except in terms of their own ambitions. Any romantic feelings he might have had for any of them were tempered by his sharply honed sense of caution against making the same mistake twice.

Frances Brokaw was something else altogether. He had never encountered anyone like her before—she was sweet, gentle, vulnerable, yet had a quiet, capable strength and possessed a variety of interests. When they met soon again, they threw all their caution to the winds. They quickly fell in love and shared every possible moment with each other.

At the completion of the filming the two trekked the Continent together. Their first stop was Paris, where war preparations were already being made. They then motored through France to Munich, took a quick side trip by air to Budapest, returned to Munich and drove from there to Berlin, getting good glimpses of German military maneuvers all along the route.

Henry and Frances, profoundly happy to have found each other and dizzily but dignifiedly in love, decided while they were in Germany that they would marry. The two returned to New York by ship in early September and immediately applied for a marriage license. Fonda was due back in Hollywood shortly to start a new picture. He set up temporary residence at the Gotham Hotel in Manhattan, a long step up from the Casa Gangrene, while waiting for the prewedding technicalities to clear.

The Fonda-Brokaw wedding on the afternoon of September 17, 1936, was an event of no little importance to the upper strata of New York society. More than a few tongues clicked in disapproval as Frances Seymour Brokaw walked down the aisle of Park Avenue's Christ Church on the arm of her brother to be given away to the laconic movie actor. Criticism of the Seymours for even allowing the marriage was even louder. But the wedding went off without demonstration. Joshua Logan came in from California to be best man to his old friend. Frances' sister, Marjory Capell Seymour, attended her.

The ceremony was followed by a crowded reception at the Roof Garden of the Pierre Hotel, after which it was off by plane to Omaha for the newlyweds so that Frances could meet Henry's two sisters and other members of the Fonda family. His father had died the year before, his mother the year before that. Neither of them had lived to see him achieve the realization of his dream.

From Omaha Henry and Frances continued on to Los Angeles, where he was to make three films over the next eight months. During their courtship in Europe they had talked incessantly to each other about themselves, revealing their backgrounds, their influences, their values and their tastes. Their initial attraction to each other was refined during those weeks by their discovery of how very much alike they were. They were both basically shy, ingoing people who valued directness and honesty. They had both grown up with parents who were remote and who mistook the withholding of affection for instilling discipline. Each of them had felt the sting of hurt and disappointment in their early struggles for identity and self-determination. They confessed their insecurities to each other—or at least the ones they were aware of—and vowed to create a life together that would be rich and meaningful in the simple pleasures they held dear. They mutually despised ostentation and the accumulation of material things for the sake of appearance—she because of what she had seen growing up in the privileged world of the East, he because of what he had observed in the plaster Athens of Los Angeles—and they swore to forge a different kind of life. And, of course, they wanted children. Although Frances already had a five-year-old daughter, she now wanted to populate the world with young Fondas.

On their arrival in Los Angeles they found a modest house to serve as temporary quarters while they looked for land of their own on which to build the kind of homestead they had decided on. At first doubtful about the idea of living in Southern California, Frances soon fell in love with the pleasant subtropical climate and the rich, aromatic verdancy of Los Angeles.

When Henry was not at work filming, he and Frances were out combing the Santa Monica Mountains for property. They finally found a secluded nine-acre vale on a hill above Sunset Boulevard in Brentwood that suited them perfectly. It had 360 degrees' worth of spectacular views, yet was level enough to put to all the uses they envisioned for it.

When they inquired about purchasing it, however, they were told it was not for sale. They were disappointed but vowed that someday they would own the property.

By April, 1937, Frances Fonda was pregnant. Henry was delighted by the news, but at the same time he was growing tired of film acting. He had lost his fascination for the technical aspects of moviemaking and was impatient with the boring routine of life at the studios. He was making a great deal of money, but perhaps because of his strict sense of ethics, he felt he was not doing anything to earn it. Movie acting lacked challenge and excitement, especially for an actor who was basically playing himself. If he had been a performer who depended on histrionics to get his effects, it might have been different. For Henry, acting in Hollywood meant mostly standing around waiting for the next camera setup. He yearned for the excitement and tension of the stage and live audiences.

When Fonda let his desires be known, Leland Hayward arranged for him to return to Broadway in a new play called *Blow Ye Winds*. The play would open that fall. Since Henry had no film commitment for the summer, he would be able to warm up for it by starring in a summer stock version of *The Virginian*, first at the Westport Playhouse in Connecticut, then at Mount Kisco, where only four summers before he had been the scenery designer.

With a busy rehearsal schedule coming up, he and Frances returned to New York early in the summer. While Frances arranged to sell at auction all the antique furniture and art objects she had accumulated during her first marriage, Henry did his stint at Westport and Mount Kisco, then went into preparations for *Blow Ye Winds*. When the production opened, he received high praise, but the play did not. As a result, it had a short run. For Henry the whole experience had been enervating, and he could now go back to picture making with his artistic batteries recharged.

Frances' pregnancy had moved into its advanced stages. Although Henry had to return to California to start filming *Jezebel* with Bette Davis, she preferred to remain in New York so that she could have their baby under the direction of her regular doctor. Since the birth was to be by Caesarian section and the exact date for it was set well ahead of time, Fonda would be able to return from California in time for the delivery. Thus it was, then, that on Sunday, December 21, 1937, Henry Fonda's first child, a daughter, was born at Doctors Hospital in New York City. It was a day American newspapers were filled with detailed stories and outraged editorials about an incident that had just occurred on China's Yangtze River. The Japanese had fired on the American gunboat *Panay*, killing and wounding many among its crew and passengers. Suddenly the American public had thrust before it the prospect of war in the Far East. ROOSEVELT BARS PEACE AT ANY PRICE! the headlines shouted.

2.   The Farmer's Daughter

> *I spent my childhood wanting to be a boy, because I wanted to be like my father.*
>
> —JANE FONDA

THE Fondas named their daughter, born on the cusp of Sagittarius and Capricorn, Jane Seymour Fonda.

Frances' family proudly claimed direct descendancy from, among others, Edward Seymour, Duke of Somerset in early sixteenth-century England—whose sister, Lady Jane Seymour, was the ill-fated third wife of King Henry VIII. Frances had persuaded Henry Fonda to read Shakespeare's account of the corrupt and corpulent king's reign, in which Lady Jane played a prominent role, so as to acquaint him more dramatically with the intriguing complexities of her ancestry. Fonda, increasingly aware of his own tenuous descendancy from ancient nobility, was fascinated to learn in this direct way of his wife's blood connections. He enthusiastically agreed to Jane Seymour Fonda as the name of his daughter. It was a natural.

The name worked in other ways, too. It enabled Frances Fonda to carry on an old upper-class family tradition of giving girl children, as middle names, the maiden names of their mothers. Henry Fonda had somewhat the same tradition—his middle name was Jaynes, after his mother. Although his sister's name was Jayne, he couldn't very well name his daughter Jaynes, but Jane was close enough an approximation to give the whole business a neat sense of balance. From the moment of her birth, though, he could not resist the nickname Lady Jane, which stuck in his mind from his reading about Lady Jane Seymour in

Shakespeare. So Lady Jane his infant daughter became, the heiress apparent of what royal blood remained in the veins of her parents.

Upon her passage into the world Lady Jane Fonda was, as any healthy baby, an amalgam of parental features all slightly distorted by the rigors of delivery. But within a year her face began to define itself and the heavy preponderance of Fonda genes was soon revealed. Her high forehead could have come from either parent. She had more her mother's coloration than her father's, and her almost pale blond hair (which would darken as she grew) was certainly part of the Seymour inheritance, as were her large ears. But she was without any question a Fonda. She had her father's long and slightly bobbed nose. She had his wide-set, highly expressive blue eyes. And she had his long, oval, steep-jawed face with its sad, taut, downturned mouth—a mouth which, whenever it broke into a grin, suddenly contradicted its own implications.

Frances Fonda brought Lady Jane back to California shortly after her birth. The family settled into another rented house, made a second unsuccessful attempt to acquire the land they had fallen in love with on the hill in Brentwood and, instead, went ahead with a smaller house nearby—a simple frame Cape Cod bungalow. When Fonda was not busy taking home movies of his daughter and showing her off to all his old friends, he worked at his trade. Indeed, during the next two years he engaged in a virtual nonstop round of filmmaking as the studios struggled to keep up with the demand for his screen presence. In quick succession he completed ten films, the most noteworthy of which were *Jesse James*, *The Young Mr. Lincoln* and *Grapes of Wrath*, the picturization of the celebrated John Steinbeck novel which, as a result of his performance, boosted Fonda into film immortality. Another picture in this series was *Drums Along the Mohawk*, John Ford's cinematic recounting of revolutionary times in the Mohawk Valley of upper New York. Fonda played an heroic pioneer settler who led a hardy group of farmers and their families in defense of their lands against the ravages of British-subsidized Indians and Tories. It was a soft irony, but one that must have amused him.

While the actor-father was spending most of his time at the studios, Frances was busy bringing up Jane. According to some witnesses to those early days of their marriage, Frances Fonda was never terribly engaged by Henry's work. She loved Henry dearly, of course, but by both background and inclination felt herself an outsider to the emotional and frequently raucous world of film and theatrical performers. Except for a few of her husband's close friends from his earlier days in New York, such as Joshua Logan, John Swope and Leland Hayward, she did not feel comfortable with film and theater people. Logan recalls, "Frances was not really interested in the theater, so she was always embarrassed to talk about it. She'd talk of children, operations, jewelry, the stock market. I often wondered what she and Henry talked about, because these are the only subjects Henry couldn't talk about."

Frances was a dutiful wife, however, and made great efforts to overcome her patrician sensibilities, though not when it came to her daughters. During the first few years of her life Jane Fonda was given the same kind of upbringing her mother had been given as a child—she was committed to the care of governesses, was trotted out for company, was gently but firmly taught the infant niceties and learned through the centuries-old upper-class tradition of osmosis to be a mild, well-mannered child.

In February, 1940, soon after Jane's second birthday, Frances Fonda gave birth to another child, a boy. She and Henry named him Peter Henry Fonda and, again, it could be seen at an early date that the Fonda genes predominated. Aside from gaining a brother, Lady Jane Fonda acquired a leading man for all the home movies Henry Fonda shot of them in his spare time.

In order for Henry Fonda to play the role of Tom Joad in *Grapes of Wrath*, a part he had been coveting since the book came out, he had to sign a seven-year contract with the Twentieth Century-Fox company in 1939. The contract was a form of extortion that he would soon come to regret. Despite the rave reviews he received for Tom Joad, a performance he had thought out with painstaking care and executed with a verisimilitude that had rarely been achieved in movies, Twentieth Century forced him into a string of second-rate films that made him boil anew with frustration. Such pictures as *Lillian Russell*, *The Return of Frank James* (an exploitation of his earlier success as the brother in *Jesse James*), *Chad Hanna*, *Wild Geese Calling*, *You Belong to Me* (with Barbara Stanwyck, his most frequent leading lady), *The Magnificent Dope* and *Tales of Manhattan* brought Fonda into 1942 seething with dismay at the turn his career had taken. Without a doubt he was making more money than ever—indeed, he took second place to no one in Hollywood on that score, not even his wife, who was a wealthy woman in her own right by virtue of her inheritance of her first husband's fortune—but he was unhappy, bored, restless and mad at himself. The moguls at Twentieth Century had tunnel vision about him, of that he was sure: They saw him either as the stereotyped rustic or as the bumbling, endearing foil for their snappy, sophisticated female stars. He had tried on several occasions to buy out his contract, but to no avail. Lately he had been taking out his frustrations on the people he worked with. Even though he hated most of the roles he was given, he approached them with sincerity and integrity and had little patience with the hack cynicism he encountered at the studio as each picture was ground out. He would come home from a day's filming feeling sour and unfulfilled. Encountering his wife's lack of interest in his work, her breezy misinterpretations of his distress and her practical "rise-above-it" advice—perhaps owing to his inability to articulate his feelings—he began to keep his own counsel.

Not everything was dismal, though. After four years of turning down the Fondas' attempts to buy the hill property in Brentwood, the Mountain Park Land Company, its owners, finally agreed to sell. The Fondas had revisited the property many times since they first saw it in 1937. By now well acquainted with its potential, they eagerly snapped it up and embarked on plans to build their dream house.

Again, Fonda tenacity and patience had paid off. One would think that their pent-up passion to own the land and to build the miniature colonial model farm they had envisioned for it would have resulted in rapid, pell-mell house construction. Just the opposite happened. With the same kind of patience and meticulous attention to detail that characterized Henry and Frances Fonda's approach to life, they spent two years putting their dream together.

First they made innumerable visits to the site, which overlooked the city of Los Angeles to the east, the Pacific to the southwest and the canyons of the Santa Monica mountains to the north. They analyzed the views from every angle. They and the children sailed kites and recorded the directions of the wind currents. They studied the sun at different times of day to learn how its rays affected the different sectors of the property. They made as thorough a survey of the land's livability as was possible.

After much trial and error they picked out just the spot for the swimming pool. They found a flat piece of land where the wind was weakest and penciled in the tennis court. They decided on the site of the main house. They located the best area for the gardens, the barn, the greenhouse. Before a single bag of cement was mixed, trees were moved and transplanted, flower beds were set out, a citrus grove was planted, and the vegetable gardens were mapped. Most people build a house first and then call in the landscapers and say, "Make the land blend with the house." Not so the Fondas; they wanted their house to fit the terrain and its flora. With the property burgeoning with trees and shrubs, all carefully arranged according to their plan, they then set out to build their house.

Henry in the meantime had become involved in something else. A novel had just been published. It received very little fanfare, but had the same kind of spare, direct narrative simplicity and complex moral pathos as *Grapes of Wrath*. The book was *The Ox-Bow Incident* by an obscure professor named Walter Van Tilburg Clark. No one had any faith in the potential of the book as a commercial film except Fonda and director William Wellman. The two browbeat Darryl F. Zanuck into making it, despite the grim, uncompromising story which Zanuck felt—rightly as it turned out when the film was first released in 1943—would be sure death at the box office. His claim that it would also tarnish Henry Fonda's bright image, however, was wrong.

Fonda agreed to appear in *The Magnificent Dope*, a picture he had no taste for, in exchange for the chance to play the bored, cynical cowboy in *The Ox-Bow Incident*. Wellman likewise agreed to direct a potboiler in exchange for the directorial assignment on *Ox-Bow*. Wellman, Fonda and the rest of the company plunged into the project with the dedication and craft of fourth-century monks copying the Gospels. They produced a film that has since become a classic and, in the intervening years, made its money back thrice over.

While Henry was immersed in *The Ox-Bow Incident*, Frances Fonda was busy with plans for the new house. She approached the task with efficiency, flair and controlled excitement. She saw her house as a personal statement of her and her husband's taste for simplicity, utility and unpretentious elegance. Having decided on something along the order of a colonial farmhouse, she conferred with architects and designers continually on the best way to translate the idea into reality.

Lady Jane—or just plain Lady, as she was now called—was becoming aware of her surroundings. As she approached her fourth birthday, it became clear to her parents that she was an extraordinarily bright young child, a bit more introspective than they might have hoped, but curious and self-sufficient. The governess Frances employed to look after Lady and Peter was competent and trustworthy and was able to free Frances from much of the petty detail of child rearing so that she could concentrate most of her formidable energies on the housebuilding.

Not that Frances ignored her children. On the contrary, she remembered her own childhood and gave them a great deal of time and attention. Her elder daughter, whose nickname was Pan, was already a pretty ten-year-old and was occupied much of the time with her school affairs. Pan doted on Lady and Peter, exhibiting all the endearing traits of young girls who love to play "mother" in imitation of their own mothers. Frances was able to bask in the lovely relationship the three children had. Too, Pan, with her impeccable manners and genuine air of breeding, served as an excellent model for Lady Jane as the two grew up together.

Frances was determined to rear the children as the thoroughbreds they were. She had implicit trust in her own ability to give them the right direction without overloading them with the snobbery and sense of *noblesse oblige* that were endemic to most upper-class families she had encountered in the East. And of course her husband, with his rough-hewn but charming distaste for artificiality, would be the leaven of the children's proper development.

Lady Jane adored her father. She would take every opportunity she could find to snuggle up to him. At first he was a bit awkward with her, fearing even to pick her up until she was well past a year old, but then he became cautiously responsive to her. He was not permissive, though, and when a bit of discipline was called for, he would set his mouth and glower at Lady Jane with a look of impatient disdain. This was usually sufficient to put an end to whatever transgression she was involved in.

As she grew older, however, the disdainful looks became more frequent and were often accompanied by terse lectures—by her father's standards reasonable explanations—on behavior and responsibility, especially as they pertained to a young girl. The more Jane sought her father's attention, the less he seemed to recognize her motives and the more to attribute her actions to simple fractiousness. He would correct them with a quick, impatient outburst that would send his daughter briefly inside herself with the sulks. But soon everything would be back on an even keel.

Jane possessed one quality that surfaced early in her character and alternately worried and amused her parents. This was a kind of rebellious determination. It first revealed itself in her infantile demands —if she wanted something she would work with innocent tenacity to get it, sometimes approaching it directly, other times indirectly. No matter the desire, she would keep at it until she either had it or was absolutely rebuffed. The quality sometimes flashed as an obsession, and although the resulting behavior would not last long, when it occurred it exasperated her parents. She could not be reasoned with. She would become unreachable and brood in a manner that indicated indifference to the consequences.

Frances' concern over this was mild. Henry's was deeper, for he often perceived in his daughter's behavior a quality of character that he saw in himself and was not happy about. He would react to it with almost automatic disapproval. The more he did this, the more he saw in himself his own father's responses to him when he was a child. It was not pleasant for him to observe himself turning into a stern, impatient father when for so long he had promised himself to treat his own children with the affection and understanding he believed he had lacked. But there was nothing much he felt he could do about it except to resolve to stop such throwback behavior before it occurred. To resolve to exorcise an inherited instinctual behavior pattern is much easier than accomplishing it, however. When Henry Fonda couldn't do it, he gradually, perhaps subconsciously, turned the blame onto his children for provoking his impatience in the first place. So, although life in the Fonda household was for the most part peaceful and gracious during the early years of Lady Jane's life, a small element of discontent had insinuated itself.

None of this interfered with the plans for the farm. The outbreak of the war had already been foreseen by Henry and Frances as a result of their trip through France and Germany in the summer of 1936. Pearl Harbor gave them pause, however. With rumors rife of an impending Japanese invasion of California, and with the rumors given credibility by America's loss of its Pacific defense perimeter in the early months of 1942, the Fondas seriously considered abandoning their plans and moving back to New York, if for no one else's sake but the children's. But the Fondas weren't the only ones who thought about it, and when they saw so many other members of the film community packing up to go, they resolved to stay. Panic and flight were undignified and, in their book, expressions of moral weakness.

Henry Fonda had never been particularly political. His wife was even less so. The only overt political act he had indulged in, aside from voting, occurred in 1938, when he joined a group of other stars in getting up a petition to President Roosevelt insisting that the United States sever economic relations with Nazi Germany. Although he had been genuinely dismayed by the ugly mood he had witnessed earlier in Germany, he had no illusion that the petition would have much more effect than to garner publicity for its organizers. As it turned out, much of the publicity was negative. To petition against Germany in 1938 was not a popular stand to take, especially among the movie moguls of Hollywood who, although most were Jewish, dreaded the possibility of losing the great profits their industry drew out of Germany. As a consequence of his identification with the petition, Henry Fonda gained a reputation as a "liberal," although his real political convictions, such as they were at the time, leaned toward the middle-of-the-road.

Nevertheless, he was fiercely patriotic, and when war broke out in 1941, he was eager to make his contribution. He was already thirty-six years old and, with three children to support, was ineligible for immediate conscription. Rather than volunteer straight off, he was persuaded that at least until the course and duration of the war had become more definite he would be doing a greater service by staying in Hollywood and churning out pictures for the sake of the country's morale.

Frances and Henry proceeded with their plans for the farm and the dream house, and when it was completed, it turned out to be almost exactly as they had envisioned it, the replica of a colonial New England homestead with all the amenities of the 1940's.

The main house faced on Tigertail Road, which wound steeply up the mountain from Sunset Boulevard. From the road a white-graveled drive curved in through post-and-rail fencing and passed under a cupolaed porte cochere that separated the main house from the garage and servants' quarters. The main house itself, two stories high, was constructed of a harmonious combination of fieldstone, stucco and shake-and-shingle siding. The house was a series of wings, each with its own wood-shingled roof at a different level to give a rambling effect. The garage had its entrance for cars at the rear and was heavily protected by shrubbery at the front. With the breezeway connecting it to the main house and its old barn-siding exterior, it created the impression of an attached barn.

Beyond the house and slightly to the rear, across a small lawn, was the playhouse, which was meant to serve both as a cabana for the swimming pool and as an informal entertainment center for children and adults alike. The playhouse was a single-story structure put together in the same stone-wood-stucco style of the main residence. Its front overlooked a swimming pool that was dug and finished to look more like an old-fashioned swimming hole than a modern pool, and to its rear was the tennis court. Beyond, running to the lip of the canyon, were the gardens and fields where Henry Fonda intended to pursue his agricultural hobby and a small playground and jungle gym for the children, complete with a pair of painted wooden carrousel horses Frances had imported from the East.

Number 600 Tigertail Road was a happy place, especially for Lady Jane Fonda. There was something for everyone there; especially for Jane there was breadth and space in which to play out her childhood. Once installed there, the Fondas took to spending their days in country clothes and busying themselves with the little tasks that make a perfect place even more perfect. Henry passed most of his time outdoors cultivating his vegetable gardens, running his tractor and adding an improvement here and there about the grounds. Frances tended to the flower and shrubbery beds and managed the household with the proud and aggressive efficiency of a curator. Both Fondas enjoyed the satisfactions of detailed and patient work, and they insisted their children develop an appreciation of it.

By the time Jane was five she began to take exception to the name Lady. She had started at the Brentwood Town and Country School and found that the name elicited giggles and snide comments from her schoolmates. To a child as sensitive and attuned to rebuff as she had grown, the nickname created in her a sense of juvenile mortification. She had to remind her parents over and over again to stop using it, at least in front of others.

Each of the three children had a room of his or her own on the second floor of the main house; Henry and Frances had their living quarters downstairs in a separate wing that faced out onto the pool and the playhouse. The interior of the house was a highly romanticized rendering of early Vermont. The living room, with its pine-paneled walls, massive wood-and-brick fireplace, large colorful hooked rug, barrel tables, heavy ceiling beams, bookcases, colonial antiques and big sofas and easy chairs, was a warm and comfortable sanctuary. The Fondas dined at an antique trestle table in the small wallpapered dining room that looked out onto the front lawn. The kitchen and adjoining pantries, in the rear of the house, were spacious models of modern efficiency.

As were Henry and Frances Fonda's quarters. The Fondas' master bedroom was a large, square bay-windowed room dominated by a mammoth stone-and-wood fireplace set catty-cornered into the wall opposite their bed. The room was painted in yellow, green and white, and again, hooked rugs were scattered over the polished plank floors. Off the bedroom to the rear were dressing rooms and baths, and at the back of the house a separate entrance and exit for Henry Fonda. Frances also had a small office in this part of the house, from which she ran the day-to-day affairs of the household.

Jane's bedroom was at the top of the steps leading from the pine-paneled entrance foyer downstairs. The room was at the rear of the house and afforded her a splendid view northwest and northeast into the neighboring and distant mountains. Jane slept in an old-fashioned maple four-poster done up by her mother with a matching canopy and dust ruffle of frilly cream voile. Two walls were papered in a red-and-white colonial floral print. Built-in bookcases, painted white, lined the door wall, and opposite the bed was a gaily upholstered window seat set between two large cupboards. Another of the Fondas' ubiquitous hooked rugs covered most of the floor.

It was a warm, open, inviting homestead the Fondas had created, but aside from an occasional uncharacteristic shout from Jane or Peter, it was a quiet and not very busy place during the next few years. It appeared as though the war were going to last for a while. Late in 1942, after completing filming on one of the many morale-building war pictures that were being shot in those days—this one called *The Immortal Sergeant*—Henry Fonda enlisted in the Navy. After a short training period in San Diego he was sent to the Pacific to serve as a quartermaster third class aboard a destroyer.

The Fondas had built their little farm in a relatively undeveloped area of Los Angeles. Although it was within walking distance of Sunset Boulevard down winding Tigertail Road, it provided the seclusion they desired, not only for themselves, but for their children. Not that Frances and Henry were antisocial—indeed they enjoyed entertaining occasionally, especially Frances, who, when Henry was home, put together big, casual pool-and-barbecue parties in the playhouse that were an elegant mix of California and Eastern life-styles. But they lived quietly for the most part and strove to avoid the garish social and night life of Hollywood; they were determined that their children should be as untouched as possible by the deceptive glamor of being the offspring of a movie star. Thus, what was a secluded location for Henry and Frances represented isolation for Jane and Peter.

Except for daily forays down the hill to her school and an occasional trip to the beach, the Fonda farm was just about all Jane Fonda saw of Los Angeles in her early years. Coincidentally enough, Leland Hayward, Henry's agent, married Henry's first wife Margaret Sullavan in late 1936, and the two started to produce their own family. The Haywards set up house near the Fonda farm, and in the wartime absence of the two husbands, their respective wives and children looked after one another. They became in many ways one big family.

The war passed unnoticed for Jane, but not her father's absence. Except for an occasional short visit by Henry Fonda while in transit from one duty station to another, Jane did not see her father for three years. During this time she led a happy and carefree existence, troubled only occasionally by loneliness for her father and the insecurities of her own shy nature. Life was a daily round of school, swimming, roaming the property and playing with the Hayward children. Jane and Brooke Hayward, Leland and Margaret's eldest daughter, became constant companions.

Frances Fonda bore the war and her husband's absence with the stoic resolve that was part of her Seymour heritage. Her life became her children, her house and looking after her extensive real estate and stock market holdings. She brought to these tasks a singular efficiency that amazed her friends. She organized the house so that everything was in complete order at all times, supervised the staff—servants, governesses and gardeners—with executive aplomb and directed the children's activities with stern but affectionate control. She had an inventive business head and easily took charge of the family finances.

Her day was as organized as a corporate president's. She got to her office, which was adjacent to her bedroom, no later than nine each morning. She would be met there by her secretary, who would open and lay out the mail while Frances was on the phone ordering provisions, checking a discrepancy in a bill or seeking information from a broker on a potential stock purchase. She would then go through that day's correspondence, dictate replies and pay bills. Next, she would turn her attention to the day's activities. If a dinner party were in the offing, she would dictate the menu, the guest list, the kind of table linen to be used, the type of flower arrangements. Her secretary would then type up the lists and give them to Frances. With the prepared lists in hand she would tour the house, instructing the cook on the menu, telling the gardener which flowers to cut, the maid which linen and flatware to lay out. Walking through the house, she would also notice, with her fine eye for detail, whatever irregularities might exist—a half-filled cigarette box, a candy tray slightly askew, a brown leaf on one of the plants. She would immediately pluck the leaf, straighten the tray, take the cigarette box to the pantry to be filled. Then it would be upstairs to inspect the condition of the children's rooms. If she noted any irregularities—a sock tossed carelessly under a bed, a toy left off its proper shelf—there would be a note of admonishment for the offending child. Next would be a tour of the grounds—to check the pool for cleanliness, the playhouse for order, the greenhouse for the condition of the plants, the gardens for absence of weeds.

So went the days of Frances Fonda. She was no less a perfectionist than her husband and in many ways was probably more capable because she was able to touch a greater variety of bases with her skills. When Henry Fonda came home from the war in 1945, he found a perfectly functioning household, with everything in readiness for him to resume his hobby as a part-time farmer.

He also found a daughter who had grown measurably since he last had seen her; not only that, he saw that she was developing into a bundle of contradictions. She was eight now and usually well behaved, but she was occasionally given to sudden bursts of willfulness. She had been trained to contain her emotions and to maintain careful control over her behavior, and most of the time she succeeded. But occasionally there would be an outburst, and she would quiver with barely suppressed rage, her true instincts locked in combat with her trained responses. Since he despised neuroticism in any form and found displays of it embarrassing, these not infrequent behaviorial aberrations on Jane's part disturbed him. Other than that, life went along temperately at the mountaintop homestead.

Jane was doing well in the third grade at the Brentwood School, and if she had any awareness that her father was an important movie star, she didn't reveal it. The Brentwood School was filled with the offspring of film and theatrical celebrities, so not much notice was given Henry Fonda's daughter.

Jane was aware of what her father did, however. Between seeing one or two of his Western films on the home projector and watching him intently guide his tractor through the gardens, she had formed an image of him as an outdoorsman who, in his adult way, shared her own fantasies about cowboys and Indians, horses and cows, buffalo herds and branding parties.

With her father back on the farm, Jane began to neglect her dolls and other young-girl interests for the dream life of a boy. Except when there was a special social occasion, her standard mode of dress around the house was cowboy hat and boots, blue jeans and flannel cowboy shirt. Peter followed suit, and much of their time was spent with Jane leading him on play forays to distant corners of the property. They made imaginary raids on Indian villages, defended their own forts from the marauding Indians, mounted mock cavalry charges on their carrousel horses, rounded up wandering buffalo and saved pretty damsels in distress from the clutches of Black Bart villains—just as they had read about in the books and seen in the movies.

Often the Hayward children participated in these games. It was a happy time for Jane because she had a talent for acting out the various roles and would take the lead to get things going. Occasionally she would become bossy, but most of the time she was able to direct her cohorts through the persuasion of her enthusiasm. It pleased her to have other kids following her, even if most of the time it was only her little brother, and the more response she received, the more inventive she became. She liked the feeling of authority these games produced in her and could go on at them for hours, resenting the peal of the old school bell in the cupola that was the signal around the farm that it was time to abandon the game and report to the house for an adult-inspired activity—usually lunch or dinner.

When her father was at home puttering around the gardens or refinishing an old piece of furniture in his shop, she trailed after him like a duckling, shyly but incessantly asking questions about this or that, imitating his distinctive amble and more often than not getting in the way. To Fonda, his agricultural and carpenterial pursuits were a form of therapy. He would set himself a task and then plunge into it with a concentration and dedication that brooked no interruptions. Consequently he often grew impatient with the persistence of Jane's juvenile curiosity and testily sent her scurrying with a curt dismissal.

Her worship of her father was not to be denied, however, even if it had to be accomplished at a safe distance or through the vehicle of her own consuming fantasies.

Jane had finally got people to drop the nickname Lady, more as a result of her boyish interests and energy than through persuasion on her own part. She had definitely graduated from the "little lady" role she had been molded in by her mother during her earlier years. She was tall for her eight years. The silky champagne hair of her infanthood had darkened to a burnish, and she began to grow a bit pudgy, losing the doll-like quality she had earlier possessed.

Henry Fonda's first acting assignment after his return in 1945 was the starring role in *My Darling Clementine*, in which he played the legendary Wyatt Earp, marshal of Tombstone, in his search for the killer Clantons. When the picture was released in 1946, he scored heavily with the critics, who generally agreed that his version of the much-portrayed Earp was the definitive characterization. Before the war Fonda had established himself as one of America's foremost Western actors. His natural drawl, at once hesitant and authoritative, his slightly stooped, wary stance, his loping gait and his uniquely authentic face, strong but not blatantly heroic—all contributed to his believability. When these were coupled with his actor's sense, which was restrained and unmannered—almost indifferent (although he could be anything but indifferent about his craft)—audiences were magnetized. Fonda was certainly not a magnetic man in real life, at least not in the sense of the high-energy screen Lothario. But through the chemistry of diffidence and honesty he had become a magnetic actor.

He had also proved that he could reverse the coin of the character he was most generally identified with to show another side of that type. He could play contemporary comedy with a droll credibility and give his characters in serious dramas an engaging identifiability. His face was American bedrock in the minds of millions of moviegoers, and the magic of his attraction was the security that face, and the style associated with it, provided. Audiences believed in Henry Fonda and were never forced to endure a "performance."

My Darling Clementine was the first movie Fonda had made with John Ford as director since *Grapes of Wrath*, and it was the first for director and star together in an area in which both had had individual successes—the Western. During the month or so before the start of filming Fonda was required to grow a beard, much to the consternation of Jane, who suddenly detected an air of menace in her father's hirsuteness. Only long, patient explanations by Frances finally persuaded her that her father had not turned into an ogre. The explanations also served to impress on Jane just exactly what it was her father did for a living. She was a bit disappointed to learn that her father was not a real cowboy, only a play one. But inasmuch as he was in his own way doing essentially what she liked to do, her admiration and respect for him deepened. Fortunately the beard came off shortly after filming was begun.

In 1946 Fonda signed to play the leading role of the runaway priest in *The Fugitive*, most of which John Ford was filming in Mexico. Frances joined her husband on location. They both learned to like the native burros, and when they returned home they told their animal-crazy children about them in such an enthusiastic way that the two kids begged to have some of their own. A short time later Henry heard that MGM was willing to get rid of a pair of burros called Pancho and Pedro.

Summoning Jane and Peter one night, he said, "I'll get you the burros provided that you both take care of them. They'll be your responsibility. Is it a deal?" Jane and Peter ecstatically agreed. They got their burros, made a little stable for them in one of the farm sheds and treated them like their own children. Jane fed and watered them religiously each morning before leaving for school and on her return would be back in her cowboy duds exercising them. From her father's point of view the acquisition of the burros was a good way of imbuing the children with responsibility and giving them pleasure at the same time.

Both Fonda parents were in agreement on this. Neither felt pleasure should come cheap. Nor did they believe in doting on their children. Their convictions on this gradually muddied, however. The high ideals they originally had for the upbringing of their offspring, which they had discussed and agreed on during that romantic period ten years earlier, had somehow become diffused. True, they were both ten years older—Henry was forty-one, Frances thirty-nine—and aging, coupled with the experience of parenthood, has a way of eroding ideals. Nevertheless, if they had lost some of the vigor of their notions about child rearing, they were still good parents. They instructed the children in their duties and responsibilities as human beings. They were neither overly permissive nor excessively strict, although sometimes their patience wore thin in the face of their other concerns—Frances' with house and business affairs, Henry's with his work and hobbies.

Something else had become diffused, too—their relationship. They didn't really discuss it, for it was untoward for either of them to raise the black flag of discontent. But discontent was growing. Minor arguments over the children were easily handled, for they really had no differences on that score. Their dignified approach to Jane and Peter was something that came out of their own lives and inheritances, and it was easy for each of them to fend off the children's youthful hungering for attention and affection. Again, pleasure should not come cheap. Nor should praise. Nor affection and attention. Not all the responsibility should rest on the parents, though, and Jane was now at an age when she should begin to understand that a relationship, even a child-adult relationship, is a two-way street. One must give as much as one expects to take.

But from two parents who were themselves basically ungiving, how was Jane supposed to learn this? It was not a question she at her age was able to ask. Even if she were, her parents would probably not have been able to answer it.

Her questions came in a different manner. They were put in the form of behavior and attitude, the way all emotionally suppressed nine- and ten-year-old children's questions are. But her father could not perceive the questions being asked—he was at heart a pragmatic man. In spite of the endearing, sympathetic image he projected, he was not attuned to the more subtle needs of juvenile life.

Being a woman—if a tautly strung one—Frances Fonda was more sympathetic to emotional undercurrents, yet her basic training in life had given her a strong distaste for their expression, especially when such expression revealed self-pity or despondency. She had been brought up to be strong, independent and, if the need be, self-sufficient. She was, like her husband, discomfited by displays of negative emotion; even reckless jubilation embarrassed her. She believed in the dignity of man, not just as a philosophical concept but as a practical virtue, and had tried to instill this belief in her children. Pan, the daughter of her first husband, certainly took the lessons well—she was a model teen-ager with all the graces of her heritage. But Jane and Peter—they seemed to be cut from a different cloth, as indeed they were.

Frances Fonda could organize a household and run a charity or direct a party for fifty people with the ease and precision of a mathematician balancing a bank account; Henry Fonda could cut a garden furrow straight as a die and fill a dramatic character to the brim with humanity. But neither was able to reach across the emotional gulf between them and their children. For some reason they had become locked into their own repressions and were unable—or perhaps unwilling—to crack the lock. They each saw the weakness in the other but were unable to see it in themselves. Or if they did see it, they were unable to admit it.

To compound the difficulty, Henry was again growing bored with film acting. He hungered for more demanding challenges, which he was sure he could only find on the stage. The more restless he became, the less tolerant he was toward the individuals around him, including those within his family. He had long before resigned himself to Frances' lack of interest in his work and was probably even grateful for it since her indifference relieved him from having to discuss it. Down deep, though, it angered him.

But appearances must be kept up, and the Fondas, sailing through 1947 on uneasy waters, kept them up. There was tension, but not enough to divert the ship from its course. Henry Fonda made two more movies and ferociously channeled his growing discontent into his fields and gardens. Jane grew chubbier and, on the receiving end of increased parental criticism, turned to her equally anxious brother and her burros and her secret hideouts for solace. Frances Fonda withdrew further into her command of household activities—the house itself seemed to become the only member of the family, aside from Pan, that she could relate to.

Then came the change in everyone's fortunes.

3. Eastward Ho!

Henry is a man reaching but unreachable, gentle but capable of sudden wild and dangerous violence. His face is a picture of opposites in conflict.

—JOHN STEINBECK

JANE FONDA at ten continued to be absorbed in her cowboy dreams. Occasionally her mother dressed her up and sent her off to children's parties in Beverly Hills and Bel Air, but she hated these functions and would spend most of the time hovering shyly and uncomfortably on the fringes of the festivities. When reports of her timidity filtered back to her mother and father, they were greeted with the anger and frustration anxious parents invariably feel about children who do not seem to be fitting in.

Parental pride is an easily bruised quality. Jane resented her parents' insistence on thrusting her into crowded rooms of babbling children. The sense of inadequacy that had been brewing in her made it virtually impossible for her to react in any but the most antisocial way. Although both Henry and Frances themselves were basically shy and private people, they were perfectly capable in the exercise of social intercourse. They were determined, therefore, that their children grow up practiced in the social niceties and able to hold their own in a roomful of their peers. Jane's relative isolation during the previous few years had put her at a disadvantage insofar as meeting the demands of certain social situations was concerned, and it was time to correct that.

When Jane reacted with displeasure, and sometimes panic, over being sent on these training forays to other children's homes, her parents let their embarrassment conquer their understanding of her childish anxieties. Her recalcitrance constituted an injury to their pride, a slap in the face of their desire and expectation that their children should be perfect junior editions of themselves. Their recognition of their own anxieties and insecurities as human beings did not extend to admitting the possibility of their existence in the children. So they became more determined that Jane, and later her brother, should continue with their social education despite their resistance. Henry and Frances agreed that Jane's timidity was just a stage she was going through, the result of a hypersensitive nature, and that the trauma and agony of being forced to participate in upper-class childhood society was a necessary price to be paid in exchange for the proper education. Besides, her inexplicable fears and resulting behavior were an unflattering reflection on them.

For Jane, the parties and other functions she was sent to were a juvenile form of hell. She could not understand her parents' insistence on her attendance at these social activities when she had made it so clear to them that she wanted no part of them. Pressed for explanations, she could only shrug and make what would emerge as vague childish excuses that would be dismissed before she got halfway through them. She hated her own inarticulateness about this problem; it only made her feel more inadequate. And she hated her parents' failure to see between the lines of her reticence and their unwillingness to understand and comfort her fears in a way that was meaningful to her. But she was an obedient child. Though she froze up each time with the diabolical shame that childhood insecurities provoke, she grudgingly obeyed their wishes.

Early in 1947 Henry Fonda made the last film he owed Twentieth Century-Fox on his much-detested contract and resolved to reinvigorate his career by going back to his real love, the theater. His restlessness had reached the point that even he now realized his truculence at home was partly his own doing. He was growing bored with his farming diversions and was becoming less and less communicative with his family. He ached for something that would give him the kind of self-esteem he only seemed to get from the stage.

In a reflective moment he might have assessed his life. He might have acknowledged the luck factor but would have been unimpressed with the heights his career had reached. In spite of the money he had earned, the family he had created and the land he had developed, he had not achieved the dream that motivated him twenty years before: to be a successful Broadway actor. In a certain sense his life had been a failure; he had sold out to expediency. His pleasures had come too cheap, which was a contradiction of everything he believed in. How much his own guilt over this self-perception contributed to his growing dissatisfaction is a matter of conjecture, but he was obviously disappointed in himself. In that reflective way we all have, he was taking his disappointment out on those closest to him. He had become a nit-picking perfectionist at home, as critical of his wife and children as he was of himself. What was worse, he saw what was happening and was unable to do anything about it.

Jane's childhood friend Brooke Hayward recalls that Jane's father was "melancholy and saturnine, always about to explode or angry for no reason." Another of her schoolmates has a similar recollection. "We were all afraid of Jane's father," she recently told an interviewer. "We always felt he was a time bomb ready to explode. But it was years later when we actually saw him lose his temper over some forgotten trivia. He was booming, purple-faced, with veins sticking out on his temples. It was the only time I was ever privileged to see what may have been a constant for Lady Jane."

Henry Fonda's real self was in extreme variance to his screen image of the calm, taciturn, engaging leading man. Yet it was precisely his hypercritical nature that had enabled him to sculpt that image. Of course Jane had no image of her father other than the one she perceived at home. "I loved him desperately," she has said. "I was very much under his spell. . . . We wanted the intimacy he had with his pals, but it never happened."

Fonda's pals were men like Richard Rodgers, Oscar Hammerstein, John Wayne, James Stewart, John Ford, Ward Bond, John Hodiak, Joshua Logan and Leland Hayward. They all visited the farm at one time or another, and Stewart even lived there for a while after the war. Henry and his cronies would sit around the playhouse playing cards, drinking and talking shop. Jane, hungry for attention and for any opportunity to share in her hero-father's life, often intruded on these sessions until a severe reprimand from Fonda sent her away, hurt and grieving that her father could embarrass her so, confused by the apparent fact that she was unimportant to him.

Criticism, reprimands, admonishments, warnings—these all seemed to grow in proportion to Jane's reaching out. Where she once worshiped her father, she now began to fear him. Her fears often expressed themselves in the form of bad dreams. "As a young girl most of my dreams evolved from the basic need of being loved and being frustrated in fulfilling that need." A recurring dream was one in which she found herself in a large banqueting hall faced with mountains of food but unable to reach any of it. Another consisted of long, exhausting and fruitless chases after delicately beautiful butterflies. In contrast with her quarries, she would be dressed in drab, ungainly clothes, and her hands, distorted to abnormal size, would refuse to work.

With her fears came stronger feelings of inadequacy and insecurity. Superficially her father demanded a great deal of her, and the few times she succeeded in carrying out his wishes they would go unnoticed. When, at the end of 1947, her father left for New York to go into rehearsals for a play he had found, she was not sorry to see him go. Nevertheless, she missed him desperately.

Earlier in the year Fonda received word from Joshua Logan that Logan and Thomas Heggen had written a play based on Navy life in the South Pacific during the war. They were sure the title role would be perfect for Fonda's return to Broadway. When Fonda flew to New York to see about another play, Logan read him his and Heggen's play, which was called *Mister Roberts*. Fonda enthusiastically agreed to do it. He returned to Brentwood, made one last Western for John Ford, *Fort Apache*, and was quickly on his way back to New York to start rehearsals.

Mister Roberts opened on Broadway in February, 1948, and was an immediate smash hit, with Fonda earning the best reviews that could possibly be hoped for. It was a transforming experience for him. Never in his life had he experienced such joy as he found in the process of putting together *Mister Roberts*. On opening night the audience did not merely give the play an ovation; they shouted themselves hoarse. The curtain kept going up as the actors took bow after bow. The audience wouldn't leave. Finally Fonda had to make one of his rare curtain speeches: "This is all Tom and Josh wrote for us. If you want, we can start all over again." As John Chapman reported in the next day's *Daily News*, "I hung around awhile, hoping they would."

Mister Roberts was a reunion of old friends now embarked on an exciting, profitable business and artistic venture. Leland Hayward produced the show. Logan, aside from co-authoring it, also directed it. Fonda was the star and was now faced with the happy prospect of a long run. Within weeks orders were coming in for seats that would not be available for at least two years. Fonda decided that the only answer would be to bring his family East.

At first he was hesitant about suggesting it to Frances. He knew she would not take kindly to having to pack up and move. On the other hand, it would be good for the children to get out of their remote rural environment and see a little more of the world. He was thinking of Jane especially; it would be a fine opportunity to move her out of her tomboy isolation and into closer proximity to the society she would eventually have to grow up in.

Fonda was right; Frances didn't take too well to the prospect of moving East. But she had no choice because Henry had no intention of giving up the play. He not only was basking in the success he had achieved as the star of *Mister Roberts*, but was back in the milieu that gave him his only real pleasure. The smell of greasepaint and the power of performance had been recaptured, as well as the backstage camaraderie he had missed for so long. Now that he had these again he was not going to let them slip away.

The Haywards had decided to divorce. Although this was a sad note in the life of Frances Fonda, it made it easier for her to accept the necessity of moving back East. Margaret Hayward was already making plans to move with her three children to Greenwich, Connecticut. Frances and Henry therefore arranged to take a house in Greenwich so that all the children would be able to remain close to one another.

Frances spent the spring of 1948 organizing the move, and she did it with her customary efficiency. With Henry in New York and Frances preoccupied with the myriad tasks involved in disposing of her beloved homestead, Jane and Peter were pretty much on their own. Jane, for her own reasons, was gloomier than her mother over the prospective departure from the farm. As far as she was concerned, it was home; it had never occurred to her that she would have any other. She was lonely for her father, yet happier than she had been for the past two or three years. Nothing she had heard about Connecticut increased her taste for it, even though she would soon have Brooke Hayward and the others back with her and would have more access to her maternal grandparents. There would be a new school, new people, new friends she would have to make. Why couldn't they all just stay here?

The move was made in June, and by midsummer Jane was settled with her family in a big house in Greenwich. There a whole new way of life began. She no longer had the freedom of the Brentwood acres, she was no longer permitted to run around in her Western outfits, and she found herself being chastised more and more often for her unintended breaches of the strange new Eastern etiquette. Her mother, anxious that she quickly fit into the sophisticated customs of Greenwich society, forced her to dress up when neighbors came by and generally imposed her own self-consciousness on Jane. When the Hayward children finally arrived in Greenwich and Brooke greeted Jane with an enthusiastic "Lady

Jane!" the unhappy girl icily replied, "My name is Jane . . . J-A-N-E
. . . if you don't mind."

Jane was enrolled at the Greenwich Academy in the fall of 1948. Like
the Brentwood school, the academy's student population consisted
mostly of children of well-to-do and socially ambitious parents; unlike
Brentwood, it was not accustomed to the children of celebrities. With the
Fonda name practically a household word throughout the country,
therefore, Jane suddenly found herself the object of the kind of treatment
she had never before experienced. It was not so much that her
schoolmates treated her differently; it was the adults—teachers, school
administrators and parents of the other children. At first, preoccupied
with her own shyness, Jane was unaware of this, but it was not long
before she noticed a certain deferentiality in the way her teachers
approached her, the covert glances from parents picking up their
children. The parents' attitudes eventually filtered into their own
children's consciousnesses, and in a matter of weeks Jane was somewhat
of a celebrity.

Of course, her mother was aware of the likelihood of this happening.
Although there was about it something that secretly pleased her, she
tried to impress upon Jane the importance of not letting it affect her.
This, of course, only made Jane more aware of her special place in the
world in which she was now living.

Jane, on no account of her own, suddenly found herself the most
popular member of the sixth grade at Greenwich Academy. For her this
was fortuitous, for her quick acceptance enabled her at least partially to
overcome her shyness and move more easily into the society of
eleven-year-olds. But as is often the case with insecure preadolescent
children who suddenly find themselves in the limelight, her enthusiasm
for her new role sometimes overboiled. She became rambunctious
around the classroom and often led eager-to-follow classmates in
conspiracies of maldeportment that resulted in more trouble for them
than for her. One classmate recalls, "There was this shed on the school
grounds where we all used to go to listen to Jane tell her dirty
traveling-salesman stories." Whether these stories were ones she had
picked up by eavesdropping on her father and his cronies is uncertain,
but soon complaints began to be made about Jane by other parents.
They were at first delighted to have their children associating with the
famous Henry Fonda's daughter, but their vicarious pleasure was
eventually dislocated by what they considered to be the insidious effects

young Jane was having on the children. Word of their displeasure eventually filtered back to the Fonda household, and a new round of parental criticism began.

Frances Fonda returned East in the expectation that her husband's success and acclaim in *Mister Roberts* would somehow put new blood in their marriage. On the few occasions in California when they had sincerely tried to discuss the turn their relationship had taken since his return from the war, he had blamed his growing restlessness and incommunicativeness on his Hollywood situation. He admitted to a dread of ever again falling back into the poverty he had experienced during the Depression years and blamed this dread for his willingness to settle for the easy and plentiful money of a Hollywood career. But it was exactly the spiritual limitations of his Hollywood career that he found so unsettling. Frances was led to believe that until he was able to break out of the cocoon of security he had wrapped them in, he would be unable to recover in himself the man of ideals and dreams he had been when they married. Frances felt she understood the paradoxes her husband had been wrestling with; although she could not quite comprehend his reasons for taking it all so seriously, she tried in every way she knew to sympathize and encourage him. She was sure, then, that *Mister Roberts* would be the vehicle of his liberation from the demons in his life. She was crushed when she discovered, therefore, after trustingly giving up the Brentwood homestead, that it was not.

Rather than liberate Henry Fonda from the pattern of alternating moodiness and elation that had established itself in his nature, *Mister Roberts* intensified it. In a sense the play became his whole life. Although it was an interesting play, tinged with the sense of tragedy one of its authors, Thomas Heggen, would later succumb to, it was not an immortal piece of dramatic literature. There would be many productions of *Mister Roberts* after this one, with many stars cast in the title role, but the play would never have the singular magic it had in its first production. This magic was embodied in Henry Fonda, in the total and absolute believability he brought to the role. It was one of those rare times in the history of the theater when an actor actually became, in every possible dimension, the character he was playing. Audience appeal to Fonda in the role was irresistible. Henry Fonda *was* Mister Roberts.

It didn't take long for Fonda to realize this. Once he did, which was before Frances and the family moved East, the weight of his new responsibility fell on him like a sandbag. Rather than release him from the slavery of his critical and responsible nature, his stewardship of the role—indeed of the entire play—ground him deeper into the mire of paradox. With his sense of obligation intensified as a result of his responsibility, he virtually took charge of the production—more thoroughly than if it had been his own family—and ran the company like a stern but benevolent father.

At times, apparently, he became a martinet. Film director Henry Hathaway, a friend of Fonda's, remembers that "Hank ran that *Mister Roberts* company like a hard-driving infantry officer commanding combat troops. I was in New York at the time shooting a film. For a bit part in the picture I was using one of the actors from the cast of the play. It worked out fine, because the man could shoot with me during the day and do his performance with Fonda—he had only one line to say—each night. But one matinee day I inadvertently kept the man overtime, and he didn't get back to the theater in time to say his one line. That night Hank called me in an utter fury. He really raised hell. He threatened to have me fined and the actor fired and kicked out of the union. He said I was irresponsible and uncaring and everything else he could think of. But then, the following week, he called me, and we had dinner together. He never mentioned one word about our battle. But what a temper!"

Fonda could not help bringing his concerns home with him, once his family had settled in Greenwich. Riding high with his command of *Mister Roberts*, it was impossible to demand less from his wife and children in the conduct of their lives. Frances, Jane and Peter thus found a man who was at turns vocally critical and moodily, judgmentally silent. His emotional preoccupation with his stage family cut him off from his real family, and often the only emotion he was able to articulate was impatience. When he criticized or gave advice to one of the company members, he found he was listened to, that he received the sort of responses that he meant to elicit. As backstage *doyen*, keeping his charges in line and the production running at the high peak of perfection he had sought in his own performance, he was happy. This was the kind of man-to-man situation in which he was best able to operate. "*Mister Roberts* was a love story backstage," he has said. "We were all just crazy about the play. If anybody let down, he had thirty other guys on him. It was like being in love. You had this good feeling in your guts practically all the time."

He found "this good feeling" overturned just about every time he went home. Peter, lonely for his animals and unsettled by the move to Greenwich, was becoming fractious and in need of constant discipline. Fonda dispensed it in the only way he knew how but succeeded only in exacerbating his son's willfulness. Jane, trying to make the adjustment from tomboy to proper young lady, took many missteps that seemed to require reprimand and lecture. Frances, bitter with her husband's increasing remoteness and feeling betrayed by the letdown in her expectations, grew more anxious and high-strung. And as the unresolved tension increased, she became—and she hated this in herself—more bitchy. She still loved Henry, but the more she tried to reach him, the less responsive he became.

The children were soon engulfed by the tension. They walked on eggshells, waiting for their father to blow up over something or other, and were grateful for his silences. Yet his silences were scary, too, for by now even in them criticism seemed implicit and rejection confirmed. "He was always making us feel guilty," Jane later said. " 'Jesus Christ,' he used to say, 'when are you going to straighten out?' "

Fonda's arguments were not with his children, though. They were the arguments of a forty-four-year-old man with himself over his own guilts and contradictory drives. A man who revered the idea of home and family, he had discovered himself a failure in securing the idea. Perhaps he had made a mistake in marrying Frances, but that was something only he could be held accountable for. He was willing to admit to his responsibility in the collapsing dream, yet this form of self-criticism appeared only to heighten his dissatisfaction with the whole business.

He saw no incongruity in holding the same high expectations of his children that he demanded of his stage colleagues. Indeed, his expectations of Jane and Peter were even stricter. There was only one way to do something—the right way and, if possible, the perfect way. That Jane and Peter were having difficulty fulfilling these expectations reinforced his conviction that the Seymour inheritance and influence were, more and more, dominating their lives. He had liked Frances' family but had always felt a bit suspicious of their easy ways and the rigorless, intellectually flat lives they lived. Now, with them on the scene more frequently, he saw his children responding to their consoling ministrations, and it angered him. It was, again, pleasure coming cheap, and it interfered with—often contradicted—his own standard of love and child rearing. The children's responsiveness to his in-laws was a rejection on their parts of his strict style, and it gave him greater cause to resent Frances for letting it happen.

Jane entered the seventh grade at Greenwich Academy in the fall of 1949. Approaching twelve years of age, she had settled herself into Greenwich life and, though not particularly happy, managed to comfort herself with her few friends and her daily round of activities—school, horseback riding, pet raising and so on. She had put away most of her cowboy-and-Indian fantasies and substituted for them with more genteel Eastern ambitions. At riding school she often had a chance to watch a group of hunt club members gather on horseback in their colorful riding habits and set off behind a pack of yelping dogs in pursuit of fox. This sight gave birth to an ambition to one day embark on a career as a master of fox hounds. She would also watch with fascination the way the local veterinarians handled any of the returning horses or hounds that had injured themselves in the hunt. She admired the combination of authority and compassion they exercised in their approach to the animals and resolved to become a veterinarian when she grew up. She nurtured these dreams but kept them mostly to herself. She still felt a powerful love for her father, but it was now mixed with a sense of intimidation, and she was learning to meet his remoteness with a remoteness of her own. If she was aware of its infuriating effect on him, she did not let on.

She was involved less and less with her brother, and her mother, though bravely trying to keep up the appearance of a happy and fulfilled woman, was rapidly becoming consumed by her own depression. Thus, Jane's main adult contact began to occur with her grandmother, who was more frequently on the scene. In sixty-three-year-old Sophie Seymour's sense of balance and her still-vigorous enthusiasm for the marvels of childhood, Jane Fonda finally found someone who loved her on her own terms.

Henry Fonda was spending less time at home in Greenwich. Rumors started to float back to the increasingly distraught Frances Fonda that her husband was seeing another woman. Her friends had known about it for some time and, aware of the thin line she was walking, tried to keep it from her. The rumor was soon confirmed, with sadness, by Henry himself. He had become enamored of twenty-one-year-old Susan Blanchard, the stepdaughter of his friend Oscar Hammerstein, and intended to go on seeing her.

Frances accepted the news with stiff resolve, careful at all costs not to raise a fuss and let Jane see her deep distress. Nor Henry, for that matter. Nor her parents and friends. She calmly discussed the ramifications of Henry's announcement with him. There was only one thing for him to do. He moved out.

4. A Death in the Family

It seemed easier on the kids not to tell the whole truth. But the bottom line of it all is: I wasn't telling the truth.

—HENRY FONDA

HER father's departure just before her twelfth birthday was explained to Jane in the calm, rational terms that quarreling parents use to soften the impact of a separation: Her mother and father were not getting along well . . . trial separation to see if they couldn't work out their differences . . . no effect on their love for Jane . . . father would be nearby and she'd see a lot of him . . . they'd all remain friends . . . she was not to fret. . . .

And she didn't—at least for a while. In fact, she quickly learned to like the separation. First of all, it was as though a weight had been removed from her, and within a short time her attitude around the house improved. Second, seeing her father on new terms was a novel experience. Suddenly he was no longer disciplining her or ignoring her. He was taking her places and doing things with her. If occasionally his patience wore thin, well, that was all right, at least now she had some time alone with him without the constant overriding pressures of before. He seemed to take more of an interest in her. There were still the silences, but even these seemed different—they were more the awkward kinds of silences, silences that occur between two people who don't have anything to say; they were less filled with judgmental implications. Jane began to relax a little with her father, and he with her, although the strain of diffidence remained between them. She was careful not to show too much of herself to him.

With her father out of the house Jane began to change into the proper young lady her mother and grandmother had hoped she would be. Long, quiet talks with her grandmother about the family situation were meant to impress on her the importance of her place in the family and the role she was expected to play, and they had a positive effect on her. She also became aware of her mother's state of distress. Although she didn't

44

completely understand it, she felt an increased responsibility to please her mother and tried very hard to do so.

If Frances Fonda really hoped that the separation was to be a trial one, she was quickly disabused of the idea. Henry Fonda, being as discreet as he could about it, continued to see Susan Blanchard in New York. Susan, though just out of her teens, was a beautiful girl with a sophistication and charm beyond her years. She had got to know Fonda while dating another member of the *Mister Roberts* cast—her brother was one of the show's stage managers—and had at first been confused by his ambivalence toward her. In the beginning their relationship consisted of nothing more complicated than an occasional exchanged glance or casual hello. But she had been intensely aware of a certain electricity coming from his eyes when he looked at her, as well as a deep sadness to which she found herself responding. As sophisticated as she was, she was still young enough to be flattered by the celebrated actor's guarded attentions.

When it became obvious to Frances that there would be no diverting her husband from his new course, her depression intensified. He asked her for a divorce. She resisted for a while, but the pressure and anxiety were beginning to take such a toll on her spirit that by December, 1949, following the advice of her parents and a doctor, she agreed. A public announcement was quickly made by Fonda in New York. The actor now felt free to declare the seriousness of his intentions to Susan Blanchard.

Sophie Seymour thought that with this out of the way, the decision made, Frances Fonda would be able to resume a normal life. But she did not realize the depths of her daughter's despair. For the next month Frances outwardly tried to maintain her equilibrium, calling on all her training and heritage to bury her depression. But the effort was too much for her. She was no longer the master of her feelings, and the more she tried to balance herself on her emotional tightrope, the less of a foothold she was able to maintain. Finally, she broke altogether and on February 3, 1950, was taken in a state of extreme distress to the Craig House Sanatorium in Beacon, New York.

Grandmother Seymour had moved into the Fonda house earlier to help look after Jane and to console her daughter over the breakup of her marriage. She virtually took charge of things while Frances started on the long road of therapy at Craig House. Frances' diagnosis was "severe psychoneurosis with depression."

Beacon, New York, is an old river town on the Hudson River, about sixty miles north of New York City. During the late nineteenth century wealthy industrialists built their mansions and estates on the east bank of the Hudson north and south of Beacon. After the Depression, when many of the estate owners' fortunes were wiped out, the estates were put up for sale and could be acquired cheaply. Simultaneously the idea of private mental hospitals in peaceful sylvan settings was gaining currency. Advocates of the relatively new and uncertain sciences of psychoanalysis and clinical psychotherapy had at least partly proved that their methods could be effective in the cure of certain mental and emotional illnesses. Not everyone who suffered from mental imbalance was necessarily insane, and many could be restored to normality through proper diagnosis and effective therapeutic treatment. But such treatment required that the patient be isolated from the surroundings in which his or her illness had surfaced and be placed in an environment that was peaceful and conducive to feelings of security, without the institutional bleakness of government-supported urban hospital wards. Consequently many practitioners of psychiatry got syndicates together to purchase some of the Hudson River estates at deflated prices for the purpose of refurbishing them as private sanatoriums. The syndicates incorporated these rural estates and ran them as nonprofit hospitals. They provided comfortable livelihoods for psychiatrists and, because of their high operating costs, convenient rest-and-rehabilitation homes for mentally distressed members of the upper classes. Craig House Sanatorium was one of these.

Frances Fonda had been at Craig House for a month and a half and seemed to be making progress. She had bounced back from her initial incapacity fairly quickly and impressed her psychiatrist, Dr. Courtney Bennett, with her desire to overcome her difficulties. By the first week of April, with the soothing scent of spring creeping up the Hudson Valley, Frances was beginning to talk about returning home. The doctor agreed that she was coming along nicely and that perhaps by May she would be ready to go back to her family.

At 6:30 A.M. on the morning of April 14 the sanatorium's night nurse, Amy Grey, entered Frances' room with a wake-up glass of orange juice. She was surprised to find the bed empty but assumed that Mrs. Fonda had risen by herself. She placed the juice on the night table and started to cross the room to knock on the bathroom door, which was closed. She noticed a piece of paper lying on the carpet near the door and paused to pick it up. It was a note, addressed to her and written in Frances Fonda's fine, graceful script. "Mrs. Grey," it read, "do not go into the bathroom, but call Dr. Bennett."

Amy Grey looked suspiciously at the bathroom door for a moment. Then she left the room to find Dr. Bennett. Bennett arrived a few minutes later and found Frances sprawled unconscious in a pool of blood on the bathroom floor, her throat slashed. Bennett felt a flutter of pulse in Frances' wrist and worked frantically with towels to stanch the flow of blood from the deep wound in Frances' neck. But before any other lifesaving measures could be taken, Frances was dead.

Another note lay on the top of the toilet seat. In it Frances apologized to the doctor and to her parents. "This is the best way out," it concluded.

Henry Fonda was notified by his mother-in-law later that morning. He turned to stone. Sophie Seymour ordered her daughter's body taken immediately to a mortuary in Hartsdale, New York, near Greenwich. That afternoon a private funeral service was held. Frances was cremated, and her ashes were buried in the Seymour family plot in a Hartsdale cemetery. Fonda was at the service but was in such a state of shock that he barely heard a word that was said. Jane was kept at home.

It all happened so suddenly that no one was prepared for it. Fonda went back to New York that evening fighting his guilt and anger, unsure of what to do. He had never missed a performance of *Mister Roberts*. "I didn't know what to do," he has said, "so I asked Leland."

"Naturally I told him to go on," Hayward recalled in an interview. "A guy's got to keep busy at a time like that. He played that night before an audience that didn't yet know what had happened, and he got control of himself. He had to, once he got out there. If he'd waited, he'd have felt later audiences thinking, *That poor guy up there.* He'd have been a pushover for a dose of self-pity, which never helps anyone."

Fonda played his 883d consecutive performance of *Mister Roberts* that evening. To say that it was his best performance would be a romantic exaggeration. It was simply a performance. Henry Fonda considered himself, more than anything else, a responsible professional.

Shortly after her mother's death the news was broken to Jane. Her father and the Seymours evidently agreed that Jane was not old enough to handle the concept of suicide, especially when it dealt with her own mother, so they decided on a ploy. Although the true story had been featured in the local papers, they told Jane her mother had died suddenly of a heart attack, then cautioned all who knew the real story to cooperate in keeping it from her. Jane was stunned but took the news calmly and, with the encouragement of her grandmother, quickly turned her attention back to her school and extracurricular activities.

With Frances gone, the house they had been living in was disposed of and a new one, also in Greenwich, acquired. Mr. and Mrs. Seymour moved in with Jane and Peter and became, in effect, their foster parents. Their presence during the next year was a calming influence on Jane. Eugene Ford Seymour was already eighty years old but was lively and alert. Sophie Seymour looked after him with wry humor and no-nonsense compassion and took the same approach to Jane and Peter.

Jane, starting the eighth grade at Greenwich Academy in the fall of 1950, had lost much of her preteen awkwardness and was beginning to blossom into a pretty but still pudgy girl. She was faithful to her books, had a tight circle of friends and, except for an occasional sadness about her mother, was quite happy with her grandparents. The Seymours bore no obvious ill will against her father and did everything they could to encourage Jane's devotion to him. Fonda visited the children frequently during the following months and kept close tabs on their progress. He was still the stern father, but now at a remove. For a while he kept a rein on his perfectionism when he was around them, but he found it easier to be more sanguine about Jane than Peter, his ten-year-old son.

Peter had been a source of worry to both his parents since the move from Brentwood to Greenwich. If Jane had been unhappy about moving, her younger brother was miserable. And although he was devoted to Jane, he was also jealous of the attention she received from their father at what he imagined was his expense. It didn't matter that much of the attention focused on Jane took the form of annoyed reprimand; he would rather have had that than the almost complete indifference he usually received. After the Fondas settled in Greenwich, Peter embarked on a compulsive pattern of behavior which drew his father's wrath but little else. As far as he was concerned, that was at least something.

Once Peter's father wised up to his son's childish motives, however, he refused to play the game. He would meet Peter's acts of rebelliousness and petulance with not much more than a cold glare, and eventually he learned to ignore them altogether. Once Fonda moved out of the house, Peter, a lonely and unhappy youngster, found his only solace in his mother. Frances, however, was in the process of crumbling under her own unhappiness, and there was not much she could give him. When she died and when Jane explained to him in her mock-adult way that she wouldn't be coming back, Peter was shaken with a sense of loss almost beyond his ability to comprehend.

Jane adjusted well to her mother's death, but Peter did not. His youthful anguish cast a pall over what Henry Fonda hoped would be a quick return to normality for his children. The Seymours worked as best they could with Peter, but he was too much for them. Plans were made to send him away to boarding school.

As Jane's thirteenth birthday approached in December, her father introduced her one day to Susan Blanchard. He informed Jane that he and Susan planned to marry shortly and expressed the hope that Jane and Peter would come to love her as much as he did. Jane accepted the news without any resentment and shyly sized up her stepmother-to-be. Susan was only ten years older than Jane and had a delicate, refined beauty that astonished the young girl.

Jane's hair had finally settled into its natural color—light brown tinged with russet and blond. She was still taller than most of her female contemporaries, but with her distinctive Fonda features she felt herself to be homely and clumsy. Meeting Susan Blanchard was a revelation that left her filled with preadolescent awe and a dream of one day becoming as beautiful herself. Rather than resent Susan, she admired her. And she was doubly thrilled when Susan took an interest in her.

Henry Fonda and Susan Blanchard were married on December 28, 1950, while his children were on their school vacations. The newlyweds journeyed to St. John's in the Virgin Islands for what they thought would be a quiet honeymoon. Their stay was interrupted shortly after they got there, however, by an urgent message from Greenwich. Peter had shot himself.

As Peter tells it, he may have been trying to commit suicide. "I was visiting the R. H. Kress estate in Westchester. I'm not sure if I was really trying to kill myself or not, but I do recall that after I shot myself, I didn't want to die—and I came very close to dying. Jane tells me the doctor came out of the operating room and said I was dead, that my heart had stopped beating. My sister is prone to dramatize, as I am. He may have said things were looking tense, but regardless of what the doctor said, that's how she took it. She thought it was all over for me. Anyway, I was conscious after I shot myself (with a .22-caliber pistol). I was also very scared, and I got the chauffeur to drive me to a hospital in Ossining."

The bullet pierced his liver. "It took the doctors a while to understand it was a gunshot wound; there wasn't a lot of blood. I was beginning to get a little dopey, but I remember that they didn't know what to do. There was just one doctor around who knew how to operate on bullet wounds, and they finally got him on the phone. He had been the Sing Sing prison surgeon for years, and Ossining Hospital at that time was right next to Sing Sing. Anyway, the man saved my life. I was in intensive care for four weeks."

With the help of the Coast Guard, Henry Fonda was rushed to his frightened son's bedside. The trip must have been an agony for him. First his wife and now his son—would there be no lid on the price he would have to pay for his newfound happiness and freedom? He was profoundly ashamed of Peter but resolved to make more of an effort to get involved with his children. As for Peter, "I guess my father's remoteness from me had something to do with that incident, but now I see that the life of an actor is a very strange thing, and I can see how it interferes with raising children. But my father's nature is, or was, incommunicative."

Jane was taken aback by her brother's brush with death but was discouraged from talking or even thinking about it. Once Peter recovered, their grandparents forbade the children from dwelling on it, just as they prohibited discussion of all unpleasant events. Life struggled back to normal.

With the approach of fall, 1951, arrangements were made for Jane to enter the Emma Willard School for Girls in Troy, New York. Emma Willard is an expensive boarding and day school whose principal function is to prepare its students, mostly daughters of wealthy and socially prominent families throughout the East, for entrance into such colleges as Wellesley, Smith and Vassar—in those days still exclusively women's colleges. Yet it is not merely a finishing school; it has a fairly rigorous program of instruction and a wide-ranging classical curriculum.

During her freshman year at Emma Willard, while waiting for a class to begin, one of Jane's classmates was thumbing through a movie magazine. She handed the magazine to Jane and said, "Hey, I didn't know your mother killed herself." Jane, surprised, said, "She didn't. She had a heart attack." Her classmate smiled knowingly, indicating the magazine. "So why does it say she committed suicide?"

Jane looked at the story with the lurid details of her mother's death. She read it with a fascination that quickly turned to horror. Later, when she questioned her father about it, he admitted the truth and gently explained his and her grandparents' reasons for keeping it from her. Jane went about for a while with her mind and emotions in a state of intense confusion. Once she was able to start sorting it all out dispassionately, she felt betrayed. She was certainly not old enough to start chastising her father for his dishonesty; besides, she was still vaguely afraid of him. There were no dramatic scenes; in fact, Jane was now enlisted in the conspiracy to keep the news from Peter. Nevertheless, her view of Henry Fonda began to change.

5. A Proper Young Lady

> *By the time I was fifteen I thought I was dreadfully grown up, which meant I was already learning to suppress my natural feelings.*
>
> —JANE FONDA

THE Emma Willard School is a compact cluster of imposing neo-Gothic buildings set on a hill above the small, shabby city of Troy, New York, across the river from Albany. Its ivied walls contain an ambience that is steeped in comfort, permanence and security. With its traditional English campus architecture and its hallowed Christian pedagogical customs and rituals, it is a bastion of old-fashioned upper-class privilege.

It was while she was at Emma Willard that Jane Fonda began to learn what it meant to be the daughter of Henry Fonda. Like Greenwich Academy, Emma Willard was used to having in its classes the daughters of the wealthy, and even an occasional celebrity's child was no cause for excitement. Nevertheless, Henry Fonda had a unique kind of fame. His image as a strong, quiet, virtuous, larger-than-life character with a casual, disarming humor and a calm, controlled approach to even the most desperate situations of life—an image that had been carefully cultivated through twenty-nine starring motion-picture roles, then reinforced by *Mister Roberts*—was universal. Consequently the people at Emma Willard not only were highly pleased to have Jane under enrollment, but expected her to be the young female embodiment of this image. Their expectation fell perfectly into line with the school's avowed purpose of producing "young ladies of expanding mind and healthy body, schooled in the social graces and prepared to take their places in the world of modern young women."

Jane Fonda, then, entered the school at a considerable disadvantage compared to most of her classmates, yet she managed to survive the rigors of special judgment that were applied to her. She had already grown accustomed to the critical eye, the judgmental voice, and had little difficulty in adapting to the school's anxiety that the daughter of Henry Fonda be a credit to Emma Willard so that Emma Willard could in turn be a credit to Henry Fonda.

Nor did she have any difficulty subscribing to the school's training in the social graces. Emma Willard's philosophy was fully in accord with the things Jane had been taught at home, first by her mother, then by her grandmother. By the time she entered Emma Willard she had shed most of her tomboyishness and was a pliant receptor of the school's discipline. Save for her abiding love for animals and the fearless ease with which she moved around the school's stables, one would not have guessed that she had grown up in a rustic, outdoor world—however carefully contrived and comfortable that world might have been.

Jane later said about her time at Emma Willard, "It was ghastly—all girls, and that's unhealthy." Perhaps it was, but when Jane was fourteen and in her sophomore year, the company of boys was the last thing she sought. She still had powerful feelings of inferiority about herself, and at this point in her life boys only exacerbated them. Superficially she was a placid girl during her first two years at Willard; at the same time she was driven by a desire to please. She was industrious in her schoolwork and ambitious in tackling special campus assignments, but for the most part she kept to herself. She was slow to approach a classmate, start a friendship or ask a favor and was generally more respected than liked. She hovered on the fringes of things, happy when included in some activity but unable to assert herself without being invited.

Later on in her life Jane would profess a belief in astrology. An astrologist who knew her at fourteen might have suggested that Jane was in the process of struggling through the very strong conflict posed in her nature by her Sagittarius-Capricorn apposition. To the skeptic such an explanation might sound absurd, yet on the basis of her adolescent development the notion has some credibility. She exhibited strong Capricornian traits at times, at others Sagittarian ones. In her childhood her orientation was markedly on the side of Sagittarius, but as she grew up and began to relate to the authority figures in her life—especially her father—her Sagittarian nature was repressed and her Capricornian influences surfaced. The astrologist would say that her early adolescence passed mostly within the grip of the goat sign, but that as she matured and grew away from dependence upon her father, her Sagittarian instincts regained their former power in her life and locked horns, so to speak, with her Capricornian influences. The result was a tortured, incipiently neurotic, alternately ebullient and despondent young woman.

Whether that was the case or not, by the time Jane was a junior at Emma Willard she was making hesitant efforts to step out of her self-contained world. She was aided to a great extent in this by her stepmother, Susan, who was not yet far enough removed from her own adolescence to ignore Jane's silent pleas for help. Susan went to great lengths to be a friend to Jane once she had settled into being Henry Fonda's wife, and Jane responded to her friendship like a hungry infant to the bottle.

Shortly after his marriage to Susan Blanchard, Henry Fonda purchased a town house on East Seventy-fourth Street in Manhattan, a few steps off Lexington Avenue. He had decided to remain in New York and continue to work in the theater. The new house was to be his headquarters. He and Susan had the house refurbished, including bedrooms for Jane and Peter so that the children could spend their school vacations there, and moved in during the fall of 1951. The train trip from Troy to New York City took only three hours, so Jane was able to spend many of her long holiday weekends and school vacations visiting her father and stepmother.

At fifteen Jane was still taller than most of her schoolmates, and although she often felt self-conscious about her weight and her "awful" looks, she was gradually growing into a handsome girl. She was required to wear her dark-gold hair short in accordance with the school's custom. Her short haircut, coupled with the long, prominent Fonda jaw and soft pugged nose, gave her an appearance that vacillated between being "cute" and pugnacious. Within a few years the rest of her facial features would catch up to her already fully developed jaw and she would lose the extreme pudginess of her cheeks. But now, living in a world in which looks meant everything, she was thoroughly dissatisfied with herself.

Whenever she came to New York to stay at her father's house, she found the mood much more relaxed than when her father had been living with her mother. For one thing, Fonda had found a new hobby to fill the gap left by his retirement from agriculture—art. It was an activity that was much more demanding of his penchant for painstaking perfection, and he pursued it for long, solitary hours at a stretch. He had part of the attic of his new house converted into a studio, and Jane could spend an entire weekend on Seventy-fourth Street without seeing her father except to say hello and good-bye.

For another thing, Fonda was, at least for a while, happily married and engaged in another successful Broadway play—*Point of No Return*. In Susan he had found a young woman who was bright and energetic, as well as beautiful and genuinely interested in his work. She knew and understood the theater and was happy to circulate in the world of performers, directors and producers. In the bargain she related well to his children and even took some of the burden of their upbringing off him.

Jane not only discovered in her youthful stepmother an effective mediator between herself and her father, but also found a sympathetic and helpful friend. Susan introduced Jane to the glories and mysteries of New York City. She took Jane along on her rounds of hairdressers, department stores, specialty shops, luncheons and movies and included her in as many other grown-up activities as she could squeeze into a weekend or vacation. Jane soon began to return to Emma Willard from her stays in New York with dreams of one day becoming as sophisticated and charming and beautiful as Susan. She fell in love with her father's wife. It was a love that carried her through the rest of her years at Emma Willard on the wings of dreams and continues to this day.

"It was wonderful," Jane has said about her relationship with her stepmother. "I remember Susan—twenty-five and a ravishing beauty—at a Parents' Day at school. I was so proud of her I almost flipped."

Jane's attachment to her father's third wife represented probably the happiest time of her young life. Susan built up Jane's confidence in herself, and their easy relationship quickly became the envy of Jane's schoolmates. When she returned from her trips to New York with stories of the fantastic times she had had and the incredible people she had met, disguising her enthusiasm behind a casual narrative, Jane's stock at school quickly went up. Whereas before she had kept pretty much to herself, more out of timidity than the snobbery her classmates thought her manner reflected, she now found herself being sought out and, in the unspoken way children have, invited to become a member of the inner circles of Emma Willard.

It was not long before Jane started thinking of Susan Fonda as more than just a stepmother. Susan recalls, "After a while Peter asked me if he could call me Mother, and Jane said she was going to call me Mother, too. The Seymour side of the family got very angry."

Upon Frances Fonda's death new custodial arrangements with regard to Jane and Peter had to be worked out. When Frances took her life, the children were already living with the Seymours. Relations between them and Fonda were strained but civilized. They became a bit more strained when Frances' will was probated and Henry discovered that he had been pointedly excluded from it, though Jane and Peter were left with hefty trust funds. Nevertheless, the adults had to be practical and not let their feelings toward one another affect the children. Henry agreed that Jane and Peter should continue to live in Greenwich with Frances' parents, and this arrangement worked to everyone's satisfaction until Peter had his encounter with the pistol. Once Fonda was settled in his new house in New York, he began to exercise his right to custody of the children. There was a bit of tug and pull between the father and the grandparents. As time went on, the children divided their time, when not away at school, more or less equally between the Seymour home in Greenwich and the Fonda house in New York. By the time Jane was sixteen, though, she was spending most of her out-of-school time with her father and Susan. That was where the action was.

Jane started her junior year at Emma Willard in the fall of 1953 in a much more improved state of mind than when she first enrolled. She was now thinking of college, and like many of her schoolmates, she was concentrating on Vassar. A pair of new ambitions also began to take form as she thought about the future: One had to do with the ballet, the other with art.

The dream of becoming a ballerina was a common fancy among girls her age, and Jane was no less assiduous than the others in her single-minded approach to her daily ballet class. She enjoyed the discipline, the hard work, and the feelings of grace and coordination the classes gave her. The satisfactions were great, and occasionally she got a taste of the power of performance that made them even greater. She understood that to seek distinction in ballet demanded an almost superhuman dedication, and at that point in her life she was eager for something to which she could dedicate herself. She ignored her teachers' gentle discouragements that she would be too tall to become a really first-rate ballerina and pursued her classes with monkish devotion.

The other ambition was slower in forming but later became even more powerful. It flowed from her father, primarily. Henry Fonda had by now immersed himself in painting—it was no longer a form of recreation for him; it had become a serious avocation. He had always had a talent for drawing and had gained a practical knowledge of paints and colors during his scene-designing days in the thirties. He greatly admired the work of Andrew Wyeth, and when he first started painting, he seriously sought not so much to imitate but to emulate Wyeth's style. It was a style well suited to Fonda's nature—melancholy, demanding, deceptively real.

Fonda was serious enough about painting to commend it to Jane as a worthwhile ambition. She had a talent for it. Both Frances and Henry had tried to give their children an early appreciation of art, starting back in the Brentwood days, and it was one form of expression that Henry continued to encourage in Jane throughout her adolescence. Although father and daughter had increasing difficulty relating to each other in many ways, Jane had lost nothing of her deep love for and attachment to him, however incapable she was of expressing it. She responded to his encouragement.

The people at Emma Willard were after her for some time to take part in the Campus Players' dramatic productions, but she had resisted. She resisted because she knew, being Henry Fonda's daughter and living in the shadow of his acclaim as an actor—no matter how comforting that shadow sometimes was—she would be judged on the stage according to standards different from her schoolmates. On the few occasions she had tried to talk to her father about acting, he clammed up or brushed over it, suggesting art as a more worthwhile ambition. So art it was, at least for a while.

Jane hated the isolation of Emma Willard and complained often to her father about it, hoping he would take her out and enroll her in one of the many girls' schools in New York City. But Fonda would not bend. He had finished *Point of No Return* and was about to embark, in the fall of 1953, on a cross-country tour of the *Caine Mutiny Court-Martial* prior to bringing the new play into New York. In addition, he and Susan planned to adopt a baby and were waiting for arrangements to be completed. In view of this, there would not be much time available for Jane if she were to live in New York.

Jane swallowed her disappointment and continued at Willard. Once she accepted her father's decision she expanded her activities at school. She pressed on with her ballet and art studies, tolerated her academic courses and started to engage in a few extracurricular activities. She finally gave in to requests that she join the Campus Players and auditioned for a play. Since Willard was an all-girls school and there were few boys' schools nearby, girls were required to play the male parts in student productions. Jane was a bit abashed, therefore, when she was given a male role for her stage debut. It was the title role in Christopher Fry's *The Boy with a Cart*, a staple of the school-and-college dramatic circuit.

The play called for threadbare costumes and lots of makeup, so it wasn't difficult for Jane, with her short hair, to be disguised as a boy. It was understood by all connected with the productions that they were mounted not as faithful reproductions of the original works but to give the girls the opportunity to gain some experience in acting before an audience. Anne Wellington, former headmistress of Emma Willard, recalls that Jane acquitted herself well as the Boy in the Fry play. She was nervous and self-conscious but had a definite presence and showed obvious talent.

Her next stage outing was in her senior year, when she won the role of Lydia Languish in Sheridan's farce *The Rivals*, another costume production. Again she did well, according to Miss Wellington—"in fact, her performance was memorable." Jane was immensely pleased at the reception she received and was doubly excited to learn that she was able to hold an audience's attention, even make it laugh. She relayed her excitement to her father, who had experienced similar feelings thirty years before. He calmly acknowledged her enthusiasm but was judiciously aloof to any suggestion of an acting career. Her enthusiasm waned.

It was not long, though, before it was revived. In the spring of 1955, as Jane approached her graduation from Emma Willard, she received a phone call from her Aunt Harriet—her father's sister—in Omaha. Harriet, whose married name was Peacock, had followed her brother into the Omaha Community Playhouse back in the late twenties and remained active in it for three decades. She was a member of the fund-raising committee and was planning to ask her brother to return to Omaha for a week during the early summer to do some benefit performances. Having heard about Jane's sudden interest in acting, she thought it might be amusing to include her in the week's festivities.

Jane had been accepted at Vassar along with several of her classmates. She was looking forward to starting there in the fall, but her plans for the summer were vague. Her aunt's phone call was a godsend. Harriet Peacock asked her if she would like to be in the Omaha theater's benefit production of *The Country Girl* with her father. It would be only a small part, but it would lend a nostalgic family quality to the production, and the people in Omaha would be delighted to see Henry's daughter on the stage with him. Jane jumped at the suggestion but was cautioned by her aunt not to whisper a word to her father yet since she hadn't discussed it with him.

When Harriet did raise the subject, Henry was at first worried about it. He agreed to do the benefit but wasn't sure it would be good for Jane to have him around for what would amount to her stage debut. Harriet told him that she had already talked to Jane and that she was eager for the chance. Henry demurred further, suggesting that it might be better for Jane to be cast in another play. Harriet countered with the argument that having all three Fondas involved in the production would be good publicity. Since the point of the benefit week was to raise funds for the theater, the more publicity it received the better. Her idea was to have Henry playing the male lead in *The Country Girl* with Dorothy McGuire, a well-known actress who had also got her start in the Playhouse, in the title role; Jane would have a small part, and Peter would be included in a backstage capacity.

Fonda finally agreed with the proviso that Jane not simply be given the part but that she be required to earn it. Harriet thereupon called Jane back at Emma Willard and auditioned her over the telephone. With that requirement out of the way, plans were set for the production.

When Jane was graduated from Emma Willard in June, her face still had a hint of the pudgy, boyish pugnacity of her childhood, but her figure had thinned out considerably and she had developed a modest bosom. She was well-mannered in the style of the prototypical Emma Willard girl and, with the exception of a few irritating seventeen-year-old's affectations, was well thought of. Her vocabulary was liberally laced with Eastern schoolgirl superlatives like "marvelous," "fantastic" and "adore," and her voice, usually calm and modulated, carried faint overtones of London. She was still shy and sometimes haunted by feelings of inferiority, but her education had taught her how to mask her insecurities under a veneer of schoolgirl sophistication.

Soon after graduation she was on her way to Omaha with her father and brother. "On the plane to Omaha," her father recalls, "something about the way Jane was listening to me—as one adult listens to another—got me to talking about myself and the rough time I'd had getting started in the theater. I'd never talked to her just that way.

"At rehearsals I was determined not to pull professional rank on Jane, but now and then she'd look at me for help, and I couldn't *not* make suggestions. She soaked up direction like a dry blotter.

"In one scene Jane had to enter crying. That isn't easy—walking on at the height of an emotional breakdown. I didn't want to watch. I didn't think she would be able to handle it. I was sure she'd just end up looking phony-dramatic. But I was last off the stage before her entrance and first on afterward. Well, Jane came on wailing and wet-eyed, as though she'd just heard that Vassar was not going to admit her that fall. I couldn't believe it. I couldn't believe she was acting. I thought all her anxieties had broken through the Fonda façade and were tumbling out. But the minute she cleared the stage her face relaxed, she looked at me and said, 'How'd I do?' She didn't understand that she'd done what many professionals couldn't do in a lifetime."

6. Last Train from Poughkeepsie

I was brought up where people didn't express what they really felt. You hid everything. You hid your fears and your sorrows and your pains and your joys and your physical desires. Consequently I was a zombie, living somebody else's image, and I didn't know who I was.

—JANE FONDA

NINETEEN fifty-five was a signal year in the lives of all three Fondas, although the signals were increasingly discordant. For Henry Fonda, it was the year he reached his zenith as a film star with his screen portrayal of Mister Roberts. It was also the year his personal life began to disintegrate again after four modestly contented years. For Jane, it was the year that marked her unsteady passage from restrained, polite schoolgirl to restless, anxious, searching young woman. And for Peter, by then a blade-thin, volatile fifteen-year-old, it was the year the momentum of his adolescent despair shifted into high gear. The personal troubles that haunted each of the Fondas rubbed against the others until, by the end of the year, the emotional climate of the family was thick with unexpressed rage.

During the Broadway run of *Mister Roberts*, Henry Fonda often talked with Logan and Hayward of one day doing the film version. By the time the play was ready for transfer to the screen, however, Hayward, who had sold the property to Warner Brothers with himself as producer, thought Fonda was too old to play the twenty-seven-year-old title character. Fonda had also been too long away from films, Hayward and Warner's decided; he was a stage star now, and the film would be better served by the presence of one of the hot box-office names of the day in the title role—William Holden, for instance, or, ironically, Marlon Brando.

Fonda had been so strongly identified with the character of Mister Roberts, nevertheless, that the film's director—Fonda's old friend John Ford—insisted that he play the role. Ford even went so far as to inform Hayward that without Fonda he wouldn't direct. Hayward gave in. Fonda quickly agreed to terms and set out with the rest of the company for location shooting on Midway Island in the Pacific. His happiness over getting to play Mister Roberts after all was not to last very long, though. By the time the film was finished he would be bitter and disillusioned about one of his closest friends—John Ford.

After developing the character of Roberts onstage for nearly three years, Fonda had very strong convictions about how the role should be played and how the play should be translated to the screen. When he arrived at Midway to film scenes on a Navy vessel, he took one look at the script, saw the changes Ford had made and became, as Leland Hayward recalled a few years later, terribly depressed. "After the first day of shooting he came to me and said, 'My God, Leland, Jack's ruining *Roberts.* We've got to figure out a way to talk some sense into him.' " Later that night John Ford collared Hayward and said the same thing about Fonda. "He said that Hank had an obsession about the character and so on. Tempers were short."

The next day was even worse, according to Hayward. Fonda, after being so long a part of *Mister Roberts*, regarded the original play almost as sacred. He grew even more resentful over what he considered to be Ford's attempts to overplay laugh scenes and to turn the crew of the USS *Reluctant* into a brawling, low-comedy burlesque troupe. For his part Ford was angered by what he took to be Fonda's incursions into the director's bailiwick; he felt betrayed by the man who was playing the part only on his insistence and was infuriated by Fonda's attempts to undermine his directorial authority. "The following evening," according to Hayward, "Hank and I went to Ford's room to talk about the script. Ford *had* made changes, like putting in three pretty nurses instead of one. Hank and I started to talk with him, and we were all pretty upset. Suddenly Ford flung himself from his chair and took a swing at Hank. Hank belted back, more in self-defense than anything else. And there I was, trying to separate them and stop this utterly ridiculous scene. It finally subsided, but Ford and Fonda have barely spoken to each other since."

Soon after the fight Ford left the film, and another director was brought in. The picture was completed and opened in 1955 to great acclaim, reestablishing Fonda as a first-rank film star after seven years on the stage. But he remained unhappy with it. "When people take liberties with a property you're so close to," he said, "it hurts. And liberties *were* taken. For one thing, it was too broad. I discovered, for instance, that the nurse in the play was multiplied by five in the film, because Hollywood thinks that if one nurse is funny, five nurses will be funnier. And there were a lot of other things done that were not in the play—I won't go into details. I recognize the fact that audiences liked it, even audiences that had seen the play, but they weren't the purists that Leland and I were. It may be picayune, but that's the way I felt, and still feel. I was glad it brought me back to films, though. . . . I was the forgotten man, as far as films were concerned."

Perhaps it was Hollywood's tampering with Fonda's by-now highly ingrained sense of purism that set him so on edge early in 1955. Whatever it was, he seemed incapable of separating his professional perfectionism from his personal relations, and wherever he looked within his own intimate, tightly knit but incommunicative circle, he found discontent. The *Mister Roberts* experience had been an unnerving one, and the residual bitterness he carried with him infected just about all of Fonda's relationships for several years thereafter—not the least of which those with Jane, Peter and his wife.

Jane's graduation from Emma Willard and the time she spent at the Omaha Playhouse with her father constituted a pleasant interlude in an otherwise troubling year. During her last few semesters at Willard she had overcome some of her timidity about boys and had begun to accept an occasional date, although the dating ritual was severely circumscribed both by the school's stringent rules and curfews and by its inaccessibility. Most of her dates were with young men from the nearby Rensselaer Polytechnic Institute and were more in the nature of field exercises in the protocols of a young lady's expanding social experience than actual boy-girl relationships. And although Jane had overcome some of her shyness, her sense of inadequacy in the presence of boys was still powerful. Her easy banter within the society of her schoolmates became an uneasy reticence once she stepped off the school grounds in the company of a boy. She was more than ever concerned with her weight, her complexion, her looks and what she felt were her dubious attractions to members of the opposite sex, and her anxieties were compounded by her certainty that her popularity with the eager young polytechnicians was due solely to the fact that her name was Fonda.

This was only one facet of Jane's seventeen-year-old life that was troublesome to her. Her relationship with her stepmother, Susan, which had been a happy and salutary one for four years and had contributed so much to helping Jane through the rigors of adolescence, was threatened by the sharp discontent she was witnessing between Susan and her father. Henry Fonda had grown restless and short-fused again, and the results were the inevitable silences and moody withdrawals that Jane had lived through before her mother died. Jane's loyalty to Susan was suddenly thrust into conflict with her visceral love of her father, and as she sensed the imminent breakup, she felt powerless, frustrated and unhappy.

Henry and Susan had adopted a baby girl in November, 1953, and named her Amy. Much of life in the Fonda house in New York during the next two years revolved about the child, and Jane, although away at school much of the time, became the same kind of surrogate sister to Amy that her own stepsister, Pan Brokaw, had been to her. Having been through the breakdown of one marriage at an age when she really hadn't understood what was going on, Jane was not supersensitive to the breakdown of this one. In the best Fonda style, all intimations of it were kept hidden, and Susan Fonda made great sacrifices to keep it together. But by midsummer of 1955 Jane could see exactly what was going on. Her growing sense of the impermanence of things in her family life, coupled with the contradictions she began to divine on her own in her father's character—especially the perfection he demanded of others but seemed more and more to lack in himself—deepened her confusion.

Then there was her brother. Peter had managed to get through the Fay School, a boys' secondary school in Southborough, Massachusetts, the year before. He was now at the Westminster School, another boarding school for boys of high school age, in Connecticut. Although she did not see much of Peter, Jane still felt a strong protective tie to him, the more so now that he had become the prime object of their father's impatience and disdain. Jane's graduation and her brief fling at acting with her father in Omaha had caused Henry Fonda to modify his expectations of her. Indeed, Jane could almost palpably feel the change in his attitude toward her; suddenly he was treating her more as a grown-up. But as he did so, his despair over his unruly son intensified. When they were all together, Jane often found herself forced into the role of mediator, trying to explain Peter's often manic behavior to an incomprehending father, trying to explain their father's angry seethings to a masochistic brother.

Once the film version of *Mister Roberts* catapulted Henry Fonda back to screen stardom, he had his pick of movie offers. The one he chose, in spite of the loftiness of his intentions, succeeded only in compounding his unhappiness and intensifying the tensions and frustrations within the family.

Fonda agreed to play the role of Pierre in Dino de Laurentiis' epic production of Tolstoy's *War and Peace*. The picture was to be shot in and around Rome, beginning late in the summer of 1955, and Fonda decided to show Jane and Peter the Italian capital for a few weeks before they returned to their respective schools in September. Consequently, shortly after finishing their stints at the Omaha Playhouse, they flew to Italy and settled in for the rest of the summer on a rented small estate on the outskirts of Rome.

Five years had passed since the death of Peter's mother. His reaction to her death was neither the guilt and embarrassment of his father nor the stifled sadness of his sister; it was one of ten-year-old panic and emotional dislocation. He didn't understand much about death at the time; all he knew from the cautious and fragmented explanations of well-meaning adults was that his mother was gone forever and that he was alone. All talk of Frances Seymour was from that point on cut off, more as a result of guilt and shame on the part of the adults than of a desire to protect the children's feelings. Jane had learned of the true circumstances of her mother's death when she was thirteen, and if the knowledge affected her in any profound way, she was by then old enough and sufficiently imbued with the Seymour-Fonda tradition of suppressing and ignoring the unpleasant to prevent it from showing. Peter, on the other hand, was not. Thus began for him a long ordeal of juvenile misery and misbehavior that was only a prelude to what was to come after his visit to Rome with his father.

In much the same way Jane discovered how her mother had died, so did Peter. Sitting in a barber's chair in a hotel in Rome, he picked up a movie magazine and read about his mother slashing her throat in an insane asylum. When he looked to his father for an explanation, he received a curt evasion. And when he realized that his sister had been party to the secret, the last bastion between himself and his anxieties crumbled. He brooded around Rome, able to take comfort from no one. Left to his own devices, he began to drink wine by the quart and wander through the humid city in a drunken daze. One day he found himself in front of St. Peter's, where, he claims, he was picked up by an air attaché from the American embassy and his wife. Luring him to their apartment, they gave him his first sexual experience. Jane, in the meantime, did little in Rome "except eat figs and get fat and watch Gina Lollobrigida, a neighbor, through binoculars."

Henry Fonda was preoccupied with preparations for *War and Peace*. In September he sent Peter and Jane back to their schools and plunged into the filming, which would last well into 1956. He quickly regretted having taken the part and spent the next six months vainly trying to overcome the sour taste it left in his mouth. Fonda wanted to play Pierre the way the character was written in the novel—clumsy, stammering, bespectacled, stout—but found that producer De Laurentiis had other ideas. "It seems they didn't want a Pierre who looked like Pierre," Fonda said. "One who looked like Rock Hudson is closer to what they had in mind. They went into nervous shock when they saw my original makeup." Fonda knew he was all wrong for the part, but he felt it would be a worthwhile challenge to do something good with it in what he initially thought could be a great picture. "I decided that with the right kind of spectacles, some strategically placed padding and my hair combed forward, I could play Pierre the way he should be played. I got some glasses from the property department and started to wear them in a scene, and when De Laurentiis saw them, he blew his top. So I was forced to take them off. And for the rest of the six months on the picture it was a fight. If he wasn't on the set when I started a scene, I put the glasses on. Sometimes I'd get away with it all through a scene, but sometimes he'd come on the set and I'd have to take them off in the middle of a sequence. It was a running battle between De Laurentiis and me to try to make a character out of Pierre instead of a romantic leading man."

The film's eventual critical reception was not favorable, and although Fonda shared in the less than laudatory notices given the cast, most recognized that he alone seemed to be trying. *Time* magazine, for instance, said that he gave the impression of being the only member of the huge cast who read the book.

While Fonda agonized in Rome through the fall and winter of 1955, Peter and Jane rattled through their own separate but similar agonies in the United States. But whereas Peter wore his clashing emotions on his sleeve, Jane continued to keep hers buried within herself. She entered Vassar College for Women in September, with her friend and growing rival Brooke Hayward, and nervously settled down to conquer the academic and social intricacies of college life.

Physically, Vassar was the Emma Willard School twenty times magnified. The college is nestled in a large, parklike setting on the outskirts of Poughkeepsie, New York. It is a few miles north of Beacon, where Jane's mother had taken her life, and a good deal closer to New York City than Troy. The Vassar campus is enclosed within an eight-feet-high wrought-iron fence and is a pleasant mix of Georgian and Neogothic architecture set amid expansive lawns, fine old trees and winding drives and paths. In 1955 it was the sort of school to which young women of privilege and intelligence were sent to complete their formal education, acquire a sophisticated cultural overlay and prepare for "marriage, motherhood and menopause," in the words of one of its more sardonic graduates.

It is doubtful that many of the girls who started at Vassar in 1955 were thinking about the menopause component of that axiom, and mother-hood was probably considered only in terms of the avoidance of embarrassing pregnancies. But marriage was certainly in the forefront of the minds and emotions of most of the girls who were installed by their parents in Vassar's sylvan setting. Indeed, from most of the parents' point-of-view, this was the entire justification for spending upwards of $10,000 to send their daughters to Vassar over a period of four years—to ensure their growingly nubile offspring exposure to the most favorable conditions for making a desirable marriage. A good education was fine, but Vassar's strong point was the inbuilt attraction of its students to young men of social and financial potential from such men's colleges as Yale, Williams, Amherst and Wesleyan. "Everyone was in such a hurry to get married," Jane said. "If you didn't have a ring on your finger by your junior year, forget it."

Jane, having grown up in an environment in which social achievement and standing were no trivial matters and using her still-youthful stepmother as a model for her own dreams, was no different in her expectations from most of her classmates. Yet there was another side to the coin. She had also grown up in the company of show people. She had a famous father and had already appeared with him on stage. She could drop the names of celebrated actors, directors and producers with the same ease and familiarity that other girls used when talking about the high school boyfriends they left behind. She had actually dined at Joshua Logan's, had roughhoused with Jimmy Stewart, had been patted on the head by John Wayne, had been pecked on the cheek by Audrey Hepburn. To a residence hall full of fanciful seventeen-year-olds, most of whom nurtured secret fantasies of film stardom for themselves or at least wondered what it would be like, Jane quickly became an object of both admiration and envy.

She had by now learned to be fairly at ease in the company of girls but was still, in those first months of her freshman year at Vassar, more quiet and introspective than outgoing. Aside from Brooke Hayward—now a beautiful and talented girl who had already decided to become an actress—she had few close friends, and those friendships she did make were mostly with one or two of the handful of girls who also came out of show business families. At first she applied herself to her studies— French, music and art history were her favorites—with a single-minded devotion. The responsibility of making good, a constant ingredient of the lectures she had been receiving from her father, still weighed heavy. But she was soon distracted by the variety of emotional stimuli she was bombarded with and rapidly lost interest in the imperatives of academic excellence.

It became obvious to Jane during the winter of her freshman year that the marriage between her father, who was still in Rome, and her stepmother, who was in New York with two-year-old Amy, was not going to last. It had already deteriorated into long, tension-filled silences punctuated by brief outbursts of anger before Fonda left for Italy, and now stories were surfacing in the gossip columns to the effect that Henry Fonda had succumbed to his own aristocratic Italian heritage by romancing a beautiful Venetian baronessa. When the stories got back to Jane, she was doubly hurt—first, because Susan, with whom she identified so strongly, was suffering, and second, because her father had not thought enough to keep her informed of what was going on. Jane was old enough to realize that her father was doing nothing more than trying to be discreet in his unwillingness to include her in the secrets of his personal life. But she was more inclined to interpret his incommunicativeness as dishonesty, especially in the light of past experiences. She grew increasingly worried over her ambivalent feelings toward her father and felt bitter about the pattern of dissembling she felt he had established between them.

In many ways Jane was still emotionally underdeveloped; the emotional dislocations she had suffered between her eleventh and seventeenth years because of the loss of her mother and remoteness of her father had not yet been resolved. The result was increasing attacks of anxiety about everything under the sun—herself and her own place in the world, her father, her brother, her stepmother and, most of all, the seeming impermanence of things. For someone brought up to pursue the virtues of order and perfection, the constant breakdown of these virtues within her own family left her with a shaky faith in herself and her world.

Susan Fonda was striving to keep the marriage together, trying to maintain for Jane and Peter the sanctuary of the house on Seventy-fourth Street. Shortly after her marriage to Fonda in 1950, Susan told an interviewer, "How could I be expected to resist such an impetuous guy? There I was in the kitchen, in blue jeans and my brother's old college sweat shirt, scrubbing out an oven, when Hank walks in and tosses me this box and says, 'Try this on for size.' It was an engagement ring. That's my Hank, just a moonlight-and-roses boy." If Susan admired the casualness of her husband-to-be in proposing marriage, she certainly understood his casualness five years later as he began to extricate himself from the marriage. Casualness had always been a hallmark of Fonda's style, both personally and as an actor. Underneath the veneer, though, a rope-stiff resolve and a self-protecting wariness operated in tandem, enabling him to sail through life relatively untouched by the unhappiness he left in his path.

As Jane celebrated her eighteenth birthday during her Christmas vacation in December, 1955, she was able to look back on a year in which her world had changed markedly. The differences between the high school senior at Emma Willard and the college freshman at Vassar were considerable. She had reached her full height of five feet seven and a half inches and almost her full development. Her Omaha acting stint had given her an increased self-awareness and even a touch of self-confidence. Through a program of stringent dieting she was losing the residue of baby fat she had carried through Emma Willard and was delighted to find herself becoming a slim, coltish young woman. It was an appearance she had to work hard to maintain, however, since she enjoyed eating and the Vassar cuisine, though it was a notch above ordinary institutional food, was heavy in starches. Like many other girls at the college, Jane became caught up in obsessive anxieties about her weight. She began to practice the trick of eating a full meal, then hastily retreating to the bathroom to vomit it up before it had a chance to do its deadly work on her system.

The rules and restrictions on the girls at Vassar were much less strict and confining than at Emma Willard. Weekends, especially, were much freer, and the girls were allowed to leave the campus almost at will, so long as the proper permissions were sought and granted. Jane responded to her new freedoms with gusto. With her father still in Italy, she spent as many weekends in New York as she could, often visiting Susan and Amy in their new residence. As she found that young men were attracted to her, she began a cautious round of dating. This was not the polite, awkward ritual of the year before; it was the painful and sometimes messy rite almost every shy and insecure teen-ager goes through.

At first, Jane was like everyone else at Vassar—her social life was motivated primarily by a desire to conform to and compete in a world of ambitious, sophisticated young women on the make. But she quickly learned that, because of who she was, the competition factor did not really apply to her; she was singled out as someone special and was besieged with the attentions of young men who came down for weekends from Yale and the other colleges of the Northeast. As far as conforming was concerned—well, she soon grew bored with that imperative. She set her own pace, and it was not long before she drew far ahead of the rest of the Vassar field in the date-and-romance race.

Not that a long-standing romance was her goal; indeed quantity and variety, rather than singularity and permanence, were the things she sought in her relations with young men. If Jane entered Vassar a good deal less sophisticated and practiced than most of her classmates, she rapidly altered the balance. Once she discovered the joys of dating and the sweet satisfactions to be had from the stature an intensive social life provided her among her peers, she pursued them avariciously. And as she had done once or twice previously when she'd discovered herself in a special limelight, she went overboard.

When Henry Fonda returned to New York in the spring of 1956, he brought back with him the frustration and silent rage that had been building in him for more than a year. His mood was not lightened by what he found at home. He was disturbed at the reports of Jane's less than dedicated approach to her studies at Vassar, but since she was getting by, he kept his own counsel on that score. Peter's problems at Westminster were another matter altogether; the young Fonda seemed to attract trouble the way honey attracts a bear, and nothing Henry did or said to him seemed to have any effect.

Fonda resolved to try to make something positive out of the coming summer. He arranged to take a house on Cape Cod so that he and the children could have some time together, and when Jane expressed an interest in having another go at acting, he used his influence to get her a summer apprentice's job at the very place he had started when he came East in the summer of 1928—the Dennis Playhouse.

By spring of her freshman year Jane was of two minds about acting. She had enjoyed her previous summer's stage venture in Omaha and had especially liked the camaraderie she had achieved with her father. That she gained few distinctive notices was of no particular moment; nevertheless, she had been hurt by suggestions in the local press that her presence in *The Country Girl* had been worthwhile only as a curiosity piece. Although she loved the feeling of being onstage in front of an audience, of giving a performance, she had no confidence that she had a talent for it. And as Henry Fonda's daughter, she could not bear to make a fool of herself.

Her father had immediately recognized talent in Jane when he performed with her in Omaha, but he was reluctant to share his recognition. He was mildly amused at her interest in the theater, yet was not a man who dreamed of seeing his children follow in his footsteps. Indeed, since he had experienced the hardships himself and having witnessed heartbreak over and over, his instincts were to discourage Jane whenever she talked about an acting career.

Jane took his discouragements seriously, if sometimes dejectedly. There was so much that was unspoken between them that she was never certain whether he actually disapproved of her loosely formed acting ambitions or whether his negativism was merely protective. Whichever, she was now able to talk a little about the theater and acting, and it pleased her that she finally had a common ground on which she could relate to her father. That he usually dismissed her enthusiastic percep-tions as the naïve ramblings of a neophyte or changed the subject altogether discouraged but did not deter her. And as more and more people at college wondered why she was not pursuing an acting career, she decided that a few months in summer stock would settle the question in her mind once and for all.

Since he was living nearby, Henry Fonda saw Jane act in one of the Dennis Playhouse's apprentice productions and gained a greater appre-ciation of the talent he perceived in Omaha the year before. Neverthe-less, he continued to maintain his silence in the face of her growing enthusiasm for acting. She played the part of a maid in a Restoration comedy. "When she came on, the audience reacted in an almost physical, audible way—a straightening up and intake of breath. What a position to be in, trying to remind yourself that you were her father! If you were any other SOB you'd say, 'Get that girl into the theater,' and you'd use a ship to get her there. But of course I never let her know that."

Later that summer Fonda accepted an invitation from the company to play the lead in a play called *The Male Animal* for a week, with Jane as the ingenue. At first Jane was hesitant about appearing with her father;

she felt she was being given the part as a courtesy and would again be considered a curiosity piece. But the opportunity was too great to pass up. She was eager to be onstage with her father again, involved with him in the only way he was able to share his life with her. The production was a great success. Although Jane again was noticed primarily because she was on the same stage as her father, the three weeks of rehearsals and performances were the happiest moments she had spent with him since she could remember.

Day Tuttle, the managing director of the Mount Kisco Playhouse during the summer Henry Fonda pulled his iceman ploy, was on the Cape that season with his family. When he read about his old scene designer appearing at Dennis in *The Male Animal*, he brought his wife and children to see it. He remembers strolling about the grounds of the playhouse early one evening when a voice boomed out from one of the dressing-room windows. "Hey, Day, you old good-for-nothing, what are you doing here?" It was Henry Fonda.

"We had a wonderful reunion," Tuttle recalls. "He introduced us to Jane and that evening we saw the play. It was just marvelous, and Jane was delightful. She and her father played beautifully together, and you could just see that she had the same vitality and presence that had made her father such a star."

When Tuttle talks about Henry Fonda his praise and admiration are clouded by the sadness of a sympathetic friend. "Henry Fonda is such a wonderful man," he says. "He was wonderful when I first knew him at Mount Kisco—we were all so pleased with the great success he had—and he's still wonderful. He's a marvelous actor and such a kind, generous, considerate human being. Back in those early days when I knew him best there was no one I liked more. He would do anything you asked him to do, and no matter what you asked him to do he would do it with a dedication and perfection that are rare even in saints. That's why I can't understand why his life has been such a mess. My wife and I knew his first wife, Margaret Sullavan, well. She was a darling. We were at his wedding to his second wife, Frances Brokaw. We all thought that it was a perfect marriage for Hank. But look what's happened—he just can't seem to stay married to one woman. And his children! The grief he's had from his children is shameful. I really feel for the man. I have no way of knowing what went wrong with Hank Fonda, what happened along the way, but it distresses me that he has had so much unhappiness. I can't think of a nicer human being, and for all this to happen to him is just a tragedy."

Feelings such as these have been echoed by many of Fonda's old friends. No one seems to know what it is in Henry Fonda that gives him his chameleon character. "I'd hate to be a girl and married to him," his best friend John Swope remarked about him. "All his marriages ended the same way—beset with quietness. After a while, he just couldn't say anything to the woman. There was no communication. And he can be cruel. He can cut someone right out of his life and not appear to have it affect him at all."

Later in her life Jane recalled seeing a well-known actor perform in a play on Broadway. "He was brilliant and strikingly like my father. Yet I asked myself, 'What is so different about my father's performances?' Suddenly I knew. There is a pervading undercurrent of deep, deep sadness in him. If it weren't for the sadness, he would be cold, lifeless. But the sadness coming through creates an identifying thing with an audience. It is a quality like an animal that has been deeply wounded."

This perception might have helped Jane understand her father better a few years later, but by the end of the summer of 1957 she was more confused by him than ever. She had hoped for some help, some indication of whether she was justified in her enthusiasm for an acting career. He told her that she could probably get somewhere as an actress but indicated through his lack of enthusiasm that such a career was not what he had in mind for her. Whether he wanted the life of a young society matron for Jane or was simply trying to protect her from the torment he had seen so many other young actresses go through in their struggle to succeed is unclear. Whatever the reason, his reticence left Jane with more questions and fewer answers than she'd had at the beginning of the summer.

She returned to Vassar that fall to start her sophomore year with little interest in anything serious and shortly began to feel she was doing nothing but marking time.

"The college put on a Lorca play and I played the lead, a young Spanish girl who stood in a window and sang songs and cuckolded her husband. I knew almost nothing about the motivations of the character I played. By then I was self-conscious enough to look for things in the character, but I didn't know how. There was nothing behind the emotions I showed. I didn't know how to show that the emotions came from something and that the words had meaning. I really hadn't decided to become an actress at that point." On the one hand, she wanted to; on the other, she didn't. "What I really wanted was to get out of Vassar."

With her father's marriage to Susan finally ended and Peter further shattering the family's fragile solidarity with his compulsive misbehavior, what meager taste Jane had for academic matters quickly got lost in her efforts to counteract her loneliness and unhappiness. By her own account, she became totally irresponsible during her second year at Vassar. "When I discovered that boys liked me, I went wild. I went out all the time. I never studied." Jane has often claimed that she was a late developer, both intellectually and emotionally. Perhaps her behavior at Vassar when she was eighteen and nineteen, then, was the behavior of earlier-maturing youngsters of fourteen and fifteen who rebel to receive the attention they are not getting otherwise. "When Jane was at Vassar," her friend Brooke Hayward once was quoted as saying, "she had a reputation for being easy. It was almost a joke."

Henry Fonda returned to Hollywood to make a pair of pictures in the fall of 1956, so there were few restraints on Jane in Poughkeepsie except those placed on her by the school. And the school was hard put to contain her. She became a "sophisticated delinquent," in the words of another observer, hardly ever studying, cutting classes and often getting into trouble with the college authorities. Stories of sexual promiscuity that have come out of that year are the products of hyperactive and often resentful imaginations and are mostly unfounded; sexually, Jane certainly was no shrinking violet by the time she was nineteen, but neither was she the abandoned harlot she has often been pictured as. She had one love affair that was as desperate as it was foolhardy, and for a while she even pressed the boy, a Yale student, to marry her. But, as she said later, "he had the good sense to decline."

By December Jane was caught in a growing dilemma. She was secretly thinking more and more about trying to become an actress, but a number of things militated against her. The Vassar ethic was not the least of these, nor was her lack of confidence in herself. "When I was at Vassar, I was taught to believe that girls who want to be happily married and have families must not become actresses. But the more weddings I went to, the more I realized this just wasn't my bag. But I still didn't know if I had any talent." She continued to suppress her desire, growing all the while more restless and unhappy. She drifted into the spring of her sophomore year at odds with herself, bored with Vassar and most of her schoolmates and starving for some kind of direction.

One day early in 1957 Jane's father announced that he would be marrying Baronessa Afdera Franchetti, the young beautiful noblewoman he had met in Italy when he was filming *War and Peace*. The wedding took place in Fonda's New York house on March 10, and both Peter and Jane came down from their schools to be present.

Afdera Franchetti was twenty-four years old when she married Henry Fonda. Many of Fonda's friends had been remarking with wry, almost sad humor on his growing penchant for girls much younger than himself. His own children, both now in the flower of their respective rebellions, were not above wisecracks themselves, although they made sure to make them out of their father's hearing. According to one friend, Jane and Peter made a private bet that when the time came for Fonda to take his next wife, she would be younger than Jane, and the one after that would be younger than Peter. They had a hilarious time speculating on the age of his ninth or tenth wife, regaling themselves with stories of their father feeding her from a bottle and diapering her in the bedroom.

Their jokes were laced with bitterness. Neither Jane nor Peter liked Afdera very much—she had replaced Susan, who had been even more of a mother to them than their own mother—and they felt uncomfortable in her presence. Afdera was flamboyant, fey and suffused with a vague languid Mediterranean decadence that was completely alien to their sensibilities; besides, her English was tiresomely inadequate for decent communication. They distrusted the way she insinuated herself into the Fonda household and hated the way their father let her take charge of things. He was a puppy at her feet, and the contrast between the way he treated her and the way he treated them only sharpened the intensity of their resentment.

Jane and Peter went back to their schools unhappier and, in Peter's case, more anxiety-stricken than ever. It was not long before Henry Fonda began to get the feedback. Jane did her best to get thrown out of Vassar in the spring of 1957. Unprepared for an examination, she is said to have filled her blue book with drawings and handed it in. The college refused to flunk her or punish her and gave her a makeup exam instead. She took to sneaking out of Vassar on weekends when she didn't have permission. One weekend she discovered that the authorities found out she was absent when she shouldn't have been. She decided to steal a beat by calling in with a tearful explanation before they had an opportunity to confront her with her transgression. "But before I got a chance to say I was sorry, the professor said he understood that my father had just married for the fourth time and that I was emotionally upset. I wasn't, really; I'd just gone away with a boy for the weekend."

Peter Fonda was even more avid in his self-destructiveness. He says that when he went home for the wedding, he tried to talk to his father about the difficulties he was having at Westminster. However much Peter's problems were the result of his adolescent paranoia, he got no sympathy from Henry Fonda, merely a curt lecture on the responsibilities of growing up.

Peter returned to school and started swallowing phenobarbital to calm himself down. After a couple of fistfights with teachers he was threatened with expulsion. Peter called Jane at Vassar—his father had left on a wedding trip to Europe—and pleaded for help. Jane borrowed a car and drove the next day to Peter's school in Connecticut. She found Peter hiding in some bushes, talking to himself in a drug-induced daze. With their father in Europe, Jane called their Aunt Harriet in Omaha. Harriet told her to put Peter on a train to Omaha, that she and her husband would look after him until their father returned.

This was the second time Henry Fonda had been interrupted on a wedding trip by Peter's problems. He flew from France to Omaha in a state of high agitation. He and his sister decided that Peter should remain in Omaha with her and her husband. They would see that he got psychiatric help and would look after his schooling. Peter reluctantly agreed with the decision, but things would get worse for him before they got better.

Fonda returned to New York to find more trouble. Jane informed him that she was going crazy at Vassar and had to get out. She didn't know what she wanted to do with her life, but she realized that she was wasting it in Poughkeepsie and would never get through college. Remembering his own frustrations as a college youth and because Jane was his daughter, Fonda was probably more attentive to her unhappiness than he was to Peter's. When she asked him to finance a year in Paris, where she could pursue her art studies and study French, he was amenable to the idea. After all, many young college girls took a year off from school to study in Europe, and since Jane seemed genuinely interested in something he thought worthwhile—something which she could later pursue as a valuable hobby—why not? He was disappointed with Jane's inability to stick with Vassar, but recalling his own college days, he could not be too hard on her.

Jane was surprised by her father's compliance and couldn't wait for the spring semester to end. For the first time in a long while she had something to look forward to. With a change of life in the offing, she applied herself to her studies and wound up the year with good grades. Then, in June, her expectations high and her anticipation delicious, she took her last train from Poughkeepsie and flew off to Paris.

7. First Plane to Paris

I went to Paris to be a painter, but I lived there for six months and never opened my paints.

—JANE FONDA

ALTHOUGH Jane persuaded her father that her ambition to become a painter was real and that a year of study would give fruitful support to that ambition, her argument was most likely just a pretext to get away from school, home and problems. "I was nineteen, an age when you know you are not happy but you don't know why, and you think a geographical change will change your life." Henry Fonda suspected as much. He was convinced Jane had at least a small talent for art and was pleased that she seemed interested in it, but he remained unsure about the wisdom of her move to Paris. The problem of Jane was just one of his concerns, however, so it was easy for him to quash his misgivings and collaborate in the pretext. "Frankly," he recently admitted, "I've never really dealt with personal problems at all. They just keep happening to me. Eventually, if you sit there long enough, they just fall off. I can't deal with problems, and that's the plain truth."

Jane's living arrangements in Paris had been made for her before she left New York, and when she arrived in late June she moved into a dark, elegant apartment in the fashionable Sixteenth Arrondissement. The apartment belonged to an ancient countess who boarded young American girls. It was in a somber building on the Avenue d'Iena, halfway between the Arc de Triomphe and the Trocadéro, almost directly across the Seine from the Eiffel Tower. The location couldn't have been more pleasant for an impressionable American girl wetting her feet in the sophisticated pleasures of Paris, but Jane soon learned to hate it. "It was an apartment with everything covered in plastic, where everything smelled, where young ladies were not supposed to talk at the table and where I was absolutely miserable."

Her living conditions were not all that made her miserable. She found herself a prisoner of her barely adequate college French. It is one thing to blunder through a French conversation class in an American classroom, another to make oneself intelligible to feisty French store-keepers and taxi drivers. She was thus in a state of constant distress over her inability to communicate. She worked hard during the summer to improve her French, but no matter how proficient she managed to become in the technical aspects of the language, she was unable to rid herself of her self-consciousness and her giveaway Vassar accent.

When she started her art studies in the fall at the Académie Grande Chaumière and the Académie Julien, she found the instruction, which was in French and mostly idiomatic, much too rapid for her tenuous grasp of the language. However sincere she might have been in her desire to study art, she was lost in the classrooms and studios of the two schools and found life much more interesting on the vibrant streets of the Latin Quarter outside. Her concentration thus diverted, she easily lost interest in her studies and proceeded to spend most of her time learning the language in the crowded bistros and *zincs* of the Left Bank.

The Paris of the twenties was, of course, famous as the home of post-World War artistic and literary exiles from other parts of Europe and America. The eventual commercial success of many among this polyglot creative population served as an inspiration to succeeding generations of artists and writers, especially those who believed that cultural conditions in their own countries were too sterile to be conducive to the development of new forms and ideas.

The Paris of the mid-fifties was again the center of an American artistic and literary movement. Hundreds of young writers, painters, sculptors, actors and musicians, fleeing the malaise of the post-Korea Eisenhower years and infused with what came to be known as the Beatnik philosophy, settled in Paris with the idea of re-creating the twenties and nourishing themselves on its ambience.

It might have been a fine idea—this pilgrimage to the Jerusalem of the arts—but if its success is measured by the criteria of the twenties, it didn't work. The production of significant works of art and literature was minimal, at least from the American contingent of émigrés. The mood and atmosphere of the earlier Paris, which were essential ingredients in the decade's reputation as a watershed period in art and literature, were simply not to be found in the 1950's. The Paris of the twenties was a jubilant city, still feasting on the glory of its victory in the "war to end all wars" and exuberant with the promise of an unfettered future.

Paris in the fifties, on the other hand, indeed all France, was a gray, exhausted, bitter and cynical place. No sooner had the Second World War ended than the French were embroiled in the fruitless task of protecting and preserving their colonial interests in Indochina. By 1951 France had an army of 390,000 men in Vietnam and was waging a full-scale and increasingly unpopular war against the Communist Vietminh revolutionaries led by Ho Chi Minh. In 1952 Bao Dai, chief of state of the French-sponsored government in Vietnam, withdrew from the scene for lack of local political and popular support. In December, 1953, with the French Army suffering thousands of casualties a month and opposition to the war growing increasingly vocal in Paris, the Vietminh cut Vietnam in two. The shame of the French was irreversibly stamped on the national consciousness in May, 1954, when the French army's last stronghold in Vietnam, Dienbienphu, fell to the redoubtable Vietminh. It was a shattering blow to France's prestige; the entire futile nine-year effort of the French to hold onto their distant colony left a stain on the national spirit that would take years to eradicate. Led by Premier Pierre Mendès-France, who was elected on his promise to end the war and evacuate the now-divided Vietnam, France signed the Geneva accords, ending formal hostilities, in July, 1954.

But informal hostilities continued. The French kept their forces in what was now South Vietnam and tried to establish a local government with Ngo Dinh Diem as Premier. When it became apparent that Diem was not following orders from Paris, the French put pressure on him, increasing their unpopularity in the South. In 1955, as Diem's position in Saigon grew stronger and France's weaker, the United States began to take part in the proceedings. Although the United States had given massive economic and material aid to the French struggle for the previous five years, it had not played an active military role in Vietnam. Once the French stumbled, however, the U.S. government, led by President Eisenhower and Secretary of State John Foster Dulles and using the CIA as a secret mini-army, filled the breach. In October, 1955, with massive financial aid and paramilitary support from the United States, Premier Diem declared South Vietnam an independent republic with himself as President. Now it was the United States' turn to become embroiled in a thankless war. France, bitterly ashamed by the evidence of its weakness in foreign affairs and resentful of the United States for undermining its position, withdrew totally from Indochina and sullenly licked its wounds. The French, always highly attuned politically, remained profoundly polarized and grew even more so as the problem of Algerian independence raised its head.

Such was the mood in Paris when Jane Fonda arrived in the summer of 1957. A strong undercurrent of anti-American feeling flowed through the normal tension of the city. Many of the earnest young American expatriates who had gone there to suckle at the breast of Paris' cultural mystique had packed up their brushes, chisels and typewriters and moved on. Jane had no overpowering artistic pretensions when she went to Paris, and whatever ambitions she did have did not require that she immerse herself in the traditional bohemian life so many youthful artists and writers believed was the magic carpet to inspiration and productivity. By the time she arrived not much remained of the American colony except for those who were financially independent enough to afford to stay and those who were too poor to leave.

Feeling lonely and unsettled, insecure in the language, empty of ambition, at loose ends emotionally, Jane found a remedy to her unhappiness in what was left of the American colony. And for the members of the colony, the presence of Jane—a pretty American girl with obvious breeding and culture, and in the bargain the daughter of a celebrated film star—was a pleasant and welcome diversion.

Among the leading lights of Paris' cultural life was a coterie of hyperimaginative young men and women involved in putting out a quarterly called *Paris Review.* By 1957 most of what remained of the serious literary and artistic effort of the expatriate community revolved around the *Paris Review.* Its editor and financial lifeguard was George Plimpton, a talented essayist and the scion of an old, wealthy American family who, several years later, would establish himself in America as a popular and humorous reporter of Walter Mitty adventures. Through Plimpton and his band of intellectually high-powered cronies, Jane gained entrée into Paris' expatriate smart set, which crossed with casual aplomb all the lines that traditionally separated the city's economic and intellectual classes.

Jane, just short of her twentieth birthday, moved into the group with gratitude and a desire to please. Much of her time was spent hanging around the office of the *Review,* bantering, flirting, running errands. She found the company easy, the talk amusing, the social life exciting. The sophistication of the group was far above her own, but she was clever and observant. She imitated it as well as she could and soon was able to keep up with the fast-paced and often esoteric chatter that swirled around her head. She was more immediately adept at the nightly partying and Left Bank bistro crawling.

Artists, literary people, filmmakers—these were the people who made up Jane's circle of acquaintances in Paris during the fall of 1957. She met not only Americans, but Frenchmen as well, and many of the latter pursued her with barely concealed lust. The cafés and ateliers of the Left Bank became her home, and she spent less and less time in the musty confines of the apartment on Avenue d'Iena. One night, at a gathering of film people at Maxim's, she met the French film director Roger Vadim—a man whose reputation preceded him wherever he went. Vadim had been the "discoverer" and first husband of Brigitte Bardot and probably more than anyone else in Europe was responsible for the emergence of the erotic feature film. The night he and Jane met he was with his second wife, Annette Stroyberg, also a film star. A tall, slender man with a long, melancholy face, Vadim looked at Jane with cold appraisal, then interest. Jane, self-conscious under his gaze and aware of his reputation as a shameless womanizer, bristled, then ignored him. Vadim, who among other things was known to have a knack for prescience, filed her away in his memory.

If Jane was any more than vaguely aware of the political mood in Paris that fall, she showed no sign of it. Most of her American friends who had left the United States because of its political apathy and cultural sterility proved for the most part to be politically apathetic themselves. And French politics, with its continual haggling, scapegoating and word splitting, was a bore. They had more pressing concerns. There were a few French Communists who hovered about the *Paris Review* group, but no one took them very seriously. When discussions got around to politics, most of the Americans' eyes glazed over. Jane's eyes glazed quicker than most.

Once past her twentieth birthday, Jane's "year" in Paris abruptly came to an end. Word had got back to her father that she had abandoned all pretense of studying art and was running with Paris' fast crowd. Fonda heard rumors of sexual promiscuity and other forms of malfeasance on Jane's part and is said to have exploded with rage. He ordered her back to New York and read her the riot act.

Jane settled uneasily into her father's house on Seventy-fourth Street. As if to show her good intentions, she enrolled at the New York Art Students League to resume her art studies. She also signed up at the Mannes School of Music, which was next door to her father's house, and at Berlitz to study French and Italian. To underline her seriousness, she worked for a while for the New York office of *Paris Review*, traveling the width and length of Manhattan soliciting ads from publishers and bookstores.

A friend who worked for a fashion magazine asked her to model some clothes when the magazine needed someone to pose free for some layout pictures. One of the editors saw the pictures and expressed an interest in using her in a larger way. Although she still did not think of herself as attractive, she liked the idea of being a model and decided to pursue it. She also met an ambitious young actor by the name of James Franciscus, with whom she started a romance.

In the early months of 1958 she proved to herself that she was capable of doing hard work and sticking to it, even though it was without any long-term purpose. Her purpose was to please her father, and since she was at a point in her life when, more than ever, she required some outside direction, she derived a certain amount of satisfaction from the discipline she imposed on herself. But if she was looking for words of praise or approval from her father, she very seldom got them. After all, she was simply doing what she was supposed to be doing, and Henry Fonda could never see the point of bestowing praise on someone merely because he did his job. If Jane came home with an animated tale of what she had accomplished that day, her father would acknowledge it with a distracted, unresponsive grunt and turn to other things. So although Jane was almost obsessively busy during those days, her grip on her future grew shakier, and she more unhappy, dissatisfied and restless.

"It was frustrating," she once recalled. "I wanted to jump in and start playing concertos instead of studying scales. I wanted to paint masterpieces, but painting became steadily less enjoyable and more difficult to do. I thought people who looked at what I painted expected something of me that I couldn't live up to. As soon as I finished a canvas, I'd be hypercritical of it. Underneath everything I still thought about becoming an actress. That was what I wanted to do more than anything else, so I spent a lot of time figuring out reasons why I shouldn't: It was selfish and egotistical, it gave no enjoyment, I wasn't pretty enough, and so on. The truth is, I was just afraid to try."

Complicating things was the atmosphere at home. While Jane was in France, her father had enjoyed another film success with his performance in *12 Angry Men*. It was more of a *succès d'estime* than a financial one, however, and since he had co-produced and financed the film himself when he was unable to find any studio interest in it, he was distracted by financial anxieties. The picture had cost only $340,000 to make, but it was not doing well at the box office. For one thing, *12 Angry Men* had been shown originally as a television play; it had already been seen by millions, and interest in the movie version was mild. If it had been booked into small art theaters, as such a picture would be today, it might have run for months on the strength of its reviews. But treated as just another commercial release and booked into conventional large movie houses, it never had a chance to find its audiences. As a result, it quickly closed without much notice. The picture barely brought back its money, and Fonda, as its producer, never received a cent of profits or of his deferred salary. To a man of his pecunious and pragmatic nature, this was indeed unsettling.

Something else had him unsettled as well. In January he opened in a new play on Broadway—*Two for the Seesaw* by William Gibson. It was a two-character drama in which he played Jerry, an aging lawyer who, his marriage having failed, faced a lonely and desolate future. His co-star was Anne Bancroft, who made a personal tour de force out of the much meatier role of Gittel, a neurotic Jewish girl. Fonda's reviews were sparkling, but he was miserable in the play. Jerry, he felt, was a one-dimensional character of dubious psychological motivation, while Gittel was fully realized. In Fonda's view the contrast was so striking that it took a supreme effort for him to play the part night after night. He had only agreed to the role originally on playwright Gibson's assurances that he would expand the character during rehearsal rewrites and give Jerry the dimension Fonda felt he needed. But the expansion never came. Fonda was angry with Gibson for failing to keep his word. In spite of the laudatory notices he received, he felt betrayed and couldn't wait until his contract was up.

These two events, along with Peter's continuing troubles in Omaha and the discovery of Jane's Paris adventures, had conspired to turn Henry Fonda crankier than usual. "If you're looking for that old show business warmth, you won't find it in Hank," an old acquaintance said of him at the time. "More and more, lately, he's just been interested in work. I think one of the reasons he's been married four times is that you can't marry the man. You can marry his little finger, maybe. The rest of him is brooding over other things."

Another observer noted that there had come over the private Henry Fonda a sobriety which only his innate and grainy charm could keep from going altogether dour. Fame, which would grin and glisten out of someone else, seemed quarantined at a cold distance from him. He even seemed to live faintly apart from his own home, which had lost its simple raffish town house character and been transformed into a sumptuous mansion where silent European servants glided about attending him and his Venetian baronessa.

Jane's relationship with her father's fourth wife remained distant. To most of the Fondas' friends, the twenty-five-year-old Afdera was seldom more than a blond, exquisite and mysterious shadow—the product, as one acquaintance remarked, of Henry's congenital optimism and, perhaps, his need to have a woman who worshiped him with no questions asked. Worship him she did, and Fonda responded with a phlegmatic, paternal devotion that seemed to infuriate Jane. She perceived a double standard at work in her father's contradictory attitudes—one set of responses for her, his daughter, and a totally different set for his wife, who was barely older than she was.

Afdera, though cool and elegant, had a *dolce vita* streak in her. Leland Hayward recalled attending a dinner party at the Fonda house for some Italian friends of Afdera: "For dessert they had ice cream and chocolate sauce. There was dancing, and all of a sudden those nutty Italians began throwing ice cream and sauce on the walls. I thought Hank would commit murder. But he just stood there and smiled and enjoyed it." Whether out of embarrassment or because he actually found his wife's antics amusing, such a reaction was totally unlike Fonda. It was such reactions as these that added extra fillips to Jane's confusion.

Life was soon to change radically for Jane, however. Her restless indirection was about to transform itself into driving ambition. As with her father before her, luck and coincidence, along with some fortunate connections, would become the dominant factors of her life. She would no longer be the Lady Jane of her father's early visions.

Part II
Jane Fonda/1958–1963

8. The Strasberg Connection

Lee Strasberg changed my life.

—Jane Fonda

IN 1958 Lee Strasberg, a short, diffident man who might have been mistaken for an aging waiter at the old Lindy's Restaurant, was the talk of the film and theater world. A more unprepossessing "star" could not have been imagined. Of course, he was not a star in the conventional sense. Indeed, he was not even an actor; nor, for that matter, a director or producer. Some called him a teacher, but such an appellation was inadequate to describe what he did. Others resorted to words like "guru," but these implied the possession of mystical powers and exaggerated what he did. Still others used the term "high priest," and if one can imagine a run-down former Greek Orthodox church on the seedy West Side of Manhattan as the modern equivalent of the ancient Jewish Temple, then the phrase came close to applying. Not that what Strasberg did had anything to do with religion. Yet his single-minded devotion to a theatrical philosophy was soaked with a religious zeal that attracted a host of fanatical and famous disciples.

Strasberg was born in Austria-Hungary in 1901 and reared in the Jewish slums of New York, the son of poor immigrant parents. Yiddish was the language and Socialism the politics of the Jewish immigrants, and Strasberg became steeped in both. With an early fascination for the stage, he started his career as an actor in the colorful Yiddish theater. Then he worked his way into the English-language theater. During the Depression, when almost everyone in the theater became equal by virtue of common poverty, and when the barriers of the Broadway stage against working-class Jews began to fall, Strasberg graduated into the legitimate theater. In the early thirties he was a founding member of the famous Group Theatre, a troupe that was modeled along the lines of a Socialist collective and drew its twin inspiration from the teachings of a then-obscure Russian theatrical theorist named Constantin Stanislavski and the struggle for social justice in America.

Just as Henry Fonda's association with the University Players of Cape Cod would play a dominant role in his future career, so did Lee Strasberg's association with the Group Theatre in his. And as with the University Players, many members of the Group Theatre went on to become celebrated in the theatrical and film world—John Garfield, Franchot Tone, Clifford Odets, Elia Kazan, Harold Clurman, Luther and Stella Adler, among others. And, of course, Lee Strasberg.

But Strasberg did not leap to eminence, as some of the others did, as an actor or director. Most of his professional work after the Group Theatre broke up was as a minor director or stage manager of various and sundry shows. After the war he scratched out a living teaching acting, still using the ideas of Stanislavski, at one of the many acting schools that sprang up in New York thanks to the GI Bill of Rights.

In 1948 a few people formerly connected with the Group Theatre got together to start what became known as the Actors Studio. This was not a school, but a sort of communal workshop where actors could congregate in their spare time—of which many had a great deal—and practice their craft. Strasberg had been teaching at a school called the Dramatic Workshop. Although the workshop operated under the auspices of the New School for Social Research, it had been founded and was run by a German director and refugee from Nazism named Erwin Piscator—later to be driven out of the United States for his unswerving Communism. At the school were many young students who would eventually achieve stardom.

Piscator was of the Teutonic school of drama and was one of the early developers of what became known as Epic Theater—which meant strident, bravura presentations of political-message plays with all the production stops pulled out. Strasberg, on the other hand, was interested in furthering the more contemplative, introspective techniques of the post-Revolutionary Russian theory of theater, whose ideological father was Stanislavski. Since the founders of the Actors Studio had similar interests, in 1950 they invited their old colleague to join them as the Studio's artistic director. Strasberg gladly accepted the invitation.

For a while the Actors Studio and the Dramatic Workshop vied for ideological leadership, but as Piscator began to run into political problems with the government and the idea of Epic Theater lost its force, the Actors Studio philosophy prevailed. When Piscator was forced to leave the country and the direction of the Dramatic Workshop passed to his wife, the Workshop became just another acting school and the Actors Studio rose to the forefront. Because of the stars who emerged from it in the late forties and early fifties—Marlon Brando, James Dean and others who appealed to the young—it quickly became a modern-day temple of the theater. And its director, Lee Strasberg, became indeed the high priest of the excitingly new style of acting projected by these stars. It was not long before the powers of Strasberg and the Studio were enrobed in myth.

By the mid-fifties the Actors Studio was not just a place where stars were conceived and born; it was a place to which already established stars and substars made pilgrimages in order to learn the magic formulas of the "Method," as the Strasberg acting theories were erroneously dubbed by the press. It was also a place admittance to which almost every ordinary actor and actress dreamed of. Thanks to the press, most people imagined the Studio to be a school, a place to which one went to take acting lessons. This was not the case at all. Lessons, properly speaking, were not given. The atmosphere was more like that of a seminar, with Strasberg doing most, if not all, of the talking. His "students" hung on every word—stars and obscure alike. "Sessions," as they were called, were held twice a week in the converted church; the rest of the members' time was spent rehearsing scenes or exercises which they would eventually present to Strasberg's critical eye.

Since the Studio was a members-only establishment, since membership was severely limited to those who could pass its high audition standards and since thousands of actors and actresses were eager to partake of the Stanislavskian magic, Strasberg hit upon the idea of giving private classes. No sooner had he announced this than his doors were stormed by hundreds of eager acolytes willing to pay $35 a month to enroll. Strasberg was soon teaching three two-hour classes a day, five days a week. For his monthly $35 each student was allowed to attend two classes a week. For every student taking a class, there were five waiting to get in. Strasberg had already become famous with his so-called Method. Now it was time to become rich.

Strasberg's wife, Paula, a former actress, assisted her husband and was soon the all-round factotum of the great man's system. Although Lee had become the high priest, many thought Paula Strasberg the power behind the throne. Her style was the perfect complement to her husband's shy, phlegmatic disposition. A tiny, stout, gregarious woman, she became den mother to dozens of striving, often starving actors and actresses, both well known and obscure, who passed through the Strasberg classes.

One of the Hollywood stars who made the obligatory journey to New York in the mid-fifties to "learn my craft" at the feet of Strasberg was Marilyn Monroe. After observing a few sessions at the Studio she publicly endorsed the Method, as it was by then universally called in spite of Strasberg's disclaimers, and enrolled in his private classes. So strongly did the troubled and insecure actress respond to Lee's mystique and to Paula's ingratiating, motherly sympathy that she gave herself up to them. In no time at all she enlisted Lee as her official acting theoretician, Paula as her personal drama coach and both as friends.

The Strasbergs were also noted as the parents of Susan Strasberg, an engagingly fragile young actress who had, at an early age, made an auspicious Broadway debut with her creation of the title role in *The Diary of Anne Frank*. During the spring of 1958, while Henry Fonda was appearing nightly in *Two for the Seesaw*, he spent his days making a movie in which Susan Strasberg was his co-star. The film was called *Stage Struck*, a remake of an earlier Katharine Hepburn hit about a young actress seeking Broadway fame. It was being redone primarily as a vehicle for Susan Strasberg's motion-picture debut in a starring role. Normally, Fonda would not have been interested in such a project, especially in the prospect of playing second-fiddle to an untested teen-ager. But he was bored and restless with *Two for the Seesaw*. He did the movie primarily as a favor to its director, Sidney Lumet (who had directed him in *12 Angry Men*) and also because it gave him the opportunity to film in New York. As a result of the making of this film, a conspiracy of events was put in motion that would profoundly affect, of all people, Jane Fonda.

Jane got to know Susan Strasberg as a result of her father's involvement in *Stage Struck*. Although Henry Fonda had no taste for Lee Strasberg, the Actors Studio and the whole school of Method acting, he liked Susan Strasberg and spoke well of her to Jane. The two became friends, and Susan introduced Jane to several of her friends in the theater. Although Jane found these busy, animated young actors and actresses fascinating, their single-mindedness made her uneasy. "I didn't like what I saw the acting profession do to people who went into the theater," she said at the time, perhaps a bit defensively. "All the young actresses I've met are obsessed with the theater. They think and talk only about one thing. Nothing else matters to them. It's terribly unhealthy to sacrifice everything—family, children—for a goal. I hope I never get that way. I don't believe in concentrating your life in terms of one profession, no matter what it is."

Jane's exposure to these youthful and nervously aggressive theater people excited and unnerved her. She envied them their freedom, their easy sophistication, their dedication, yet she was still instinctively trying to justify her resistance to attempting an acting career. She felt talentless in the face of the talent they exuded, shy and tongue-tied against their natural gregariousness, inferior to their superior gifts. Nevertheless, as summer approached, she became more intrigued by the idea of trying.

That summer Henry Fonda took time off from *Two for the Seesaw* to make a movie in Hollywood. He rented a house in the exclusive Malibu Beach colony and brought Jane and Peter out to join him and Afdera. Also staying at Malibu for the summer were Lee and Paula Strasberg, there to attend Marilyn Monroe, and their children, Susan and Johnny. Their house was just down the beach from the Fondas'.

Jane resumed her friendship with Susan Strasberg, and they spent many of their days together on the beach or at each other's houses. Jane met many among the constant stream of visitors to the Strasberg abode, which they ran practically as an open house. The conversation, which seemed to go on without pause around the clock, was all about theater and movies, actors, actresses and directors, theory and gossip. Jane did a great deal of listening but felt incapable of contributing to it. She admired the raucous Jewish warmth of the Strasberg household, however, which was in stark contrast with the studied and formal casualness of her own.

One night she went to a party and met longtime Hollywood director Mervyn Le Roy, who was there with his children, Warner and Linda, both about Jane's age. The conversation turned to why Jane hadn't done any acting since the summer at Cape Cod. Jane replied earnestly that she didn't think she was up to being the kind of actress she would have to be as the daughter of Henry Fonda; to be anything less than perfect would be to be nothing at all. Le Roy scoffed and asked her if she wouldn't like to play Jimmy Stewart's daughter in *The FBI Story*. He was serious. Jane, suddenly presented with a job proposal, didn't know what to say. All she knew was that the thought of it scared her.

She tried to talk to her father about it, but he was enigmatic. "If you're going to be an actress, you don't want it to be as Jimmy Stewart's daughter in *The FBI Story*," was his reported answer. She mentioned it the next day to Susan Strasberg and some of her chums on the beach. One of them was a young man named Marty Fried, a directorial protégé of Lee Strasberg who had been staying at the Strasberg house. He wondered aloud why Jane hadn't got into acting long before: She was obviously attractive and was filled with a natural vibrancy and vitality that could take her a long way. Jane countered with her carefully thought-out misgivings about being Henry Fonda's daughter. The question became part of the discussions and conversations that trailed through the next few days among the young people. Personal magnetism, grace, singular good looks, intelligence, distinctive and attractive mannerisms—Jane had all these qualities. Even if her name wasn't Fonda, she had enough to be a candidate for success. The real question was: Did she have the obsessive need to act, the inner fire, and the drive and ambition to succeed?

The only way to find out would be to try. And there was no better way to try than under the tutelage of Lee Strasberg.

Admission to the Actors Studio was by audition only. It was a form of audition that turned every actor who approached it into a nervous wreck. So many were seeking entrance into the Studio that, by 1958, even to be accepted for audition was a feather in one's cap. The audition was not simply a matter of giving a reading. One was required to prepare a scene, usually with another actor, then present it to a jury of Studio members. Many tried, few succeeded. The exclusivity of the Actors Studio was part of its mystique.

Admission to Strasberg's private classes was another matter altogether. As long as one could pay the $35-per-month fee and could survive a brief interview with him, one was eligible for the classes. All that remained was the long wait for a vacancy to open up. For very special people—people like Marilyn Monroe—vacancies were made.

Susan Strasberg talked to her parents about Jane. Paula called Jane over to the house and questioned her. The questions were incisively personal and cut through the shield of Jane's wariness. Then she talked to her husband, who agreed to give Jane an interview and retired with her to a quiet corner of the house.

When Strasberg talks to someone, especially someone he doesn't know well, he gives the impression of talking past one. His voice, with its strong trace of Mittel-europa, is flat and expressionless. As he talks, he unconsciously arranges his face into expressions of distaste, so that to someone who doesn't know him well he appears unfriendly and impatient. If that someone happens herself to be shy, fearful and insecure, the experience can be unnerving. Strasberg is not an imposing man; indeed, with his thick glasses, his bland Slavic face, his gray-tinged complexion and a postnasal drip that punctuates his sentences like a metronome, he is totally unprepossessing. Yet because of his fame and the aura of his myth, he projects a sullen authority that commands respect and attention.

As Jane answered Strasberg's questions about herself, she found herself opening up. He was gruff, almost surly—not unlike her father—but his questions and comments had an interested, uncritical, probing edge that her father's had never had. "He talked to me as if he were interested in *me*, not because I was Henry Fonda's daughter. He could sense I wanted to act but was afraid to."

"The only reason I took her," Strasberg has said, "was her eyes. There was such panic in the eyes." Part of her panic may have been as a result of her fear of being inspected by this man of spectacular reputation whose judgment had been sought by stars of the magnitude of her father. When Strasberg consented to have her in his classes starting that fall in New York, without the usual wait for a vacancy, Jane, for one of the few times in her life, felt a sense of real self-esteem. She had survived the first test—the spotlight of Strasberg's cold but sympathetically perceptive judgment. The dogmatic seriousness and dedication she detected in him when he talked about "the work" filled her with a sense of sober anticipation. What this mysterious "work" consisted of, exactly, she wasn't altogether sure. But although she had often listened to her father ridicule the Method, she sensed that it was important and that something momentous was going to come from her exposure to it. The wheels of purpose, however vague, slowly began to revolve within her.

Strasberg conducted his private classes in the tiny theater of the Dramatic Workshop, which was situated over the cavernous Capitol Theater on Broadway and Fiftieth Street in Manhattan. Although he had severed his formal teaching relationship with the school, he remained on friendly terms with its managing director, Saul Colin.

Colin had been a friend and associate of Piscator. He was an elderly self-styled theatrical impresario from Rumania and Paris whose imperious ways and waspish manner rubbed most American theatrical people the wrong way. With Piscator gone and Piscator's wife, Maria, an indifferent administrator, Colin had assumed direction of the Dramatic Workshop more or less by default. He was pleased to give Strasberg the use of the Workshop's theater at a nominal rent in exchange for the reflected glory Strasberg's presence shed on what was by now a second-rate drama school.

In spite of his idiosyncrasies and his low station in New York's theatrical pecking order, Colin had a beguiling European charm and multilingual urbanity that made him tolerable to the Strasbergs. During the fall-to-spring season when Strasberg held his classes at the Workshop, he and Colin lunched together every Monday at nearby Lindy's, where they reminisced and exchanged stories about their former days in the theater—Strasberg's in New York, Colin's in Europe.

After Colin took control of the Workshop, he tried to turn it into a kind of commercial Actors Studio. The teachers were for the most part out-of-work actors and actresses—many of them members of the Studio—who employed Strasberg's theories and techniques. The students were, by and large, young starry-eyed émigrés from the hinterland of America who were led to believe that a year or so at the Dramatic Workshop was the first step on the ladder to Strasberg's private classes, then to the Actors Studio and eventual theatrical and movie stardom. Because of Strasberg's almost-daily presence at the school and the constant flow of traffic between his classes—with many well-known personalities milling around the halls—the Workshop students were easily convinced that they were at the heart of the most important theatrical happening in New York.

Next to membership in the Actors Studio, enrollment in Strasberg's private classes was the most desirable status a young actor or actress could hope to achieve in 1958. Once admitted, one would practically sell one's soul to raise the monthly $35 required to stay in. Thus, the Dramatic Workshop, the site of the classes, was the focal point of New York's theatrical elite during the late fifties and early sixties. Often, when someone particularly newsworthy was attending the classes—Marilyn Monroe, for instance—the local newspapers and wire services would send reporters and photographers to infiltrate the Workshop. One enterprising columnist even went so far as to enroll a legman as a student in the school so that he could obtain a daily supply of gossip and surreptitiously snapped photos while Miss Monroe was there. In addition, hundreds of other people—mostly actors and actresses—sought to crash the classes.

Strasberg frequently complained to Colin about the incursions during their weekly lunches. Colin took it upon himself to provide security by interviewing each new Strasberg student and carefully checking the faces of those who came in and out. Since crashing was often done with the complicity of bona fide students, this didn't work very well; a student who wanted to get one or two outsiders into a class would divert Colin's attention while the others slipped through the theater's entrance.

Strasberg conducted his classes in the small darkened theater from a seat in the first row, facing a low stage upon which some activity—a scene or exercise—would be in progress. Behind him, filling most of the theater's fifty or so seats, were his students, most of them in rapt attention. Who was there legitimately and who was not remained a vexing question; in the theater's dimness all the faces were anonymous. Finally, Colin suggested that Strasberg arrange for one of his more physical male students—one who knew the faces and names of the students—to act as a sort of security man and bouncer in exchange for free attendance at all the classes. This arrangement was made, and for a while the unauthorized-attendance problem improved.

It was into this atmosphere of elitism, high ambition and ballyhoo that Jane Fonda, accompanied by her friends Susan Strasberg and Marty Fried, came in the fall of 1958. She didn't have to be introduced; the news of her coming had already preceded her, and her face, which bore the indelible Fonda trademark, was immediately recognized. Jane was an instant celebrity, if only because of her name. The jealousy quotient, always high in Strasberg's classes, became unspokenly feverish.

She went through the hurried, obligatory interview with Saul Colin. He was not unmindful of who she was and he immediately switched on his highest charm. As he later recalled, "She was like a frightened deer hiding behind a nervous, forthright manner. She was tall and well dressed and made up like one of those society girls I always see coming out of the shops on Madison Avenue. She spoke in rapid bursts, with the strong accent American girls think made them appear well bred. She had a lot of, how do you say, phoniness . . . but the way her eyes locked onto mine, as if trying to reach for a life ring before drowning, made me sympathetic. I could feel the intensity behind her snobbish manner . . . and the anguish. The poor girl really felt quite out of place. But she had something. . . ."

Another person who recalls meeting Jane that first day—one of Strasberg's students—says, "Jane came in with Susan Strasberg, I think, just before the class began. Lee ignored her, but everybody else immediately knew who she was, and you could feel the tension that was always there swell up like a balloon. I had never seen her before, but we'd all heard the talk about her coming, and everybody was looking forward to it. I mean, she was Henry Fonda's daughter and all that, and everyone was dying of curiosity. I was surprised to see how much like her father she looked—the resemblance was uncanny. That's what we were all talking about after class, how much like her father. . . . I came out, and there she was talking to someone. She smiled at me, and I could see she was a bit nervous and apprehensive. I was surprised how tall she was as I passed her. She was dressed very elegantly, wearing sort of a pink suit and high heels, with her hair up, but she looked as though she didn't know what to do with herself. Which was funny, because if *she* felt awkward, *we* felt even more so. There was something about her that right away said 'class,' and, if anything, I think a lot of us felt a little less of ourselves in her presence. You know how you're always measuring yourself against other people; well, there she was, feeling insecure, when it was us who were feeling even more insecure. I think the way she made us feel—her name and the kind of classy aura she had—was a source of a lot of hidden resentment on our parts there at the beginning. Oh, we pretended to be friendly and all that, but I'll bet almost everyone in the class was dying for her to make a fool of herself."

9. From Student to Star

Acting gave her the kind of applause she never got as a human being. I've never seen ambition as naked as Jane's.

—BROOKE HAYWARD

ABOUT her start with Strasberg, Jane says, "I was awfully frightened. I didn't know what to expect. For the first month or so I thought it was all pretty ridiculous. But suddenly something happened, and I became thoroughly involved in it."

What happened was that, with tortured misgivings, she performed her first "exercise" before Strasberg, and the class and suddenly discovered she had the power to affect people—especially the people whose approval she sought.

Performance of an "exercise" was required of every new Strasberg student; it was the student's initiation rite into the mysteries of the Method. Until one performed it, thereby exposing oneself to the critical scrutiny of Strasberg and the assembled students, one was not accepted by the others as a genuine member of the class. The exercise consisted of anything the student wished to do, within a specified framework, and was in two basic parts. The first was usually a physical action—jumping up and down alone on the stage and chanting the words to a favorite song, for instance. This part of the exercise was designed to expose the level of inhibition to which the student was tied and to see if he or she was capable of conquering it. The second part consisted of a "sense memory" or "private moment," in which the student acted out in pantomime some action that had a particularly emotional meaning. This was designed to plumb the student's ability to define and express an emotion and was considered a measure of talent.

The new student approached the day of his or her first exercise with dread, for it was truly a different and revealing experience. No matter how thick a mask of self-assurance one wore in everyday life, the exercise stripped it away and exposed the student's insecurities and self-consciousness for all to see. It was a moment of truth for the untested actor, and it was not unusual for the more timid among Strasberg's students, fearing exposure and ridicule, to put the performance of their first exercise off for months, even years. And there were those who never got up the courage to do it at all; they attended the classes faithfully but remained rooted to their seats, content to receive their pleasure vicariously.

It took Jane a month to conquer her fears about doing her first exercise. At first she remained superficially calm and superior as she watched others go through their agonies—her father's criticisms of Strasberg's methods were fresh in her mind, and she found herself using them as a balm to her insecurities. Yet she envied those who had the courage to go on in the face of their fears, then get caught up in the enthusiasm of having done so; she saw how it filled them with confidence and cockiness. More, she envied the attention they received from Strasberg. It became clear to her that this was the only way to get the great man's attention—to expose yourself and run the risks.

As she sat inactive through the early classes, Jane began to get the hang of things. She soon learned that Strasberg was not to be feared. To her surprise, he did not react to the students' often inept exercise performances with the expected ridicule; rather, he gently criticized. It was the presence of the other students, many of them accomplished actors, and the secret thoughts she imagined they would harbor if she took the stage—possibly breaking out into sarcastic laughter (it had happened with others)—that held her back. "I didn't believe in myself. I couldn't stand the thought of exposing myself, of being attacked and torn to pieces."

But she was also in a hurry to receive an indication from Strasberg of whether she had anything besides her name upon which to build an acting career. And she was anxious to prove something to her father, who treated the stories she brought home about Strasberg's methods with amused condescension. So, with the encouragement and guidance of the few friends she had made, she set a date for her exercise and busied herself with its preparation. As the appointed day approached, she grew more nervous and fearful and even thought of calling in sick. But her courage prevailed. When the day came, feverish with anxiety, she took the stage.

"You see so many exercises I forget what it was she did," a longtime member of Strasberg's classes says. "I do remember that the class was particularly crowded that day. A lot of people from the other classes had heard about it and were there to see her fall on her face. But she didn't. In fact, she was terrific. You could see this change go through her. The first impression she gave was her nervousness, but everybody is nervous the first time—I did exercises for six years and was as nervous the last time as I was the first. Then you could see her start to relax and get caught up in it. Pretty soon she was letting it all hang out. Everybody was pretty impressed. Not only with the actor's talent she showed, but with her guts. Now that I think back on it, it was inevitable that she be good. It had to happen that way, what with so many people secretly hoping she'd be bad."

That first excruciating performance revealed a lot about Jane. It revealed her desperation and panic, of course. But more important, it revealed an instinctive gift—the ability to move around on a stage, block out distracting external stimuli and zero in on her own space and time. Although the performance was rough-edged and overblown, marred at the start with the anxious amateur's self-consciousness and tendency to rush, it contained very definite intimations of talent. Most remarkable of all, her presence dominated the small stage; even with other students on it, all eyes were drawn to her.

Strasberg made no departure from his usual dry and clinical tone when he began to analyze Jane's exercise for the rest of the class. But his voice grew more lively as he went along, the way it always did whenever he perceived what he felt was an unusual talent. His critique was at first a letdown for Jane; it was only after the class, when everyone flocked to her and congratulated her, "accepting" her into the group, that she felt she had shown something. And when one of Strasberg's closest observers added that he had seemed more ebullient than usual, and explained what that meant, she soared with happiness.

"My life changed radically within twenty-four hours," she says of the experience. "It was just a night-and-day difference. Before, I'd been scared and extremely self-conscious—I was one person. And then after that exercise I was somebody else. I worked harder than anybody else. I was more ragged than anybody else. I was the rattiest, wannest, most straggle-haired. . . ."

Jane was hooked. She plunged almost obsessively into the life of Strasberg student and striving actress. "I've never seen anyone involve herself so much," her friend Brooke, also a student, said. "She worked at it seven days a week."

"God, it was like a light bulb going on," according to Jane. "I was a different person. I went to bed and woke up loving what I was doing."

Her enthusiasm for acting didn't merely grow; it exploded. "Now I know that nothing that happened to me before last fall really counts," she was to say a year later. "It's a fantastic feeling when you've finally found out where you're going. You're happier. You're more productive. You're nicer. Whether I'll make it is something else again, but at least I'm finally channeled." But if she was pleased with the hard ambition she finally found, she remained disappointed in her higher hope—achieving her father's approval and respect.

Henry Fonda had already made it clear to Jane that he didn't believe in acting schools. He had little confidence in the theories of the Method, which she started to expound as though she had been the first to uncover them. He was glad in a paternal way that she had finally discovered an interest, and although he occasionally indulged her enthusiasm for acting talk, he would quickly become bored with her evangelism, shutting her off with an indifferent shrug. And if he was in one of his dark moods, which were occurring with more frequency and lasting longer, he would barely respond to her at all. As Jane began to find herself, she was hurt by her father's indifference.

"I used to come home from Lee's classes so full of what I was doing," she recalled a few years later, "and my father would say, 'Shut up, I don't want to hear about it.' There was one time, for example, where I had just done a marvelous scene in class. And it was like I was on fifty Benzedrines. I bumped into my father and got into a taxicab with him. I was panting with excitement. I wanted to tell him all about it. And I could see his curtain come down. He smiled, but I just didn't get through."

When questioned about this later during an interview for the *Saturday Evening Post*, Fonda, tears swelling his eyes, said, "Well, I don't understand this. Maybe I'm—maybe I do things that I'm not aware of that mean something to other people. I don't know what she means by a curtain coming down. It may be that I'm trying to hide my own emotion, and to her it's a curtain coming down. Now, *I'll* relate the story, because it started long before Jane started studying to be an actress. She was with a young beau of hers who was just getting started in the theater, and he and I were talking about using an emotion, having to feel an emotion on the stage. I told a story about the process I go through, likening it to a seaplane taking off. There's a section on the underside of the seaplane called a step. When the plane starts its takeoff, it is very slow in the water, very sluggish, but as it picks up speed, it gets up on that step and starts to skim across the water before lifting off. I used to feel that if I could get myself going, I could get up on that step and nothing could stop me. Then all I had to do was hold back, hold the controls down, because then I was going, I was soaring. Anyway, about a year later I found myself in a cab with Jane going downtown, and Jane said, 'Do you remember the story that you told about soaring?' And she said, 'Now I know what you mean. It happened to me today.' Well, I can get emotional right now remembering Jane tell it, and probably the curtain came down to hide that emotion. Because for my daughter to be telling me about it—she knew what it was like! Well, I wasn't going to let her see me go on like this."

The interviewer, Alfred Aronowitz, asked, "Why not? Don't you understand she wants to get to you?"

"Well, gosh," Fonda replied, "she does get to me."

"I know," Aronowitz said, "but she wants to know she's getting to you. She's such a demonstrative person."

"Well," Fonda said, "I'm not."

Whether it was due to professional impatience or fatherly reticence, Fonda's continuing indifference to Jane's striving was like water sprayed on the seeds of her bitterness. She still did not give up the hope of someday winning her father's esteem. But her increasing self-confidence, most of which she now derived from Strasberg, gave her the will and determination to set her own course, independent of her father's reactions. It would be an exaggeration to suggest that Strasberg became, at least for a while, a substitute for Jane's father, yet his influence did become the dominating one in her life.

"You see," she claimed at the time, "with Lee nothing more was demanded of me than what I felt innermost. Lee Strasberg, someone who was not related to me, was saying, 'You are sensitive, you are good, you are worth something.' No one had ever told me that before. He was the only person I'd ever known who was interested in me without having to be. Lee somehow imparts dignity and gives you confidence in yourself."

After her return from Malibu and before starting her classes with Strasberg, Jane moved out of her father's house. Earlier in the summer a girl she knew at Vassar, Susan Stein, had come down to New York with the intention of obtaining an apartment. Susan was the daughter of Jules Stein, the wealthy founder of the Music Corporation of America. Known in the entertainment world as MCA, it was one of the largest talent and booking agencies in show business, with agents on both coasts representing many of the biggest stars in motion pictures, theater and television, including Jane's father. Susan suggested to Jane that they share an apartment. Jane broached the subject to her father and got his permission to move with Susan and another girl, Jenny Lee, into a small duplex in a converted town house on East Seventy-sixth Street, just two blocks from her father's house. In her mind, this was an important first step in the process of gaining her independence.

Another large talent agency of the day was an organization called Famous Artists. Working there at the time was a young agent named Ray Powers. Powers represented actor Jody McRea, the son of Joel McRea. Jody McRea's girlfriend at the time was Jenny Lee, one of the girls Jane had moved in with. Powers recalls, "One day Jody McRea asked me to see Jenny's roommate, Jane. At first I didn't realize the Jane he was talking about was Jane Fonda. I said I'd see her, and we set up an appointment. When Jane came into the office, she had just started taking Lee Strasberg's classes. She told me she wasn't really intent on becoming an actress but was taking the classes more as a kind of therapy than anything else. After realizing who she was, I said that, God, she could be something great and I would give her a guarantee she would be a movie star. She continued to be doubtful, but I kept calling her and meeting with her and saying, 'You really can do it, you know.' She kept going to Strasberg's classes that fall, and gradually, between the stuff she was getting from him and my constant encouragements, she began to believe that maybe she really could do something. As a result of all that, I became her first agent. She could easily have gone with MCA—after all, it was owned by Susan Stein's father, and it was her father's agency. But I found out right away that her father didn't take her acting at all seriously—he thought it was just another lark—and he wasn't helping or encouraging her in any way."

Powers says that after Jane began to think seriously about an acting career, he had to devise a new image for her. "She was known around New York as a sort of fashion debutante, and I had to get her to stop having her picture taken at balls and other society functions. Nobody in the entertainment business would take her seriously, being a debutante, so I got her to stop wearing all that makeup and those chic clothes and asked her to start wearing the uniform of the serious young actresses of the time, which was the black leotard outfit—you know, the bohemian look. Well, she did, and we had pictures taken of her, looking very stark and kind of dedicated and sent them around to all the movie studios. And that's how it all really started."

Young actors and actresses competed furiously with each other not only to get stage and picture roles, but also for work in television commercials. "One day," Powers says, "Jane came in and asked if I could send her around for some commercials. It seems she was overdrawn at the bank, had just bought an expensive sofa for her apartment and was desperately in need of money. So I sent her around for jillions of commercials, but none of them would use her. She was very discouraged about it, but then she started to get photo-modeling work, and things began to look better for her."

Jane was tall. Her thick, dark-gold hair fell to her shoulders when she wasn't wearing it up in a tight knot. Through constant dieting she had reduced her weight to about 115 pounds. Her cheeks had lost most of the fleshiness of her teen-age years, and when her hair was up, her face had a ballerina's fashionably gaunt expression. Her steep, broad forehead was like a smooth palisade above her wide, deepset blue eyes. The rest of her face was slightly elongated, angling from high, prominent cheekbones to long, square jaw, its length accentuated by the triangular shaping of her mouth. Most photographs taken of her at the time found her posed with her head tipped down so as to minimize the hang of her chin. Her teeth were large for her mouth, especially the upper ones; when she smiled, which she did with a suddenness that was unexpected, her slightly convex teeth jumped out in a flash of brilliant white.

Her long graceful neck climbed out of a supple, well-shaped body. Her breasts were high and compact, and her wide-shouldered, high-waisted torso curved to well-rounded hips. Her legs were shapely but had a dancer's thickness, especially in the calves and ankles. Her feet were large, as were her hands, but she possessed long, slender, expressive fingers that belied the curious chunkiness of her upper arms. She was, at twenty-one, an at once fragile and sturdy beauty and indeed had a look that was different from what one expected to see in fashion magazines of the time. It was a decidedly girlish look, appealingly scrubbed and unexotic, and her long, serious face in repose gave her an added touch of vulnerability and innocence.

With her deep-seated insecurities about how she looked, Jane alternated between narcissistic worry and indifference. She took to wearing the pseudobohemian garb that most of the other young actresses around New York affected, eschewing the jewelry and cosmetics of former days and dressing in the plain sweater-skirt-and-leotard outfits that were the uniform of the day.

Jane's romantic life grew increasingly active during the fall and winter of 1958. According to Ray Powers, "She had just broken up with Jim Franciscus when I met her. I think the reason they broke up was that, although he was an actor, he was also from very much the same social background as she was, and after a while she found that sort of dull and boring. Then she started seeing lots of different people. By then she was so enthusiastic about acting she was trying to get all her socialite friends into it too. I was dating Brooke Hayward a lot, so I saw a good deal of Jane socially, as well as professionally, and got to meet many of the people in her circle. After going around with several different young men, she finally started having a romance with a fellow named Sandy Whitelaw, who was sort of a socialite who was interested in the theater."

As Jane saw the real possibility of an acting career opening up, she grew less and less interested in the idea of "getting married and having babies," a notion Powers says she was still clinging to when he first met her. And according to Jane, after going through several abortive relationships during the previous three years, "I was terrified of being vulnerable. I had never been able to sustain a relationship. I'd always gone through the first stages, the passion, the expectation, and then become disappointed. I vowed I wouldn't get married unless someone gave me a good reason to."

Although he had become resigned to Jane's animated metamorphosis, Henry Fonda still considered her acting studies nothing more than an experiment and did not expect her interest in this one to survive any longer than her other experiments had. Her unalloyed enthusiasm and her growing impatience to make her mark as an actress, although she had not acted in anything yet, continued to dismay him. Still distrusting anything that came easy or cheap and trying to protect his daughter from what he was sure was her naïveté, he occasionally lectured her about the years it would take to learn her craft and the special critical demands that would be made on her because of her name. The latter was something she was already well aware of; as for the former, she had little use for her father's cautionary advice in the face of the encouragement she was receiving from outside his house. It's likely, moreover, that his indifference to her stories of Strasberg's wisdom and genius convinced her that Henry Fonda was, in certain respects, out of touch with things. And as far as intellectual and emotional nourishment were concerned, Jane was getting much more from Strasberg than from him. Strasberg had become a positive, encouraging force in her life, opening her up to all the possibilities that lay before her, whereas her father remained dour and discouraging about them.

Fonda's cautions seemed especially hollow when, early in 1959, his friend Joshua Logan heard through his wife that Jane was studying acting. Logan had acquired the rights to a popular novel called *Parrish* and was planning to produce and direct the screen version. Always a close friend of the Fonda family and one of Jane's honorary godfathers, Logan had often suggested to her that she take up acting. He had been, he says, surprised by her consistent lack of interest. He was doubly surprised, therefore, not having seen her in some time, to learn that she was in Lee Strasberg's classes.

Parrish was a sentimental young boy-young girl love story played out against a background of upper-class pathos. Logan was looking for a youthful actor and actress to play the two well-bred leads. He already had Warren Beatty, the unknown younger brother of actress Shirley MacLaine, in mind for the boy's part, and it occurred to him that Jane might just be right for the girl. It may also have occurred to him that to introduce the brother of Shirley MacLaine and the daughter of Henry Fonda together in their first movie roles would give the picture a wonderful publicity touch.

Logan says he immediately called and talked to Jane about it. Unnerved by the sudden, unexpected prospect of doing a movie, Jane looked to her father for advice. He was noncommittal. He told her it was a decision she would have to make on her own, although privately he couldn't think of anyone whose hands he would prefer her to be in than those of Josh Logan. She made her decision and, after doing some further readings, was given a screen test by Logan, who recalls that he was pleasantly surprised by Jane's poise.

Screen tests are made primarily so a producer can gain an idea of the qualities an actor or actress will project on film and to determine if those qualities will enhance the character meant to be portrayed. Acting ability is a secondary consideration, particularly for a newcomer; what the producer looks for above everything else is physical magnetism. The more powerfully this is projected, the better, for this is the magic essence of film stardom. Like talent, it is indefinable and unpredictable. It is a gift few possess, and in those few it is not possessed equally. Its highest expression occurs when, on screen, one's every gesture, every pause, every acceleration are an event, when to stand still and relaxed is to be mysteriously surrounded by one's own space.

If Jane didn't impart an overwhelming presence in her first screen test, which she made with Beatty, she did well enough. She had had no experience before a camera, but she used the few tips her father gave her—mainly to relax and not to "act"—to good effect and passed the test to Logan's satisfaction. Indeed, Logan was so pleased with the way Jane came across that he immediately signed her to a seven-year personal contract which called for her to star in a picture a year. Ray Powers, who by then was Jane's official agent at the Famous Artists agency, thinks the contract called for her to receive $10,000 a year. Fonda history was repeating itself, although this Fonda was one up on her father. "I could barely contain my enthusiasm after seeing her test," Logan says. "I tested Brooke Hayward the same day—she and Jane were friendly rivals and I thought it was only fair of me to do, especially since Brooke was my actual goddaughter and Jane was only my informal one—but Jane surely stole the show. I knew immediately that she was destined for stardom."

Without yet having appeared in a professional capacity, Jane Fonda had become a film star. All that remained was for the public to confirm it.

10. *Tall Story*

I found out that acting was hell. You spend all your time trying to do what they put people in asylums for.

—Jane Fonda

JANE'S confirmation had to wait a while, as in fact did Warren Beatty's. Logan had both of them set to play the young lovers in *Parrish*, but to ensure the picture's box-office appeal, he wanted established stars like Vivien Leigh and Clark Gable to play the two leading adult roles. When he couldn't get them and when script problems arose, he decided to abandon the project and concentrate on something else.

Although Ray Powers recalls that Logan had some misgivings about Beatty's screen potential because of the young actor's "cross eyes," as a result of his screen test Beatty was eventually signed to a contract by MGM. He went to Hollywood to wait for another picture. Jane, in the meantime, armed with Logan's promise that he'd soon find something exciting to star her in and propelled by her growing ambition to be accepted into the Actors Studio, worked more intensively than ever in Strasberg's private classes.

She was still not getting any television commercials, but her modeling activities were rapidly expanding. She went to see Eileen Ford, the owner of the leading model agency in New York, and was promptly enlisted in the Ford stable. "She was something," Miss Ford recalls. "She was terribly insecure about her looks and the impact she had on people and was astonished to learn that people would be interested in using her and paying her as well."

Within a short time, Jane's modeling career was racing far ahead of her acting career. With the help of Eileen Ford's aggressive marketing tactics, Jane was soon appearing in major magazines, and it was not long before she made a few covers. With several covers to her credit in the period of a few months, she became a minor celebrity in her own right around New York. "I used to hang around newsstands watching the people who bought the magazine. I thought I looked pretty, but not really beautiful." Her visibility on the newsstands, along with the knowledge of her contract with Logan, was ample evidence to her classmates, many of whom had been toiling for years without recognition, that she would soon be on her way.

Still innately shy and unsure of herself, Jane sensed the resentment that mounted in class, especially from some of the other actresses. She took to rushing in and out of class without stopping to talk to anyone. "Naturally they assumed she was already acting like a star," recalls a classmate, "when the truth was that she was ill at ease." She did not let her discomfort deter her ambition, however. She continued to work harder than anyone else and was onstage almost every other week with a scene or exercise.

In April, true to his promise, Logan acquired the film rights to another property—a play called *Tall Story*, which had been running on Broadway through the winter. It was adapted by the well-known playwriting team of Howard Lindsay and Russel Crouse from an earlier novel by Howard Nemerov, about college basketball and gambling scandals, entitled *The Homecoming Game*. The leading roles were those of a college basketball star mixed up in a bribe attempt and his cheerleader-girlfriend. Logan originally wanted to use Warren Beatty again but says the moguls at Warner Brothers were against the casting of two unknowns in the leads. He had to decide between Jane and Beatty and chose Jane. For the male lead, he decided on Anthony Perkins.

Logan sent Jane to see the play the night before it was due to close, without telling her he had her in mind for it. She sat next to Tony Perkins, the young, lanky film and stage actor who a few years before had co-starred with her father in a Western movie called *The Tin Star*. "I knew Josh had already cast Tony in the movie version of *Tall Story*, but I didn't realize he had me in mind. I must confess I hated the play, and I thought the girl's part was too small. The next day Josh sent me the script for the movie, and wow! What an astoundingly large part for the girl. I loved the script. I couldn't believe I was going to have such a large part."

If Jane's critical faculties seemed limited by the performer's perennial concern about the size of a part, she was responding no differently from the way any other actor or actress would have. And like most, once she knew the part was hers, she grew anxious about it. It had been one thing to dream of attaining stardom—the dreams bore no responsibilities and no exposure to criticism. But now, with the chance at hand, fears of failure began to nag at her. Suddenly she was confronted with the prospect of exposing herself to the public, and she felt uneasy. She started to lose sleep, waking up at night with unpleasant dreams—mostly reprises of her childhood dreams of rejection and persecution. She also suffered, according to Ray Powers, from a severe case of boils, a chronic condition that had a habit of surfacing whenever she was particularly anxious. "I knew some people in the movie business would be nice to me because my name was Fonda, but I wanted to make it on my own merits. There's loads of difference between growing up in a theatrical family where someone else is doing the great things and doing something yourself. After I signed the contract, I began to have doubts about myself."

Jane's anxiety was intensified by an experience she had in June. Filming of *Tall Story* was not to start in Hollywood until September, so Ray Powers arranged for her to play the ingenue lead in a two-week stock revival of *The Moon Is Blue* at the North Jersey Playhouse in Fort Lee, New Jersey. Hurriedly prepared, inadequately rehearsed and indifferently directed, the production provided Jane with her first professional acting job. Without her father's presence to divert the spotlight from her, she was on her own. She quickly learned that she knew a good deal less about acting than she thought. A number of her acquaintances came to see her and were understandably liberal in their praise and congratulations, but she knew she hadn't been good. Ray Powers says, "When you come right down to it, she was miscast. She had none of the right qualities for the virginal girl she played, but we wanted to get her some exposure before audiences before she started on *Tall Story*." She tried to use all the things she had learned from Strasberg, but somehow nothing worked. She could not conquer her nervousness and relax into the role. "I flopped around the stage in control of nothing," she said shortly afterward. "Control is what I'm after. Control is the whole kookie secret."

The experience was a sobering one. In preparing for *The Moon Is Blue*, she worked diligently on the "acting problem" the part presented. But she became so embroiled in the theoretical dimensions of the character— trying to solve such questions as motivation and intention—that she never got a firm grip on it. As have numerous young performers schooled in the Strasberg tradition, she confused the Method, which is nothing more than a design for acting, with acting itself. The truth, depth and intensity of a characterization do not stem from the Method; they come out of the intuition and understanding of the actor who is playing the character. The Method, as Strasberg devised it, merely tries to give the actor, through training and practice, a capacity for these qualities. There is no such thing as Method acting, as if it were some special technique; there is only acting based on Method training. It's a small distinction, but an important one, and young actors often are as fooled by it as the public. Jane was not yet fully aware of it. She thus sought to act through the Method rather than through herself. Her resulting discomfort and the lack of assurance it revealed dominated her performance. The few notices she received in the local newspapers made reference to her sweet-looking appearance and her resemblance to her father—these were inevitable—and even used words like "promising." But none failed to note the awkwardness in her performance.

It was a salutary experience, nevertheless, for instead of feeling defeated by what she considered to be her failed debut, she resolved to improve herself and refine her understanding of what it took to be an actress. Moreover, it gave her an appreciation she hadn't had before of her father's obsessive perfectionism about his craft. She may not yet have been ready to follow her father's advice about working gradually toward a career, but she understood his notions about "babying up on a part" as opposed to trying to swallow it whole, then flamboyantly spitting it out and calling that a performance. She would henceforth be less inclined to lecture her father on the wonders of the Method. "It's supposed to be terribly difficult being yourself onstage," she told someone after her Fort Lee debut, "but now that I know how hard it is I admire my father enormously."

Not that she lost faith in the Method. On the contrary, she understood more clearly now what it was and how it could help liberate her from the prison of her still bottled-up emotions. And when she heard Strasberg say that her father was more of a Method actor than most self-styled Method actors, except that he was a natural one, her faith was given a boost.

According to Powers, Logan was planning an intensive publicity campaign for Jane. She was to leave for Hollywood in July for wardrobe fittings and preproduction publicity for *Tall Story*, which Logan would be producing and directing for Warner Brothers. Shortly before departing, she met with Logan and Tony Perkins in Logan's New York apartment to discuss the script. Perkins recalls, "There was a photographer there, and he wanted publicity pictures of us necking on the couch, sort of a preview of a scene in the movie. Jane kind of turned pale. It was her first encounter with one of the absurdities of this business, and it was as if she said to herself, 'Well, is this what being an actress means?' You could then see her take a deep breath and say to herself, 'Well, I guess it is, so OK, let's get it over with.' "

Jane's first exposure to the publicity grind—a necessary adjunct to an acting career but one she hadn't given any thought to—was a harmless one. But it awakened a new concern. Her father had been a famous actor for twenty-five years, yet had managed to shield his children from the glare of publicity. He had little taste for personal promotion; although he grudgingly cooperated in a certain amount of the ritual stars were required to participate in, he never enjoyed it. Logan, on the other hand, now a veteran producer, doted on publicity. Launching Jane as his new star, he wanted to make sure that she was able to handle the publicity-related activities that would be a necessary part of her rise. So he sat her down and outlined his plans and expectations, coaching Jane on how she should act and what she should say in the many interviews she would soon be giving in Hollywood. Since, in *Tall Story*, she was playing a wholesome all-American girl spiced with a dash of wanton sensuality, he told her how to promote that image to interviewers and photographers. Of course, she should have no difficulty on that score, he confidently assured her, since those were exactly her qualities. Jane remained unconvinced.

Logan's enthusiasm about Jane and her prospects encouraged Henry Fonda. Logan was certain that she would have a happy debut in movies and would quickly become a star. Fonda had every reason in the world to respect Logan's judgment, and his friend's optimism lifted some of the burden of his skepticism about Jane's chances. It relieved a bit of the gloom that continued to pervade his personal life as well. Fonda had returned to Hollywood to star in a new television series, *The Deputy*, for which he had high hopes. According to his press agent, John Springer, he was partly motivated by the fact that his agents had arranged an extremely lucrative deal. In spite of the financial inducements, however, Fonda rapidly found his desire for money again in conflict with his actor's integrity, and he became unhappy. *The Deputy* had promised to be a high-quality adult Western series, but it soon suffered from the urgencies of scheduling so that scripts could not be polished and production was hurried. When it went off the air after two seasons, Fonda was so disgusted that he vowed never again to do another television series.

His mood was further darkened by his son Peter. Now nineteen and a sophomore at the University of Omaha, Peter showed no signs of settling down. He had spent a turbulent, unhappy three years living with his aunt and uncle and was still flouting the authority and fighting the influence of his distant father. "I was programmed to be a Boy Scout," he says. "That's all my old man wanted me to be.

"Everybody has a problem with their parents, and I had a very typical problem, the 'nobody understands me' routine. I enjoyed being born with a platinum spoon up my ass, but I remember being very down on my father. . . . He was a very busy man and I was a hypersensitive kid who needed somebody to talk to, so I reacted quite bitterly to him. . . . The first big shock my sister, Jane, and I experienced about my father was discovering that Henry Fonda wasn't perfect. It really disoriented us."

The only thing Peter seemed to enjoy in college was acting. He acted in several plays put on at the school, but offstage much of his time was spent creating trouble for himself. He was secretly in love with Bridget Hayward—Margaret Sullavan's second daughter—with whom he'd grown up, but was forced to stifle his feelings because of the distance between them. His classroom life was a continual round of disputes with teachers, and out of school he devoted most of his time to pranking. On one occasion he and a schoolmate planted a fake bomb in the Omaha Greyhound bus terminal, then tipped off the police and watched the ensuing action. The caper was a sensation in the Omaha press, he says.

He also managed to get a local girl pregnant. The incident in Rome with the air attaché and his wife "blew my life out when I was fifteen and I was expected to come home and date these nice girls in Omaha. And my father's off in the woods someplace, and even when he's sitting in the same room with me, he doesn't know what to say, and my hair's cut short the way he wants it, and my aunt keeps telling me I should take out this Zelda Farnsgrabber because her father's a member of the Establishment and she's a nice girl, right? Well, the only chick I ever knocked up was Zelda Farnsgrabber, and I got it the first date, and I stayed out until five in the morning, and when I got home, it was all right with my aunt because it had been this Zelda, and here I'm going to have to pay five hundred dollars to send her to Puerto Rico and I haven't got the money. So I sold a Christmas present, a shotgun or something I didn't want . . . and bought my freedom from Zelda."

Henry Fonda continued to have his troubles then. But at least Jane seemed to have straightened out and was on the verge of a promising career. He even began to show interest in her work. Jane was surprised, on the eve of her departure to Hollywood, to find her father more expansive and talkative than he had ever been about the movie trade. He urged her to ignore the whispers of nepotism that would invariably surface in the press when her association with Logan became better known. He also advised her to trust Logan and follow his wishes as a director. "But," he cautioned, "don't allow yourself to feel pushed."

"I wondered what he meant by that for a while," Jane has said. "Then I realized. When you're in front of a camera, you automatically feel you have to *do* things, because the film is turning. He was saying not to be intimidated by the camera, not to be forced into doing things that are unnatural, which is the mistake every novice film performer makes." It was a lesson her father had learned during the filming of his first picture, *The Farmer Takes a Wife*, when director Victor Fleming kept telling him he was hamming.

Fortified with Logan's and her father's encouragement, yet still uncertain of her ability and fearful of the consequences of public failure, Jane prepared to leave for Hollywood. As departure day approached, her tension grew even worse than when she had done her first Strasberg exercise. The day before she left, "I raced around Manhattan like mad, then ended up in tears at home. I worried about falling flat on my face and having everyone ask, 'What's all the talk about?' "

On the day Jane was born in 1937, the newspapers told of the Panay incident in China and editorialists wondered in print about the implications it was going to have for the United States in the Far East, especially in light of the "Roosevelt Bars Peace at Any Price" policy of the government. When Jane left for Hollywood twenty-one years later to assist at the birth of her acting career, the newspapers were speculating on a similar question. Two United States "military advisers" had just been killed in a terrorist attack at the Bien Hoa military base in South Vietnam, becoming the first Americans to die in a war the American people were scarcely aware of. It is doubtful if Jane, preoccupied with her anxieties, noticed the stories.

Upon arriving in Hollywood, the first order of business was not moviemaking but publicity. Jane met with representatives of the Warner Brothers publicity department to create an official studio biography. The two-page document began: "Jane Fonda is a blonde, beautiful and talented answer to Hollywood's search for new personalities. Joshua Logan is so confident in Jane's ability and popular appeal. . . ." Studio biographies are devised primarily for use by the press. Jane insisted that no mention be made of her mother's suicide and that the fact that she was Henry Fonda's daughter be soft-pedaled. But the press, as subsequent events would prove, was less interested in Jane as a "new personality" than in the fact that she was, indeed, Henry Fonda's daughter.

Shortly after her arrival, Warner Brothers gave a large cocktail party in her honor so that Joshua Logan could formally introduce her to the press and to some of Hollywood's leading luminaries. The next day some of the local newspaper accounts snidely hinted that Jane's debut had been a disaster and drew the inevitable comparisons with her father, who had been there.

"The stories about my being nervous were true. It had never happened to me before. Usually I'm not nervous, because I don't know what's going to happen. But that day I'd been through wardrobe fittings and walked into a roomful of men and couldn't even see one female. Everyone was looking at me, and I just got this tremendous feeling of cynical indifference from everyone. I burst into tears. Then I saw my stepmother. I went over to her, and she gave me a sedative, which relaxed me. Most of my fear at the press party was because the value of such a gathering depends a lot on what you have to sell. If you're Marilyn Monroe, a press party is great. Her strap can break or she can just stand there, and they all know her. But who cares if my strap breaks? The only thing you have to sell is personality, and I felt they were thinking, 'What's all this fuss about plain Jane?' "

Jane's public introduction to Hollywood was unnerving and inauspicious. But cajoled and prodded by Logan and the Warner's publicity executives, she kept her nose to the wheel. Her next tasks were the obligatory interviews with the leading movie columnists—Louella Parsons, Hedda Hopper, *et al*.

Louella Parsons, whose column appeared in hundreds of newspapers throughout the country, was the *doyenne* of the Hollywood gossips. So important was she considered by the studios that to be interviewed and written favorably about by her constituted a virtual seal of approval. The studio publicists cultivated her like a rich spinster aunt with a terminal disease. She didn't go to her subjects; they came to her. Jane was driven to her house by a Warner's publicity man who carefully coached her in the car about how to act with "Lolly." It struck Jane as all being a bit distasteful and dishonest, but she went along with it.

"I shall never forget the way she looked when she breezed into my house from the beach where she had spent the day trying to get a suntan," Louella Parsons wrote later. "She was wearing a white blouse and yellow skirt, with her hair wrapped in a tight turban, which she called her 'babushka.' In her hand she carried a bright blue balloon which she said she found on the curb outside my home—the color effect was most becoming." The publicity man had done his job well.

"Jane is a pretty edition of Hank," Parsons wrote. "She appreciates that Henry Fonda is her father and that she received her first chance . . . because her name is Fonda. She has the same soft brown eyes [*sic*], light brown hair, and her profile is amazingly like that of her father." Jane was learning to her dismay that she was not going to be judged on her own merits and that even as astute an observer as Louella Parsons was supposed to be was no guarantee of accurate reportage.

The inevitable questions about Jane's love life and her feelings about marriage were asked. "When I marry," Jane replied, probably never having given it serious thought before, "I want it to be for all time. I have grown up with divorce, and I want to feel sure before I marry."

The rest of the column painted Jane as a wholesome, normal American girl who "loved swimming, tennis and painting," who "looked about 14 but is quite a mature young lady," and who tried to put to rest the rumor that she didn't get along with her stepmother Afdera by saying, "She improves with acquaintance."

The column, which appeared in the national press on September 13, 1959, was Jane's introduction to the nation of movie fans who hung on Louella Parsons' every word. "Quite a girl, my old friend Hank Fonda's daughter," Parsons concluded. "Beautiful, talented and charming. I invited her to come see me again soon." The seal of approval was stamped and official.

Jane's next stop was Hedda Hopper, Louella Parsons' bitter rival and Hollywood's second most influential syndicated columnist. After her, the rest of the Hollywood press corps was given its first shot at Jane. She quickly grew bored with the sameness of the questions and dissatisfied with the image that began to form, yet she dutifully played out her role as the grateful and cooperative newcomer, taking special pains to seem at once sophisticated and starry-eyed.

Meanwhile, there was a movie to make. Filming on *Tall Story* started in late summer. "I found it all very strange. I felt alone, surrounded by lights and unfriendly faces. I didn't question Josh, though. I'd known him all my life, and I thought that if he believed I could do it, I could. But the role itself didn't mean very much. I just came to the set whenever I was called."

Henry Fonda visited the *Tall Story* set one day and watched his daughter play a love scene with Tony Perkins. He was a bit nonplussed to see how casually she took on the warm-blooded passion the scene called for, but was delighted at the ease with which Jane seemed to have picked up acting. Although he didn't mention it directly to her, he proudly told a reporter, "Jane has made more progress in one year than I have in thirty." High praise indeed, if a shade hyperbolic. What was important was that Jane had finally got a public response out of her father.

It was not much comfort, however. Nor were Logan's gentle encouragements. The further Jane got into the filming, the more at sea she felt. Midway through the thirty-five-day shooting schedule, "I was in a total panic. I constantly felt like I was falling off a cliff. And there was this *camera* that was like my enemy. I *hated* it. I was always trying to hide from it, and I hated the way I looked on the screen when I saw the rushes."

This was a normal reaction for a newcomer to movie acting. So were her feelings about the tediousness of film making. "Everybody told me how much time there would be when you had nothing to do, but it's the sort of thing you don't really believe until you're involved in it. Once I spent an entire day waiting to be called for a shot, and a newspaperman who turned up on the set wrote that I was bored. I wasn't bored." She couldn't have been, for she was in a continual state of terror.

"Tony Perkins was wonderful in many ways; I learned so much from him. He was a total professional. Take the lights, for instance. You're always working with those enormous lights in your eyes. Some people keep squinting. I went to Tony and said, 'What do you do?' And he said, 'You do it, you just do it. You forget about the lights.' And that did it. I just forgot about them." So much for Method acting.

Indeed, whatever notion Jane had brought to Hollywood about using the things she had learned in her Strasberg classes soon went out the window. She had too many other things to worry about. "It was so much more complicated than I'd imagined. I always thought that you go on and pretend the camera isn't there when you shoot a scene. But that's not so, I soon learned. You have to play to the camera when you act. You relate to it in a certain way, with consciousness of the lights and all sorts of technical matters. You learn such fascinating things—like the fact that the audience's eyes tend to go to the right side of the screen, so you try to get over to the right side of the set. That's a subtle form of scene-stealing. Or you might play a scene in which you are face to face with someone; then you do it again for close-ups and different angles. You still have to get the same intensity of emotion each time, the same sincerity, even though you are acting in those second shots all by yourself. When it was my turn to cue Tony for his close-ups with me off camera, I would read my lines and really put feeling into them. But when he cued me, he just read his lines and I couldn't work up the proper reactions. When I realized that, I told him I'd make a deal with him. If he would read my cues properly instead of just in a dead voice, I'd do the same with his; otherwise, I would just throw them away."

Logan, like Henry Fonda, had little faith in the Method. He considered its deliberate, mannered style self-conscious and unnatural and would have none of it from Jane. He wanted her simply to be as he saw her—a pretty, lively, excitable version of her father. He wanted her to say her lines, hit her marks and find her key lights. He and the editors would take care of the rest in the cutting room. He knew that in Jane he had an actress of great seriousness and little confidence. Somehow her interior panic dominated her presence before the camera and disguised her insecurity. He recognized this early in the shooting and used it to Jane's advantage. It gave her character a slightly different shading from the one he had hoped for, but by and large it was better.

As for getting a performance out of her, he and his editor would solve that in the cutting room. He continued to praise her; he knew from reviewing the dailies that she had all the requisites of stardom and that this picture, no matter how inexperienced she appeared, would successfully launch her. There was no doubt about it in his mind.

Jane wasn't so certain, in spite of Logan's assurances. And as shooting continued, she grew even less sure. Not only was she intimidated by the camera and the lights, but she was convinced that the crew, many of whom were veterans who had worked with her father, were treating her like a child and laughing behind her back. Perhaps it was merely paranoia on her part, a compound of her fear of being measured against her father and her still deeply felt horror of being exposed to ridicule, but it deepened as the days progressed.

It did not take her long to realize the picture was not going to be good. An air of defeatism pervaded the set long before the filming was completed, and with the help of her highly developed sense of guilt she was certain she was at least partly to blame for it.

The basic fault, however, was not Jane's. Despite her insecurities, she worked gamely to overcome her inexperience. As the star cheerleader at the college where the film's action took place, she displayed an energy and skill that gave her characterization a ring of truth. She spent whole days learning and practicing the routines a real-life cheerleader goes through, and when she performed them for the camera, they had a polish and verve that made her believable. And as the basketball hero's girlfriend she projected a seductive innocence that was almost as credible. She took Logan's stage-oriented direction well, revealed a good sense of timing and a definite flair for comedy. The fault lay more in Logan's judgment in failing to recognize a tired script and in casting Perkins in the role of the basketball star. Perkins had appealed to Logan for several reasons, not the least of which were the director's sense of irony and his eye for the neat publicity tie-in.

One of Henry Fonda's early films had been *I Dream Too Much*, which also suffered from a flaccid script and a miscast co-star. It featured, however, one of Hollywood's premier character actors—Tony Perkins' father, Osgood Perkins. Osgood Perkins died of a heart attack shortly after making *I Dream Too Much* with Henry Fonda; in fact, he died the same year Jane Fonda was born. Tony Perkins was five years old at the time and grew up to be an actor himself. In 1957 he co-starred with Jane's father in *The Tin Star*, an appealing Western in which he played an idealistic young sheriff to Fonda's cynical but good-hearted veteran. Casting Perkins with Jane in her first movie permitted Logan to indulge his delicious appreciation for such professional incest.

Perkins was an actor very much in the Henry Fonda mold, which delighted Logan even more. He was tall, razor-thin, vaguely wary and inherently sad, and his hesitant acting style and tentative personality were reminiscent of Fonda as a young actor. Not trusting the public to guess his intentions, Logan and Warner Brothers made sure that these coincidences were made note of in the film's prerelease publicity.

Logan's intentions could not be faulted, except for one minor point. Perkins, for all his melancholy screen appeal, was simply not athletic enough to be believable as the college basketball star. Upon release of the movie six months later, Perkins' ungainly cavortings in the basketball scenes would give the film a laughable transparency that overshadowed whatever good points it had—which, with its weak story, were few enough. In spite of his skill and appeal as an actor, he was plainly miscast, and the blame had to rest ultimately with Logan. The screen-wise crew perceived Perkins' limitations immediately and concluded that Logan either didn't know what he was doing or else was simply using the film as a vehicle to launch his "discovery," Jane Fonda. They were glad for the work and were not inclined to let Logan know of their feelings. They let their cynicism bounce off the actors instead.

Today Logan reflects on the picture: "It was not one of my prouder moments as a screen director. I should have known better than to get involved in *Tall Story*, and I did it more out of a sense of obligation to Warner Brothers than anything else. Nevertheless, I'll always remember it with a bit of fondness for what it represented—Jane's debut. I'll tell you this. With the exception of Marilyn Monroe, I have never worked with a more talented actress than Jane Fonda."

By the time filming was completed, Jane was emotionally exhausted and distraught. She misunderstood the crew's frequent *sotto voce* cracks. She was sure they had been directed at her out of contempt for her incompetence, when the fact was they were meant for the production itself. She felt herself a thorough failure. She loathed Hollywood and the whole filmmaking process. Like a wounded animal, she fled back to New York and the sanctuary of Lee Strasberg.

11. *There Was a Little Girl*

Even today it hurts me to talk about Jane. When it was over, I tried to kill myself.

—TIMMY EVERETT

WHEN Jane returned to New York in November, she felt nothing had been proven with respect to her acting ability. Her baptism of fire—the filming of *Tall Story*—certainly provided her with credentials among her Strasberg classmates, but she was sure the credentials would prove false once the movie was released. Even if she got good notices, she would not feel she had achieved much. Nevertheless, she was not unmindful of the change in attitude on the part of Strasberg's students when she returned to her classes. As a result of all the newspaper stories out of Hollywood, she was no longer just another student-actress who happened to be the daughter of Henry Fonda; she was now obviously on her way to becoming a star in her own right. If they expected her to start acting like a star, however, her classmates were disappointed. Jane plunged more diligently than ever into her classes and became much friendlier than she had been before she went to Hollywood.

Shortly after her return, *Look* magazine came out with a two-page feature story on Jane and her experiences in Hollywood. It was her first major national exposure, and it was only a matter of days before she found herself being recognized in the streets of New York and even hounded for autographs. The dividends of the Logan-Warner Brothers' publicity campaign were beginning to pay off. Within months she would be on the cover of *Life* and would be the subject of feature stories in most of the other major magazines. Superficially, she remained unaffected by the star buildup. There was no sudden imperiousness or throwing of tantrums; because of her exposure to her father's stardom through the years, she was fairly level-headed about her own. Deep within, however, the buildup increased her anxiety—she had visions of it all exploding into ridicule once *Tall Story* hit the screens.

Jane swallowed her apprehension and tried to get the most out of her busy life as an independent young actress and model. Although she had no desire to marry, she had discovered since her return from Paris that she possessed a powerful need for a man in her life. Both of her serious attachments in the previous year and a half had been to aspiring actors. Her romance with Franciscus had ended on a bored note; her affair with Sandy Whitelaw, although still active, was without any special excitement. Most of her less serious and briefer relationships had been with actors too, and by the fall of 1959 she seemed genuinely upset about her ability to sustain a relationship.

She blamed this on the young men. "Actors are so boring," she said at the time. "It's very important for a young actress to have men around her. So many actresses tend to forget they're women, and most actors are so self-centered they don't have the time to remind them."

One of her former boyfriends saw it another way. "Jane was so insecure and hungry for love that she tried to swallow you whole. She was a tremendously sweet and lovable girl, very intense when she was in love, but very demanding too. She took much more than she was able to give. Oh, she was generous with her time and money and all that, but it was as if she used these as substitutes for real emotion. There was something deep inside her that she kept to herself and would give to no one."

Another old friend recalls, "I hate to sound Freudian, but my guess is that Jane was looking for a father—someone strong and secure and domineering whom she could follow. She needed to be told what to do. But all she got were guys who were as insecure as she was, and she would eventually become infuriated by them and drop them. She needed to be led."

With her whole life by now uncompromisingly dedicated to an acting career—a particularly parochial concern to someone only twenty-one—Jane was limited in her choice of men. The high incidence of homosexuality among the men of her circle limited her even more. And she had little interest in anyone who wasn't in the theater. "If I had done what I was led to believe I should do, I would have married a Yale boy when I was twenty. He would have gone into investment banking or his father's business, I would have settled in suburbia, taking care of a lot of kids I wouldn't have liked, hating my husband, drinking too much, having a lot of affairs and ending up a wreck."

Although she professed little public admiration for actors, and even less for the homosexuals among them, she continued to involve herself with them. "I spent most of my free time mothering some of the boys in my classes. I'm probably the biggest little mother in all New York. Almost every one of them has some kind of problem. They need someone to listen to their troubles." Despite the trace of sarcasm in Jane's words, one of these young actors was about to become, as he tells it, the first real love of her life.

Timmy Everett was the son of poor, itinerant working-class parents. He was born in the upper Midwest and grew up in North Carolina. With a love and talent for theatricals which he nurtured through high school, he came to New York when he was eighteen to break into the theater. He was an engaging youngster who could do everything—sing, dance, act—and it was not long before he had a topflight agent and a featured role in an important long-running Broadway play, *The Dark at the Top of the Stairs* by William Inge. He followed his success in this with a starring role in a second play, *The Cold Wind and the Warm*, and was then signed to an exclusive motion-picture contract by Otto Preminger. His first job with Preminger was to be a featured role in the film version of *Exodus*.

During his three years in New York Timmy Everett achieved a great deal and was on the threshhold of a splendid career. A slight fair-haired young man of medium height, he would not be immediately noticed in a roomful of people. But he had an energy and electricity that practically jumped out of his body and made anyone nearby quickly aware of his presence. His face was attractively boyish, and his sleeve-worn vulnerability could melt the heart of even the most jaded person. He had only one problem: He was extremely insecure about himself. In a world of witty, gregarious, preening show people, he became as high-strung as a racehorse.

Like many young actors in New York, Everett spent almost every cent he earned on lessons of one kind or another. He studied singing. He was forever in dance studios. And he was a member of Strasberg's classes.

"I knew Jane from class, but just to say hello to," he recalls. "During the summer of 1959 I was in Hollywood and went out to visit Tony Perkins, who was a friend of mine, while he was making *Tall Story* at Warner Brothers. I met Jane there, and I was surprised that she remembered me because she used to look right through me in class. Back in New York that fall, I went to a Thanksgiving party one night, and she was there with someone else—her boyfriend. I had been admiring her from a distance all this time, but I'd always thought she was, well, too good for me. I would have liked to have done a scene with her for Lee, but I'd always been afraid to ask her. At the party—it was at dancer Geoffrey Holder's house on the West Side—I got a little high and worked up the courage to ask her about doing a scene. She said she'd love to."

Jane and Everett decided to do a scene from *Adventures in the Skin Trade* by Dylan Thomas. He was living in a crowded railroad flat his parents rented on the lower West Side of New York. There was no room to rehearse there, so he had to go up to Jane's apartment on Seventy-sixth Street. "It was a beautiful place, the most fantastic apartment I'd yet seen in New York, with an upstairs and a downstairs.

"We'd been rehearsing the scene all week. I'd come, we'd rehearse, talk a little; then I'd leave. Well, this one night after we finished rehearsing, Jane asked me if I'd like to stay for a drink. I said sure, so she made me a drink, then turned on some music. We talked a while, the lights were low, then all of a sudden we were looking at each other in this strange way. I just got consumed by this wave of tenderness and desire, and so did she. We ran upstairs to the bedroom, tore our clothes off and stayed in bed for three days."

It was the beginning of a sweet, vibrant and turbulent love affair that spanned almost two years and had lasting effects on both of them. They lived together on and off for the next year and a half until pleasure turned to pain and, for Everett, pain to suicidal despair. "It was just fantastic at the beginning," he remembers. "We were so much in love, and she taught me so much about the right way to live. That Christmas she showered me with expensive presents—I mean, I wasn't used to that kind of lavishness. I hardly had a thing to my name, I didn't know how to act in company, my clothes were threadbare, I had no sense of style or anything, and she taught me a lot. I taught her, too. I taught her something about emotions, I think—you can see how emotional a person I am—and I taught her about lovemaking and how to show love."

In December, just before Jane's twenty-second birthday, Joshua Logan came to her with a new proposition. He was going to direct a play for Broadway, a complex psychological drama about what happens to a well-bred young girl who's raped by a hoodlum, then accused of inviting his attack. The play was by Daniel Taradash and was called *There Was a Little Girl*. Logan wanted Jane to play the lead role; it would be a perfect chance for her to make a splash on the stage just at the time *Tall Story* was due to be released.

Henry Fonda was back in New York and had opened in a new play himself. "Jane met with her father to discuss whether she should take the part in *There Was a Little Girl*," Everett recalls. "I thought it was a great break for her, but her father was against it. He didn't make any big deal out of it, as far as I could see, but it had Jane upset. Whether he was against it because he didn't think she was ready to carry an entire play, which the part demanded, or because he didn't like the idea of her being associated with the kind of character that the girl in the play was, getting raped and all, I don't know. There was some discussion, and I know he was pretty adamant, but he made a point of telling her the final decision was hers. She agonized over it, and I knew she was weighing her feelings about disappointing her father against her desire to take the part. Finally, she decided to take it. I encouraged her, and I think her father blamed me just a little."

Jane told it this way: "My father thought the play and the part weren't right for me; it was about rape and I was to play the girl who was raped. I think he wanted to protect me from what he thought would be a disaster. But I thought, 'Who am I to turn down such a part—the leading role in a Broadway play?' It was a great opportunity. I knew that practically every young actress in New York would have given her eyeteeth for the part, and after I read for it, Josh and the producers wanted me. Three days before I accepted the part my father called me up and begged me to turn it down. But I didn't."

According to Ray Powers, Henry Fonda was incensed that Logan would want to cast Jane as a girl who is raped. He was further angered over the question of money. "Jane really had mixed feelings about doing the play," Powers says. "She was getting a lot of pressure from her father over the rape thing, and in addition Logan was only going to pay her something like a hundred and fifty dollars a week, an incredibly low salary for a starring role on Broadway. Jane was sure the only reason Logan wanted her was because he could get away with paying her so little. First she wanted to do the play, then she didn't, and it went on that way for a while. Logan started reading other actresses but kept coming back to Jane. Finally, Jane decided to take the part. The whole thing was sort of messy over the business of money, and Jane became a little disillusioned with Logan."

Logan assembled a cast, and rehearsals got under way in January, 1960. "I'd say doing that play was a big turning point for Jane," Everett claims, "much more so than *Tall Story*. It was the first really important live acting job she'd ever had, and the whole play revolved around her. Even though the play didn't run, she learned what it was to be an actress, what her emotional problems were all about. And she really learned that she had emotional problems. Up until that time Jane the person and Jane the actress were two separate people. When she did that play, the two became one and stayed that way afterward. That's when she really started to change."

Once rehearsals were over, Logan took the company to Boston for a brief out-of-town tryout. "I loved the rehearsals," Jane once said. "I loved working with a group, and I began to see for the first time that when a group works together with real love, art happens. I savored every morsel. It was like belonging to a family. I was doing exactly what I wanted to be doing. I enjoyed making myself fit the part, making myself frail as a woman, and vulnerable, and weak. I had always thought of myself as strong and independent, a self-sufficient type, the way I was brought up. Now I began to have some idea of what there was to do in life and what I had been missing. I loved the routine of acting in a play every night. I had had so little responsibility in my life that I loved having demands made on me—to be someplace at a definite hour, with something definite to do. I began to feel a connection with myself. I felt accepted."

Powers claims that Timmy Everett had begun to act as a sort of manager of Jane's life. He thinks her principal attraction to him came from the fact that she felt a desperate need for psychological reinforcement as an actress, so unsure of herself was she still, and that Everett provided it. Everett saw himself not only as a performer, but also as a teacher and coach. Jane responded eagerly to this notion, and Everett thus became, for a while at least, her unofficial mentor, as well as lover. His increasing influence in Jane's life disturbed Logan, her father, and others involved in her career, but she resisted all efforts to disconnect her from Everett.

Everett went to Boston to be with Jane and says that on opening night she received a standing ovation. "I've never seen anyone so happy. She was really good in the part. The play had its weaknesses, so did the part for that matter, but she brought more to it than was there. And the beauty of it was that it was instinctual; you could just see it coming out of her once the curtain went up."

The experience transformed Jane. She received excellent reviews in Boston, and one of the reviewers even failed to mention her father. "The Boston critics said I was fragile, when I'm really strong as an ox. They said I was coltish, febrile, virginal, translucent—*me!* I realized I had created something that moved an audience. From there on I wanted to do nothing else in life but become the greatest stage actress there ever was."

More important than the notices was the fact that playing the part forced her to crack the vault of years of suppressed emotion. "Now that I was determined to be a successful actress, I had to find out how to bring out all the emotions I had learned to inhibit in polite company. It's difficult. I used to be so polite about acting during that first year I was studying. Whenever I read for a part, I'd tell the director that so-and-so was much more suited for it than me. You didn't catch me doing that anymore. I learned that there were fifty girls just as good and maybe better waiting to take my place. I stopped worrying about whether I was being asked to read because I was Henry Fonda's daughter. I began to get more confident and aggressive."

She enjoyed the way acting brought her out of herself, but it also created further difficulties. "I began to see that the problems of Jane Fonda the person were the same as those of Jane Fonda the actress. Acting, when you're serious about it, is tough. It hurts. It has to hurt; otherwise, you're not acting. All you've got to draw upon is yourself. If you're shallow, if you've got no emotional depth, you're not going to act very well, especially in a part that is highly emotional. It will come out all surface and without truth. The serious actor tries to get at the truth of a character. To do that you have to really reach into yourself. I was not used to reaching into myself, and when I did with this part, I was at first surprised to find that there was something there, then astonished to learn how thoroughly well hidden it had been."

According to Everett, acting in *There Was a Little Girl* created a bundle of new anxieties for Jane. She was at once delighted and frightened by the things she was learning about herself, and she became much more emotional in her personal life. "It was like the play was a heavy dose of intensive psychotherapy. Once she had it, she had to have more of it."

Jane had a lot of prodding from Logan during rehearsals. She remembers that at one point he said to her, "I don't think you can do it,

Jane. You're going to fall behind your old man. When the curtain goes up, there'll be a ghost of your father sitting in the chair."

"I got so mad," Jane said. "I knew he was using every trick he could to make me do my best, but I hated some of them." She also felt the first conscious stirrings of being in competition with her father.

The play had its New York opening on February 29, 1960, at the Cort Theater. It was Jane's debut on Broadway, and she could not have hoped for a happier beginning. Although the play was roundly blasted as a trite, cliché-ridden melodrama by the New York critics, Jane's personal notices were glowing. Brooks Atkinson, the authority of authorities, wrote in the next day's New York *Times*, "Although Miss Fonda looks a great deal like her father, her acting style is her own. As the wretched heroine of an unsavory melodrama, she gives an alert, many-sided performance that is professionally mature and suggests that she has found a career that suits her." John McClain, another critic, hailed her performance as a "personal triumph," calling her "a resplendent young woman with exceptional style and assurance. Jane Fonda has a fine future but not, regrettably, in this play."

At the customary post-premiere party at Sardi's, everyone stood and cheered Jane when she entered. The play would last for only sixteen performances, but despite its failure, it launched Jane as a genuine stage figure. During the two weeks of the play's run she had the thrill not only of knowing that she had achieved her dream, but of seeing her name on the billboards just four blocks from where her father was starring in *Silent Night, Lonely Night*. "Part of being an actress is to be in flops, as well as hits," she rationalized after the play shut down. "From here on in I'm going to spend all my time in every dramatics class I can squeeze into. I'm going to work like mad at becoming a good actress."

Work like mad she did, according to Timmy Everett. "She did scenes with me, with others and by herself. I had already sort of made it on Broadway, and now that she had it was beautiful. We were really happy together, and we shared everything. The only rough part was when we went over to her father's house. Here I was, sort of a starry-eyed young novice having to talk with Henry Fonda. I was just twenty-two myself at the time, and shy and nervous and uncomfortable in that plush house. I really felt out of place, and Jane really went out of her way to make me feel at home. But I just couldn't communicate well with her father. He didn't talk much, and he sort of remained aloof from everything. We used to sit down to dinner with him and Afdera, and sometimes other people, everybody all dressed up and these servants and everything sort of hushed and somber. Jane would run her hands up and down my thigh under the table, and I would have to kill myself to keep from bursting out laughing.

"I wasn't sure whether Jane's father liked me or not; that made me even more nervous. He never said much to me, but I remember one night when I thought he was going to strangle me. It was at a party—it was during *There Was a Little Girl*, when Joshua Logan was leaving to go to the Coast or something—and Henry Fonda was there. Jane gave a little sentimental speech about Logan; then all of a sudden she burst into tears and went on in this very theatrical way. I mean it was all genuine emotion and everything. Well, later on her father came rushing up to me with this evil look on his face, and he grabbed my neck in a headlock and said something like, 'What have you done to her to make her act this way!' You see, Jane never showed her emotions in public before, and when he saw her do it, he really got upset. I think he blamed me because he knew how gushy I was and he figured she got it from me."

Everett was a few months younger than Jane. With his puckish face and juvenescent manner, he appeared younger still. He had been born poor, confesses that he had little culture below his theatrical veneer and had a volatility that would have made Librium jittery. Henry Fonda was disturbed by Jane's relationship with him. In the beginning Fonda remained stoic, but as time went on and he saw how possessive Jane was becoming about the young actor, his dismay became vocal. His disapproval caught Jane just at a time when it would have the worst effect on her pride and sensitivity. She had become filled with the power of her potential as an actress. She loved Everett. And she was involved in the process of trying to work her way through the tortuous thicket of emotional self-discovery. For the first time in her life she felt a real compulsion to defy her father's wishes; she was not going to live under the thumb of his influence forever. But she would require assistance.

"It was just after *There Was a Little Girl* closed," Everett recalls, "that Jane and I started to see psychiatrists. She'd been talking about it all winter, and we also began to see that we had problems between each other. The main problem was with her, though. I mean, she was growing confused about herself and her emotions. She wanted to be able to feel more, and she knew she couldn't until she was able to get rid of some of the inhibitions against feeling that had been instilled in her all her life. Don't get me wrong, it's not that she was a mummy or anything like that—she had plenty of compassion and feeling—it was just that she had difficulty getting into the really deep feelings she knew she had buried.

For instance, one of the things that really had her puzzled was why she didn't feel more about her mother and the fact that she killed herself and why she killed herself. I remember her telling me that when she first found out about her mother, she just laughed and then tried to shut it out. She realized this was not a normal reaction, that it was a kind of symptom of emotional dishonesty—that's it, she was bent on learning how to become emotionally honest. This became the most important thing for her. I think she felt a little ashamed that she still wasn't able to stand up to her father when she disagreed with him, and she felt she couldn't be emotionally honest with him. When she tried to talk to him about the way she felt, he would turn off and leave her stranded. I talked about emotions a lot with her, and she could see that in my own way I was very honest emotionally—I mean, I may have been insecure, but I didn't try to hide it like Jane did. I let it all hang out, and I think Jane wanted to be like that, too. You know, let it all hang, and damn the consequences. I'm really the one who put the idea of seeing a psychiatrist in her mind, and pretty soon she was more eager to do it than I was. But we did it together; she went to her doctor, and I went to mine; then we'd talk about the sessions afterward."

The Strasberg approach to acting is extremely sympathetic to psychoanalytic theory. His techniques of dramatic analysis are centered in his perceptions of what is hidden in his students' personalities and characters. He endeavors to break down the wall in each student between the actor and the person and to make them one. When he delivered a critique of an actor, his language was rife with psychiatric jargon about intention, motivation and the unconscious. (For this, many of his critics have condemned his system as "nothing but two-bit psychiatry.") His classes bore a more than passing resemblance to the group therapy and psychodrama sessions that were becoming popular in those days, and it was not unusual for the more affluent among his students to undergo psychoanalysis once they had been introduced to the pseudoanalysis of the Method.

The language of the Method was a highly particularized and metaphorical one, which added to its elite fashionability. If an actor was serious about the Method, he quickly learned to speak the language. Jane's reasons for starting psychoanalysis reflected her familiarity with the language. "An actor's violin is his body, inside and outside, and when you play and it's flat you say, 'Well, I better find out why it's flat. And what do I do to tune it up?' I was brought up in a very restricted kind of way—you know, one doesn't raise one's voice, one never says what one feels. If someone says something I don't like, I would never challenge it. Now this is a great impediment, because to be a good actress you have to go out onstage and, to use the cliché, hang out your dirty laundry, your clean laundry or whatever. In other words, you've got to be free to show whatever it is that has to be shown, you can't hold things back. I've discovered that the problems of Jane Fonda the actress are exactly the same problems of Jane Fonda the human being. I know that the better I can become as a human being, the more fulfilled I will become as a person and the better I will become as an actress."

On another occasion she said the reason she went into analysis was that "I figure this know thyself business is very important for an actress. Daddy's been married four times, and I don't think it's had any bad effects on me; but analysis might show that it has. And that would be useful to know, wouldn't it?"

Tall Story was released in the spring of 1960, while Jane was still basking in the reviews of *There Was a Little Girl*. The picture was universally vilified, and though Jane was not roasted the way she had feared, she was not given particularly good marks either. The most encouraging review came from Howard Thompson in the New York *Times*, who called the movie "a frantic attempt at sophistication and a steady barrage of jazzy wisecracks about campus sex. . . . The gangly Mr. Perkins jounces around convincingly enough, but near Miss Fonda he generally gapes and freezes, and who can blame him? The pretty newcomer shows charm and promise in her film debut." Most of the other reviews were content to draw comparisons between Jane and her father. The most charitable was *Time* magazine's comment: "Nothing could save this picture . . . not even a second-generation Fonda with a smile like her father's and legs like a chorus girl." Jane was distressed by the reception, but she quickly put it out of mind. She was convinced she was a stage actress. "Everything is best for me when I'm onstage. That's when I come alive."

She and Everett spent the rest of the spring in a furious round of acting studies, dancing lessons, sessions with their analysts and trips out of town. "We used to take my father's old car," Everett says, "and leave town every chance we could. We took weekend trips out to Long Island, up to the Catskills, down to Atlantic City—we were really having a good time. I was staying with Jane most of the time at her apartment, but sometimes when Susan Stein was having company, we'd go down and stay at my parents' place. There wouldn't really be any room there, so we'd sleep on the couch in the living room. My parents would walk in and out in the morning, and Jane would pop out of bed and give them a big hug. She really liked them, and they liked her. One thing about Jane—she always had this respect for, I don't know, common people, people who *had* to work, who had tough lives . . . she always had this thing about the underdog, which was something I really liked about her. She didn't feel self-important, and she had none of those silly affectations a lot of theater people had."

At the end of the theater season Jane was given the New York Drama Critics Award as the most promising new actress of the year for her performance in *There Was a Little Girl*. "It gave her a big lift," Everett says. "But by then she was so involved with other things she didn't stop to enjoy it. She had a play to do in summer stock at the Westport Playhouse. I had to go to St. Louis to play the lead in a summer production of *The Adventures of Tom Sawyer*, so we were apart for a while. But then she flew out to St. Louis to see me, and we had a great time together. As soon as we got back to New York, she had to start rehearsals for another play."

The new play was Arthur Laurents' *Invitation to a March*, a comedy about conventionality versus nonconformity. "As soon as I read for it, I knew I had to have the part," Jane says. "The part of Norma Brown was the story of me—of a conventional girl, a sleeping beauty who is awakened to love by the kiss of a boy." Timmy Everett was considered for the role of the boy, but it was decided he and Jane were too intimate in their private lives, and the role went to another actor. The production, which had an exceptional cast that included Eileen Heckart, Celeste Holm and Madeleine Sherwood, opened in New York on October 29, 1960. The reviews were decidedly better than they had been for *There Was a Little Girl*, and the play ran for three and a half months. Jane's personal notices were even more glowing than the play's. Whitney Bolton called her "the handsomest, smoothest and most delectable ingenue on Broadway," while Walter Kerr described her as "delectable." George Oppenheimer of *Newsday* said she had a "glow that almost dims the moonlight. Here is surely the loveliest and most gifted of all our new young actresses." And Kenneth Tynan, in the *New Yorker*, was rhapsodic: "Jane Fonda can quiver like a tuning fork, and her neurotic outbursts are as shocking as the wanton, piecemeal destruction of a priceless harpsichord. What is more, she has extraordinary physical resources."

Despite the favorable critical reception she received, Jane, feeling like a veteran now and with a revealing show of Fondaesque dissatisfaction, was unhappy with the play. "I knew just what I wanted to do with the role, but other people had other ideas, and I think we lost the human reality of the girl. When the play opened, I was acting the role the way the others saw it. I was doing what they thought the audience wanted me to do, rather than what I wanted to do, so I came out like a thin, slick, Ginger Rogers ingenue. I wanted the humor to come from the conflict in the girl, her struggle with herself, but instead I had to do a funny painted poster of a girl. Anyway, I went on doing what the others wanted me to do. Finally, what I came to like about the play was just going to the theater and knowing what I would be doing day after day. I had a sense of belonging."

If Jane thrived on the sense of belonging the play gave her, she also found that it fed her anxieties about herself, which were intensifying as a result of her psychoanalysis. "I enjoyed the opportunity of working with two fine actresses, Eileen Heckart and Madeleine Sherwood. I had so little experience and knew so little about the technique of how to sustain a performance. I learned that they were able to sustain their performances whether the audience was or wasn't responding and laughing at the expected times. They could play to a full house or to a small house. At first I used to wonder at the way they did it, and then I found I was able to do it once in a while myself. In the beginning, when I first went out onstage, I always felt like apologizing to the audience. I suppose I felt unworthy to appear before it. If I sensed resentment on the part of anybody in the audience, I'd start to fade out. For a long time I felt I had to know who was in the audience. Sometimes I'd go up to the balcony to look at the faces and guess how they were going to respond to me. If I saw mean faces, I'd feel terrible."

Timmy Everett remembers the months Jane spent in *Invitation to a March* as a transitory period in their relationship. "Things were beginning to happen with Jane that I don't think she even expected. She was really into her analysis, and she was beginning to dredge up a lot of emotion. Sometimes it was almost too much for her, but she kept at it with the determination of an addict looking for a fix. Oh, we were still in love, still hanging out—in fact, that Christmas was the greatest Christmas I ever had. Jane was always worried about my appearance and my shabby clothes—I think a lot of the flak she was getting from her family and friends about me had to do with the way I dressed—and she was always buying me an expensive shirt or sweater so I'd look better. That Christmas she went out and bought me an eight-hundred-dollar cashmere overcoat. My God, that was the most expensive present I had ever had in my life. It was a beautiful coat; in fact, I still have it to this day. We had Christmas dinner at her father's house, and it was fabulous. Jane was getting along much better with Afdera and had even studied some Italian so she could talk with her more. The whole family was there, and I was nervous as hell about making a fool of myself in front of all these elegant, sophisticated people. Afdera, whenever I saw her, always seemed to be reading movie magazines. But she was also quite effervescent and witty when she wanted to be, and everybody else was so, you know, sure of themselves. At one point during dinner they were passing around plates and I ended up balancing a plate while somebody put some food on it, and Jane said, sort of as a joke, 'Try not to drop the plate, Timmy.' Well, that's exactly what I did, I dropped the plate and I felt, Oh, my God! I look over and there's Jane's father with this scowl on his face, and I figure that's it for me. But they all made a joke of it, and pretty soon it was forgotten."

Those were the good memories Everett has. A less pleasant one is the fact that he and Jane had begun to quarrel. "It was early in 1961 when it started. I guess toward the end of *Invitation to a March*. Jane was unhappy in the play. I mean she liked going to the theater, but she didn't feel comfortable in the part and was generally feeling depressed. Also, her analysis was getting her down—she was in a hurry to get it all out, but it was coming slowly and she was feeling frustrated. I was feeling pretty frustrated myself. I was supposed to have played one of the lead roles in *Exodus*, but Preminger dropped me at the last minute in favor of Sal Mineo. I guess he thought Mineo was more of a name. Anyway, out of that atmosphere we began to argue, and pretty soon we were fighting like cats and dogs. She was demanding a lot of me emotionally, and of course I had my own emotional problems and wasn't able to give her what she needed all the time, when she needed it, and she'd get furious with me and I'd get furious with her. We were awfully young and immature in many ways. It was an unhappy spring. I could feel her start to draw away from me, and that killed me because I was still desperately in love with her. I still think to this day we might have worked it out with a little time, but I don't know. She had a lot of pressure on her, both inside and out, and so did I. But we were really in love with each other, even then when it was really bad, and if we'd been able to love ourselves the way we loved each other, we might have stuck it out. But then Voutsinas came into the picture, and, well, that was it."

12. The Voutsinas Factor

Andreas destroys every friendship.

—ARTHUR LAURENTS

JANE met Andreas Voutsinas during her classes with Strasberg. He was an aspiring director, considerably older than Jane, who was born of Greek parents. Brought up in Ethiopia and educated in London, he had managed during the mid-fifties to induct himself into the escalating intimacies of New York's theater salons from the home base of his cold-water flat on West Forty-sixth Street in Manhattan. Although he worked irregularly in the theater, he was a fixture around the Actors Studio and had achieved local fame as the constant escort and mentor of several well-known actresses, Anne Bancroft among them. He was flamboyant and worldly, spoke several languages and affected an air of weary European dissipation. He dressed in the Strasberg style—dark shirts, ties and jackets—and accented his proletarian garb with berets and cigarette holders. A director by choice, he occasionally landed an acting job and would invariably be cast in roles that were heavily suggestive of homosexuality or satanic decadence.

"Voutsinas saw himself as the European version of Strasberg," a member of the Actors Studio recalls. "He considered himself Lee's principal protégé, although Lee didn't, and was out to have the same influence on people Lee had. Of course, a lot of people thought he was a laugh. There was something basically silly in the way he went about it—he was so transparent about manipulating his way around that you couldn't really dislike him for it. He obviously had some attraction, though, because look who he was associated with. These were serious relationships, too. I mean Annie Bancroft swore by him there for a while."

During 1960, while Jane and Timmy Everett were at the height of their stormy love affair, Jane was offered the female lead in *No Concern of Mine*, an Actors Studio project that was to be staged during the summer at the Westport Playhouse. Voutsinas was the director.

"We were still so in love," Everett remembers, "that I didn't notice anything happening at first. I went up to Westport to spend some time with Jane. We'd be lying around with no clothes on, and Voutsinas would walk in and take off his clothes. I had a pretty good body then—Jane used to say how much she loved my body—and Voutsinas had a really ugly body. We used to joke about it. But he was really into Jane as an actress. I mean, he was directing her in some really deep way, and the way he talked to her about herself made an impression on her. Later that summer, when she came to see me in St. Louis, she was much more enthusiastic about him. She was talking about how he had brought out a lot of sensitivity areas in her that she didn't realize she had."

During the run of *Invitation to a March*, Jane decided she was ready to make her bid to get into the Actors Studio. She had been to the Studio on many occasions as an observer and was convinced that the work she was doing in Strasberg's private classes was child's play compared to what she could accomplish in the Studio. Besides, admission to the Studio was the *sine qua non* of achievement for any young New York actor—proof that one was truly among the elite of the theatrical world.

Voutsinas persuaded her to do a scene under his direction from *No Concern of Mine* for her audition. Her first audition was given to a panel of Studio members in January, 1961, and Jane passed with the hearty recommendation that her second and final audition, before the Studio's governing board of Cheryl Crawford, Elia Kazan and Strasberg, be held as soon as possible. With her second audition she was immediately accepted into the Studio. Elia Kazan said at the time, "I always thought of her as an interesting theater personality, but not until now did I realize she could be a major talent." This was high praise indeed, much more important to Jane than what the theater critics said about her, and she felt indebted to Voutsinas for having managed her success. For his work in directing Jane, Voutsinas' reputation around the Studio did not suffer either.

Jane had for some time been receiving weekly paychecks in accordance with the terms of her contract with Joshua Logan—at least that's what some of her friends and associates from those days recall. Logan confirms it. Her contract with him was for $10,000 a year. Added to that was the money she was making as a model, plus money she received from the trust fund her mother had left her. All in all, she must have been delighted with her sudden financial independence. With the money she had accumulated and as a gesture of her growing independence, she announced that she was paying her father back for supporting her after her departure from Vassar. With the rest of her savings, she purchased a cooperative apartment of her own on West Fifty-fifth Street, just off Fifth Avenue, and proceeded to decorate it with expensive antiques and paintings. "I'm twenty-two and I'm spoiled," she explained. "I never had to know what a dollar is about. The only way to learn is to do it myself. It gives me a good feeling to pay my own way."

Peter Basch, a well-known photographer of actresses who had been hired to do publicity photography for *There Was a Little Girl*, got to know Jane well. Just after she moved into her new apartment, Basch persuaded her to collaborate on a photographic essay he had been commissioned to do for *Cavalier* magazine. The theme of the feature was to be Jane Fonda playing different well-known movie roles as famous directors might see her. The photos would be timely publicity exposure for Jane, and she enthusiastically agreed. One of the roles they agreed to photograph was from the film *Les Liaisons Dangereuses* directed by Roger Vadim, a picture that was causing quite a controversy because of its nude scenes. The scene called for Basch to photograph Jane partially nude. Basch recalls that Jane was pleased with the way the photos turned out and gave clearance for them to be used in *Cavalier*. "But," he says, "her father heard about it and disapproved. Next thing I knew, *Cavalier* called and told me that one of Henry Fonda's press agents was trying to persuade them not to print the pictures. I consulted with Jane and she was quite angry at her father. She told me to go ahead, I told *Cavalier* it was all right, and the pictures appeared. But I understand Jane had quite a flap with her father over it."

As Jane grew more concerned about money, she realized her contract with Logan was financially limiting. Like all such personal-service contracts, it contained a clause that allowed Logan to "lend" her to other producers for whatever salaries they were willing to pay for her services. With Jane becoming more of a name, her salary worth was escalating. Her earnings would be paid to Logan, however, not to her, and she would continue to receive the weekly stipend their contract called for. If Logan were paying her $10,000 a year and her services on a future project called for her to receive $100,000, Logan, presumably, would keep the difference.

In addition, Logan's autonomy over her career enabled him to lend her out to whomever he wished. Although she was grateful to Logan for having launched her, by early 1961 her faith in his judgment, as a result of *Tall Story* and *There Was a Little Girl*, was shrinking. Logan was still a highly thought-of producer-director, but among Jane's Actors Studio circle many considered him out of touch with what was really going on in films and the theater. These convictions were not lost on Jane; she had cast her future with the Studio and was increasingly embarrassed to be associated with the more traditional Logan, even though she must have known that among all the Studio devotees of Stanislavski, none had actually studied with the Russian, whereas Logan had.

In March Jane's uneasiness, justified or not, was confirmed. Logan lent her to another high-powered producer, Charles Feldman, for the motion picture version of Nelson Algren's popular novel, *A Walk on the Wild Side*, to be directed by Edward Dmytryk under the auspices of Columbia Pictures. Jane was ambivalent. She was reluctant to do another picture—her memories of *Tall Story* were still fresh in her mind. Yet she was eager to test herself again before the cameras now that her confidence in her talent had grown.

Everett says that by the time she signed to do *Walk on the Wild Side*, "Jane and I were having lots of trouble. Voutsinas had really gotten into her, almost against her will. She would keep telling me, 'Don't let him get in control of me. I don't want him around me.' Then she would turn around and praise him because he was really teaching her how to express herself and work on all the different aspects of her emotional nature. I think Jane's fascination with Andreas had to do with the fact that he brought out the meanness of her personality . . . he showed her a completely different side of herself. She was sick of being the goody-goody girl; it nauseated her that people only saw her in one way. Andreas taught her how to express all the hidden rage she had in her, how to be mean and ugly without feeling guilty about it, and she liked what this did for her. It gave her a completely new dimension. Once she learned to handle it as though it were a natural part of herself instead of some kind of abnormality to be kept buried, it gave her a sense of power and confidence she'd never had before. Jane used to be paranoiac about herself; she was always worried about what other people were thinking or saying behind her back. Now, people who are like that are people who are afraid of being found out, and they go to all kinds of lengths to keep from revealing themselves. But Jane knew that as an actress she couldn't continue to keep herself hidden. This was the great problem during our relationship, and once she started psychoanalysis and began to dig things out, she wanted more and more. Then she wanted to get it all out at once, the good and the bad, and Voutsinas helped by constantly getting her to act out of the depths of everything she had been instinctively trying to hide. This is when Jane really began to change. She enjoyed the ability to be herself without feeling guilty about the impressions she made. It gave her a kind of internal toughness and security she'd never had before. We started to have terrible fights. Of course, I was just as much to blame as she was because I didn't really understand what was going on. She used to say our relationship had become like a roller coaster—you know, the incredible highs and the depressing lows—and it was. But all that time she was gaining more security, while I was losing whatever I had, which wasn't much to begin with. Voutsinas had a real hold over her, and I started to become paranoiac about what they were saying about *me* behind *my* back. I was feeling threatened by Voutsinas and desperate about the prospect of losing Jane, and I started doing lots of stupid things."

Freed of some of her insecurities about herself, Jane was not yet confident enough to go it alone. She arranged for Voutsinas to go to Hollywood with her for the filming of *Walk on the Wild Side* as her drama coach. As such, Voutsinas became her constant and personal mentor—some said Svengali—and more or less took control of her career for the next two years. He orchestrated her development both as a personality and as an actress, much to the grief of co-workers, friends and family, and was instrumental in shaping the image of the new, outspoken Jane Fonda that developed on her second visit to the movie capital.

Jane arrived in April with Voutsinas in tow to start *Walk on the Wild Side.* Although the script was based on the Algren novel, it was a loose interpretation that exploited the more lurid aspects of the book. It turned out to be a tawdry melodrama, the principal purpose of which was to shock what the authors and producer thought was the exposed nerve of America's confused sexual mores. It was filled with unbelievable characters, who were, for the most part, portrayed by unbelievable, miscast actors, not the least of whom was Jane Fonda in the role of a petulant thief and prostitute. Jane saw the role as a chance to deflate her image as a sweet all-American girl and prove that she could play characters on the seamy underside of life. To underline her new image, which Voutsinas was helping her sculpt, she started to sound off in the press.

"Two years ago Jane Fonda was a terrified youngster facing movie cameras for the first time," Hedda Hopper wrote about her during the filming of *Walk on the Wild Side.* "She didn't like Hollywood, didn't know if she'd like motion pictures or even if she was serious about acting.

"This time it's another story. Jane has found her acting feet, is at home not only on stage, screen and TV but also in an interview. . . . She came in to see me a tall, glossily groomed young woman in an olive-green suede tailored suit, hair brushed severely away from the face and coiled in a knot at the back of her head. It was soignée and very different from the shoulder-length bob and ingenue appeal of the Jane of two years ago.

"Jane no longer works as a model, says she doesn't know how she ever did it since a session in the portrait gallery now terrifies her. 'Still photographs show only what's there in the physical structure; you can't move and you can't speak. . . . I realize that if I'm going to be a success it won't be on terms of looks.'

"At 23 she isn't thinking of matrimony; in fact she rocked me back on my heels with her outspoken ideas about marriage. 'I think marriage is going to go out, become obsolete,' she said. 'I don't think it's natural for two people to swear to be together for the rest of their lives. Why should people feel guilty when they stop loving each other?'"

The interview appeared throughout the country on July 9, 1961, under the headline JANE FONDA THINKS MARRIAGE OBSOLETE. Hedda Hopper's breathless reaction to what she called Jane's "radical views" may have been disingenuous, but the column provided fresh fodder for the Holywood publicity mills. Attributed to her were such statements as "If you're going to get married it should be done properly. You must be able to make compromises and sacrifices, and I'm not ready to do that. I couldn't maintain such a relationship; I don't think I'll ever be able to do it and it doesn't bother me too much." And "I enjoy my independence and the moment anyone tries to restrict it, I resent it and run the other way. Some people have a need to feel needed, but I don't." And "Hollywood's wonderful. They pay you for making love."

To call Jane's ideas "radical views" in 1961 was certainly an overstatement, but enough readers were incensed by them to write thousands of protesting letters to Hedda Hopper and other columnists, who dutifully reported on the controversy. Of course the moguls at Columbia Pictures, where *Walk on the Wild Side* was being filmed, were delighted. As were Jane and Andreas.

Another press observer on the scene at the time marveled at the difference two years had made and described her as "every inch the antithesis of the 'sleeping beauty' type she played in *Invitation to a March.* Beautiful she is—but alive and vibrant. She is poised, frank and alert; cool, but with great warmth. Her piercing eyes have a candor and refreshing honesty."

Jane's new outspokenness extended itself to her work as she put herself more and more in the hands of Voutsinas. Peter Basch was on the set of *Walk on the Wild Side* to take still photographs. "There was a great deal of tension on the set," he remembers. "Jane was very adamant about playing her part according to Voutsinas' interpretation, and this caused a fair amount of trouble between herself and the director, Dmytryk. She was very defensive about Andreas, and just about everybody connected with the picture resented having him around all the time. I liked Andreas, and I think he probably did some good things for Jane, but I think he was also using her to his own ends. He was very imperious and didn't seem at all bothered by the resentment he invoked, but it bothered Jane, even though she tried to hide it."

Timmy Everett says, "I was out there to do a TV show, and I saw Jane a few times with Andreas. She was still warm and outgoing toward me but was totally wrapped up with him and the part. She was still the same frantic, neurotic girl, but she was stronger now, and tougher, and didn't let things get her down the way she used to. She had total confidence in Andreas by then, and he was beginning to become possessive about his role in her life. I don't say that out of sour grapes or anything. In fact, I always liked Andreas. It wasn't him so much, I mean, he wasn't really working hard to seduce Jane or put her under his spell. It was really Jane who responded to his weird, demanding personality. I knew things were over between Jane and me, but I just couldn't accept it."

A crew member who was on the set of *Walk on the Wild Side* recalls that Jane "was delightful to work with in every respect but one. She was warm and considerate, but she insisted on having this creep Voutsinas around all the time. I don't know what their real relationship was—I find it hard to believe that there was anything sexual between them, even though there was a lot of hugging and kissing going on. He was supposed to be her coach, and there was always a lot of whispering back and forth between takes and so on. I didn't get it. Voutsinas was a sort of preening little guy all filled up with his own self-importance, and he had this kind of evil manner about him. But Jane listened to everything he said, and she was really serious about him. Maybe because in the picture she was playing a whore and had to project a lot of blatant sexuality, she was relying on him to show her the way. He had this pinched, grayish face and mincing manner that made you feel he had done it all."

Another report lends credence to the effect her Actors Studio training and Voutsinas' influence had on Jane. "She was always talking loudly about the morons in the picture business," said Hollywood columnist

Sidney Skolsky. "She refused to wear undergarments in scenes after being directed to do so, and went far past the line of duty and good behavior in the fight sequence with Sherry O'Neil. Jane bloodied Miss O'Neil's nose, hurt other important parts of Miss O'Neil, and caused one of the production staff to remark to me, 'Her performance didn't help the Fonda name.' "

Jane herself admitted at the time that "there was a lot of stir because I had Andreas working with me. But I feel you have to learn as much as you can; if you're not good, people turn against you, but if you try to be good in a way that doesn't seem to them to be necessary, they lash out at you. I don't like the idea of turning people against me, but I've gotten over the feeling that everybody has to love me."

The making of *Walk on the Wild Side* not only was complicated by Voutsinas' presence on the set, but also had constant script problems. As rewrites were made, Jane's role shrank from its original size. "But it doesn't matter," she said. "Kitty Twist is a wonderful acting part—a tough young girl who ran away from an orphanage and reform school and had to steal to survive. She's like a cat, ends up ratting on everybody and getting everybody killed. I never would have thought anyone would offer me this kind of part. I've always been wanted for the ingenue, the girl next door."

Jane was pleased by her performance in the film, although the critics did not agree with her when the picture was released the following year. The general tone of the reviews was reflected by Bosley Crowther in the New York *Times*: "As the heroine, the tall, thin actress who calls herself Capucine is as crystalline and icy as her elegant mononym. Laurence Harvey is barely one-dimensional, and Barbara Stanwyck is like something out of mothballs. Jane Fonda is elaborately saucy and shrill (a poor exposure for a highly touted talent). Edward Dmytryk's direction makes you wonder whether he read the script before he started shooting. If he did, he should have yelled."

Nevertheless, Jane professed to enjoy making the picture. "The director and I waged a little secret fight to get Nelson Algren's book, which I knew so well, back into the picture. I think we did, too." Under Voutsinas' guidance, "I got a little humor into my role. People will remember Kitty Twist." The rest of the critics joined Crowther in finding Kitty less than memorable.

Jane continued to mine the press in order to transform her public image. She still accepted questions about what it was like to be Henry Fonda's daughter but made it clear that she was getting bored with the association. She soon began to make irreverent jabs at her father in print, perhaps because he had publicly stated his confusion over the direction in which his daughter was going. "I know it's very strange that a girl should feel competitive against her father, but that's the way I feel. I always feel that I have to prove to him that I'm right. Somehow he can't seem to separate my being a daughter from my being an actress."

If Henry Fonda had been troubled by Jane's relationship with Timmy Everett, he was infuriated over her attachment to Voutsinas. Earlier, when she was still with Everett, Fonda had read about Jane's psychoanalysis in a newspaper article. "You need it like a hole in the head," he told her, but she had defied his wish that she give it up. Now she was talking publicly about her analysis, and out of her pronouncements about its virtues came veiled hints that life with father was what drove her into it in the first place. "Daddy should have been analyzed forty years ago," was one of the quotes attributed to her.

During the filming of *Walk on the Wild Side*, Jane was shown a script for the forthcoming film version of Irving Wallace's best seller *The Chapman Report*, which would be directed by the veteran George Cukor for Warner Brothers. Earlier she had been offered the lead in a new Broadway play by Garson Kanin, *Sunday in New York*. The opportunity to play a nymphomaniac housewife in *The Chapman Report* compelled her to decline the *Sunday in New York* offer, in which she would have had to play another vapid, well-scrubbed ingenue. Voutsinas persuaded her that to develop her dramatic potential, she should seek more parts with heavy overtones of sexuality. This, in his view, was where reputations were made.

"My friends told me I was crazy to say no to *Sunday in New York*," Jane said at the time. "But I could see why they wanted me for it, and I didn't feel like doing that part again. When I was sent the script of *The Chapman Report*, people said, 'Why do it?' My reason was that I wanted to play the nymphomaniac, which I'd heard was the only good part in it. So I dressed up in my best nympho style and went to see George Cukor, the director. He looked at me and laughed. 'You are going to play the frigid widow,' he said. I was disappointed. But it was George Cukor, and you can wait a lifetime to work with him, so I took the part."

Jane continued the lease on the swank apartment she had rented just off Wilshire Boulevard in Beverly Hills. Once she knew she was going to be in *The Chapman Report*, she told an interviewer, "I didn't think I'd ever feel this way about Hollywood, but I really love it now and may be here all summer. I never enjoyed working so much before; it's partly that

I've changed and partly the town. There's something different about this place. Maybe I know different people, but there's more new blood, more people willing to try new things and responsive to new ideas." About her acting she was still uncertain, in spite of her growing confidence. But because of Voutsinas and, she claimed, her analysis, she was considerably braver than she'd once been. "I'm always in a panic. And I'm always ready to go out and make a mistake, even though I know I may be criticized. I do it because I'm always thinking my life will be over before I have a chance to do some of these crazy things. For instance, I knew that playing Kitty Twist would make me look very ugly. I thought that my career might be ended because of it, but I went and did it anyway."

From *Walk on the Wild Side*, Jane went right into *The Chapman Report*. There had been considerable controversy in Hollywood over the propriety of filming Irving Wallace's novel about a Kinseyish team in Los Angeles conducting a survey on the sex habits of American women; it was considered rather racy fare for the Hollywood of 1961. (How tame it would seem only a few years later!) In addition, the picture had been tied up in an internecine squabble between Darryl Zanuck, who was originally going to produce it with his son Richard for his old studio, Twentieth Century-Fox, and the present studio head, Peter Levathes. Levathes had canceled the picture on the eve of production at Fox. After several weeks of public name calling, Zanuck arranged with his old friend Jack Warner to have the production moved to the Warner Brothers studios in Burbank, where filming began in August.

In spite of the preproduction controversy over the film, the picture on release seemed fairly placid, and the problems of the ladies involved, which ranged from nymphomania to frigidity, were presented without startling innovation. All four of the female stars—Shelley Winters, Claire Bloom, Glynis Johns, and Jane—played their roles adequately. George Cukor was an old hand at putting "women's pictures" on the screen, and he did *The Chapman Report* in a style that hardly justified the controversy.

But for Jane, making the film was another pleasurable experience, if for no other reason than Cukor, who had directed some of the greatest film actresses of the thirties and forties. "There aren't words to describe what it means to work with him," she said. "He's a mystical character. He creates a woman. When you're working with him, it's like an aura wrapping you and the character and him together. He goes through the whole thing. He shoots everything fifteen or sixteen times. You know he'll protect you. He has impeccable taste and a sense of subtlety. He forces himself to love and believe in you. He's interested in talent. He had me out to his house and told me, 'I've let you do certain things now that if you did them three years from now, I'd knock your teeth in.' He teaches you discipline as an actress—I don't mean arriving on the set on time, I mean how to play in front of a camera and get the most out of a character."

Cukor was equally glowing in his assessment of Jane. "I think the only thing she has to watch is that she has such an abundance of talent she must learn to hold it in. She is an American original."

In order to do *The Chapman Report*, Jane was forced to terminate her association with Joshua Logan. It ended on a temporarily unhappy note. Logan says today that the problems over the contract stemmed from the fact that he had guaranteed her one movie a year but was unable to come up with a second picture. "I tested her for *Fanny*, and although the test was delightful, she just wasn't right for the part." He also says that he had received a very high offer from producer Ray Stark for Jane's contract. He told Jane about it and offered to let her buy back her contract for a like amount rather than sell it to Stark.

Jane says she asked Logan as a friend simply to release her from the contract. Logan declined, and made a counterproposal that would allow Jane to buy her contract out at a price lower than Stark's offer. "I was kind of hurt for a while by Josh's attitude," Jane told Hedda Hopper. "All that baloney about his being my godfather, that was just publicity. I grew up around him, so somebody decided it would be a good gimmick. He's just a friend of the family who was not enough of a friend to let me pay less money to get free. It was then I realized that you can't count on friendship when it comes to business dealings." According to Powers, negotiations were conducted and Logan was eventually persuaded to accept $100,000 to release Jane. "I feel fortunate, at my age," Jane said afterward, "to have been able to buy out. I paid for my freedom, but freedom is the most important thing."

Joshua Logan denies Jane's version of their contract differences—the amounts of money involved, interpretations of the nature of the so-called contract and so on. Evidently he is saving his side of the story for his memoirs, which he is in the process of writing.

Jane apparently was still feeling acrimonious toward Logan when she returned to New York after completing *The Chapman Report*. Henry Fonda was in Europe filming *The Longest Day*, but the word was around New York that he was extremely displeased with some of the statements she had made about Logan and was downright furious about her relationship with Voutsinas, who had now become a fixture in Jane's life. Peter Fonda, who was living in New York at their father's house, filled Jane in on their father's mood, which had been black, to say the least.

Henry Fonda was undergoing another of those quiet crises in his life. Peter had left the University of Omaha during his junior year in 1960 and gone East to get a start as an actor. After a summer of acting and scenery painting with an upstate New York stock company, he showed up at his father's house and announced that he wanted to remain in New York and try for a stage career. Fonda reluctantly agreed to support him and arranged for him to get an agent. But father and son still did not get along well: Peter believed his father was constantly making him feel like a failure. During the fall of 1960, the great love of Peter's life, Bridget Hayward, committed suicide at just about the time he was reading for a Broadway play. "I went home, and my father said, 'Sit down and have a drink.' He never even talked to me, so I couldn't understand why he wanted me to have a drink, but I sat down and he kept saying, 'Poor Leland, poor Leland.' Bridget's dead from an overdose of pills, and I was falling thirteen floors to the ground, and all he's saying is 'Poor Leland.' "

Distraught and failing to get the part he had read for, he called his aunt and uncle. They wired him $150 so he could return to Omaha to talk to the psychiatrist whose care he had been under during the previous three years. Peter remained in Omaha until the following spring, when his agent called and told him the producers of the play he had tried out for in October wanted him to read again for the part. He returned to New York and got the role, which was for a play called *Blood, Sweat and Stanley Poole*. The play opened in October, 1961, to unenthusiastic reviews, but Peter's notices were filled with praise. A week later he married Susan Brewer, a Sarah Lawrence student who was the step-daughter of Noah Dietrich, longtime business associate of Howard Hughes. Henry Fonda, still holding to his distrust in anything that happens too fast or easy, was not happy about the developments in his son's life.

Nor was he happy about his own career. After twenty-five years of acting, during which he had created dozens of memorable performances, his roles had begun to take on a sameness that left him bored. Since *Mister Roberts*, his movie roles had been perfunctory, and there was not much around in the way of stage parts. Upon returning from Europe and the filming of *The Longest Day* at the end of 1961 and more out of desperation than conviction, he accepted the lead in a play called *A Gift of Time*, Garson Kanin's dramatization of the life of a novelist dying of cancer. When the play opened in February, 1962, Fonda was unanimously praised, but the depressing nature of the story discouraged critics and audiences alike, and the play died a quick death. Disillusioned and unhappy, Fonda went back to Hollywood, according to John Springer, with the cynical idea that if that's the way audiences felt, he'd give them *Spencer's Mountain.*

As Springer tells it in his pictorial book *The Fondas*, when Fonda signed with another agency after his longtime representative, MCA, was dissolved by the government, he agreed to follow his new agents' advice about the number of pictures he would do in relation to the number of plays. He had insisted on going through with his commitment to star in *A Gift of Time*, even though the new agents, correctly as it turned out, predicted that audiences would not want to see a play about a man dying of cancer.

When the play closed, his agents insisted that Fonda sign for the movie *Spencer's Mountain*, despite the fact that he thought the script was "old-fashioned corn—it'll set the movies back twenty-five years." While working on the picture, he picked up a New York paper in his agents' office one day and noticed an item announcing the opening of a new play by Edward Albee. "Oh, Albee," remarked his agent when Fonda questioned him about it. "He wanted you to do that play, but we turned it down."

"But why do you turn down plays for me without even letting me know?" Fonda said. "You know I'm always looking for a good one."

"We felt you should do this picture," the agent replied. "And the play won't run—there's nothing to it except a husband and wife fighting with each other."

The play, of course, was *Who's Afraid of Virginia Woolf?* Fonda was furious with his agents when he read the reviews and was even more incensed when friends like Jimmy Stewart and Joshua Logan came back from New York and told him how perfect he would have been in the male lead. As soon as he finished *Spencer's Mountain*, Fonda returned to New York and immediately went to see Albee's hit. "I sat there, sliding further and further down in my seat. I think I would have given up any role I've ever played—Tom Joad, Mister Roberts, any of them—to have had a chance at that part."

When Albee was told of the incident, he said, "I had sent the play right to Fonda—it's the first time I really had a star in mind—and I was so hurt when it was sent back without a word from him."

Jane returned from Hollywood after *The Chapman Report* in time for her brother's debut on Broadway and his wedding three days later. Installed in her new apartment, which by now was completely redecorated, she spent much of her time at the Actors Studio. Although Voutsinas was the number one man in her life now, Timmy Everett continued to hover on the fringes.

"By this time I was a wreck," he says. "I was still hanging onto her, even though she'd made it clear that she only wanted to be friends. I was drinking pretty heavily and generally feeling very self-destructive. One night, just about Christmas, I went up to her apartment to talk to her. Voutsinas was there, and seeing them together after the two great Christmases she and I had really blew my mind. I was pretty drunk. I don't know what made me do it, but I rushed into the kitchen, grabbed a knife and started hacking at my hand. By the time they got into the kitchen there was blood all over the place. I know there are better ways to try to kill yourself, but I was so blind I couldn't even see what I was doing. Jane wrapped my hand up in a towel and took me in a cab to Roosevelt Hospital. I called her the next day to apologize, and she said she thought we'd better not see each other anymore. I saw her later that week at a New Year's Eve party at the Strasbergs—she was there with her brother—and we talked for a minute, but after that I never really talked to her anymore. Afterward, I mean for about three or four years, life was pretty rough for me. I drank pretty heavily and finally ended up with a nervous breakdown. I just couldn't get her out of my system, and it took six months in a hospital before I got back on my feet again."

Jane returned to Hollywood with Voutsinas in the spring of 1962 to play the female lead in the movie version of Tennessee Williams' Broadway comedy *Period of Adjustment*. She had auditioned for the play the year before when it was being cast. "At that time it was Greek to me—I didn't understand it at all. I didn't know whether it was a comedy or what. I'm sure I gave a bad reading. Then, when I was offered the movie and saw the script, I was frightened. But after I read it, I liked it. I was too young to know what it was all about when I first read the play, but since then I've learned a few things."

Nobody would include *Period of Adjustment* among Tennessee Williams' major works. But had it been written by a less celebrated playwright, it's doubtful that it would have been dismissed by the critics and public as abruptly as it was when it opened in 1961. The plot explored the "period of adjustment" in the marriages of two couples—a nervous pair of newlyweds and a longer-married twosome on the verge of breaking up—and when it was prepared for the screen by scriptwriter Isobel Lennart, it remained a perceptive and intelligent comedy.

Jane had her hair cut and dyed blond for her role. "As a bride who cries most of the time throughout *Adjustment*," she said about herself, "I don't know how pretty I'll look. The whole story covers a period of twenty-four hours following the wedding, and everything goes wrong. It's a story of the lack of communication between male and female—the old idea that a man must show off his masculinity and a girl must be dainty and weak. They're both so busy living in this framework that they go right past each other."

Of the four movies Jane had done, this was her favorite. Directed by George Roy Hill, who had mounted the Broadway production, she enjoyed playing the nervous, nubile Southern bride in a cast of mostly Actors Studio people. "It was an enormous challenge for me, especially because with my two previous films I felt I had tried but not gotten a good grasp on the characters I was playing. That was partly the fault of the scripts, but I knew I had made a lot of mistakes too. With *Adjustment* I felt that I finally got hold of a character and . . . well, I liked what I did. I became an actress because I needed love and support from a lot of people, but at the beginning I never dreamed I'd end up in the movies. A stage career is what I wanted. But somehow making movies gets to you. It's ego-battering—you're up one day and down the next—and it's much tougher work for an actor, because with all the various things involved it's harder to create a performance. When I did *Adjustment*, I finally began to feel like an experienced film actress, and I decided movies were for me."

13. The Fun Couple

Don't mention Andreas when you talk to my father. It will bring your conversation to an abrupt end.

—JANE FONDA

DURING her stay in California for *Period of Adjustment*, Jane was offered a part in another play. It was a comedy called *The Fun Couple*, written by an aspiring playwright, Neil Jansen, and a thirty-seven-year-old California dentist, John Haase, about a young married couple who are terrified that if they grow up and assume responsibility they won't have fun anymore. Dr. Haase, an attractive man with a wife and five children, evidently wrote out of his own experience. The role of the wife was not unlike that of the bride Jane was playing in *Period of Adjustment*. The play was fast-paced and called for youth, freshness, fantasy, farce and tenderness. Voutsinas evidently convinced Jane that with the experience she was gaining as a comedienne in *Adjustment*, the role of the young wife in *The Fun Couple* would suit her perfectly and would give her her first real opportunity to star in a hit play on Broadway. He also convinced her that it would be an excellent vehicle for his own debut as a Broadway director.

Jane was in love with Voutsinas and felt, as well, deeply indebted to him for what she was convinced was his role in the expansion of her talent. So she agreed to star in the play, provided Andreas was allowed to direct it. If it was the hit everyone thought it would be, it would be a great feather in both their caps, and Jane was especially anxious that Andreas' directorial talent finally be recognized. She was tired of hearing him constantly put down by people like her father and others in the business. The producers accepted her conditions, contracts were signed, and Jane and Andreas spent much of their time in Hollywood during the filming of *Period of Adjustment* preparing their approach

143

to *The Fun Couple*, which would open on Broadway later in the fall.

Jane kept busy refining her new image as the irrepressible and outspoken daughter of Henry Fonda by continuing to distribute controversial quotes to the press. Her statement of the year before about marriage being obsolete was still following her around, and she was afforded numerous opportunities to embellish it, which she did. She also began to pontificate more caustically about her father and brother. She criticized her father's marital record—he had just broken up with Afdera—and called him an unhappy, unfulfilled man. With equal fervor she criticized her brother's materialism and characterized him as a hapless neurotic forever trying to find himself.

Peter Fonda was appalled; he thought he *had* found himself. He had come into his share of his inheritance from his mother and had moved with his new wife to California. There, with his hopes high, he began to seek a film career and to emulate his father's life-style. "I was a conservative, a registered Republican," he says about his first years in Los Angeles. "Short hair, wearing business suits all the time, fur coat for my wife, house in Beverly Hills, tennis court, a garageful of fine cars. I thought of myself as one hundred percent upright—American and straight. I was into acting out other people's notions about who I should be, doing the right thing, being a member of the right clubs, joining the right party, meeting the right people. Being a socialite, the Blue Book thing, I believed in it, I accepted it."

When Jane's remarks about him were printed, reporters came to him for a reaction. "To each his own," he would say with a leering glance, making certain the reporters read in his face his disapproval of his sister's relationship with Voutsinas. The press sensed a war brewing and made the most of it. As a result, before he had got a single acting job, Peter was a minor celebrity in his own right. But he was hurt by his sister's condescension.

Nineteen sixty-two was another unhappy year for Henry Fonda. His marriage to Afdera had failed. He had missed out on the lead in *Who's Afraid of Virginia Woolf?* There was no decent stage role for him to play. He had been forced to make *Spencer's Mountain*, in his view a worthless picture. His bile over Jane and Voutsinas was growing more sour, and now he was being called by friends to be told about her latest press utterances, which were usually aimed at him.

Maureen O'Hara, his co-star in *Spencer's Mountain*, recalls his mood on the picture. "I knew Hank well in the old days at Twentieth Century, when he and I worked there with Tyrone Power, John Payne and Victor Mature. We used to visit each other's homes, and we all knew each other's kids. When *Spencer's Mountain* came along, I was delighted that my daughter, Bronwyn, who was studying to be an actress, got a small part in the picture. Hank hadn't seen her since she was a little girl. On the first day of shooting I was sitting and talking to Hank. Bronwyn arrived late, and not wanting to disturb us, she perched herself on a fence a few yards away. Suddenly I caught Hank looking at her with an expression I couldn't mistake. 'Oh, ho,' I said to myself. To Hank I said, 'Don't you know who that is over there?' I must have had an expression he couldn't mistake, because he said, 'Oh, no, not Bronwyn? I was just going to ask her for a date for tonight.' 'You will not!' said I, and that was definitely the end of that."

One of the crew members on *Spencer's Mountain* remembers that "often he'd be sitting on the set and someone would be talking to him, and suddenly it would be like a curtain dropped in front of his face. He'd look through whoever was talking to him and not answer and stare off into nowhere for maybe half an hour. The guy was really restless and troubled. He was carrying a lot around inside him."

Jane was not surprised at the breakup of her father's marriage to Afdera. She had seen it coming—the long silences, the quickened temper, the wandering eye. But it angered her that he continued to disapprove of her personal life when his own was such a mess. Now publicly committed to a life without hypocrisy and unable, she claimed, to communicate with her father on any level but the most superficial, she compulsively continued to take her anger out on him in the press. Peter spoke similarly about his father. "The only difference is," he once announced, "that living out in Malibu, my father sends his chicks home at night. His duplicity blew our minds."

Fonda kept up a façade of calm in the face of the blasts he was receiving. He was proud of his children, he said repeatedly, especially Jane, who "by now is a bigger star than I ever was and has an unlimited future. And Peter seems to have settled down and has a good chance for an acting career."

But privately he was confused and hurt. "I'm between planes somewhere, and before long there's a reporter to interview me, and he has a clipping that says Jane Fonda thinks her parents led a phony life. Or that she thinks her father should have been psychoanalyzed thirty-five years ago. Now it's all right for her to think it, but I don't think it's all right for her to say so in interviews. After all, I *am* her father. I mean, that's disrespectful. And some of the things she's been saying—well, they just aren't true."

By mid-1962 Jane's personal style had changed radically from that of the uncertain schoolgirl of five years before. She was now an outgoing, opinionated, freewheeling beauty who seemed, on the surface anyway, to have exorcised all her insecurities and to be eager to make her mark as a star. She attributed her transformation to analysis and Voutsinas, in that order, and fully enjoyed the attention she was getting. "I'm not at all like my father," she said. "I like fame. I don't go along with this stuff of hating to be recognized. I like to be recognized. I like to give autographs. My father always hated it. I never understood that. If you want privacy, you can make it for yourself.

"I used to think I was an introvert. Now I know I was just a shy extrovert. When I first went to Hollywood, I wasn't sure of my ability. I lacked confidence, so I said provocative things to create attention. Thanks to analysis, what I say now is really me.

"Before I went into analysis, I told everyone lies—but when you spend all that money, you tell the truth. I learned that I had grown up in an atmosphere where nobody told the truth. Everyone was so concerned with appearances that life was just one big lie. Now all I want to do is live a life of truth. Analysis has also taught me that you should know who to love and who to hate and who to just plain like, and it's important to know the difference. Because then you learn to really love some people, really hate some people and just become passive about others."

Before completing *Period of Adjustment*, Jane had an unhappy experience. The fall of 1961 was a particularly dry one in the Los Angeles area, and a huge brush fire broke out in the hills and canyons above Sunset Boulevard. Dozens of homes in Bel Air and Brentwood were consumed in the flames, and hundreds of others were severely damaged. The old Fonda homestead on Tigertail Road was one of those destroyed. Jane's grandmother and grandfather—the Seymours—had reacquired the property after Henry Fonda sold it in 1948 and had been living there for some years. "My whole childhood went up in smoke," Jane says. "When my grandmother got on the phone to tell me about it, I was more emotional than she."

According to Voutsinas, the incident provided Jane with a release of sorts. "It's like with her mother," he said. "When I became close with

Jane, I waited and waited for a burst of emotion about her mother. But she had it sidetracked. When Jane would talk about anything in her past, in some strange way her memory would not include her mother. When we went up to see the place in Brentwood, she was upset. But then she packed all her memories about growing up there away. It was like her life started from twelve years old on."

Filming was completed toward the end of June, but there would be no rest for Jane. Believing that she and Andreas would have an opportunity to share a working holiday in Greece and also, according to Ray Powers, to help pay off her financial obligations to Joshua Logan, she accepted a leading role in a motion picture called *In the Cool of the Day*, which was scheduled to start shooting there in July. However, a snag developed. Voutsinas had never done any military service. He had been promised a part in the movie but then discovered that he would immediately be drafted into the Greek army if he accompanied Jane to Greece.

At first, Jane refused to go without Andreas, and her agents tried to get her out of the movie. But it was an MGM picture for which its producer and director, John Houseman and Robert Stevens, claimed they had high hopes. They insisted Jane fulfill her obligation. So, with her hair dyed dark brown and styled in severe bangs by the MGM hairdressers, she flew to Athens without Voutsinas to get it over with. There would be some location filming in London in August, and she would be able to meet Andreas there, after which they both would return to New York to start rehearsals for *The Fun Couple*.

Once in Greece, it quickly became clear to Jane that *In the Cool of the Day* was one of those movies put together more out of a desire to give everyone a holiday than any ambition to accomplish something worthwhile. Houseman, the producer, had a reputation which, in the words of one widely read motion-picture critic, was "practically synonymous with compromised quality; a producer whose ambitious conscience does not let him rest until, in his commercial pictures, he has tampered with something or someone serious." The film was a turgid, sententiously romantic soap opera which featured—besides Jane in the role of a tubercular young lady—Angela Lansbury, British actor Peter Finch and an endless supply of Greek scenery. In a short film career already perforated by several low spots, *In the Cool of the Day* would prove to be the lowest for Jane.

Happy to have it over, Jane returned to New York to start

preparations for *The Fun Couple* and was promptly honored by the Defense Department by being named "Miss Army Recruiting of 1962." She appeared at a ceremony of Army recruiters, appropriately decked out in a satin sash that read MISS ARMY RECRUITING, and delivered an animated speech on the virtues of Army life and the need for a strong military force as a deterrent against America's enemies. That out of the way, she embarked on rehearsals for *The Fun Couple* with Voutsinas, actors Ben Piazza and Bradford Dillman and actress Dyan Cannon.

Any hopes Jane had that *The Fun Couple* would finally give her a hit play to boast about were quickly dashed. There was trouble from the beginning, and all four cast members grew progressively more desperate through rehearsals as director Voutsinas called for rewrite after rewrite from the fledgling authors.

"We started out with a lot of enthusiasm and talented people involved," Jane recalled sadly. "But the two authors had never written a play before, and when it came to rewrites, the thing got worse instead of better."

Others connected with the production felt that Jane had suspended her critical faculties for the sake of Voutsinas and that Voutsinas, anxious to have a Broadway credit at any cost, stupidly pressed on in the face of disaster. "My God," says one, "the thing should never have opened. They all should have chalked it up to experience. The writing was inept and amateurish. Voutsinas' direction was murky and unresolved. It was as if he were using the production as his own personal toy. He obviously thrived on playing the great director, but he was directing a Broadway production the way he might direct a scene for the Actors Studio. It was tentative and at the same time bizarre."

The Fun Couple had its opening on the night of October 26, 1962. It was an unmitigated disaster. The audience, many of them Actors Studio friends of Voutsinas, Jane and the other actors, hooted and snickered. The comments of critic Richard Watts in the next day's New York *Post* were typical of the reviews: "The most incredible thing about the play is that two such talented young performers as Jane Fonda and Bradford Dillman were willing to appear in the title roles. Even the sight of Miss Fonda in a bikini doesn't rescue *The Fun Couple* from being an epic bore."

"There's no use doing a play in New York unless it's a good one," Jane bitterly rationalized afterward. "It takes too much out of you.

So far, I've never been in a successful play. I guess I'm doomed to flops."

Although it's true the play was not a good one, Jane should have known better than to use it as an excuse for the failure of the venture. The real blame lay with Voutsinas for using Jane to advance his own career and partly with Jane herself for being blind to his motives. "Voutsinas' hold over Jane was complete," says Peter Basch, who saw them often around the Actors Studio. "She was a sweet and lovely girl and an enchanting actress, but she was tough and uncompromising when it came to defending Andreas, which she always seemed to be doing. She had put herself completely into his hands, and she seemed terribly unhappy over the fact that so many people thought ill of him. It's my guess that her pride kept her with Andreas long after she began to lose faith in him."

"What can I tell you about Andreas and Jane?" says an actress who knew them both. "He was the weird character—he gave me the willies. He looked like Satan incarnate, which I think is what got him the reputation he had. He had this accent and a kind of mad scientist aura. And he really worked at being mysterious and hypnotic. But there was something pitiful about him. I don't know if Jane dug him because he was pitiful—she had this thing about underdogs, you know—or because he was exotic and had a veneer of Oriental mysteriousness. Whatever it was, they made the most unlikely pair you could imagine—she with her sexy aristocratic beauty; he with his wizened features and his sort of Transylvanian manner."

Jane's depression over *The Fun Couple* found little relief over the next month or so. The three movies she had made in Hollywood during the previous year and a half had all been released. *Walk on the Wild Side* was unanimously denounced by the critics, although some saw promise in Jane's performance. And *The Chapman Report* was greeted with a universal yawn; Jane was noticed, but barely. Only *Period of Adjustment* elicited positive comment and provoked the serious recognition she had been hoping for.

Stanley Kaufman, film critic for the relatively obscure *New Republic*, wrote about movies with the high seriousness of a curator. He was the first to examine Jane's work in the light of rigorous standards. "A new talent is rising," he wrote in November, 1962. "I have now seen Miss Fonda in three films. In all of them she gives performances that are not only fundamentally different from one another but are conceived without acting cliché and executed with skill. Through them all can be heard, figuratively, the hum of that magnetism without which acting intelligence and technique are admirable but uncompelling. In *Walk on the Wild Side*, a film beneath comment, Miss Fonda played a girl of the road, vicious, foxy, tough. In *The Chapman Report* which (to put it in a phrase) is not up to the level of the novel, she plays a frigid young middle-class widow. The girl's pathological fear of sex, exacerbated by her hunger for love, is expressed in neurotic outbursts that cut to the emotional quick, with a truth too good for the material. In Tennessee Williams' comedy *Period of Adjustment*, which is amusing enough, Miss Fonda plays a nervous Southern bride, anxious in more than one sense. Her comic touch is as sure as her serious one. Besides the gift of timing, she has what lies below all comedy: confidence in one's perception of the humorous—where it begins and, especially, where it ends. Her performance is full of delights. . . . It would be unfair to Miss Fonda and the reader to skimp her sex appeal. She has plenty. Not conventionally pretty, she has the kind of blunt startling features and generous mouth that can be charged with passion or the cartoon of passion as she chooses. Her slim, tall figure has thoroughbred gawky grace. Her voice is attractive and versatile; her ear for inflections is secure. What lies ahead of this appealing and gifted young actress in our theatre and film world? Does she stand a chance of fulfillment, or is she condemned—more by our environment than by managers—to mere success? With good parts in good plays and films, she could develop into a first-rate artist. Meanwhile, it would be a pity if her gifts were not fully appreciated in these lesser, though large, roles."

Kaufman's article was a godsend, and although the *New Republic* was read by few people, the Famous Artists agency made sure that every important producer and director in Hollywood received a copy. Copies were also sent to the Harvard *Lampoon*, an undergraduate humor magazine that had given Jane its annual "Worst Actress of the Year" award for her performance in *The Chapman Report*. It was also a vindication, of sorts, for Voutsinas, who was beginning to feel nervous about his position in Jane's life. And for Jane, it had special significance over and above its favorable appraisal of her talents: For the first time someone had appraised her film talents without mentioning her father.

Jane and Andreas continued to live in her elegant apartment on

Fifty-fifth Street. The apartment was decorated to the last detail and was filled with Regency and Louis XV antiques. Her bedroom was sumptuously European in style and was dominated by a huge brass four-poster framed by acres of gold satin caopy and covered with a huge fur rug. In the living room one's eye was immediately drawn to a tiger and a leopard which lay silently at guard, mouths open and fangs bared, on the polished wood floor—a pair of rugs chosen for her by Voutsinas.

As a result of her favorable reviews for *Period of Adjustment*, Jane was besieged with new movie offers. She was urged by her agency to stick to comedy roles of the type she had played in *Adjustment*, for it was in these that her talents really shone. She was bright, energetic, vibrant, and her screen presence projected sexuality and innocence with equal attractiveness. This was obviously what audiences wanted to see, for the quality played on their fantasies and sent them home happy. Jane followed her agents' advice and signed with MGM, at a salary of $100,000, to play the lead in the film version of *Sunday in New York*, a frothy sex comedy by Norman Krasna that was enjoying a profitable run on Broadway that year. But first there was another project—an all-star Actors Studio revival of Eugene O'Neill's *Strange Interlude.*

With few exceptions Jane was, at twenty-five, completely her own person. True, she had inherited much of her father's looks and mannerisms—for instance, the sad, long face, the large, blue and riveting eyes, the way he put his hands to his lips when speaking, as if to serve his words better, the way his mouth tightened when he talked and the way his eyes moistened when the talk became emotional. But her own distinct qualities made these only vague reminders of her genetic inheritance. Where her father spoke slowly, with a kind of throwaway inflection, she spoke in rapid-fire bursts, her voice a curious mixture of finishing-school detachment and thrumming conviction. Her eyes darted, where her father's remained fixed and distant. Her movements were purposeful and quick, with a dancer's grace, while her father's were at once shambling and economic. In conversation she had a way of ducking her head and then sliding it up and forward for emphasis, whereas her father, except for the use of his hands, remained Buddhalike. Her laugh was full-blown, nervous, deep-throated, while her father's, which seemed to come from no deeper than his teeth, was scratchy and tentative.

Similarities and dissimilarities of personality aside, Jane seemed to be following some secret print of her genes that forged a nature totally different from that of her father. Fonda had matured into his late fifties with a rock-ribbed Midwestern consistency; although he was an actor, bedeviled with the usual actor's insecurities (how could he be an actor otherwise?), he stubbornly denied his neuroticism and clung to his belief in himself as a self-contained fortress of sanity in the less than sane world he inhabited. For him, acting served as a safety valve for his neuroticism, a distraction not unlike farming and painting—a form of occupational therapy that enabled him to keep his anxieties at a safe distance from himself. Like a good liberal, he believed in the separation of church and state—in this case the distancing of man from actor. Jane, on the other hand, found in acting a way of coming to terms with her insecurities. She did not believe in the separation of woman from actress; indeed, her goal was to unite the two in herself. She was convinced the actor acts because of his neuroticism, not in spite of it; thus, the more she was able to expose of herself on the personal level, the better a person she would be because of the expansion of her acting sensibilities. She used acting not as an occupational therapy to divert her neuroses but as a form of analysis to confront them. To her, acting and living were synergistic; although they had different forms of expression, the two worked together like gas vapors and sparks in the piston of an engine. Her job was to keep the engine as finely tuned as possible so as to ensure perfect combustion.

Combustive Jane had become. Although she'd managed to bring many of her insecurities to the surface, she was not yet able to release them. She'd freed one hand from the bonds that tied her to her past and was desperately wriggling the other loose. As she did so, her father tightened the knot.

Fonda was interviewed early in 1963 and was asked about Jane's statement: "Don't mention Andreas when you talk to my father. It will bring the conversation to an abrupt end." Fonda responded by saying, "Well, it won't come to an abrupt end, but we'd have a short pause until we got to another subject." When Fonda did talk about Voutsinas, he cursed him, characterizing him as an evil molder of Jane's personality. He held him responsible for the incomprehensible changes that Jane was going through and refused to have him in his house. "I couldn't talk enough about Jane and the good things she has," her father said. "But in one area she has a blind spot." This area was her choice of men. "She's going to get hurt," he concluded bitterly.

Voutsinas readily admitted that he had fantasies of becoming what he called "the power behind the throne." But on the other hand, he said, "I can't be that much of a Svengali; I really can't, you know. And I'm hurt, very hurt by Jane's father's rejection of me. And so is Jane."

Jane remained silent in the face of the growing criticisms of Voutsinas from friends and father. She was furious with her father but could not discuss her feelings with him; he would simply turn away with an angry, sarcastic remark about the fool she was making of herself. She knew that in her acting achievements she had finally given him something to be proud of, but the realization of that dream was compromised by his recalcitrant attitude toward Andreas. Finally, in a mood of resentful despair, she gave up her attempts to win him over and turned more avidly than ever to Andreas for solace.

Jane's debt to Voutsinas stemmed from the fact that he had forced her to cross the boundaries of her inhibitions and was sympathetic to her attempts to break completely out of the mold in which she'd been formed. They both still took their theatrical nourishment from Lee Strasberg. In addition, they were undergoing psychotherapy together and were striving to marry the esoteric perceptions of analysis with the imperatives of the Method, convinced that such a union would elevate them into the rarefied atmosphere of art. Most stars learn early in their careers that merely to be a performer creates its own torment; to be a performer and an artist is double the penalty. As did Marilyn Monroe before her, Jane Fonda agonized before the mirror and ached through her entire body before each public appearance, even if it was only in a scene at the Studio. After the praise that was heaped on her for *Period of Adjustment*, she was finding that success, rather than provide security, gives birth to new insecurities.

"It's become much harder for me now," she said early in 1963. "Just to get up in the Actors Studio and do a scene is so hard. Mainly because I know that there are people there who have far more talent than I do. I know that I do have something else. I have star quality, I have a personality, I have presence on the stage, which may make me more important than they are. What I have is obvious, it's like a commodity and it's in demand. But in terms of acting ability, they have more. That's why it's so hard."

She was not boasting about her star potential, nor was she being modest about her acting ability. She was hardheaded and practical enough to recognize the signs of her success and what they meant and realistic enough as well to comprehend her limitations. But as happens with most stars, the middle ground between her image and her reality became a quagmire of self-doubt. The questions Stanley Kaufman had posed—does she stand a chance of fulfillment, or is she condemned to mere success?—haunted her. Under the influence of Strasberg and Voutsinas, she aspired to art, but her knowledge of herself and her awe of what she considered the true art of the actor made that higher ground seem unreachable.

The production of *Strange Interlude* provided a particularly trying test of Jane's confidence. Although the Actors Studio was basically a noncommercial workshop where projects were put together and performed exclusively for the membership, it occasionally gave birth to productions that were suitable for full-scale presentation on the commercial stage. *Strange Interlude* was such a project. It had started as an acting exercise for Geraldine Page, a Studio member who was considered one of the finest actresses in the theater, and had evolved into a full-scale production directed by José Quintero. With Miss Page starring as the troubled Nina Leeds, Jane won the part of Madeline Arnold, the girl with whom Nina Leeds' son falls in love.

Geraldine Page, an actress of diverse and powerful colors, had practically cornered Broadway's neurotic-leading-lady market. She was no longer just another capable performer; she had become a specific type in the minds of playwrights, directors and producers. The scope of her talent was vast, and her performances invariably inspired awe on the part of other actors. Jane Fonda was doubly in awe of her. Her ability to dominate a stage and to plumb emotions Jane had never conceived of gave Jane feelings of profound inadequacy.

Rehearsals for the long and taxing play spanned most of the winter, and the production opened to enthusiastic reviews on March 12, 1963. The impeccable cast also included Betty Field, Ben Gazzara, Pat Hingle, Geoffrey Horne, William Prince, Franchot Tone and Richard Thomas, all members of the Actors Studio. Howard Taubman in the New York *Times* called it a "brilliant revival" and declared that "Jane Fonda happily contributed her vivacity and beauty to the final two acts."

Jane was disappointed in the blandness of her personal notices but realistically acknowledged that she could hardly expect more while sharing the stage with Geraldine Page, who gave a bravura performance. She was content with the opportunity to perform with a superb group of actors in a highly professional production—"an atmosphere in which art had a chance to happen." She realized, nevertheless, that she was not about to gain the acclaim as a stage actress she had dreamed of. She had once said, "I'd like someday to be as great an actress as Geraldine Page or Kim Stanley." Now that she had seen what it took to be a Geraldine Page or a Kim Stanley, she felt slightly foolish for ever having had such a dream for herself. She felt young, inexperienced and seriously distanced from achieving the kind of controlled virtuosity they were capable of. There were too many Geraldine Pages in the New York theater—actresses who had the magic gift of ripping a character apart, then putting it back together with a uniqueness that made it their sole property. It had to do with that mysterious gift of intuition a great actor possesses, the ability to perceive totally the truth of a character and a scene and to bring them out with full-bodied and unerring certainty. Jane had been intellectualizing for two years about making art, but art in acting had nothing to do with the intellect. It was pure and simple instinct coupled with an emotional depth and comprehension that she did not yet possess. She had talent, yes, and she had an actress' temperament—in short, she could act. But the sobering experience of *Strange Interlude* convinced her that she did not have the sort of acting genius that made art possible.

Shortly after the opening of *Strange Interlude*, the first revealing, in-depth story about Jane appeared in the *Saturday Evening Post* under the by-line of Alfred Aronowitz. The article probed beneath Jane's public image and presented a fairly accurate picture of her joys and her torments. In the same issue was the first long article to be published in the popular American press about the United States' activities in Vietnam. The article was entitled "The Long and Lonely War in South Vietnam," and it described in alarming terms, with pictures, what was happening in the Vietnam of 1963. An accompanying editorial warned: "Americans are going to have to get accustomed to the fact that the war will be a long one."

Jane, in the meantime, was busy adjusting her sights. She went directly from *Strange Interlude* into the filming of *Sunday in New York*, the picture that would finally establish her in the eyes of the American public as a full-fledged movie star. *Strange Interlude* was the last play in which she would appear.

Although Jane despaired of ever possessing the awesome emotional resources of a Geraldine Page, she was by now a highly charged young woman who exuded a smoldering sensual urgency that registered well on the screen. She used this quality to good advantage in the filming of *Sunday in New York*, a picture that became the template of her movie future as a sex-and-skin star.

Sunday in New York, most of which was filmed in Manhattan with Cliff Robertson and Rod Taylor in co-starring roles, had been a trite little Broadway sex-situation comedy that was transformed by director Peter Tewkesbury into a stylish but still trite Hollywood sex-situation comedy—a bit more daring than similar comedies from previous years but cut from the same cloth. In it Jane played a single girl living in New York and caught in a web of stock-farce sexual intrigue. The story was necessarily short on frankness and long on suggestion, and the harmless salaciousness of its dialogue gave the script whatever humor it had. In many respects Jane's character of Eileen Tyler was the most difficult she'd ever had to play because of its one-dimensional mock innocence. The character was cousin to the cheerleader in *Tall Story*—Jane's intervening film roles had been more on the order of character parts—but she managed to infuse it with an amusing credibility. "Making the picture was completely fun from start to finish," she said, "which is more than I can say for the other films I've made. The part could have been boring, but it wasn't. I'm sure this movie will help my career."

Help her career it did. When the picture was released in February, 1964, her reviews were unanimously favorable, even though the film itself was dismissed as inconsequential. Stanley Kaufman came in with another commendation for Jane, somewhat mitigating the lingering effects of the reviews she had received earlier for the film she'd made in Greece: "Jane Fonda's last film, *In the Cool of the Day*, was an insurmountable disaster, but it does not disprove her comic powers in *Period of Adjustment* and the current *Sunday in New York*. Miss Fonda has wit, even when Krasna doesn't. It is in the immediacy of her voice, her readings of lines, her sharp sense of timing. The combination of her slightly coltish movements and her unpretty but attractive face gives her a quality that cuts agreeably across the soft grain of other young actresses. Her presence has the instant incisiveness and interest that are usually summed up in the term 'personality.' This last is certainly not identical with talent. Alec Guinness has large talent, little personality. Miss Fonda has considerable of both. It is still worth wondering—up to now, anyway—what will become of her?"

By the time Kaufman re-asked the question he had first posed a year and a half before Jane was well on her way to providing an answer.

Part III

Jane Plemiannikov/1963–1969

14. Second Plane to Paris

I love working in French. I feel a certain kind of freedom—the way you feel when you learn to speak a foreign language and find you can say things you wouldn't dare to say in English.

—JANE FONDA

ALONG with its other implications, the assassination of John F. Kennedy on November 22, 1963, was a particularly demoralizing event for millions of young Americans of increasingly libertarian instincts. Kennedy was their demigod. His youthful, wry style of leadership and his sophisticated but wittily self-effacing manner created an appeal that ignited the imaginations of a generation of people hungry for the promise of a new national life-style. Dwight Eisenhower, with his down-home grin and his look of eternal befuddlement, belonged to their parents. Now, with Kennedy at the nation's helm, it was young America's turn.

More than anything else, young America appreciated style, and Kennedy practically dripped with it. When he was assassinated, America aged overnight. No matter how false the myth of Camelot would turn out to be, it was as if young America's life-sustaining juices had been perversely extracted through the barrel of a rifle and replaced with the manic fluids of despair.

Kennedy's murder was the watershed experience of the new American consciousness that had formed out of the do-nothing fifties. That consciousness had already drawn the plans for a reinvigorated society and was merely waiting for Kennedy to implement them. When he was killed, the reaction against commercialism and materialism that had been slowly growing since his election suddenly leaped forward with the fury of an express train. This was the new America, and as it evolved over the next ten years, it would pass through three basic and overlapping phases.

The first was the love-and-flower phase, a reaction against the violence symbolized by the assassination and the shattered promise of the Kennedy years. The second was the drug-sex-violence phase, which sought to create and define an alternative world view to represent the millions of disenfranchised young—and not-so-young—of America. The third was the activist phase, the frantic application of that world view to the monolith of America's hypocritical respectability. Glued together by the communicative power of music, ironically nourished by the never-ending Vietnam War and promoted by press and television's pandering to America's vicarious and often self-righteous fascination for the startling and outrageous, the three phases eventually became one—a diffuse, yet loosely unified subculture that dubbed itself the Third World movement. Primarily the manifestation of white, educated, middle-class youth, along the road to its final form the movement picked up others among the more seriously alienated and socially or politically oppressed —blacks, Indians, Socialists, anarchists, women, the poor, the felonious. They all fed off each other, and America in turn fed off them.

As the popular mirror of both the normalities and aberrations of America, Hollywood, with its financial appreciation for America's taste for the bizarre, quickly began to exploit and reflect the new culture. At the time of Kennedy's assassination, Hollywood had already embarked on a desperate effort to become Europeanized. The French New Wave had begun to have a serious impact on the movie industry. Television was keeping movie audiences away from the theaters in droves, and what was left of the audience for motion pictures was ignoring the traditional Hollywood product and flocking to see the "more honest" films from Europe. In their attempt to recover their audiences, American films rapidly became infiltrated by the mannerisms of the French style— blurry, slow-motion love scenes, split-second flashbacks, improvised dialogue, the roller-coaster effects of the hand-held camera, nudity and sexual frankness and a taste for the unglamorous, proletarian face. The growing European influence, coupled with the movie industry's anxiety to exploit young America's rapidly expanding interest in film as a serious art form, helped shape a new Hollywood. It was a Hollywood that would eventually become a major outpost of the Third World movement as the movement attempted to transform the life-style of much of America to conform to its radical, libertarian, hypocrisy-free vision.

Having decided to concentrate exclusively on advancing herself as a major film actress, Jane Fonda's aspirations meshed perfectly with those of the new Hollywood that was about to find its development accelerated by the Kennedy assassination. Where else would Hollywood go to learn the French film techniques at first hand than to the successful French film directors? And where else would Jane Fonda go to expose herself to these techniques than to Paris?

After finishing *Sunday in New York*, Jane left for Paris in the early fall of 1963 to star in an MGM-sponsored picture by the well-known French director René Clement. The film was to be called *Joy House*, would co-star the popular French actor Alain Delon and would be one of Hollywood's early attempts to capitalize on the American fascination with the New Wave. Characteristically, as in most attempts to make quick capital of a misunderstood mass enthusiasm, the picture would be a dismal failure.

Jane's trip to Paris was carefully planned by the experienced MGM image makers, and she arrived in a fanfare of publicity. It was quite a switch for the girl who had arrived there five years before as a lonely, unhappy student inept in the language and feeling like a fish out of water. "This time I had a girl linguist with me, and I didn't speak one word of English for two months. And all that publicity, with reporters constantly crowding in—they adore my father in Europe. All this, mind you, in my French. It was wonderful, I never felt so good."

She was an instant celebrity and could go nowhere without being recognized. During the next few months most of the French magazines had feature stories on her. The press delighted in her technically correct but often idiomatically fractured French and printed her funny cracks and malapropisms as rapidly as they rolled from her tongue. She captured the French fancy even further with a dazzling performance on a television interview show—she covered her long hair with an old straw hat, but wore a revealing blouse and bikini that showed off her long shapely legs to advantage. She amused her viewers by calling everybody "thou," a rare form of address in France, and by making such cracks as "I sent a check to my father recently—he spent a lot of money on me, and it's only natural that I should help him out."

Jane gained more publicity when it was reported that she was the reason for the breakup of her co-star Alain Delon's much-publicized romance with actress Romy Schneider. Delon, France's biggest heart throb and a young man with a reputation as a Peck's Bad Boy—he was poor-born and had connections to the French underworld—was intrigued by the aristocratic, outspoken Jane. She, in turn, was captivated by his limpid good looks and his cocky self-assurance. "I will undoubtedly fall in love with Delon," she announced to the press. "I can only play love scenes well when I am in love with my partner."

Film flackery, to be sure, but Jane thoroughly enjoyed the sex-and-sin image and was happy to cooperate in broadening it. She knew she wasn't like that—she was still Jane Fonda, after all, the well-mannered young woman of impeccable background—but being in France and speaking the French language somehow made the whole business more fun than it would have been in America. She discovered she could say things that would be inappropriate vulgarities in English but had a delicious drollery in French, and as she became more proficient in the language, she delighted in trying them out.

Joy House, which was called *Ni Saints, Ni Saufs* (*Neither Saints Nor Saviors*) in French, was designed as a taut suspense thriller in the Hitchcock vein but turned out to be an absurd, contrived melodrama. The story had Alain Delon as a small-time mobster on the lam from some cohorts he had cheated. Pursued to the Riviera, he ducks into a flophouse, where he tries to lose himself in the soup line. There, dishing up the soup, are Lola Albright, playing a Salvation Army type angel of mercy, and Jane Fonda, cast as an expatriate Cinderella. The unlikely duo spirit the handsome stranger away to their Gothic mansion to act as their chauffeur. Miss Albright, a widow, is the one with the money. Jane, billed as her "cousin," is obviously a poor relation who spends all her time in the kitchen preparing meals. After Delon arrives, though, she manages to spend considerably more time in bed—his bed. The trouble is that Delon is seldom in it. He is busy down the hall making love to Miss Albright, but he's not completely at ease because the lady keeps a shrunken head in a glass case by her bower. Delon can't worry about this too much, though, with so many other problems. The mob is closing in, somebody is trying to poison his food, and Jane keeps bouncing into his bed. Slithering around the walls of the house in a secret passage, meanwhile, is a madman who happens to be the widow Albright's lover.

When *Joy House* opened some months later, critics and public alike howled. The gumbo plot was thickened by the grafting on of some bizarre chase music. Clement's script tried to be clever, witty and offbeat but succeeded only in being ridiculous. Jane didn't fare well with the critics either. "Miss Fonda has some mysterious hold over Miss

Albright," Judith Crist wrote in one of the kinder reviews. "It's not all Miss Fonda has—or at least she so attempts to indicate by alternately impersonating the Madwoman of Chaillot, Baby Doll and her father Henry; she's a sick kid, this one."

Jane knew she was in a clinker before the film was even released. "As usual in Europe, there was no script and very little organization," she said, anticipating the reviews. "It sort of threw me because I'm used to working within a structured framework. There was just too much playing it by ear for my taste. But Clement is still a wonderful director."

During the filming of *Joy House* the publicity Jane had received on her arrival in France intensified—mainly as a result of her relationship with Delon. There was a slight pause at the end of November, when all available space was devoted to news about the assassination of President Kennedy, who had been a favorite in France, but it soon picked up again. A pop song likened her to a gazelle, and the editors of the snobbish *Cahiers du Cinéma* put her on its cover and interviewed her for eight pages, when usually they only spoke to the hautiest directors. The inevitable comparisons to Bardot became more frequent—*La BB Américaine*, she was called—and from a physical point of view, at least, they were not far off the mark. Jane was not a beautiful woman in the classic sense, but her strikingly attractive face—very much like her father's but appropriately softened—her lithe, boyish body and her flippant sensuality sparked the French imagination. With her long hair dyed blond again and the natural pout of her mouth, she did bear a resemblance to Bardot that was sometimes uncanny. The French saw in her some exotically sexy combination of Annie Oakley and Sheena, Queen of the Jungle, and the press fell all over its inkpots attempting to describe her. Most of the prose came out purple. "A young wild thing galloping too fast, bursting into flame too easily . . . a revelation," went one account. "A super BB, a cyclone of femininity, a marvelous baby doll," went another. "On the outside, she's true to her image," wrote journalist Georges Belmont, "tall, blonde, the perfect American, with long, flexible movements. Inside she is sultry and dangerous, like a caged animal. . . . I watched her move and thought in a flash of the black panther I used to watch in the zoo."

Under the circumstances, Jane was a dead cinch to catch the attention of France's leading feline fancier, director Roger Vadim, who had "discovered" large batches of the nation's most celebrated pussycats (among them Bardot, Annette Stroyberg, Catherine Deneuve) and had more or less married most of them.

Vadim was about to start a remake of the postwar French film classic *La Ronde*. The original had starred Gérard Philipe, Danielle Darrieux, Simone Signoret, Jean-Louis Barrault and Simone Simon, all established stars of the French cinema. It had been based on the German play *Reigen*, a sly, wicked comedy of errors revolving around sex by Arthur Schnitzler. Vadim intended to take advantage of the increased permissiveness toward sex and nudity on film, much of which he had been responsible for, and shoot *La Ronde* in a more contemporary freewheeling style. When he saw the impact Jane Fonda was having on the French public, he immediately wanted her in the picture.

Vadim's real name is Roger Vladimir Plemiannikov. His father was a Russian refugee from Bolshevism who became a French citizen and died when Vadim was nine. Born in the early 1920's of a French mother, Vadim studied for the French consular service until the war and the German occupation interrupted his training. After the war he worked as a journalist before trying his luck as an actor. By 1950 he had given up acting for more menial off-camera chores when he "discovered" Brigitte Bardot on a movie lot. Others may have seen her first, but none showed the enterprise of Vadim. He staked his claim by moving into the home of Brigitte's prosperous middle-class parents. She was sixteen at the time and had been trying to break into movies by doing bit parts. When she was eighteen, still a brunette and unknown, she and Vadim were married.

By the time she was twenty-one she was a blonde and, if not famous, at least notorious—thanks to Vadim. He took photos of her scantily dressed and showed them around to agents and movie scouts. He got her parts in nine movies within a three-year period and established her as an amoral child-woman. Not satisfied with her progress, or his, he decided to direct her himself in a film that would make her "the unattainable dream of every man."

The picture, *And God Created Woman*, achieved the Bardot image he was after and did almost as much for him. But the movie destroyed their marriage. During the filming of the picture's key bedroom scene, Vadim reportedly ordered Bardot's leading man, Jean-Louis Trintignant, to act as if he meant it. The actor did as he was told, and Brigitte decided that she meant it, too.

While their divorce was in the works, Vadim directed Brigitte in *The Night Heaven Fell*. During the shooting Vadim's new mistress, a Danish model named Annette Stroyberg, was in constant attendance. At dinner every night, Vadim was said to treat his wife as a younger sister and

Annette as a lover. Everyone appeared happy with the arrangement, and when news of it reached the press (Vadim had developed a certain talent for publicity), the three were heralded as examples of the new morality.

Brigitte got her divorce in December, 1957, and the next day Vadim became the father of a daughter, Nathalie, born to Annette on her twenty-first birthday. "What was there to be ashamed of?" Annette demanded. "I love Roger." Brigitte offered to be the baby's godmother but was graciously turned down.

Annette and Vadim finally got married in June, 1958, and he revealed plans to transform her into another Bardot. He changed her screen name to Annette Vadim and starred her in a grade-Z movie about a vampire woman. Just as the picture was about to be released, French newspapers broke a scandal. Annette, they reported, was having an affair with French singer-guitarist Sasha Distel, who had enjoyed brief fame as one of Brigitte Bardot's boyfriends. An exchange of letters between Vadim and Distel was leaked to the press, reportedly by Vadim himself, and the vampire movie opened to standing-room-only crowds.

In his next picture, Vadim went all out to establish Annette as Brigitte's successor. He starred her in the nude opposite Trintignant in a film entitled *Les Liaisons Dangereuses*. The picture was held up for two years by financial and censorship troubles, but when it was finally released, it cemented Vadim's reputation as a shameless, free-living, naughty-erotic Pygmalion. In the meantime, in 1960, he divorced Annette, claiming that Distel was still hanging about and that "I want to escape the ridiculous situation of the cuckold." In France, where cuckoldry was a serious matter, the masses sympathized with him. He managed to retain custody of his daughter.

When Vadim came to the United States in December, 1961, for the delayed opening of *Les Liaisons Dangereuses* (it was generally panned), he brought along his new mistress and protégée, Catherine Deneuve, an eighteen-year-old French blonde. "She is my fiancée," he announced, "and when I have a fiancée, I marry her." He also vowed that he was going to make Catherine as big a star as Bardot and Stroyberg. When Vadim failed to marry her after she gave birth to his son, she said it was all right with her. "I'm against marriage," she declared. The two lived together for another year or so, then went their separate ways—she to become a star on her own, he to seek another Galatea.

Vadim, tall and stoop-shouldered, had the magnetism and high-voltage charm of a star himself, although he lacked the matinee idol's good looks. His long face, generous nose and big mouthful of teeth gave him a strong resemblance to the French comic actor Fernandel; nevertheless, he had a commanding way with impressionable young women and, it is said, a deserved reputation as a well-endowed sexual technician. He effectively mixed quiet self-assurance with shy, boyish vulnerability and was well liked by almost everyone who knew him, except for those who had to deal with him on a financial level. His reputation as an insatiable sex enthusiast was overblown by the press, yet he did have an abiding interest in regularity and variety and enjoyed playing teacher to a series of invariably beautiful students. By 1963 he was a sort of sexual hero in France, and when it became known that he was interested in Jane Fonda, the French nation, with the help of the press, held its breath.

"I met Vadim that first time in Paris when I went to study painting," Jane once recalled. "I heard things about him then that would curl your hair. That he was sadistic, vicious, cynical, perverted, that he was a manipulator of women, et cetera and so forth. . . . Then I saw him again in Hollywood a couple of years later, and he asked me to meet him for a drink to talk about doing a picture. I went, but I was terrified. Like, I thought he was going to rape me right there in the Polo Lounge. But he was terribly quiet and polite. I thought, 'Boy, what a clever act.' Then, back in Paris the second time, he wanted to talk to me about doing *La Ronde*. Okay, I'm older, and I think, 'Christ, I never gave the guy a chance.' This time—well, I was absolutely floored. He was the antithesis of what I'd been told. I found a shyness, a—"

Vadim had few interests aside from women, sex and filmmaking, and on these subjects he had become somewhat of a philosopher. His philosophy of life was strongly hedonistic and libertine, and he was not a man to be intimidated by guilts or conscience. He had a large circle of friends, many of them sycophants, and was one of the acknowledged leaders of the free and unencumbered life-style of the Paris–St.-Tropez film circuit.

He had his contradictions, though. Celebrated as a *bon vivant,* he also had a *petit bourgeois* side that puzzled and amused his friends. He enjoyed nothing more than presiding over a house with wife and children, having friends in for dinner and informal salons. A witty, intelligent conversationalist—he spoke several languages, not including Russian—he suffered fools with charm and grace and was considerate of anyone who sought his company. By the time he met Jane he was more of a wry observer of than a participant in the life he led and always behaved with a remote dignity—even in sexual matters—that belied his public image. In many ways, not just physically, he bore a startling resemblance to Henry Fonda.

Whether it was because she thought her part in *La Ronde* was an exceptional one, or because of her disgust with America over Kennedy's assassination, or simply because the moth could not resist the flame, Jane agreed to work with Vadim. His authority, sophistication and self-assurance, which he mixed like a master alchemist with his sad-eyed vulnerability, captured Jane's fancy once she started filming. "I began making the film, and I fell in love with him. I was terrified. I thought, 'My God, he's going to roll over me like a bulldozer. . . . I'll be destroyed. . . . My heart will be cut out. . . . But I've got to do it.' And I discovered a very gentle man. So many men in America are . . . *men*-men, always having to prove their strength and masculinity. Vadim was not afraid to be vulnerable—even feminine, in a way. And I was terrified of being vulnerable."

The relationship that ensued was inevitable. Vadim was a man who held the view that modern society's conventions were outmoded and hypocritical, especially those dealing with sexuality and marriage. He had promoted his convictions through his work and his life until they were of a piece in the public mind with the man himself. He was also a man who fed off the largess of others; he was hardly wealthy and depended on the generosity of friends, often women, to see him over financial rough spots. No man approaching forty, with two marriages, two children and countless affairs behind him, falls helplessly in love; there is invariably a certain strategy and design in his response to the woman who attracts him. With his career becalmed by a string of flops, he saw in Jane an opportunity to revive it, not only with *La Ronde* but in the long term as well.

For her part, Jane was seriously questioning the attitudes and values of her upbringing. In Vadim's discourses on decadence—it was his contention that conventionality was what made society decadent, not freedom and sensuality—she found easy support for her growing need to rebel against what she felt was society's hypocrisy. In addition, she required a strong man in her life—not a repressive one like her father, but one who would control and direct her and at the same time encourage the expansion of her spirit and broaden her ability to live without the guilt and recrimination with which she had been raised.

Her role in *La Ronde* required Jane to spend most of her time in bed, alternating between her character's lover and husband. The film was being shot in French (it would be dubbed into English for its American release), and Vadim patiently spent a great deal of his spare time coaching Jane on her accent. Since it was being made to exploit its sexual content, he also spent time coaching her in the techniques and subtleties of lovemaking. Studio technicians said that they watched the Fonda-Vadim alliance develop right before their eyes and that Jane was an eager and pliant student.

Jane acquired a luxurious apartment in a seventeenth-century house on the Rue Séguier, about 100 yards from the left bank of the Seine, and it was not long before Vadim was in residence. After the filming of *La Ronde* was completed in January, 1964, the two conducted their affair in strictest privacy, much to the dismay of the press. They frequently dropped out of sight for days while newspaper speculation mounted. Occasionally the press was able to confirm—with conveniently available photos—that they spent a couple of weeks skiing together in some remote village of the French Savoy or stayed with friends in a town on the Atlantic, but mostly the stories concerned the secrecy of the Fonda-Vadim romance. This was not like Vadim at all, the newspapers contended; he must be doing it out of deference to *La BB Américaine* (Americans, after all, were not as liberated as the French).

The concept of vulnerability seemed to be the key to their mutual attraction. Of the beginnings of their romance, Vadim says, "Like all the women I have been involved with, she had a . . . vulnerability. Nothing is more attractive than vulnerability in a woman. She wants to be beautiful but is not sure that she is. She wants to be happy but manages always to be unhappy. Jane always thought that to be happy you must build walls to protect yourself from unhappiness. If I taught her anything it was to be more herself, not to be afraid. Later, she became more open. But in the beginning . . . you ask if the walls were high? They were a fortress! The Great Wall of China! She was very afraid of me but attracted, too. So she decided, 'Okay, I will do what I feel and then leave and never see him again, and the problem will be over.' So it was an easy conquest for the first few days. She was fighting the enemy by running out of the citadel and into his arms. But then, when she discovered it was not over, she retreated again behind her walls.

"Living with her was difficult in the beginning. One can fall in love fast. But to know if you can live with someone . . . that takes longer. She had so many—how do you say?—bachelor habits. Too much organization. Time is her enemy. She cannot relax. Always there is something to do—the work, the appointment, the telephone call. She cannot say, 'Oh, well, I'll do it tomorrow.' This is her weakness.

"Her strength? Jane has a fantastic capacity for surviving. She learned long ago how to be lonely. She can be very—in French we say *solide*. For me, what was attractive was her attention to other people. She knows how to listen. This is so rare, especially for a woman. She opens her mind, tries to understand. Others try to change a man; Jane accepts him for what he is."

Jane returned to the United States in mid-February to do a series of publicity promotions for the opening of *Sunday in New York*, leaving Vadim to wrap up the technical work on *La Ronde*. Although she was in love with Vadim, she was careful to avoid all mention of him to anyone but her closest friends, since she wanted a little more time to test her feelings before confirming them publicly. Besides, she knew what the press would make of it if they got wind of it. The American press was still talking about her affair with Alain Delon, and she did nothing to discourage their conclusions that she was still interested in him.

Her reviews for *Sunday in New York* were unanimously favorable. They buoyed her considerably. She went through a round of interviews in which she claimed she would never appear in a nude scene ("Personally, I couldn't appear nude—I'm too modest"), commented on some of the stories that had surfaced about her in her absence ("It doesn't surprise me to find a lack of good in people—it neither surprises me to find betrayal from 'friends' or admonitions from other") and admitted that she and Voutsinas had broken up but still remained friends. She philosophized on the mores of life, sex and marriage, unconsciously revealing the effects her brief attachment to Vadim had had on her thinking.

She also debunked some of Hollywood's anxiety over European films. "After being in France I realized how much we take our movies for granted," she said. "The French really know and love American movies. They have a set of American directors they really flip over—Hitchcock, Cukor, Stevens, Kazan, Sturges . . . to me it was incredible. And it's no superficial appreciation. They can discuss American films in detail, and a lot of movies that open and close in a week in the United States are considered masterpieces there. There's a certain flavor and type of thing we do here that is unique to them. Most of our directors and producers put a feeling of virility into their films. Europeans like our Westerns because they express masculinity and strength. You hear the most arty, highbrow talk, the most cerebral discussions about our Westerns. It's funny—for ages the Europeans have wanted to make movies the way we do, and now Hollywood is trying to imitate the Europeans."

She was glad, however, that American moviemaking was no longer centered in Hollywood. "I enjoy making pictures abroad, but I'm no runaway actress and wouldn't want to live there permanently. My home is New York."

When asked how she would enjoy acting in a play or movie with her father and brother—Peter had by then made four pictures—she said, "Good God, no. It would be awful. I couldn't stand it, and neither could they. First, Peter's still got to find himself as an actor, and it would hurt him to be subjected to both of us—Dad and me—at the same time. Maybe, Dad and me in television, but only maybe. The filming could be done in two weeks. I guess we could stand each other that long."

When Peter read his sister's remarks about still having to find himself as an actor, he blew up. He was unhappy about the roles he was being offered—mostly innocuous parts in beach-blanket pictures—and was furious with his sister's patronizing attitude, which would surely prejudice producers against him. As usual, he expressed his hurt with a series of angry blasts which the press printed with glee.

Shortly after settling in Beverly Hills with his wife, Peter had tested for the part of President Kennedy in *PT-109* but failed to get it. His first film was *Tammy and the Doctor*, for which he was paid $15,000. "I saw it and had to be hospitalized for a week and a half. I'm just kidding. I only vomited." He then went to London to appear in an unsuccessful antiwar epic, *The Victors*. He followed this with *Lilith*, a quality picture he thought would really launch his career. But his part was heavily cut, he didn't get along with Warren Beatty, the star, and he received practically no direction from director Robert Rossen. His fourth film, *The Young Lovers*, was another flop and sent Peter into a prolonged depression. His mind was full of things he wanted to say, but he was profoundly displeased with his creative output. He sank deeper within himself, began to shed the trappings of respectability he had so carefully assumed three years earlier and withdrew from the kind of society that approves of making movies for money even if they don't say anything. He moodily accused his sister of prostituting herself as an actress and loudly and repeatedly, as if trying to exorcise a demon, blamed his father for bringing him up to believe in hypocrisy and cant. As his troubles piled up again, he sought solace in the love-and-drug subculture that had begun to flower in Hollywood.

Henry Fonda, in the meantime, living alone in his New York house, had embarked on a busy schedule of picture making that kept him conveniently distant and thankfully aloof from the activities of his children. He had heard reports that Peter was experimenting with marijuana and that Jane was involved with "some French film pervert," as Vadim's reputation had him among many of America's old-guard movie people, but he had learned to roll with the punches and keep his displeasure mostly to himself.

After a month in the States, Jane was anxious to get back to Paris and Vadim. Her first tasks on her return were to make an English sound track for *La Ronde*, which was now being called *Circle of Love*, and to dub *The Love Cage*, which she had made in English, into French. Those completed, she and Vadim then left Paris for a quick trip to Moscow—a first visit for both of them. Vadim had long wanted to see the land of his paternal forebears, and his feelings for Jane gave him just the right romantic impetus.

Jane was at first reluctant to go—she still had the typical American's prejudice against Russia—but once she got there, she couldn't have been more astounded. She found Moscow completely different from what she'd imagined and discovered the Russian people to be almost the total opposite of what she had been led to expect. When she returned, she said, "I couldn't believe it. All my life I'd been brought up to believe the Russians were some alien, hostile people sitting over there just waiting to swallow up America. Nothing could be further from the truth. I was amazed how friendly and kind and helpful they were. My eyes were really opened to the kind of propaganda we've been exposed to in America. Every American should go to Russia to see for himself. They'd have a completely different idea of the people."

In interviews over the next few months she never failed to mention her discovery, but few reporters or publications printed her thoughts. As one editor said at the time, "Who cares what Jane Fonda thinks about Russia? We did her a favor by keeping that stuff out of print. The American people want to know about her sex life, not how noble she thinks the Russians are. If we printed that stuff she'd turn into box-office poison."

The trip to Russia had a profound effect on Jane, and no one who visited her in France that summer came away without an earnest lecture about how the American people were being fooled by their government, their schools and their press. She was feverish in her condemnation of America's ignorance of Russia and claimed that the United States' phobia was being fostered by the government solely in order to keep the politicians and military people in power. She saw the American paranoia about Russia and Communism—a feeling she admitted she herself had long possessed—as a giant hoax. In her view, the Russian people weren't aggressive at all. Sure, their government was just as guilty as the United States' in creating international hatred and distrust, but after all, the Russians had more reason to feel that way after what had happened to them in two world wars. If only the *people* could make the decisions about how they were supposed to feel toward each other, instead of governments!

It was the summer of the famous Tonkin Gulf incident. In May, 1964, President Johnson had received a secret thirty-day scenario from his advisers for graduated military pressure against North Vietnam that would culminate in full-scale bombing attacks. The scenario also included a draft for a joint Congressional resolution that would authorize the President to use "whatever is necessary" with respect to Vietnam. In June, top American officials met in Hawaii to review the war. Johnson at first resisted pressure from some of his more cautious advisers to seek a Congressional resolution; he secretly decided to step up the war effort without Congress' approval, despite his public pronouncements (it was an election year) that he would not commit the United States to a full-scale involvement in Indochina. In August two American destroyers, the *Maddox* and the *Turner Joy*, were attacked by North Vietnamese torpedo boats in the Gulf of Tonkin in response to Johnson's secret escalations. Johnson ordered immediate retaliatory bombing in the North, then got on television and solemnly announced to the American people that as a result of the Tonkin Gulf incident, he was asking Congress to approve a resolution pledging full support for U.S. forces in South Vietnam "to promote the maintenance of international peace and security in Southeast Asia." The measure, known as the Tonkin Gulf Resolution, was overwhelmingly approved by Congress. It opened the way for major escalation of the war and effectively gave the President the power to wage war without any further Congressional approval.

To Jane Fonda, just returned from Russia with somewhat of a convert's passion and exposed daily to the cynicism of the French over America's inability to quell the forces of Ho Chi Minh, the Tonkin Gulf Resolution must have been a puzzlement. Up to this point in her young life she had developed no strong political consciousness. Except for her natural compassion for the oppressed and her lingering schoolgirl's idealistic desire for justice and equality—both admirable qualities which she hardly ever expressed save through generality and cliché—she had never thought or acted in political terms. Suddenly she felt the stirrings of a political awareness. But unread and uneducated in this area, she was at a loss about what to do with it.

15. *La Liaison Dangereuse*

> *Vadim taught me how to live, the European way. He gave me a life in which there are no secrets between a man and a woman.*
>
> —JANE FONDA

AFTER Jane and Vadim returned from Russia they spent the rest of the summer in St.-Tropez, the old Mediterranean fishing port that had become the fashionable resort of French cinema celebrities. There Jane took up the casual life and quickly learned to overcome her natural possessiveness as various ex-wives and mistresses of Vadim trooped in and out. She became a surrogate mother to Vadim's daughter, Nathalie, now almost seven, and was quickly inducted into the international film set that headquartered itself at the Hôtel Tahiti. She loved the ease with which people moved in and out of one another's lives and admired their lack of shame or embarrassment in sexual matters. In her still strongly Calvinist view of things, this was a revelation; to be able to express oneself on any level without fear of rebuke or ridicule was the sort of freedom she had been seeking all her adult life. The honesty and directness of life—no matter how neurotic or maniacal it sometimes became—impressed her. Most of the Ten Commandments were in a state of suspension in St.-Tropez, but the Golden Rule prevailed. If someone coveted someone else's mate, more often than not the someone else would graciously step aside with Gallic civility.

"I'm terribly relaxed with Vadim," Jane said at the time, referring to him as always by the single name. "He is not a man who has to prove himself with women. He's known beautiful women; he was married to beautiful women. I would feel insecure with a man who had to prove himself, who was restless, who had things he hadn't done."

The French press was undone with excitement over what it punningly called *la liaison dangereuse*. Soon it demanded to know when Jane and Vadim would marry. Jane had retracted her "marriage is obsolete" announcement of three years before and was now conceding that she intended to marry some time. But she denied any wish to marry Vadim. "I love Vadim," she said. "He's wonderful fun to be with. He's taught me enormously, but why in heck should I marry him? His two marriages ended badly. I'm not at all sure he's made for family life, and I'm not sure of myself either, at this stage. So why spoil an almost perfect relationship by introducing a new element into it, such as the official ties of marriage?"

Her friends believed she was sincere, but the press remained unconvinced. *La Ronde* was due to open soon in France. The opening of every one of Vadim's pictures had been preceded by a spate of publicity, and the newshawks were sure that an official Fonda-Vadim union would be the launching pad for *La Ronde*. Actually, Vadim wanted Jane to marry him, but she still did not trust her feelings about him. She needed more time. As for Vadim, he was content to wait. "If all goes well, one day we will get married," he said.

"I told Jane," Vadim has said of their early days together, "that I am incapable of making love to one woman all my life. 'If I have a sex adventure,' I said, 'I will not lie to you. But one thing I promise you—it will not be important. I could not have a mistress. Also I will not behave in public in such a way as to embarrass you, because it will not be an *élégance* to you.'"

Jane not only accepted this, but made similar vows. Vadim, with his abiding need for sexual variety and his detached, professorial approach to sexual technique and sensation, taught Jane to rid herself of her American preoccupation with the meaning and significance of the sex act and to relax and enjoy sex for its own sake. To him, a lover of expertly prepared and leisurely taken meals, a sexual encounter was like sitting down to a fine dinner. It should be anticipated and enjoyed with the same delectation. It was not long before Jane, her enthusiasm for rooting out all the inhibitions of her psyche still at high pitch, took Vadim's hedonistic philosophy as her own.

Jane spent most of the fall in the countryside outside Paris. Although she didn't want to marry, she was now deeply in love with Vadim and was willing to suffer his idiosyncrasies—his financial irresponsibility and his sexual adventurism—in exchange for the emotional security and authority he provided her. She foresaw a long, if not lasting, relationship and found no impediment to establishing a household with him. Once her love was established and operating in high gear, her domestic juices began to flow. Like any young woman who believes she has found the real love of her life, Jane felt the instinctive need to wrap it in domesticity. This meant a home, a place where she and her man could live, not as two lovers having an affair, but as mates and partners embarking on a long life together. But they would need space—a house with plenty of extra rooms, where friends and family could stay, and land to give them seclusion.

Since they both were animal lovers, Jane convinced Vadim of the desirability of living in the country. In August she found a small, unkempt farm for sale at the edge of the tiny town of St.-Ouen-Marchefroy, forty miles west of Paris. The house, a quaint, run-down stone and tile-roofed cottage, was set on three acres of flat land. Jane fell in love with the house, the setting and the picturesque village and immediately arranged to purchase the property. Then she set out to restore the house to her own specifications and landscape the surrounding acreage. She worked at it with her characteristic energy and impatience, driving out from Paris almost every day to supervise the workmen and usually lending a hand herself. "The house had been built around 1830, and what really sold me on it was the color of the stone walls—a kind of beige honey color like an Andrew Wyeth drawing. I left the walls up, but completely gutted the inside and modernized it. I had to be there all the time to make sure everything was done right. But sometimes it got frustrating. Just try telling ten French workers, in your French, how to modernize a place and yet keep its original beauty. The land was flat, and there weren't any trees, so I had a bulldozer come in to move the earth around and give it a more rolling effect, and I had dozens of full-grown trees brought out from Paris and planted. It was wild—every morning you could see these lines of trees advancing up the road like Birnam Wood coming to Dunsinane."

Work on the farm was interrupted in November by a summons from Hollywood. Jane had earlier signed with Columbia Pictures to star in the film version of a little-known comic novel by Roy Chanslor called *Cat Ballou*. Production was ready to start, so Jane dropped everything at St.-Ouen and, with Vadim, left for California.

Cat Ballou might have been most notable for the giant boost it gave to the career of Lee Marvin, up to then a good, reliable secondary screen villain, but it would also prove to be the first unqualified hit for Jane Fonda. The picture was a raucous, freewheeling Western farce that spoofed every cliché its makers could think of. Marvin was cast as the most sinister badman of them all—a hard-drinking outlaw with a silver nose (his own having been bitten off in a fight) and a drunken horse. As Kid Shelleen, the hollow shell of a once-feared gunfighter he would win top stardom and an Academy Award for his performance. Jane played Cat Ballou, the very model of a demure Old West heroine—except that the sweet schoolmarm turns out to be as handy with her guns as any Wyatt Earp of movie history when she teams up with the Kid to avenge her father's murder at the hands of local land busters.

Jane acquired a house in Malibu and stayed there with Vadim while the picture was being shot. When the company moved to Colorado for location filming, Vadim went along. It was the first hard knowledge Hollywood had that Jane was living with Vadim, and the film community was abuzz with gossip. "Jane Fonda and Roger Vadim are an item," Hedda Hopper wrote a bit belatedly. "The British would discreetly refer to them as 'Jane Fonda and friend,' but Hollywood calls Vadim 'Jane Fonda's boy friend.'" Most of the gossip was not this benign, however; the people who cared about such things recalled Jane's strange relationship with Andreas Voutsinas during her last prolonged stay, and stories quickly circulated describing weird, erotic, nocturnal goings-on at Jane's beach house.

Most of Hollywood was convinced that Jane brought Vadim with her to promote his fortunes among American filmmakers and to establish him as a director. *Joy House*, the picture Jane had made with Clement, had been released, and Jane was thoroughly lambasted by the critics. There was a great deal of resentment toward her in Hollywood—on the part of the young because of her easy success as the daughter of Henry Fonda, and on the part of the older denizens because of her outspoken, independent views. Her few critical successes had been frowned at, and her more frequent failures secretly applauded. The complete debacle of *Joy House* lifted the spirits of those who wished Jane ill, and because the film was French and laden with murky sexuality, the gossipmongers were more than willing to believe that Jane had allowed herself to be seduced into a life that was as aberrant as that on the screen. Jane, of course, still thin-skinned when it came to gossip, grew angry and defensive, claiming her relationship with Vadim was "nobody's damn business but my own."

People who were close to Jane—mostly actors she had known during her Strasberg days who were now working in movies—drew another picture. "Jane and Vadim were really in love," says one, recalling a visit with them. "He treated her with deference and affection, and she was prouder than a peacock of him. From the stories I'd heard, I expected to walk in on an orgy, and to tell the truth I was a little disappointed to find everything so quiet and domesticated. Jane was really into cooking in the French style, and I envied the kind of relaxed, European ambience she created. Vadim was lovely—quiet, but with lots of personality and charm."

"I hadn't seen Jane in some time," remembers another. "I was surprised at the changes she had gone through. She was still high-strung and nervous, she still had that quiver in her voice, but she was much more open than before, and had a kind of serenity that I'd never seen. I'd say the reason she was so good in *Cat Ballou* was that she was really grooving on Vadim. She was enthusiastic about the picture, and she was talking about herself and Vadim doing a film together here, and she was just very up about everything."

"There we were on location in the hills of Colorado," says one of the actors in *Cat Ballou.* "And here was this Frenchman in horn-rimmed glasses reading *Mad* magazine—all by himself, sitting on a camp chair on the mountainside while Jane was filming. They weren't standoffish at all. Between scenes, at lunch, they joked around with everyone. Vadim's a very friendly guy."

Jane's stay in California during *Cat Ballou* was uneventful. She gave few interviews and spent most of her free time introducing Vadim to the Hollywood she liked. She had been surprised on her arrival in October to find how much the film capital had changed since she'd been there last. There had been an influx of youth into all areas of the movie industry. Moreover, Hollywood was gradually becoming the headquarters of the West Coast pop music scene. Legions of young performers and musicians, all apostles of the increasingly popular rock-and-roll, along with additional thousands of youthful hangers-on, had flocked to Los Angeles during the past year. An amorphous subculture, based on the yet-to-be-articulated gospel of peace, love and psychedelics, was just starting to form in late 1964. Jane and Vadim were fascinated by it.

Filming on *Cat Ballou* ended in December, just before Jane's twenty-seventh birthday, and she and Vadim hurried back to France— she to check on the progress of the renovations in St.-Ouen, he to do preparatory work on a new film he hoped to make with Jane under the auspices of MGM. Operating out of Jane's apartment—she wanted to have the farm ready for occupancy by late spring—they started the new year quietly. Vadim watched Jane attack the completion of the farm with amusement. He cared little for houses and surroundings and possessions. Wherever he was, as long as he had friends, good food and wine and conversation, he was content. But he indulged Jane's impatient perfectionism in organizing the farm and marveled at her industriousness and enthusiasm.

However quietly 1965 started for Jane, it would become the most tumultuous year of her life. Vadim's French producers had found an American distributor for *La Ronde*—Walter Reade-Sterling, Inc.—and the film was due to be released late in March under the title *Circle of Love*. In February Jane was called back to Hollywood to discuss the possibility of making a film with Marlon Brando. Had it been any other project, she probably would have passed it up. But she had long been eager to work with the mercurial actor, and when her agent, Dick Clayton, who had succeeded Ray Powers at Famous Artists, told her she had a good chance to get the female lead in Brando's forthcoming film, she rushed back to California with Vadim to lobby producer Sam Spiegel. Spiegel had announced plans to make a film called *The Chase* with Brando as his star and was using the time-honored publicity device of conducting a "nationwide search" for the right actress—known or unknown—to play opposite Brando in the picture.

While Jane was preoccupied in Hollywood, the Reade-Sterling organization was preparing for the premiere in New York of *Circle of Love*. The opening was scheduled for March 24 at the De Mille Theatre on Broadway. During the first week of March, the distributors unveiled an eight-story-high billboard over the theater to announce the movie. On the billboard was a huge, lifelike figure of Jane, hair tousled, lying on a bed in the nude and gazing seductively across Broadway at another billboard advertising the film *The Bible*.

Stories about the billboard immediately hit the newspapers and newsmagazines. Humorous or outraged articles, often illustrated with pictures, were printed throughout the nation. Earl Wilson, a syndicated gossip columnist, took a particularly scandalized tone when he described it: "You don't often hear a sophisticated Broadwayite shout 'THAT'S DISGRACEFUL!' But an old and trusted friend of mine . . . protested in those words when he saw the painting of Jane Fonda—her derriere amazingly bare—covering the front of the De Mille Theatre. . . . Numerous people—mostly women—have phoned in protests."

Wilson went on to wonder "what middle-westerner Henry Fonda

thought about his daughter's nakedness. Father Fonda flew to Spain the other day . . . just in time to avoid getting involved. Anyway, the word is around that oversexed movies are fighting for their life—that in films, at least, S-E-X is not here to stay."

Aside from revealing an uncertain gift for prophecy, Wilson succeeded only in providing Reade-Sterling with the kind of publicity movie distributors otherwise have to pay millions for. And Jane, when she heard of the billboard, immediately threw more oil on the fire. She announced that she was suing.

Dorothy Kilgallen, another columnist, accused Jane of being a party to the whole business and clicked her tongue disapprovingly over what she claimed was Jane's taste for cheap stunts. The fact is that Jane was genuinely shocked by the billboard—not so much because she was portrayed in the nude but because the distributors were promoting *Circle of Love* exclusively as a sex picture. At no time in the movie did she appear nude. True, she was in and out of bed a lot, and there were considerable suggestions of nudity, but she was never actually seen in the buff.

"To me," she said later, "*Circle of Love* had been a great opportunity to do a beautiful visual comedy and my first costume picture. They ruined it here—first that awful dubbed English and then that big poster of me nude! There was no such scene in the picture. In fact, I was never nude at all in the film. I resent that misleading and dishonest kind of promotion. Vadim resented it too."

Jane hired the prestigious law firm of Paul, Weiss, Rifkind, Wharton and Garrison to press her suit against Reade-Sterling. It was the same firm that would later represent Jacqueline Kennedy in her imbroglio over the publication of her memoirs. Jane's action did not take as long to resolve as the former First Lady's would, but the public followed it with almost as much interest. Jane's attorneys claimed that she had suffered extreme "anguish" and "shame" as a result of the billboard and demanded compensatory and punitive damages in the combined sum of $3,000,000. When Walter Reade, Jr., chairman of Reade-Sterling, was served papers on March 15, he declared he could "not understand what all the fuss is about."

Reade, making the most of the publicity bonanza, announced that "despite the legal differences existing between Jane Fonda and Reade-Sterling," he would host a champagne party in her honor following the press preview of *Circle of Love* and had invited both Jane and Vadim to come to New York for the event. He referred to Jane's lawsuit as "a woman's prerogative" and characterized the nude billboard as "an effort on the company's part to capture some of the adult sophistication contained in the film. We consider *Circle of Love* to be a brilliant adult motion picture and we were anxious that the sign convey this image."

In an amusing effort to forestall Jane's suit and to milk the event for even more publicity, Reade had a large, square patch of canvas draped across Jane's exposed derriere, thus drawing further attention to it and getting another round of pictures printed free in the newspapers. Jane was unamused. "It's more ridiculous than ever with that Band-Aid," she exclaimed. Reade was left with nothing to do but take the billboard down altogether, something he knew he'd have to do in the first place. The billboard came down, the dispute was eventually settled, and the movie died a quick death, with Jane receiving no better reviews than she had for *Joy House*. It's doubtful that more than a few hundred thousand people saw *Circle of Love*. Those who did pay to see it, drawn by hopes of catching Jane in the nude, were sorely disappointed. Yet the billboard remained fresh in everyone's mind. It was that, more than anything else, that established her as America's new sex symbol.

Jane was still in Hollywood angling for the co-starring role in Spiegel's *The Chase*. With two consecutive critical and box-office flops to her credit—flops for which she had been assigned a good deal of the blame—one would have thought that Jane was in trouble as an employable actress. But Spiegel's attention was caught by the publicity over the billboard. He liked controversial actors, even difficult ones. He dismissed Jane's bad reviews for *Joy House* and *Circle of Love*, contending that she had been misused and misguided by her French friends, and when he saw a rough print of her performance in the yet-to-be released *Cat Ballou*, he was convinced that she was right for *The Chase*. Spiegel gave her a contract early in April, and a delighted Jane immediately called Hedda Hopper to announce that she had just got the part of her life.

Spiegel's reputation around Hollywood was that of a producer who made few pictures but who, when he did make one, stinted on nothing. The screenplay for *The Chase* was written by Lillian Hellman and was based on a series of stories and a play by Horton Foote about intolerance and provincialism in Texas. Miss Hellman and Foote were both distinguished writers. Spiegel hired the tasteful Arthur Penn to direct the film, had Brando as his star and would be operating with a large budget so that the film would be rich in production values. Now he had in Jane Fonda, as he declared, the "right person for the right part."

"It's the most exciting and sexiest part any actress has ever had," he said at a press conference to announce Jane's signing. "Lillian Hellman has written many great roles for women, but she believes this is the best." Seldom had a Hollywood film project promised so much.

Filming was not due to begin for another month, so Jane returned to New York with Vadim to confer with her lawyers about the Reade-Sterling suit and to arrange to sell her apartment on Fifty-fifth Street. She'd decided to make France her home and to keep her house in Malibu as her American residence when working in Hollywood. While they were in New York she, Vadim and his daughter—who was visiting from France—stayed at Jane's father's house. Henry Fonda was in Europe filming *The Battle of the Bulge*.

Anxious to counteract the effects of the billboard controversy, Jane gave a few selected interviews while she was in New York. A different, more reflective Jane Fonda emerged. When asked about her relationship with Vadim, she clammed up, but one reporter raised her hackles with the suggestion that Marlon Brando would not like having Vadim on the set during the filming of *The Chase*. "That's a lot of bullshit," Jane replied with her first public use of a vulgarity. "First of all, Vadim wouldn't come on a set where I was working unless he was wanted. Second, he's a very close friend of Marlon's."

"You wouldn't characterize Vadim, then, as your coach—such as Andreas Voutsinas used to be?"

"No, I wouldn't," Jane answered curtly.

"Won't you say something about your relationship with Vadim?"

"No."

"You won't discuss it?"

"No."

When asked if she was going to get married, Jane said, "No, not at the moment. I don't guarantee that might not change tomorrow." The fact is that Vadim was pressing Jane to get married and she was wavering in her determination to stay single.

What about her attitudes? Was she still an untrammeled freethinker, not above trying to shock people? "There certainly was a time when I tried," she said, "partly to rebel against being my father's daughter and wanting to be accepted in my own right. But now I think I've made it in my own right. I don't feel the pressure to strike out with wild remarks. I feel more relaxed and tranquil than I did two years ago.

"I'm not a freethinker. I've never been particularly involved with bourgeois attitudes toward life, so I didn't have to rebel against them.

Well, I guess I have them to some extent as far as money is concerned. I wish I didn't. I dislike it—the general attitude in America that having money is sacred. It's like a disease, and it's something that bothers me about myself."

With these thoughts Jane was reflecting some of Vadim's ideas, although her interviewer didn't realize it. Vadim was not a man of strong political convictions. His view of the world was more of a cultural one, and he disliked societies built on an obsession with money. He saw the quintessence of such societies in America and had often held forth at length on this subject in discussions with Jane. He did not deny the virtues of modest luxury and leisure, but he felt that these could be achieved in other ways than through mass enslavement to money worship. It was for this reason that he was intrigued by the growing undercurrent of antimaterialism among American youth.

"What's the most important thing for a woman to remember in her relationship with a man?" Jane was asked.

She waxed long and pensively on this: "I think honesty is the most important thing and the thing that is most rare and difficult to have. So many of the relationships I've had and seen others have are really based on dishonest premises. It's the first thing to kill a relationship.

"From the beginning with a man," she went on, unwittingly defining her relationship with Vadim, "to be able to *say* everything, to be able to *hear* everything, to *talk* about everything, that's the secret. It's when you don't communicate, when you don't exchange, when you start sitting on grudges that you start harboring anger. Then the little things build up and really make it false. I see so many people living together where there is no love anymore. They just stay together and there is no spark of communication on any level. I find it absolutely appalling."

Explaining her reluctance to marry, she said, "I think a lot of the problem comes from women. . . . Women want to possess somebody, particularly in marriage. It's one of the main reasons I'm not married. I don't want to possess anyone . . . and I don't want to be possessed.

"I think the difference between a man and a woman is the difference between two stars that are as far apart as two different worlds. Women are down-to-earth, concrete, factual, tangible. Their concerns are quite different from those of men, who are much more abstract in every way. And this is one of the basic reasons for so much ill will between wives and husbands. It's very difficult to get these two worlds to meet. The ideal relationship is to recognize that you can't change it.

"A woman wants it *there* . . . wants everything in relationship to herself. I think it's glandular. We give birth to man, and we want him to come back to us. . . . Women don't have the kind of ambitions men do. When they feel a man is escaping from them they panic, they want to bring him back. The moment this happens the man feels trapped, and the woman feels frustrated. They drift apart, fighting it all the time. Yet you can become much closer in the natural apartness that exists if you know how to work at it. But it's difficult for me because I have that possessive instinct in me. I am always much happier, however, when I am able to truly—not just intellectually—respect that aspect of the man I love and not feel frustrated by it."

Jane's philosophy, derivative and half-baked as it might have been in the opinion of some, impressed many people when it appeared in print. It also confused them, fogging the image they had of a wild and conscienceless sex kitten.

Much of what she thought was the result of her own introspection and experience, but it's clear she was not an original thinker—this in spite of the allegedly stratospheric IQ attributed to her by her press agents, a bit of sleight-of-hand puffery to which Hollywood press agents habitually resort to give their glamorous clients credibility as superhumans. She was certainly intelligent, but her intelligence was considerably more derivative than singular, which is the plight of most mortals. She had a quick, pragmatic mind and a moderately humanistic sensibility that made her vulnerable to the plight of others. She believed in neither religion nor God and found what little spiritual nourishment she needed in rationalistic interpretations of the universe. Her concerns were almost exclusively with the physical, and her principal private concern was to give a tangible dimension to the mystery of her elusive emotions.

Her curiosity was almost boundless. But if experience and information equal knowledge, and experience and knowledge equal wisdom, Jane was still working, at twenty-seven, on the front end of the equation. Admittedly late-blooming and undereducated, she was a sponge for new information and experience. Her sense of discovery was keen and highly developed. With her character solidly cemented to her instincts, however, and her enthusiasm usually more certain than her knowledge, it often led her down the path of dogmatic reliance on the ideas of those to whom she was emotionally tied. This had become a pattern in her life—she had exhibited it as a youngster with her father, then with Strasberg, Everett, her analysts, Voutsinas and others—and it found its fullest expression with Vadim, who embodied a smattering of each of the men who had been important to Jane.

Both as a girl and as a woman, she had always had to identify herself in relation to the men in her life. Despite her public image, which oozed with freedom and individuality, she had very little individuality privately. Not only was she culturally forced to define herself in terms of men, like the most ordinary housewife she needed to—it was part of her nature, the result of twenty-seven years of conditioning. Her ideas were the ideas of the succession of men with whom she'd been involved but were wrapped up for public consumption, with the help of her personal glibness, as her own. She was sincere—she believed in what she said she believed in—but anyone who knew her well could tell that in a certain subtle way she was merely parroting her latest enthusiasm, usually learned at the feet of her man of the moment, in order to enhance her self-esteem.

The irony would be, in a life filled with ironies, that the very questing nature that drove Jane into her intellectual and emotional dependence on Vadim would eventually drive her out of it. But not before a painful apprenticeship in the mechanics of self-awareness.

16. Barefoot in Malibu

> *I haven't blown my full wad on the screen or in my personal life yet. But thanks to Vadim, I'm loosening.*
>
> —JANE FONDA

THE beach colony at Malibu is half an hour and several light-years away from the suburban splendor of Beverly Hills. It is a sort of West Coast–St.-Tropez where life proceeds with the barefoot and faintly bohemian insouciance that characterizes hip beach colonies all over the world. The town of Malibu itself is situated on the busy Pacific Coast Highway, but an access road slips off the highway and leads past a small shopping center to the beach. Along this road, which runs close and parallel to the curving Pacific shoreline, is the colony—a long row of smallish, tightly crowded houses of varying designs and styles that look out on the narrow strip of sand and the rim of the world beyond. When they returned from New York in May, Jane and Vadim, along with Nathalie, settled into her modest house on the beach side of the road.

With "the part of my life" and playing in a cast of superb professionals, Jane knew that she would have to give the performance of her career in *The Chase*. She was both intrigued and terrified by the prospect of acting with Brando. She found him "just about the sexiest man of all time," but she knew that appearing in the same film with him was, from a career point of view, difficult and dangerous. He had a way of filling up the screen and making whoever else was in his films appear wooden and inconsequential. He was a master of stillness. Other actors acted; Brando simply existed as a monumental presence on the screen. The expressiveness and delicacy of his emotions were without peer, but his forte was his indelible identity. Jane not only would be acting with him, then, but would be competing against him.

Brando was the most universally admired of all American film actors, but in 1965 his career was in steep descent. Following his early successes, he had left behind him a string of pictures which were interesting for his presence but otherwise of little moment. The better part of screen acting is in the reacting, and Brando's performances were regularly stifled by having so little to work against. His depictions of grief, anguish, despair, comedy and violence often seemed isolated and without any anchor outside his own personality. With his powerful naturalism confined to a vacuum, his acting had become hollow and narcissistic.

Yet he was still a magnetic and beguiling performer, and by 1965 he was desperate for a film role that would revitalize his career. As the idealistic, tragic Texas sheriff in *The Chase*—a role that fitted his private character like a glove—he thought he had found it. He was determined to make the most of it, and soon his demanding perfectionism dominated the preparations and filming of the picture.

When they first met to discuss *The Chase*, Jane was awed by Brando's authoritative confidence. "I was there when he came in for the first time to discuss the script. He will not settle for anything less than the truth. He wants to get at the root of something—not in the way most actors do, in terms of their own part, but in terms of the entire script. If he senses something is wrong, he cannot agree to do it. People say he's difficult . . . I suppose he is sometimes, but he won't settle for something less than what he feels is right. I don't have that kind of courage, and that's why I admire him so much."

Admire him she did, but she was unable to quell the sense of inadequacy she felt playing opposite him. As filming progressed into the summer of 1965, she grew less and less happy with her role and was nagged by the undercurrent of helplessness that was building in her. Away from the cameras Brando was sociable and sympathetic, and Jane was particularly attracted by his smoothly articulated social concerns— he was already involved in the movement to restore the civil rights of American Indians—but on the set he was no help to her at all with his critical, fussy, convoluted approach to their scenes.

The Chase was an allegory, heavily larded with symbolism, about the greed and hypocrisy of American society as reflected in a small, contemporary Texas town. The central character is a reluctant sheriff— Brando—who tries to bring in alive, against the will of the bigoted, lynch-minded townspeople, a local escaped convict falsely accused of murder. Jane Fonda was cast as Anne Reeves, the young low-life wife of the convict, who was played by Robert Redford. She is having an affair with the weakling son of the town's richest oligarch. Her paramour, acted by James Fox, is also an old school friend of Jane's convict-husband. As the story unfolds, Jane and her lover are co-opted by Brando into going out and trying to talk her husband into surrendering peacefully. In the ensuing action, which is thick with bloody violence and embellished by a symbolic holocaust (America consuming itself in the flames of its own provincial lust), Jane loses both her lover, who is killed in the fire, and her husband, who is shot down in cold blood by a local bigot on the steps of the jail as the heroic, battered Brando brings him in.

Despite the promise the film held, which was on the order of a classic like *The Ox-Bow Incident*, it bogged down in literary melo-drama, complete with a modern-day version of an ancient Greek chorus. From a production point of view it was first-class and was filled with rich detail, but its dices-loaded, shortcut appeal to liberal sympathies was as transparent and predictable as its characters were stereotyped. Jane's role was less than what it seemed when she signed for it, and she became in the end nothing more than a featured player with only a few fleeting scenes opposite Brando.

In June, while Jane was deep in *The Chase*, *Cat Ballou* opened. She was nursing high hopes for *Cat Ballou*. But it was the first time such a movie had been made, and along with everyone else connected with it, Jane feared that its Tom Jones approach to the Old West might not sit well with critics and audiences. Her fears were quelled by the flood of critical acclaim. The picture was hailed as a masterpiece of satire. Lee Marvin's notices were delirious in their unqualified praise, and Jane's were almost as glowing.

"In a performance that nails down her reputation as a girl worth singing about," wrote *Time* magazine, "actress Fonda does every preposterous thing demanded of her with a giddy sincerity that is at once beguiling, poignant and hilarious." It was the first performance in the nine films Jane had made that *Time* gave her its unqualified approval. And even Judith Crist, theretofore one of Jane's most caustic critics, smiled on her. "Well, let's get those old superlatives out," she wrote in the New York *Herald Tribune*. "Jane Fonda is just marvelous as the wide-eyed Cat, exuding sweet feminine sex-appeal every sway of the way. . . . This Cat Ballou is just a honey."

Jane was pleased, but she took her success calmly. Famous Artists was delighted, for *Cat Ballou* made her a full-fledged box-office attraction and pushed her future worth into the $300,000-per-picture range. Vadim was delighted, not just for Jane but because it eased his way with MGM for the new picture he was planning to do with her. Sam Spiegel and Columbia were delighted, because it meant that Jane would be almost as big a draw as Brando when it came time to release *The Chase*. But for Jane, still trying to keep up with Brando and master her role in *The Chase*, the praise was anticlimactic. She had known all along that she was a first-rate film actress, and she was too much of a veteran to be overly impressed by reviews. She viewed herself as a professional now and took the professional's clinical detachment about her performances. She had done things in *Cat Ballou* that she hadn't liked, and her discussions revolved more about these than what she had done well.

When Jane and Vadim settled in Malibu in May, their life together started off quietly. It was not long, however, before they were full-fledged Malibuites. At first, Vadim was more of an attraction than Jane. With his Bardot-Stroyberg-Deneuve reputation, his notoriety was more interesting than the conventional fame of the many film celebrities who lived in Malibu. Everyone was anxious to get to know him, and he obliged by being friendly and interested in them. He was still much more outgoing than Jane, and since he liked nothing more than a houseful of people, Jane was soon holding the same kind of perpetual party she remembered the Strasbergs running seven years before. By July much of Malibu's social life centered on Jane's house, and the colony soon became an outpost of the international film set. They had a constant stream of visitors, both from down the beach and abroad, and on weekends the house overflowed with people. Two of the more frequent visitors were Peter Fonda and his wife, Susan.

Peter had not made a movie since his last flop, *The Young Lovers*, the year before, and his film career seemed to be dying on the vine. When she returned to California for *The Chase*, Jane was upset to learn of her brother's almost-suicidal depression over his stalled ambitions. Since Peter was still not getting along with their father, her sisterly compassion, buried for the last few years as she struggled with her own problems, was reawakened. She was fairly secure now in her own career and serenely happy with Vadim, so she sought Peter out and tried to make peace with him. She sympathized with his problems, encouraged him to pursue his own destiny without regard to constant worry about what their father would say and tried to channel his white-hot rebelliousness toward constructive goals. He responded to Jane like a lost puppy finding its master again.

Since the failure of his last film, Peter had lost all interest in his pretentious Beverly Hills life-style. In February, he was in Tucson visiting his best friend, Eugene "Stormy" McDonald, heir to the $30,000,000 Zenith electronics fortune, when McDonald was found shot to death with his wrists slashed. A coroner's jury declared it a suicide, but decided that since a large stash of marijuana was found in the dead McDonald's apartment, Peter should be given a lie-detector test. Nothing ever came of it, but Peter was awarded some nasty headlines. The death of McDonald left him severely shaken—the three people he had loved most in his life had killed themselves. As an antidote to his despair, he began to cultivate the friendship of some of the young actors and musicians who were at the forefront of Hollywood's new dope-and-music culture.

Peter first tasted marijuana in London with Robert Mitchum's son, Jim, while making *The Victors* in 1963. By mid-1965 he was using it regularly and was pursuing the new youth culture with the zeal of an early Christian discovering Christ. He wore tinted motorcycle goggles and let his hair grow until it curled around his chin. He took to wearing cowboy boots and crash helmets and military caps with tuxedos, to living on raw eggs, bananas, milk and Bosco swirled up in a Waring Blendor and to talking in the jargon of the new hippie subculture. He spent much of his time learning to play the guitar and composing life-affirming folk songs.

Peter approached his first meeting with Vadim expecting to dislike him. He was surprised to find the Frenchman gentle and sympathetic, not at all like his reputation. Vadim treated him like an adult and showed a sincere interest in Peter's marijuana-oriented convictions about how life should be led. The two quickly became friends, and soon Peter was a regular visitor to the house in Malibu.

Jane's old friend Brooke Hayward had married Dennis Hopper, an actor they both had known in Lee Strasberg's classes. Hopper was a sensitive, alternately frenzied and brooding young man who modeled his style, both personal and professional, after that of James Dean, with whom he had appeared in the movie *Giant*. He'd had a modest success as a film actor, but by 1965 his personal eccentricities made him virtually unemployable in the eyes of conventional Hollywood filmmakers. Like Peter Fonda, Hopper was a convert to the new drug culture and a frequent visitor to the Fonda-Vadim beach house. The two formed a friendship and eventually a partnership that would revolutionize Hollywood filmmaking.

Another visitor to Jane's house, though not a frequent one, was her father. In Hollywood to make a new picture, he was angry about the malicious gossip floating around among his acquaintances about Jane's unusual living arrangements with Vadim. He and Jane had been in infrequent communication during the past few years. He had gamely tried to ignore the jibes of his two children and had stopped talking to the press about them, but now, hearing about Peter's public conversion to marijuana and Jane's romance with Vadim, he was nettled all over again. And curious.

"One day the phone rang," Jane recalls, "and it was Dad saying he wanted to come over. He had never met Vadim, and he wanted to dislike him. He came into our house expecting God knows what after all the things he had heard, an orgy, I suppose. But there I was slopping around in blue jeans and Vadim was sitting out on the deck, fishing, one of Father's passions in life." Fonda was as surprised as everyone else to find Vadim friendly and likable. But he was still of another generation; he could not countenance Jane and Vadim's living together without being married.

Jane had at last reached a tentative accommodation with life—at least as far as her feelings about her father were concerned—and much of this was due to the influence of Vadim. She no longer felt the need to strike out against Henry Fonda's disapproval and was even beginning to have sympathy for him. Looking back on it, she said, "You're an adult when you can see the very definite stages in the relationship with your parent.

First of all, there is complete worship, when you believe everything he says. Second is the time when you discover, 'My God, he makes so many mistakes,' and you start blaming him for the trouble you have. Third is the period you go through, at least I went through, of absolute rigid condemnation, which is a justification of having to find your own identity. Fourth, maturity comes when you can look at the relationship with your parent objectively. Mistakes were made, but, hell, nobody's perfect."

Throughout the summer Jane was continually touched by Vadim's sympathy for her father. A father himself, Vadim liked and admired Henry Fonda and found a sadness in his estrangement from his children. He was not the type to interfere in the relationships of others, but he philosophized about Jane, Peter and their father in such a melancholy way that Jane was soon willing to take part of the blame for the estrangement herself. She began to look at her father differently from the way she had before. She realized that she loved him a great deal more than she'd been willing to admit and that she'd outgrown much of her willfulness and resentment without even realizing it.

Jane had not given up analysis, but by now she was much less dependent on it and was visiting her West Coast therapist only on occasion. She had achieved a certain level of confidence and assertiveness in her life (which was what most people seek from psychotherapy), and her relationship with Vadim was having a much healthier effect on her state of mind than the probing of analysis. She had been taking a steady diet of addictive pills, all properly prescribed, during the past few years—amphetamines for energy and weight control, antidepressants for psychic support—but was growing much less dependent on these as well. Her serenity during the summer of 1965, coupled with her newly discovered feelings about her father, were such that she was considerably more amenable to the idea of marrying Vadim than she had been previously. It was not doubts over her feelings about Vadim that had kept her from marrying him. It was simply the fact that Vadim was already twice divorced. In Jane's practical view of things, this suggested a restless and impermanent nature. She was perfectly content to live with him for as long as he remained interested in her, but having grown up with a frequently divorced father and seen the effects on the women involved, she was intensely wary of marriage—especially with a man who had the same kind of record as her father.

But Vadim was still pressing, and for different reasons, so was her father. The two men were remarkably alike, not only physically, but in the quality of sadness and personal failure that had marked their lives. They both appealed to the same sensibilities in women—the maternal impulse to alleviate a man's innate helplessness and to ease his way in the world. As Jane went through her sharp change of feelings about her father, she found herself with a desire to reverse his unhappiness over herself and Vadim. She thought the best way to do this might be to get married. Her father was still noncommittal in his own feelings about Vadim, but at least he would approve of the legalization of their relationship. Once it achieved that basis, Jane thought, her father would then be free to like Vadim without reservation, and that was important to her. So, overcoming her misgivings about the likely impermanence of their marriage and privately vowing to do as much as she could to make it permanent, Jane told Vadim she would marry him.

Her decision was more impulsive than considered. In late July Vadim had left her in California and returned to Paris to work on preparations for the upcoming film he would be directing and producing with Jane as his star. She would follow him in another month, after her work on *The Chase* was wrapped up. Vadim wasn't gone for more than a week before Jane found herself moody and depressed. She missed him terribly, and to cheer her up, some of her friends began urging her to marry him. "Forget all your theories about marriage, forget all your misgivings," went the advice. "They're just the middle-class, bourgeois fears you've been fighting all these years. Stop hiding behind them and marry the man. Whether it works or not is beside the point. Why postpone happiness for fear of the future? Live for now."

Jane agreed and told Vadim over the telephone that she was ready, but that their wedding would have to take place in the United States so that their close friends could be there to celebrate with them. The delighted Vadim immediately flew back to California, bringing his mother with him. On Saturday, August 15, he and Jane chartered a private plane and with a load of friends flew to Las Vegas. In the party were Vadim's mother, Peter and Susan Fonda, Brooke and Dennis Hopper, French actor Christian Marquand, Vadim's best friend, and his wife, Tina Aumont, the daughter of actor Jean-Pierre Aumont. Also aboard were Robert Walker, Jr., and his wife, Ellie, who lived down the beach from Jane, actor James Fox from *The Chase*, Jane's cousin George Seymour, Dick Clayton, her agent, and Italian journalist Oriana Fallaci.

The marriage was performed by Justice of the Peace James Brennan, the same man who had married Cary Grant and Dyan Cannon a few weeks before, in a plush six-room suite on the twentieth floor of the

Dunes Hotel. Marquand was best man, and Tina Aumont and Brooke Hopper were bridesmaids. Peter Fonda played his guitar. Henry Fonda sent his regrets from New York, where he was starting rehearsals for a new play.

The ceremony was conducted with a tongue-in-cheek appropriate to its setting, according to *Look* magazine. "It was not just an ordinary wedding. An orchestra of female violinists undulating in skin-tight blue-sequined gowns played the wedding music. The judge was so disappointed when he heard the groom had not brought a ring that Vadim borrowed one from Christian Marquand. Jane had to hold her finger upright to keep the ring from slipping off. Vadim's mother, an energetic photographer, missed the ceremony because she spent her whole time taking pictures of Las Vegas." After the ceremony, the members of the wedding attended a striptease version of the French Revolution in which a naked woman was mock-guillotined to the music of Ravel's *Bolero.* They all stayed up the rest of the night gambling, then watched the sun rise over the desert through a haze of marijuana smoke.

To the press, which gave the wedding wide coverage—JANE WEDS BB'S EX read the headlines—Jane attributed her decision to marry to the fact that it made it easier to travel with Vadim's children, to register at hotels and, "Well, I guess because of my father. I knew I was hurting him." More recently, she has said that she felt weak and lost at the time. "I remember the day very well. I felt out of place. I had always thought that I would never marry, and instead, here I was, getting married, and saying to myself, 'I honestly don't know why I'm doing it.' I'll tell you, I was sleeping."

The newlyweds returned to Malibu the day after the wedding. Jane spent the following week finishing her work on *The Chase.* Then, early in September, she and Vadim packed up and flew to France, where they installed themselves in the refurbished farmhouse at St.-Ouen and continued preproduction work on their new picture—a film version of Émile Zola's novel *La Curée.*

Called *The Game Is Over* in English, *La Curée*'s story was a probing character study of the pampered and selfish young wife of a middle-aged French businessman who falls in love with her stepson, a young man about her own age. Vadim saw the film as an opportunity to do his first really serious work, and he toiled around the clock to perfect the script. He planned a picture lush with color and lavish with scenic decor. There would, of course, be plenty of sensuality, as there always was in Vadim's films, but for the first time in his career he was going beyond sex-and-nudity for its own sake. He wanted to use this picture to transform his reputation into that of a serious filmmaker.

With her confidence in Vadim complete, Jane approached *The Game Is Over* with more dedication than she'd shown for any previous film she'd done. It was a family affair. Vadim gave her a generous voice in its preparation and convinced her that her role as Renée Saccard, filmed as he intended to film it, would establish her at last as the topflight dramatic actress she had always dreamed of being. The role was a magnet to anyone with Jane's aspirations. She had proved herself as a comedic performer but had yet to play a successful dramatic part. Renée Saccard was an opportunity to get away from the clichéd dramatic heroines—the flashy trollope, the frigid wife—she had portrayed in her American movies. It was a chance to sink her teeth into a full-blown dramatic character, to paint a heightened and comprehensive portrait of a woman in love—her joys, her sorrows, her hopes, her fears.

The film contained several extensive nude scenes. At first, Jane was apprehensive about them, not because she didn't trust her husband but because she knew they would represent a contradiction of her earlier proclamations about never appearing nude. She'd had a fleeting moment of seminudity in *The Chase*, but that had been shot from behind and was more titillating than revealing—besides, in the Hollywood of 1965 the scene couldn't have been filmed any other way. She was anxious even about that, but with Vadim's encouragement she'd gone through with it. Among others, the scenes in *The Game Is Over* called for her to be nude with co-star Peter McEnery during a swimming-pool sequence and a bedroom lovemaking encounter.

When it came time to film the swimming-pool sequence, Vadim closed the set at Jane's insistence. Unknown to her, however, a free-lance French photographer had secreted himself on a catwalk above the set. As Jane doffed her robe to do a run-through of the scene with Vadim and McEnery, the photographer started snapping pictures. Whether he was there with Vadim's secret consent or not has never been determined, but when Jane later found out about it, she was livid. She was even angrier when she learned the photos had found their way into the hands of *Playboy* magazine and that *Playboy* intended to publish them.

Vadim, of course, was not beyond collaborating in such a stunt. And once he knew that *Playboy* had the pictures, he saw an opportunity to exploit the matter for all it was worth for the sake of the publicity it would bestow on *The Game Is Over*. Accordingly, he feigned outrage. He and Jane consulted her lawyer and shot off a letter to *Playboy* warning the magazine not to publish the photos. She claimed the pictures had been taken without her consent; if they were used, she would hold the magazine liable for damages.

During her stay in France for *The Game Is Over*, Jane began to grow more conscious of the political and social unrest that seemed to be infecting the entire Western World. With the crumbling of the French empire in Africa and the Far East, the voice of the proletarian intelligentsia of France—led by the old-guard Soviet-oriented Marxists and augmented by the newer student movement which derived its ideological inspiration from the Chinese Communist Revolution—found sympathetic ears throughout the country. In the early sixties the Communists and Socialists had taken for themselves much of the credit for the downfall of French colonialism. They transformed themselves—especially those of the student generation—from being the conscience of France to being the conscience of the entire West. They railed against the imperialism, racism and oppression they claimed were endemic to Western civilization and called for worldwide revolution and the liberation of all oppressed peoples from the undemocratic bondage of capitalism, which rewarded the few and exploited and enslaved the many. Out of this mix of political radicalism and opportunism came the *Nouveau Gauche Français*, or French New Left, whose ideological champions were, in addition to the Chinese, the Cubans, the North Vietnamese and Vietcong, the revolutionary blacks of North America and the homeless Palestinians of the Middle East. The radical impulse soon made itself felt in the French film industry as more and more filmmakers sought to couple the pathos and violence of revolution with their own romantic visions. *La lutte*, or "the struggle," became the focus of much of the new filmmaking being done in France by the mid-sixties.

Jane Fonda, who through her relationship to Vadim had already become friendly with many of the French cinema's leading left-wing celebrities—Simone Signoret and Yves Montand were two of her closer friends—admired the passion and conviction of their developing commitment to social justice. Nevertheless, Jane was still an American, and she found it difficult to reconcile her friends' political passion with their virulent anti-Americanism. Their tendency to blame the United States for all the ills of the world disturbed her, but her attempts to defend her homeland from their condemnatory generalizations were no match for their sophisticated and fact-filled arguments. Of course, there were inequities and stupidities in the American system, but there were many good things too, she would argue—only to have the good things discredited in a whorl of clever, rapid-fire logic. Jane was accused of having a provincial's view of her country; she did not possess the insight to see through her own nationalistic conditioning and perceive the evils the American system visited on the rest of the world. Wounded by their condescension, Jane took less to talking and more to listening during the long discussions that raged among the friends who visited the farm. On her own, she began to read some of the books whose authors she heard praised.

The second half of 1965 saw the first mass demonstrations against the Vietnam War in the United States. Inspired by youthful America's civil rights passion during the late fifties, an American New Left was in the process of birth in the early sixties. In 1962, a group of socialistically impassioned undergraduates and postgraduates from various colleges and universities convened in Port Huron, Michigan. Of this convention was born an organization called Students for a Democratic Society—SDS for short—which was led, among others, by a recent graduate of the University of Michigan named Thomas Hayden. Hayden was the principal author of the organization's manifesto, called the Port Huron Statement, which endeavored to analyze the relation of American capitalism to society's ills. He was elected first president of SDS and quickly became one of the principal theorists of the New Left movement, as well as an inspirational activist. Reform, rather than revolution, was the motto of the early New Left, and organizing—of economically oppressed class and racial minorities—was the methodology.

During the summer of 1963 two Buddhist monks burned themselves to death in Saigon to dramatize Buddhist protest against the repressive policies of President Diem. Pictures of the monks sitting stoically in pillars of self-inflicted fire repulsed America and turned the New Left's attention almost exclusively to the United States' involvement in Vietnam. Shortly thereafter Diem declared martial law throughout South Vietnam. Hundreds of Vietnamese students were beaten when they protested, further stirring the ire of the young American reformers. During the year after Kennedy was assassinated and the entire fabric of American life threatened to unravel, the New Left further concentrated its focus on Vietnam. And as President Johnson promised to contain American involvement in the war, all the while secretly escalating it and promoting an atmosphere of governmental equivocation, the Left appointed itself the voice of truth and conscience.

Jane Fonda, still filming *The Game Is Over* in France, had grown aware of the mushrooming undercurrent of protest and disaffection on the part of the young during her stay in Malibu the previous summer. Much of her direct exposure to it came from her brother and his friends. After she'd returned to France, Peter Fonda started to take LSD and was publicly extolling its virtues to anyone who'd listen. In November, two young, obscure American pacifists, emulating the Buddhist monks of Saigon, burned themselves to death in full view of the public at the Pentagon and the United Nations. Concurrently, the first large antiwar march was held in Washington. As these events were reported in France, Jane's circle softened its criticisms of America—at least of its youth. An atmosphere of celebration and congratulation permeated the discussions among Jane's leftist French friends. The events in the United States did not yet mean revolution was at hand, but at least it was a beginning. Jane suddenly found herself being praised for being an American. She was delighted and found it easy to identify vicariously with the expanding American political conscience she was reading and hearing about. She looked forward to returning to the States in the spring to make a new film and to observe at first hand what was happening.

17. *Hurry Sundown*

As for those things Jane said about me, you can discard them. She said a lot of things that she wishes she was dead instead; today she could cut her tongue out.

—HENRY FONDA

The new film was *Any Wednesday*, another of those coy bedroom comedies from Broadway. Jane played the young East Side mistress of a philandering, aging New York corporation executive, a role she could walk through blindfolded by now. Shooting was divided between New York and Hollywood, and when she arrived in California, she was astonished at the rapidity of the changes that had occurred in her brief absence. The pop music scene had become preeminent, practically everyone in the film industry under forty was letting his hair grow and experimenting with drugs, and Sunset Boulevard had begun to look like the main drag of a vast hippie commune.

Her brother had become a crypto-hippie himself and was deep into LSD and other mind-expanding substances.

When asked to compare the new American life-style to that of France, Jane said, "It's inconceivable that anything like this could happen in France. Whatever happens in Paris just happens in an intellectual way, it never goes public. Maybe the whole thing is just too far away from French culture and experience. In France, the middle class is everything. Everyone is essentially an individual. What's happening here springs quite naturally from a commercial culture. France couldn't and doesn't lend itself to what's happening here. Maybe the language has something to do with it. I come back here after a short time and everybody's talking differently. 'Scene' is out and 'bag' is in, or things are 'groovy' again. Can you imagine French accommodating itself to that sort of change? In French, argot is argot. It doesn't change." Jane left no doubt in anyone's mind that she liked what was going on in California. It was youthful, energetic, peacefully rebellious—all qualities of life that appealed to her. She and Vadim lost no time in exploring the new scene, with her brother as chief tour guide.

Since Jane saw him last, Peter's transformation had been radical. He had turned his back completely on his earlier way of life and was singing the praises of LSD, mescaline and psilocybin. He claimed the use of hallucinogens had helped him exorcise his demons and set him, finally, on the road to self-fulfillment. "As that first trip progressed," he told someone, "I thought more about my father and about my relationship with him and my mother and my sister. And suddenly I busted through that whole thing and related to *everything*. There was no more worry about my father, mother and sister. I began to feel really on top of all my problems. I had no further relationship with the past; I'd kicked it."

Jane's traditional pity for Peter turned to admiration peppered with envy. Her brother was shucking his guilts even faster than she had, and he was doing it in a considerably more dramatic way. He pursued his metamorphosis with a strength and single-minded intensity that left her agog. Where she had once had a subtle contempt for his weaknesses, she now praised him for being stronger than she was. She was proud of the initiative and leadership he displayed with his friends and admired the cool authority of his newly acquired manner. He was obviously becoming one of the leaders of the new, youth-oriented Hollywood. His and Jane's roles were reversed: He became the teacher, she the student.

Peter and his wife had their first child in 1964. They named her Bridget, after Bridget Hayward. By spring of 1966 Susan Brewer Fonda was expecting again. She was bravely keeping up with Peter in the changes he was undergoing and remained devoted to him. The only one in the family unhappy about Peter was, as usual, his father.

Henry Fonda had married for the fifth time the previous December. His new wife was Shirlee Mae Adams, a former airline stewardess he had known for some time. Just when Fonda anticipated some peace in his personal life—Peter seemed to have settled down, Jane had married and was sending out truce feelers, he was happily embarked on a new marriage—Peter began to make waves again. Fonda was shocked to learn of his son's involvement with drugs, but there was nothing much he could do about it except thank the heavens that the start of his new marriage had not been interrupted by another of Peter's crises.

Jane and Vadim were hoping to take life easy for a while and sample a little more of the new Hollywood after she finished *Any Wednesday* in May, but their plans were diverted by a call from Otto Preminger. Preminger was about to make a film from the best-selling novel *Hurry Sundown* and wanted Jane for the female lead. *Hurry Sundown* was a huge book—a multicharactered story about poor black sharecroppers and wealthy, paternalistic white landowners in Georgia. Its themes were race relations and civil rights in the changing South. Preminger had seen Jane in *The Chase*—in intention not very different from *Hurry Sundown* —and liked the way she handled her Southern accent. Jane jumped at the chance to work with Preminger in what she was sure would be a major motion picture. Vadim was no less enthusiastic. "Both of us consider Preminger enormously talented, dynamic, charming," Jane said. "He's one of the rare ones who can be a showman and an artist at the same time." She signed for the role of Julie Ann Warren, the dissatisfied, oversexed wife of the rich landowner who, as a result of a typical Preminger casting error, was to be played by Michael Caine, the English actor.

The state of Georgia refused to allow Preminger to make his film there, so the producer-director arranged to do it in Louisiana. Since the action of the book took place in a small town and its dusty rural environs, Preminger chose the area around Baton Rouge for the film's settings.

Along with the rest of the company, Jane arrived in Baton Rouge at the beginning of June. Rooms and offices for more than a hundred people were taken at the Bellemont, a colonial-style motel with a Confederate flag hanging in the sweltering heat above the entrance and a reputation for hospitality to movie people. But this was the first film ever made in its entirety in the South using black actors in leading roles (the two Negro leads were played by Robert Hooks and Diahann Carroll). A rumor spread that Preminger was there to make a film about "niggers gettin' the best of us white folk," and troubles immediately started. Tires were slashed on the company cars. Several cast members received telephone threats. The section of the motel where everyone in the picture was housed was like an armed camp, guarded around the clock by shotgun-toting state troopers. The actors, without exception, felt like the poor relations of an aristocratic family, hidden away from the plantation in seclusion and shame. Diahann Carroll, who rarely journeyed out after dark, said, "You could cut the hostility there with a knife. I'm not a fighter. I usually smile, then go into my room and cry my eyes out. But down there the terror killed my taste for going anywhere. Everything was supposed to be checked out before we got there. That was the company's responsibility. But they blew it."

St. Francisville, Louisiana, was chosen as the "typical Southern town" for the movie. With a population of less than a thousand, it was the kind of place where ladies still wore gardenia corsages to the drugstore, where men in ice-cream suits still sipped bourbon on their porches at sundown and where no one counted for anything unless his family lived there at least one hundred years. A fading remnant of antebellum decadence, it was white Protestant, old-guard and crumbling and was also the center of Ku Klux Klan activity in Louisiana.

To this town Preminger brought an integrated cast to film the story of post-World War II white oligarchy being outsmarted by poor-but-honest Southern blacks—a subject matter about which most white Louisianians were anything but sympathetic. Attitudes ranged from unfriendly to violent. On most film locations policemen are needed to hold back onlookers, but such was not the case with *Hurry Sundown*. "You never saw anybody," said Robert Hooks, who kept a diary of his experiences. "You could feel their eyes watching you behind lace curtains, though. Like they could cut your heart out." One prop man was sent to the local laundromat to dye some towels for a bathtub scene with Diahann Carroll and was chased out by a man waving a shotgun and screaming, "Get outta heah with them nigger towels!"

For Jane, the experience was eye-opening. Although she had already made a movie about Southern bigotry and of course had heard about it from others, she had never experienced it first hand. With infrequent visits from Vadim, she spent two tense, lonely months in Baton Rouge having her already liberal consciousness raised. "I kissed a little Negro boy on the street in front of the courthouse and the sheriff asked us to finish the scene, get out of town and never come back," she recalls. "We had this swimming pool at the motel, and I'll never forget the first day one of the Negro actors jumped into it. There were reverberations all the way to New Orleans. People just stood and stared like they expected the water to turn black!"

The cast's tension was abraded almost daily by the autocratic Preminger, who treated his actors like lowly soldiers in some grand combat scheme. Burgess Meredith, who played a cantankerous judge in the movie, said, "Preminger has developed his monster image because the only way he can control people he doesn't trust is to bully them. He thinks he's handling people, but he's only terrorizing them." According to Michael Caine, "he loves to embarrass actors in front of other people to tear down their egos. He's only happy when everyone else is miserable." Preminger kept the atmosphere in Baton Rouge as miserable as he could. He alternated between charm and top-of-the-lungs sarcasm and infected everyone else with his paranoia.

Preminger enjoyed his reputation as a cinematic tyrant. Unfortunately, his directorial techniques were equally heavy-handed. Running through the many films he had made over the years was an excruciating tendency to underline and belabor dramatic ideas and textual subtleties by means of self-conscious visual juxtapositions and symbols. As one critic said, "He makes films with a convoluted German syntax, the way Kant wrote philosophy."

For Jane, *Hurry Sundown* represented an interesting acting challenge despite the conditions under which she had to work. The part of Julie Ann Warren was her old nemesis—the sensual, highly charged dramatic character she had unsuccessfully wrestled with before in such pictures as *Walk on the Wild Side.* Under Preminger's weighty, humorless direction, she quickly realized that the character would be as obvious and stereotypical as in her previous American embodiments of it unless she added some other colors to it than Preminger had in mind. She worked hard on the characterization, consulting Vadim almost nightly by telephone when he wasn't in Baton Rouge with her, and produced a performance that at least partially managed to transcend Preminger's ponderous vision. She was helped considerably by what she had learned playing the role of Renée Saccard in *The Game Is Over*, and she invested Julie Ann Warren with about the only credibility of any of the Preminger film's characters.

Although her big scene, the scene for which the picture would regretfully be remembered, was a kind of lascivious encounter between her and Michael Caine in which she fellated a phallic saxophone between his legs—an example of the Preminger style of symbolism—she gave Julie Ann a sympathetic believability that held an otherwise fragmented and misconceived film together. It was by far the best acting she had done so far, with the possible exception of *The Game Is Over*, and she knew she owed it to what Vadim had brought out in her.

While Jane was in Louisiana, the August, 1966, issue of *Playboy* magazine came out with six pages of the unauthorized nude photographs taken of her on the set of *The Game Is Over*. They showed Jane, bare except for a flesh-colored bikini bottom, cavorting around the swimming pool with co-star McEnery, who was dressed. The photos, in black and white, were obviously candid-camera shots. The credibility of Jane's ire was compromised somewhat by the fact that the magazine also published, as part of the same feature, a posed, filtered, full-color nude photo of her that might have come from Vadim's own files. Nevertheless, she was furious, and as soon as filming on *Hurry Sundown* was completed in mid-August, she fled Louisiana and rushed back to Los Angeles to do something about it.

Her anger was due mainly to the fact that in *The Game Is Over* only her nude back was intended to be seen in the swimming pool sequence, whereas the *Playboy* pictures exposed her frontal charms to full view of the public. In the multimillion-dollar lawsuit she and Vadim brought against Hugh Hefner, publisher of *Playboy*, her lawyers claimed that "she has withheld from the public glare her nude person and likeness, and refused to permit any photography which used the exposed portion of her body." The suit claimed, among other things, invasion of privacy. Jane and Vadim argued that if an actress appears naked on screen, she does so as a fictional personality. But an actress appearing unclad and against her will in a publication—well, that was something else again. The suit was destined to drag on for months in the privacy of the courts, both American and French, but its early stages received a great deal of attention in the press, along with the pictures themselves, and Vadim happily found himself on the receiving end of another publicity bonanza for one of his forthcoming films.

He and Jane stayed at the Beverly Wilshire Hotel in Beverly Hills while they awaited word from their lawyers on the immediate outcome of the suit. While they waited, they planned their next film project together, a segment in a three-part French film based on the horror stories of Edgar Allan Poe. They also tried to interest Hollywood studios in a film version of *Barbarella*—a wildly erotic and popular French comic strip. "No," Jane replied to a reporter's question, "Vadim and I are not going to tie up our careers permanently. We will work together when it suits us, and when it doesn't, we'll work separately."

Jane was anxious to return to her farm. She was emotionally drained by her work in Louisiana with Preminger and the legal maneuverings over the *Playboy* pictures and was looking forward to the "joy of doing absolutely nothing until after the first of the year." Her father was in California with his new wife, Shirlee, to make another Western, *Welcome to Hard Times*. Shirlee Fonda—like her husband's two previous wives, just a few years older than Jane—was a simple, pretty, uncomplicated Midwestern young woman "completely without the usual phoniness of most stars' wives," according to one of Henry Fonda's friends. When she and Jane had a chance to get to know each other, it was Jane's opinion that her father had finally found an ideal wife. Shirlee was socially gregarious and in eight months of marriage had obviously loosened up Henry Fonda to the point where even he was beginning to enjoy parties and other forms of social life.

In spite of Fonda's new glow, *Welcome to Hard Times* was to become more than just another title in his long filmography. His son was probing deeper into Hollywood's youth-and-drug culture. The only film company willing to take a chance on Peter at this point was American-International, an exploitation organization that had started fifteen years before with a movie called *The Beast with 1,000,000 Eyes* and had worked its way up to *How to Stuff a Wild Bikini*. It was now involved in exploiting the new taste for drugs, sex and violence on the part of young American audiences. Peter had agreed to play a Hell's Angel type in one of several motorcycle movies American-International was making, called *The Wild Angels*, and in the summer of 1966 the company was promoting him as the leather-jacketed hero and spokesman of the new dope-and-violence generation.

On August 22, just after Jane returned from Louisiana, Peter was arrested along with three friends for possession of eight pounds of marijuana and nine marijuana plants, which were seized in a raid on a house he had rented in Tarzana. He was released in $2,000 bail pending a jury trial. With Jane's nude-picture imbroglio already front-page news, the newspapers jumped on Peter's troubles with the law and, again, the two Fonda offspring were the talk of Hollywood.

Peter was tried with the three other defendants. His defense was that he wasn't aware of the presence of drugs in the raided house. His case ended in a hung jury, although one of his friends, John B. Haeberlin, was convicted. Peter wore his hair long at the trial. He wore his funky clothes, his tinted sunglasses—everything his lawyer told him not to do. "I knew I wasn't guilty, but all my principles were at stake." Two women on the jury voted against him. He was not acquitted, because a felony charge required a unanimous vote; he could have been retried, but the prosecution decided not to pursue the case. According to the records of the Los Angeles Superior Court, Judge Mark Brandler dismissed the complaint against Peter "in the interest of justice" and on the recommendation of the district attorney. The recommendation was made for legal reasons, primarily because of the disappearance of an essential witness— a girl named Marilyn Caskey. In dismissing the complaint, Judge Brandler told Peter: "You acknowledged renting this house for your friend, John Haeberlin, and that you visited this house on numerous occasions. Large quantities of marijuana were found. . . . It is inconceivable that you were unaware of its presence." The implication was left that the judge thought Peter was guilty, but that to retry him would be foolhardy in the absence of a vital witness.

According to Peter's later version of the incident, it was a frame-up. He claims he was willing to be retried in order to prove his innocence. By dismissing the complaint, he says, "They thought they were doing me a favor, so I spoke right out and said, 'On the contrary. . . . If you want to play, I can play. And this one I'll really win because I know what mistakes I made last time.' " This was his public position. Privately he was told to shut up and consider himself lucky to have got out of it with nothing more than a dismissed complaint.

The younger Fondas' legal problems in the fall of 1966—Jane's civil, Peter's criminal—at first had a disheartening effect on their father. But he soon came to realize that the problems were his as well as theirs. Strong feelings of responsibility and family loyalty were awakened in him. He understood, finally, that his children's rebelliousness was not some kind of isolated aberration that existed without cause and of which he could continue to wash his hands. It was an expression of their natures, and their natures were refractions of him. He was beginning to acknowledge publicly that he hadn't been a good father. And without compromising his own principles, he was trying to understand Jane and Peter's attitudes and actions in terms of the effects he had had on them. His contentment with his new wife had opened him up considerably in the past year, and he surprised Jane and Peter, as much as himself, by standing up for them in their legal difficulties.

Peter's arrest and trial, for all their seriousness, had the salutary effect of bringing the entire family closer together than it had been since the Brentwood days. Fonda showed up at Peter's trial and said, "I'm here to give moral support and any other support to my son." And he meant it. He still sternly disapproved of Peter's activities, but he hoped the trial would be an object lesson for Peter and might contribute to straightening him out. "It shook Peter real good, that trial," he said shortly afterward, "and it should have. He's fine now."

Peter wasn't fine; he continued to proclaim his innocence, in spite of the inferences drawn by his trial judge, and proudly considered that by beating the rap he had won a kind of victory on behalf of the new generation over the Establishment. He was, nevertheless, pleased by his father's response to his troubles. Although he still couldn't talk to him in any meaningful way, he felt that the senior Fonda's silent support represented a breakdown in his previously uncompromising aloofness.

Peter was even more pleased at the way his trial brought Jane and him closer together. Jane zealously defended him in the press. She declared his innocence and announced that she was willing to back him for another trial. "I really dig my sister," Peter said shortly after the trial. "Probably a great deal more than she digs me, and she digs me."

During Peter's tribulations Jane was back and forth between France and the United States. She and Vadim discovered in September that their marriage was not legal in France because he had failed to register it with a French consul in the United States, so they planned to remarry in France the following spring. *Any Wednesday* was released while Jane was pressing her lawsuit against *Playboy*, and she was praised once again by the critics for her comedic talents. The movie cemented her reputation as an outstanding comedy actress, and she was immediately offered the female lead in the forthcoming film of Neil Simon's hit Broadway comedy *Barefoot in the Park*.

Shortly after she returned to California in the late fall to begin filming the Simon movie at Paramount Studios, *The Game Is Over* was released. The reviews were lyrical in their praise of her characterization of Renée Saccard and were no less praiseworthy of Vadim's contribution. "The performance by Jane Fonda is one of her very best," wrote Archer Winston in the New York *Post*. "*The Game Is Over* is a film of uncompromising artistry and originality," said Dale Monroe in the Hollywood *Citizen-News*. "It is Vadim's best picture to date and is unquestionably Miss Fonda's finest screen portrayal. The actress has of late demonstrated her agility as a light comedienne in Hollywood films.

The Game Is Over is the first opportunity she has had . . . to display her intense dramatic ability with such a probing, in-depth characterization. . . ." "Miss Fonda . . . has never looked so beautiful nor acted so well—and in undubbed French, at that," Gene Youngblood observed in the Los Angeles *Herald-Examiner*. Kevin Thomas in the Los Angeles *Times* called the picture "the finest film of Miss Fonda's career," and Brendan Gill, in the *New Yorker*, wrote, "Jane Fonda . . . has never given a better performance."

The redoubtable Judith Crist was one of the few who disagreed: "Roger Vadim firmly establishes Jane Fonda as Miss Screen Nude of '67 while equally firmly setting the intellectual cause of cinema back some 40 years. Seldom has such lavish and lush scenery, decor, flesh and photography been used to encompass such vapidity and slush. . . ."

Miss Crist notwithstanding, Vadim's promise to Jane that the role of Renée would establish her as an important dramatic actress had come true. Yet Jane's achievement in *The Game Is Over* was diluted by the film's nudity; it was not long before she discovered that it was her nude body audiences were flocking to see, not her dramatic talents. The knowledge left her a bit cynical about the intelligence of American filmgoers, and she found it easier than ever to agree with Vadim's philosophy about giving audiences visually provocative pictures and hedonistic themes. Accordingly, while she was involved in the making of *Barefoot in the Park*, she and Vadim intensified their plans to make another such picture as soon as possible.

To the press, Jane had become somewhat of an enigma. Reporters and gossip columnists had difficulty reconciling the Jane Fonda of American movies with the Jane Fonda of French films. An article by Gerald Jonas that appeared in the New York *Times* on January 22, 1967, reflected this. "Jane Fonda has managed to maintain two entirely different public images simultaneously between France and the United States," Jonas wrote. "Over here she appears in movies like *Barefoot in the Park* and *Any Wednesday*; she sounds and dresses like the pretty roommate of the girl you dated in college, and most people still think of her as Henry Fonda's daughter. Over there she stars in movies like *The Circle of Love* and the just released *The Game Is Over*. She sounds like the girl you eavesdropped on in Paris cafés; she undresses like Brigitte Bardot, and everyone knows her as the latest wife . . . of Roger Vadim."

By early 1967 Jane and Vadim were intent on making a film of the Barbarella comic strip. The forces that were shaping the new Hollywood had already become entrenched. Promiscuity, drugs and radical opinions, though previously enjoyed in secret, were now a matter of public record throughout the film capital. The national search for the innocence that had been lost somewhere in the scuffle of the Kennedy assassination, aided by the growing turmoil over the Vietnam War, was in the process of turning into a frenetic crusade and countercrusade between the old and the young, the naïve and the sly, the peaceful and the bellicose. Shortly after his trial, Peter Fonda became the image of Hippie Hollywood, and a poster of him on a motorcycle became the number one best-selling poster of this new media form. All the barriers of guilt and sin were coming down, and curiosity over drugs, unencumbered sexuality and other stimulants of the senses was given full rein. The time was ripe, Vadim and Jane thought, for a film that would repudiate the Christian sense of sin, celebrate and legitimize the new eroticism and depict a futuristic morality that would make the current concern over present-day morals seem absurd. *Barbarella* was the ideal vehicle, and as a result of the enthusiastic reviews Jane and Vadim received for *The Game Is Over*, Paramount agreed to finance the project. Dino De Laurentiis would produce, and filming would begin in the fall in France and Italy.

While Jane was working on *Barefoot in the Park*, Peter was busy on a new film of his own—an exploitative paean to LSD called *The Trip*. His co-star was Jane's old friend Susan Strasberg, and in the picture she and Peter both displayed a good deal of flesh. Peter had been absorbing Vadim's philosophy faster than the Frenchman could dispense it, and now there was only one Fonda who hadn't appeared nude on the screen—Henry—although he'd appeared in a bathtub scene in *Welcome to Hard Times*.

By 1967 the escalating war in Vietnam was becoming a central and heated issue in American life. Youthful reaction to it had hardened into widespread anger and frustration, and it was polarizing American society. The antiwar movement, started several years earlier by a handful of leftist students and old-time pacifists, had become a partly spontaneous, partly orchestrated nationwide resistance that featured flag and draft-card burnings and marches and rallies organized and coordinated across the country by the rapidly solidifying New Left leadership. The movement had formed into a broad coalition of special interest groups—the old Communist or radical Socialist parties left over from the thirties and infused with new blood, the newer revolutionary organizations of the sixties, black civil rightists, Quakers and other pacifists, hippies, adventurers and just plain social malcontents. As the American government continued to expand the war and the American Establishment continued to support it, they created a hydra-headed monster—the movement—that clawed deep gashes in the fabric of American life. And as the movement proliferated, new groups sprang up like crocuses until eventually just about every facet of American society was represented.

When Jane returned to France after finishing *Barefoot in the Park*, she brought with her the mild and fashionable antiwar sentiments most of her young Malibu film-industry friends were subscribing to. As the social libertinism of the New Hollywood began to mesh with the antiwar passion of the New Left in 1967, Jane, who was by then a strong and practicing advocate of the former, became a modest disciple of the latter. Back in France, commuting almost daily between her farm and Paris for ballet lessons, she saw evidence that antiwar fever was not just an American phenomenon but was as intense in Europe. Left-sponsored marches and demonstrations were held after each American escalation, all denouncing the United States. Committees to aid American military deserters were formed, peace rallies mounted, political seminars convened; anti-Americanism rose to a high pitch. As Jane listened to the speeches and arguments and diatribes and tried to sort out her own feelings, she began to see the United States in a different light.

The *Battle of Algiers*, a left-wing movie celebrating the liberation of Algeria from French rule, had become a popular manual of revolution and possessed an irresistible romantic appeal for anyone who believed that colonialism was a corrupt, anachronistic and enslaving system. In France, revolutionary guerrillas from every nation in the world were being hailed by adventurous, politically sophisticated youth—on a much wider scale than in the United States—and student agitation was considerably more intense. Jean Luc Godard and other well-known figures of the cinema were participating in rallies and turning themselves into film propagandists for various liberation movements, and the entire artistic and literary population of Paris was abuzz with revolutionary ardor.

The same was true in England, Sweden and Germany, although to a lesser extent. In England the actress Vanessa Redgrave was making speeches denouncing what she and others claimed was American imperialism and joining mobs that stormed the American embassy in London's Grosvenor Square. Jane, already an admirer of Vanessa Redgrave's talent, was deeply impressed by her uninhibited militancy and activism. Also the daughter of a famous theatrical family, Vanessa Redgrave became the model for Jane's first tentative antiwar activities, which were limited to attending a few Parisian rallies and listening to statistics-filled litanies about the numbers of Vietnamese the United States was killing, burning and maiming.

Vadim and Jane had long talks about the war between themselves and among their friends. Vadim, in his detached, wry way, had caught the French antiwar fever; even he was growing more critical of the United States. At first, Jane resisted the criticism. Then, as she has said, "he brought some things to my attention. For instance, when the Americans evacuated the village of Ben Suc in Vietnam and put the people in a concentration camp and completely demolished the town, Vadim said, 'Look what they're doing.' And I said, 'If they're doing it, they must have a reason.' So he gave me a book to read, a book on Ben Suc, and it upset me."

Jane and Vadim were remarried in a French civil ceremony at the town hall of St.-Ouen on May 18. Jane turned down the starring roles in *Bonnie and Clyde* and Roman Polanski's *Rosemary's Baby* so that she could remain in France, work on *Barbarella* and try to have a baby. By now she felt really at home in France. Thrilled by some good news from the States, she worked with her customary energy to make her marriage a success. Both *Hurry Sundown* and *Barefoot in the Park* had been released in America, and although Jane was generally ignored by the critics in the Preminger picture, which was harshly dismissed, she again won high praise for her work in the Neil Simon comedy. Arthur Knight, in the *Saturday Review*, wrote that "Jane . . . displays that she is in fact a charmingly fey, disturbingly sexy light comedienne, with an instinct for the timing and intonation of laugh lines that should keep her busy for many years to come." And *Time* called Jane's performance "the best of her career."

There was also disturbing news from home. Her father had gone to South Vietnam on a morale-building USO-sponsored tour. When he returned, he told a reporter, "Before I went, I wasn't anti-Vietnam—although I'm anti-card-burning and flag-burning, and I think a lot of the unwashed who go into these demonstrations are protesting for the sake of protest—but I was apathetic. Well, my eyes were opened. I discovered it was my morale, and America's morale, that needed strengthening, not the troops'. This has been said before—and I couldn't agree more—that every time there's a parade or peace rally in this country it will make the war that much longer, because this doesn't escape the attention of Ho Chi Minh. But I'm still a liberal. I don't feel I'm a hawk because I am for our involvement in Vietnam, and I don't agree that we should bomb the hell out of them. But you can't be there and come away and not at least feel, well, obviously we should be there and the job is being done and it's a good job."

When Jane read her father's remarks, she was depressed for days. She had tried to talk to him about Vietnam during her last stay in California, but he'd dismissed her ideas with his characteristic refusal to discuss anything he felt she was naïve about. And he believed she was naïve about Vietnam. He also thought her sympathy with the antiwar movement was simply another expression of her attraction to rebelliousness and unconventionality. She had tried to tell him what was going on in France and how the French felt about the United States' role in Vietnam, but he wasn't interested in hearing about it. Now, reading her father's remarks—and they sounded just like him—she resolved to learn more about Vietnam so that she could disabuse him of his Establishment views the next time she saw him.

If Jane was an enigma to the press as an actress—the sweet, funny girl next door in American movies, the sultry sex symbol in French films—her private image was equally baffling. Her marriage to Vadim absorbed her. The relationship had converted her from an anxious, uptight, frequently bitchy American girl to a calm, sophisticated, Europeanized woman. Vadim's freewheeling sensibilities had rubbed off on her to the point that she was as fully involved in sexual experimentation and fulfillment as he was. Indeed, since these pursuits were relatively new to her, she was more intensely involved, only because she had more in the way of restraint and inhibition to overcome. The idea of giving free rein to the senses and seeking pleasure, without guilt or responsibility, were almost direct contradictions of the philosophy Jane was brought up with. To take on her husband's libertinism as wholeheartedly as she desired meant a radical overhaul of long-ingrained instincts and beliefs. Yet she managed it in a remarkably brief period of time.

Not that the overhaul was complete or that she became, as they say, promiscuous. Vadim approved of infidelity so long as it was shared in, at least verbally, by both parties to a marriage. He was sometimes nettled, therefore, by Jane's residual prudity. Although she had learned to be amused by the complex sexual adventurism among their friends, she was still a one-man woman and found it difficult to derive any pleasure from extramarital liaisons, no matter how sensually exciting. "There are women who can make love and forget about it in the morning," Vadim said about her. "But not Jane. She is too . . . sentimental."

Her deepest happiness, aside from Vadim, came from her farm. Like her beach cottage at Malibu, Jane's house in St.-Ouen rapidly became open house to the highly mobile international film set. She loved playing the busy hostess. The visitor would be greeted by a howling pack of animals: countless dogs, even more cats and perhaps some impulsive ducks, rabbits and a pony. When Jane returned from trips, the dogs would leap on her in a scene that would have Albert Payson Terhune down on his knees sobbing.

Inside the ancient farmhouse Jane had created a modern, tasteful home with but one mild touch of the bizarre—a wall of glass that separated the low-beamed master bedroom from the bathroom, giving occupants of either chamber a clear view of what was happening in the other. "I almost drowned in the bathtub one day," Jane recalled to an interviewer. "Vadim came in wearing one of my miniskirts, and it was a disaster."

The element of surprise frequently manifested itself when Vadim was around. He had a wry, quiet sense of humor that delighted most in visual incongruity, and to him nothing was more delightfully incongruous than the sight of Jane entertaining Brigitte Bardot, Annette Stroyberg, Catherine Deneuve. Jane appreciated the irony, too, and claimed to enjoy the company of all three. "I know all Vadim's women," she once said. "I like Annette. I like Bardot. I especially like Catherine. Her little boy comes to visit us, too, often at the same time Nathalie's here. It's marvelous, having the children together."

It was the frequent presence of the Vadim children that got Jane to thinking about having a child of her own. She saw the farm as a perfect place for a child to grow up—it was much like the Brentwood farm of her own childhood—and although she and Vadim had decided when they first started living together that she didn't have any maternal instincts, her continuing exposure to the Vadim offspring made her realize they were wrong. "I was always terrified of having children. Being in analysis made me very aware of all the kinds of mistakes parents can make, and I was afraid I'd make them all too. But then I thought, well, at forty you may be pretty damned sorry you didn't."

By the summer of 1967 Jane decided that she wanted to try to have a child. Vadim, who loved children, was all for it. But first they had to make *Barbarella*.

18. Vanessa

So I got pregnant, and little by little, as the nine months went by, this evolution in me became the most important thing in my life.

—Jane Fonda

PAULINE KAEL, movie critic for the *New Yorker* magazine, captured the essence of Jane's screen appeal when she wrote: "Jane Fonda is accomplished at a distinctive kind of double-take: she registers comic disbelief that such naughty things can be happening to her, and then her disbelief changes into an even more comic delight. Her American good-girl innocence makes her a marvelously apt heroine for pornographic comedy. She has the skittish innocence of a teen-age voluptuary; when she takes off her clothes, she is playfully and deliciously aware of the naughtiness of what she's doing, and that innocent's sense of naughtiness at being a tarnished lady keeps her from being just another naked actress." Although Miss Kael was writing after the fact about Jane's performance in *Barbarella*, her description might have been a before-the-fact scenarist's blueprint for the character of Barbarella herself.

Movies based on well-known American comic strips were seldom as successful as their models, *Li'l Abner*, *Dick Tracy*, *Blondie*, *Little Orphan Annie*, *Bringing Up Father*, *G.I. Joe* being cases in point. Aside from the fact that cartoon characters do not lend themselves well to real-people portrayals, one element that was absent in all such pictures was sex—with the exception, possibly, of the harmlessly seductive glances of Appassionata von Climax in *Li'l Abner*. European comic strips were something else again. Perhaps because European film and book censors were stricter than those in America, many European comics became the focus of Continental sexual titillation. The strip most familiar in the United States was one that had been published for some time in the avant-garde New York magazine *Evergreen Review*. This was *Barbarella*, a sleek, audacious combination of science fiction and soft-core pornography that outraged legislators and churchmen alike.

Jane Fonda had been answering questions about being a sex symbol by disclaiming any interest in the office and denying that she ever thought of herself as one. "The overemphasis on identifying me with sex is pretty silly," she said. "I'm no sex siren just because I believe in approaching sex and the human body with honesty. Most of the women who've been big sex symbols have had problems in their own sex lives. They weren't so much women as female impersonators. It was a caricature. Look at Marilyn Monroe. She parodied femininity. I'd hate to think that my appeal was based on that kind of abnormality. I think the whole obsession with sex, and with the size of a girl's breasts, is a perversion—it's a sad comment on the state of manhood in America. The real homosexuals are the big tough guys who think they're so manly. All they're doing is hiding behind their fears. They all want to go back to their mothers' breasts, that's all. If you ask me, the whole business about sex is a sickness because it's dishonest. Everyone fantasizes about doing things they would be afraid to do in reality. That's not for me."

In *Barbarella*, Vadim and Jane saw a neat opportunity to exploit American movie audiences' sexual obsessions and parody their fantasies. According to Vadim, Jane would be playing "a kind of sexual Alice in Wonderland of the future." The picture would give them the license to make a kind of joint philosophical statement on the ridiculousness of the old-fashioned sexual and moral preoccupations of contemporary society, and at the same time allow Vadim to daringly glorify Jane's beauty and provide "a whimsical, lyrical outlook toward sex in the year 40,000 A.D."

Vadim put together an international cast and started filming in Rome during the summer. Opposite Jane as Barbarella, John Phillip Law, a young American actor who had played in *Hurry Sundown* and was a Malibu neighbor of Jane and Vadim's, was cast as the pure, blind Guardian Angel who looks after her as she gallivants from galaxy to galaxy in pursuit of righteous pleasure. With its far-out story and ethereal setting, the film required a great deal of ingenious and expensive technical effects to make it work. Not the least of these involved the picture's opening sequence, which required Jane to do an elaborate, sinuous strip in a state of weightlessness while the film's credits were run off.

"I was completely naked under the titles," Jane says, "and there's a funny story about how that happened. We were supposed to have a costume, but it didn't arrive. So we sat down and Vadim said, 'Listen, anyone who's read *Barbarella* expects her to be naked all the way through. And we're doing this as a spoof of the sort of pictures people *think* I make. So let's start off naked.' I agreed to do the scene naked, but Vadim promised that he'd cover my nudity with the titles. He did the titles once and I said, 'That's not covered enough'—so he did them again."

It was the most difficult and complicated film Jane had ever worked on. Rather than attempt to portray Barbarella in some surrealistic way, she played her as straight Jane Fonda—as American, one might say, as apple pie. She underlined the parody by taking things seriously rather than acting camp. The resulting contradiction between her fresh, bouncy innocence and the picture's lewd cartoon world of the future gave the character of Barbarella an unexpected fey sexuality that would have been leering in the hands of another, less subtle actress.

For Jane, the acting was easy, but the filming itself was filled with perils. The sets were complex, and the special-effects machinery often broke down at crucial, dangerous times. One scene called for 2,000 wrens to be blown by giant fans into a cage occupied by Jane, whereupon the birds would become so excited by the wind currents that they would peck off her clothes. For four days the fans whirred, the birds swooped, Jane emoted—but nothing happened. In desperation, Vadim jammed birdseed inside Jane's scanty costume and fired guns in the air, which bothered the birds not at all but drove Jane off to a hospital with hypertension, a fever and acute nausea. After three days of rest, she returned to work and finally completed the scene with the aid of even larger fans and a flock of peckish lovebirds.

It is a curious fact of movie-industry life that most arty, breakthrough films fail at the box office but have what their makers like to call a *succès d'estime*. Just the opposite would prove true for *Barbarella*—when it was released, the public lined up to see it in droves while the critics, except for a few who interpreted it as an expression of the high campiness that marked the times, lambasted it. "You could subtitle the film, *2001, A Space Idiocy*," Charles Champlin wrote about it in the Los Angeles *Times*. "Miss Fonda plays what you might call Flesh Gordon." Others saw it as "glossy trash" or "beautifully photographed garbage" and considered its only saving grace to be Jane's extended nudity and a witty, futuristic copulation scene between her and actor David Hemmings. "Vadim is the screen's foremost celebrant of erotic trash," Pauline Kael remarked, "with the scandalous habit of turning each wife into a facsimile of the first and spreading her out for the camera. . . .

Barbarella is disappointing after the expectations that one had of a film that would be good trashy, corrupt entertainment for a change. *Barbarella* isn't even good trash, but it's corrupt all right. . . ."

According to John Springer, Henry Fonda's press agent, about the time Jane was starting *Barbarella* his client received a telephone call from humorist and publisher Bennett Cerf, the head of Random House. Cerf's voice, usually spilling quips, was uncharacteristically sober. He told Fonda that he had just read the manuscript of a novel that an affiliate of Random House was going to publish. "It's just about the most scurrilous thing I've ever read," Cerf reportedly told Jane's father, "about an actor and his daughter, and the author has done everything possible to identify the characters with you and Jane."

"Does he refer to us by name?" Fonda supposedly wanted to know.

"No, he hasn't gone quite that far," Cerf is said to have replied. "But nobody will have any doubts about whom he expects the characters to be associated with." Cerf went on to tell Fonda that he had tried to talk the affiliate, headed by Bernard Geis, out of publishing the book. He wanted Fonda to know that when Geis refused to cancel publication, Random House had decided to sever its connection with the affiliate. "But I think you ought to read the book and see your lawyer," Cerf told Fonda.

Springer says that Fonda took the news calmly. "I don't want to read the book," he said. "I don't have time for crap like that. And there's not much point in seeing my lawyer—there have been enough scandal stories about us which actually *have* used our names in connection with all kinds of lies."

The novel in question was *The Exhibitionist* by Henry Sutton (a pseudonym for writer David Slavitt), and its publication caused more consternation in the inner sanctums of the publishing world than it did among the public. Slavitt, an entertainment writer for *Newsweek* and a man of considerable but unrecognized literary talent, was cynical about the huge sums of money being made by writers of popular trash fiction such as Harold Robbins and Jacqueline Susann. He bet Bernard Geis, an ambitious, aggressive new publisher who distributed some of his books through Random House, that he could write a best seller based on the same hackneyed formulas. Geis took him on, and in no time at all Slavitt came up with *The Exhibitionist*.

The tawdry story concerns a famous, aging film star, his equally famous film-star daughter and other assorted characters—all of whom are involved in a life of illicit and perverse sex. The character Bennett

Cerf identified with Henry Fonda was a lecherous, oft-married reprobate who at one point ends up paired with his own daughter during a masked-ball orgy and counts among his wives a beautiful European lesbian who, earlier in the sordid action, seduces the still-innocent Merry—the exhibitionist of the title and the Henry Fonda character's daughter. The plot details Merry's own rise to stardom. If Bennett Cerf saw similarities between the fictional Merry and the real Jane Fonda, he must have had a good deal more imagination about Jane's private life than anyone would have guessed. The similarities are so superficial as to be beyond recognition, except toward the end of the book when Slavitt has Merry meet a mysterious, erotic, totally impotent European film director who exploits her for his own perverted pleasure.

The book was published late in October, 1967, and became a modest best seller, helped along by the controversy started by Bennett Cerf and the subsequent public squabbles between him and Geis over what Geis alleged were Cerf's attempts to suppress the book. As an example of its genre, *The Exhibitionist* was several cuts above the ordinary. Although the convoluted plot was as ripe as anything from Robbins or Susann, its prose style was considerably more fanciful.

When she was asked if she had read it—an obligatory question in all her publicity interviews for *Barbarella*—Jane replied, "No, I don't read trash. I understand from my friends that one of the women the girl's father marries is a lesbian. Now the last kind of woman my father would marry is a lesbian."

In one of her interviews after *Barbarella*, at which Vadim was present, she was asked outright if she was an exhibitionist. Vadim interjected. "In America you are all so Puritan, so prude. You worry so much about showing the body. All actors are exhibitionists. I know, for I was an actor. But I suffered agonies as an actor, because I am *not* an exhibitionist. A voyeur, perhaps, but not an exhibitionist."

"Vadim," Jane said, as the interviewer recorded their exchange, "I don't think he means in a physical sense. He means, do I need attention?"

"Ah, yes," Vadim came back. "Well, you do exhibit yourself, as a kind of . . . experiment. You would not need to do this if you knew, really, who you are. But you do not quite know who you are, so you make tests, as in chemistry, to find out."

Vadim's comment was apparently an insight for Jane. "Yes, wow!" she said excitedly. "You're absolutely right. I never realized that until this moment—that I do in life exactly what I do when I act. I go through this extroverted, exhibitionistic period—talking like the character, and so on—as an experiment."

To the interviewer, she said, ". . . The identity I found as an actress is desperately important to me. Oh, I do feel about two hundred times more pulled together since I met Vadim, but if I had not had that identity to begin with, it might not have worked out at all. I'm certain that deep down, I *still* have no confidence. Really, that's no bull. If a situation begins badly, if I feel I'm being boring, or that I don't look good, well, I *crumble*. You want to hide, but the old ego won't let you. So you go onto a stage, or a screen, and hide behind the mask of a character. You're safe, but people are still looking at you. My father is like that. It has *got* to be the prime motivation of every actor—this need to express yourself sort of fictionally because you don't have confidence in your real self. That, and a certain exhibitionism."

Physical exhibitionism, the interviewer wanted to know?

"I'm not a physical exhibitionist," Jane said firmly.

But what about the nudity in her films?

"It certainly is not something I get any kicks from. I agree with Vadim about it. In each picture that I have been nude it was necessary to the text, to achieve the proper dramatic effect."

The question of public nudity had become a central one in Jane's life. In November, while she was making *Barbarella* in Europe, another controversy swirled around her in the United States, contradicting her disclaimers about being an exhibitionist. *Newsweek* magazine came out with a feature story on nudity and sex in movies. The magazine's cover was adorned with a seminude picture of Jane, although the story itself hardly mentioned her. The cover created a furor, especially among public school boards which approved the purchase of *Newsweek* for use in social studies courses. Cries of outrage were heard throughout the country about *Newsweek*'s libidinous assault on the minds and sensibilities of innocent schoolchildren, and the magazine was banned from many school libraries. Although Jane was somewhat of an innocent victim, the incident was another installment in the hardening of her sex-symbol image, as well as in the country's increasingly mindless polarization.

The United States was growing more intensely divided than ever. Martin Luther King's murder had inflamed the reformist spirit of young America—both white and black. Despair over the racial dichotomies that had produced King in the first place and were dramatized by his assassination, expanding anger with the government's intransigence about Vietnam, and an increasingly contagious romantic idealism that celebrated militant action and sacrifice rather than liberal theory and in turn provoked the government's repressive instincts—all combined to unite the disparate voices of American reform into an at least partially common cause. The true radicals of American society—the few Communists, Trotskyites and Socialists who had for so long been forced to maintain a low profile against the backdrop of the placid America of the two previous decades—found their revolutionary dreams infused with new life, new appeal and tens of thousands of new disciples from college campuses and hippie ghettos throughout the country. Out of the spontaneous social turmoil of the mid-sixties came new leaders—some pacifists, others proponents of violence—who saw in that turmoil the Old and New Left's long awaited opportunity to transform the American liberal conscience into a revolutionary reality.

The great march on the Pentagon in October, 1967, carefully planned and orchestrated by the New Left leadership, was the first mass demonstration against the war to draw Americans from all walks of life, not just radicals. Hallucinogenized hippies marched arm in arm with Bergdorfed housewives; doctors and businessmen in ties and vests mingled with scruffy radicals. The march became a media event, and from that point on sympathy for the antiwar movement began to permeate every level of the American Establishment. And as sentiment against the war coagulated—helped by the government's indictment in January, 1968, of Dr. Benjamin Spock, the celebrated baby doctor by whose theories millions of parents swore, on charges of counseling draft avoidance—anti-antiwar sentiments hardened as well.

In January, while wrapping up her work on *Barbarella*, Jane Fonda became pregnant. When she found out about it in February, she was at once elated and frightened. By March she canceled out of two forthcoming Hollywood films she had signed to star in, stocked up on copies of Dr. Spock and other child-rearing guides and settled in at her farm to await the birth of her child in September.

Although time, for a pregnant woman, usually slows to a crawl, for Jane it seemed to compress and speed up. Free of any concerns about filmmaking, she became more sharply aware of what was happening in the world. During the early months of 1968, student agitation at the Sorbonne and other universities was hogging the front pages of the French press. Many of her friends were actively involved in the struggle against the Gaullist suppression of the left-inspired demonstrations against the American war in Vietnam and other student issues, and as she saw evidence and heard tales of governmental brutality, she became incensed.

"I started reading the newspapers more carefully. I started watching the news on French TV: the B-52 bombers dropping their leftover bombs on the villages. I started following the testimony at the Bertrand Russell tribunal, understanding the split between what we were doing and what we said we were doing. A lot was happening inside me, secretly, through small things. . . ."

Visitors from America brought back stories of the growing violence and counterviolence over the war in the United States. Peter Fonda came to Paris, and Jane was again astonished by the way he'd changed. He was planning to make a low-budget movie with Dennis Hopper about a pair of drug-dealing hippies on a motorcycle tour across America, and although she was indifferent to his ideas for the film, she was impressed by his new confidence and sense of purpose, which gave him a strength she never imagined him capable of. He still talked in the California dope jargon she'd grown used to hearing—indeed, she had started using it herself—but he had dropped much of the hippie detachment he affected during the past three years and was now burning with dreams and ambition.

Peter was full of stories about the States. He sympathized with the antiwar movement, of course, but his feelings transcended the war. Soaked in the antimaterialistic fervor of Hollywood's drug-and-love culture, he was already envisioning a total transformation of America into a society of peace and universal love based on the magic of mind-expanding drugs. Jane thought his vision unrealistic, but was caught up by his fervor, especially when he related his dreams to his own children and to the child she was expecting. Jane had been a regular user of psychiatric drugs and had also experienced the highs of marijuana, but she was afraid of the more mysterious drugs Peter espoused. Measured against her fears, Peter's daring was reckless but, nonetheless, admirable, and Jane envied him for his pioneering courage. By the time Peter returned to California he left his sister thinking seriously about the kind of world she was bringing her child into.

As Jane grew plumper and less active during the middle months of her pregnancy, she was bombarded by more and more distressing information from the world beyond St.-Ouen. In the United States, Lyndon Johnson fulfilled the dream of the more militant factions of the antiwar movement by dropping out of the 1968 Presidential race in April, thereby bringing Eugene McCarthy and Bobby Kennedy, both freshly minted antiwar advocates sympathetic to the radical cause, to the forefront of Presidential politics. McCarthy and Kennedy shared expanding liberal-radical loyalties for a couple of months. As their presence in the battle for the White House further legitimized the radical fervor of the young, a new mystique of hope blossomed, especially around Kennedy. Then—the inevitable: Kennedy was assassinated. The Democratic Convention was turned into a bloody battleground as Hubert Humphrey was nominated to run against Richard Nixon. As a result, the various counterculture, antiwar and racial movements melded, expanded and hardened into a monolithic Third World movement that began to shake the very foundations of the country. Meanwhile, the war in Vietnam went on.

France was no more tranquil during the same period. In May, while the American antiwar movement was rallying around Kennedy and McCarthy, the streets of Paris' Latin Quarter were turned into a battleground reminiscent of World War II days. Sorbonne students and police fought a pitched battle over students' rights to demonstrate against the war, and the effects of De Gaulle's excessive use of armed power galvanized radical-liberal sentiment throughout the Western world. The result, in the United States, was an hysterical orgy of action and reaction that culminated, during the summer of 1968, in the assassination of Robert Kennedy and the riots at Chicago's Democratic Convention.

With her maternal instincts ripening as she felt her baby grow within her, Jane was repulsed and frightened by the violence she read about in America and was witnessing in France. At times she felt depressed over the prospect of bringing a child into a world that seemed to grow more discombobulated by the day. When she visualized her son—she was hoping for a boy—having to grow up in the atmosphere of intergenerational hatred that seemed to have established itself as a fact of life in America, she sometimes felt guilty for wishing to have a child at all.

Added to that was the whole question of being an American. Living in France for the past year and a half, she had been further exposed to the angry but highly rational French criticism of the United States.

"I had met Roger and Elisabeth Vailland, who were members of the Communist Party. They would come for coffee in the evenings, sometimes with workers, and I would talk with them. In Paris I also met American deserters and Vietnamese of the National Liberation Front, who knew facts that I had not been aware of. Then I saw a movie on the

Washington march, boys with long hair and professors and radicals putting flowers into the guns of the guards standing in front of the Pentagon. A lot was happening, and I learned. . . ."

Jane suffered an increasing sense of inadequacy about defending her home country and was reading more and more material in an effort to get a grip on political questions. What she read was disquieting and tended to support the critics, rather than her own inspecific notions about the glory of America. No matter how many times she pointed to the freedoms that existed in the United States, she was soon persuaded by people with whom she argued that these freedoms were relative and self-perpetuating—that is, they were almost the exclusive property of the privileged classes which, in seeking to protect them, necessarily had to restrict them. Her whole concept of freedom, ingrained in her from the perspective of her privileged upbringing, was shaken to its roots by her exposure to the radical ideas of her French friends.

Jane brooded extensively over the contradictions she began to perceive in the American system. She was by now, like most young Americans, totally opposed to war and gave financial and moral support to organizations in Paris that were formed to help American deserters. In talking to some of these young men she heard hair-raising tales of atrocities committed in Vietnam and secret weapons being used against the civilian population. She was shocked to discover that much of what she learned contradicted the official stories coming out of Washington and for the first time began to think it possible that the United States government was lying to the American people about its conduct of the war and other foreign policy matters. It was her contact with the deserting GI's, more than anything else, that provoked Jane's skepticism about the American system and stirred her liberal conscience.

One of the several people Jane got to know better as a result of her deepening interest in educating herself politically was Elisabeth Vailland. Roger Vailland, a well-known French Communist who was active in the resistance in World War II and who championed the Communist cause in France thereafter, had recently died. Elisabeth Vailland, his fifty-year-old widow, was an Italian who acquired her own Communism during the Mussolini era when she was a member of the partisan underground that fought against Il Duce's Fascism and the Nazi occupation of Italy. She had married Roger Vailland in the early 1950's and, with him, became an experienced political activist in France. After Vailland died, she carried on his work. She also deepened her friendship with Jane Fonda.

Although Jane had enjoyed her trip to Russia several years before and was astonished to discover that the Russians were as harmless as she had expected them to be malevolent, she was not particularly impressed with Soviet Communism. And in spite of her growing disenchantment with the United States in 1967 and 1968, her faith in the American dream, with all its inbuilt prejudice against Communism, was still too powerful to be seriously compromised by the beguiling logic of her French leftist friends. Nevertheless, there was a certain romance in their idealism, a certain quality of lifelong struggle and sacrifice in their political activism, that appealed to Jane. She realized that they were not promoting violence, especially the women among them, but were advocating humane change—a new world order in which everyone would share in the riches of the planet. The Communist ideal could hardly be called evil, and if Communism in practice sometimes created violence and suppression—well, this was because Communism's evolution was forever being deterred by the reactionism of the capitalist rich and the natural bellicosity of the universal male ego in whose mind Communism had been conceived and by whose hands it was molded. Elisabeth Vailland was a different kind of Communist—an activist, to be sure, but a pacifist with a woman's great compassion for the disenfranchised of the world. She was a tough-minded intellectual whose knowledge was broad and whose sense of injustice and idealism ran deep and fervent; at the same time she was a woman who was alone in the world and touched by the sadness of her widowhood. In Jane she found a confused but eager student. Jane, for her part, found in Elisabeth a sympathetic and understanding teacher. They soon became close friends, and Jane listened to Elisabeth's stories of her thirty years of political activism with a growing admiration for what a woman could do in the world besides make movies or keep house.

As Jane moved into the advanced stages of her pregnancy, a profound change came over her. A case of mumps imperiled matters and kept her bedridden for more than a month. When she was safely over it, she became almost obsessively protective of herself. She spent most of the summer in St.-Tropez with Vadim, where she good-naturedly suffered his teasing about her growing gloom over the war, her upper-class liberal confusion and guilt over her jumbled values and her fears that because of the mumps episode their child might be born injured. She took long solitary walks on the beach and generally withdrew within herself. Her upset with the assassination of Bobby Kennedy had lingered through the summer, and the news in August, when she was in her eighth month of pregnancy, of the Chicago riots and Richard Nixon's nomination at the Republican Convention, depressed her even more. Her preoccupation about America, along with her own rapidly changing feelings about the meaning of her life, became mixed up with her womanly pride in being pregnant and left her puzzled, somber and reflective as the summer neared its end.

Not all was gloom in St.-Tropez, however. Again, there was a steady stream of friends to and from the Vadim abode. Brigitte Bardot, who lived nearby, was especially solicitous of Jane. All summer long she predicted that Jane's baby would be born on September 28, her own birthday, and that it would be a girl. Jane and Vadim insisted it would be a boy, and many discussions revolved around names for the child. Catherine Deneuve insisted that Jane have the baby at the same hospital where she had given birth to her son by Vadim.

To the outside world, Jane's sensual life with Vadim went on as always, despite her enlarged condition. The usual summer complement of press photographers and reporters hung around St.-Tropez recording the comings and goings of the resort's film celebrities. Since the impending birth of Jane's baby was big news in France, they concentrated on her. Eight months pregnant, Jane hardly felt she embodied her uninhibited sex-symbol image, but the newspapers continued to print stories hinting at ribaldry in the Vadim ménage. "One reporter came to St.-Tropez," Jane recalled, "and wrote about Vadim putting his hand up the sleeve of my caftan and fondling my breast in front of other people. Well, okay, Vadim did. When the story was printed, I said to him, 'You see, Vadim, you must not do things like that in front of people.' But, my God, why the big fuss. I was pregnant and he was kidding around. The way it was written made it sound so decadent."

By mid-September Jane and Vadim were back in Paris. She was having nightmares about the baby being born in the form of a ten-year-old facsimile of Brigitte Bardot. As Vadim tells it, on the evening of September 28 he playfully put his hands on Jane's stomach and, mimicking a sorcerer, told her that she must start having the baby. "Forty minutes later, the labor pains began. I had remembered everything. I took scissors and string, in case the baby was born on the way to the hospital, and we started out. Fifty meters from the hospital the automobile stopped. Yes, I had remembered everything except to buy the gas. So I picked up Jane and carried her to the hospital—believe me, it was very dramatic—and one hour later she gave birth."

Jane quickly got over her initial disappointment that her baby was a girl. At least she didn't look like Bardot. She and Vadim named the child Vanessa, partly in honor of Vanessa Redgrave, whose political activism Jane admired more and more, and partly because they simply liked the name, which they thought went well with both Vadim and Plemiannikov. The baby had Vadim's eyes and head, but the lower half of her face was all Fonda.

Jane was transformed all over again by the experience of giving birth. "I had been wanting that child so much, for so long. . . . And something happened to me while she was growing inside my stomach. For the first time in my life, I felt confident as a human being and as a woman, and I'm sure it was because I was finally a mother. I began to feel a unity with people. I began to love people, to understand that we do not give life to a human being only to have it killed by B-52 bombs, or to have it jailed by fascists, or to have it destroyed by social injustice. When she was born—my baby—it was as if the sun had opened up for me. I felt whole. I became free."

19. *They Shoot Horses*

When it got around that I was doing Horses, *and that I wanted to cut my hair for it, you know what people said? "Jane, dahling, you're out of your mind, don't cut your hair!" I thought, oh wow, so that's what I've become—a lotta goddamn blond hair.*

—JANE FONDA

A FEW weeks after Jane gave birth, *Barbarella* opened in the United States and established her more solidly than ever in the public mind as a symbol of wicked and daring sexuality. What the public didn't know was that while her nude or scantily costumed image was cavorting with sexual abandon through the ethereal world of Barbarella, she was back on her farm in St.-Ouen nursing Vanessa, feeling decidedly unsexy and trying to deal with an entirely new complex of emotions.

The baby quickly became the consuming focus of her life. "It's made my life completely different," she said shortly after Vanessa was born. "I can't get over the miracle of giving birth. I feel fulfilled, rounder. Little things that used to bother me seem so unimportant now. I want more children. I miss being pregnant. I've never been so elated. The pleasure and pain were so extraordinary that I try to hang onto every memory of them."

Jane and Vadim spent the next few months at the farm and at their apartment in Paris, entertaining visitors and showing off the baby. After several weeks of nursing, Jane got the urge to begin working again, and she and Vadim started to plan. "Having a baby has no influence on my ambitions as an actress," she told an interviewer. "I really love acting, and I've never had so much energy and vitality as since having the baby."

Barbarella's release represented Jane's first appearance on screen in almost a year, and when it was clear that it was going to be a box-office success, she was flooded with scripts from Hollywood. One of them was an adaptation of a little-known 1935 novel by the late Horace McCoy, an obscure Hollywood screenwriter, that had more recently surfaced in Europe as a cult book of the French left. It had been praised by such pillars of the French intelligentsia as Simone de Beauvoir, Jean Paul Sartre and Albert Camus, who declared it the first existential novel to come out of America, and was required reading—as an indictment of the American capitalist system—for any self-respecting, well-informed French revolutionary. The book's title was *They Shoot Horses, Don't They?* When Jane read the screenplay, which was a faithful interpretation of the original novel, she enthusiastically agreed to make it her next picture.

Jane's role was that of Gloria, a defeated, downtrodden American girl in the early 1930's who, in utter financial and spiritual desperation, signs up for a dance marathon. The marathon dance craze, with its pain and suffering, was treated by McCoy as a metaphor for the Great Depression and the social ills that caused it. The screenplay captured the novel's burning despair almost perfectly, and the makers of the movie hoped the finished product would serve doubly as an effective metaphor for the turmoil of America's Vietnam years. Director Sidney Pollack said, "Kids don't want to be entertained today. They're pretty cynical. Hopefully, they will find it interesting and enlightening to discover that there's been another bad time in America, even worse than it is now."

Jane saw in the film a threefold challenge. First, she felt the role of

Gloria, the marathon dancer, gave her dramatic opportunities she had not had in any of her previous films. The second lay in the script. With its straightforward, naturalistic, almost laconic presentation of a slice of American life, it contained a searing indictment of the dehumanizing evils of American capitalism that coincided with Jane's rising political consciousness. It was a script with a heavy message. Yet it was not "messagey"—that is, laden with pointed, obvious speeches and dialogue that had made so many films of its type such a bore. Third, "I was sick and tired of being thought of as a sex symbol. God knows, I never thought of myself as one! I felt I had to start doing more serious work than *Barbarella*."

Jane returned to the United States at the end of the year to start preparing for *They Shoot Horses, Don't They?*, and by January, 1969, she, Vadim and Vanessa were installed again at Malibu. After a year and a half in France, Jane was glad to be back. She seemed to be losing some of her attachment for France. "When you come home, that aggressive American friendliness comes as such a shock after the coldness of the French. But it's a joy to come back. Life over there is entrenched. It's frozen; it's got arthritis. I adore it here. And all the things that are happening."

As 1969 began, everything seemed fine for Jane and Vadim. She was thirty-one now. After giving birth to Vanessa, she'd dieted down to her lowest weight ever and was pleased with her leaner, more mature look. She was ecstatically happy with the baby, and could feel her internal strength and confidence multiply as each day went by. She was a proud mother, and both she and Vadim delighted in showing Vanessa off to all their California friends. What delighted her more than anything on her return to California were the continuing signs of reconciliation with her father.

Henry Fonda had bought a house in the exclusive Bel Air section of Los Angeles and was spending much of his time there with his wife Shirlee. When Jane arrived at Malibu, Fonda, now a third-time grandfather and still happily married, had mellowed even more than when Jane saw him last. He was pleased with his new granddaughter, even more pleased with the effect motherhood was obviously having on Jane's life. "We're very close now," he said at the time, "closer than we've ever been. She doesn't talk about me the way she used to any more. She's got this marriage with Vadim, and the baby, and my God, that girl has maternal instincts she never knew she had. She's grown into an extremely intelligent, attractive woman. She's outgoing, not at all like me. . . . Look at the kind of home she's created, look at the life they lead out there in Malibu. People coming, people going, all day long, open house all the time, and Jane handling it all so beautifully, making people feel comfortable. . . ."

Fonda had even grown closer to his son, although he still disapproved of much of what Peter was doing and who he was doing it with. When Fonda's adopted daughter, Amy, now an impressionable fifteen, would visit him and his wife in Bel Air, Shirlee Fonda would not let her see any of Peter's motorcycle-and-drug films, and the two did their best to keep her away from Peter's world. Fonda detested most of Peter's friends; he particularly disliked Dennis Hopper, with whom Peter was making a low-budget, cross-country motorcycle movie which they were going to call *Easy Rider*. "The man is an idiot," the elder Fonda later said. "He's a total freak-out, stoned out of his mind all the time."

It seemed half of Hollywood was stoned out of its mind all the time, but except for her tranquilizers, diet pills and an occasional sally into the highs of marijuana and hashish, Jane stayed away from the more exotic drugs. The drug craze was in high gear in filmland, and many of her acquaintances were now regular users of hallucinogens. Jane was puzzled by the intense dependence on drugs she saw all around her, and it was characteristic of her own sense of independence that she resisted numerous urgings to get into it herself. She accepted her brother's "liberation" through LSD but was loath to try it herself. "I think proselytizers become as square as the people they're proselytizing against," she said. "Why all this proselytizing by takers of LSD? An alcoholic drinks, but an alcoholic doesn't say, 'Come on, you have to be an alcoholic, too.' Sure, I've taken pot, but I prefer a good drink."

Jane was more interested in sexual experimentation than in any wholehearted tampering with drugs. As far as she could tell, drugs did nothing but desensitize one to feeling, whereas an experimental sexual encounter, along the lines of Vadim's philosophy and all the more daring because of the lingering aura of taboo that surrounded it, heightened one's experience. She had returned to California to find that free sexuality was as fully in bloom as drugs, and although she still had a residual prudeness about it, she was much more willing to flirt with this than with the chemical expansion of her mind.

Two of the "people coming, people going" alluded to by Henry Fonda when he marveled at Jane's Malibu life-style were Sharon Tate and Roman Polanski. According to movie producer Gene Gutowski, Polanski's partner in an English production company called Cadre Films Ltd.,

"Sharon and Roman and Jane and Vadim were by this time all good friends."

Gutowski is a London-based producer of Polish origin. He had been responsible more than anyone else for introducing Polanski, then a young, obscure Polish filmmaker, to Western audiences in 1963. Polanski's *Knife in the Water*—a brooding, erotic study in sexual jealousy and violence made in Poland—had been a critical success on both sides of the Atlantic in 1963, creating interest in its eccentric director on the part of first European and then American motion-picture studios. Gutowski brought Polanski to England shortly afterward, and together they formed Cadre Films, under whose banner Polanski made his first English-language movie. The film was called *Repulsion*. It starred Catherine Deneuve—Roger Vadim's ex-mistress and mother of his child Christian—in the role of a beautiful manicurist who suffers from violent hallucinations and winds up hacking and pummeling two male acquaintances to death.

Gutowski and Polanski, aside from being associates, were good friends. Polanski, a diminutive, volatile thirty-four-year-old, was a Jew who had escaped from a concentration camp at the age of eight and survived a childhood of Nazi persecution in Poland. He had a bizarre, cynical imagination that obsessively lent itself to visually striking films of terror, witchcraft, incest and other themes about the dark underside of the soul. When *Repulsion* became a box-office success, he and Gutowski were able to raise the money to make another film, *Cul de Sac*, a blood-suffused story of murder and weirdness in a medieval seaside castle in the north of England. Polanski followed this in 1966 with *The Vampire Killers*, a macabre comedy about a university professor and his servant, played by Polanski himself, who travel to Transylvania to brick up a castle full of vampires. Polanski had written the screenplay, and the movie was produced for MGM by Hollywood producer Martin Ransahoff, mainly as a showcase for his protégée—starlet Sharon Tate.

By 1967 Roman Polanski and Roger Vadim—both purveyors of the bizarre—were well acquainted. Sharon Tate fell in love with the pugnacious Polanski, and the two started to live together, first in London, then in California, where she gained notice for her role as the drug-addicted, suicidal Jennifer in the movie version of *Valley of the Dolls* and he was offered the opportunity to direct *Rosemary's Baby* for Paramount. Jane and Vadim frequently saw Polanski and Sharon Tate around Hollywood before they returned to France after Jane's work in *Barefoot in the Park*. All four, as Gutowski says, became friends.

Sharon Tate's career, once she met Polanski, took a course curiously similar to Jane's after she had met Vadim. She started giving out quotes to the press that rang familiar notes. "Before Roman," went one, "I was disorganized and flighty. At twenty-three I'm not yet ready for marriage. I still have to live, and Roman is trying to show me how." Went another: "Americans are too inhibited, but they're slowly coming around to recognizing what a swinging world we live in. I want to be like the bright young generation in London. They're a bunch of free thinkers who are feeling their way through life and leaving an impression on the times." In the March, 1967, issue of *Playboy* there appeared a pictorial feature called "The Tate Gallery," featuring Sharon with bared bosom photographed by Polanski.

Jane had turned down Polanski's offer to star in *Rosemary's Baby* so that she and Vadim could return to Europe to make *Barbarella*. In January, 1968, after Polanski finished the film—whose starring role had gone to Mia Farrow, another of the new Hollywood's bright young lights—he and Sharon Tate were married in London. They then returned to California, where they became part of the frenetic, highly mobile group of actors, actresses, musicians and businessmen at the heights of Hollywood success. Along with Jane and Vadim, Polanski attended the Cannes Film Festival in May, at the time the students of France were revolting. As a gesture of solidarity with the students, he resigned from the festival jury. Back in California early in June, he, Sharon Tate and some friends dined one night with Robert Kennedy at a beach house in Malibu. After dinner Senator Kennedy was driven back to the Ambassador Hotel in Los Angeles, where he was shot by Sirhan Sirhan. A few days later *Rosemary's Baby* opened in a barrage of advertising and publicity. It was a huge success, and the Polanskis quickly became the toast of the new Hollywood. They remained in California the rest of that year and early into the next, staying in a rented house on a swank ridge above Beverly Hills.

The drug culture had blossomed into full flower. Top young stars of the film community just weren't in unless they were out of it. Marijuana, hashish, cocaine and mescaline were regular dietary supplements. LSD and other even more exotic hallucinogens were *de rigueur* for all who strove for acceptance and status. Peter Fonda had opened the door to the social acceptability of acid, and it was not long before just about anyone who was anyone was singing its praises, as well as the praises of living the free and sensual life to the hilt. With the success of *Rosemary's Baby*—a saga about Satan-worship and the marvels of witchcraft—the

Polanskis were soon among the leading hosts and hostesses of Hippie Hollywood. Both admitted in print that they had tried LSD and were regular users of marijuana.

Polanski's fascination with the demonic was evidently contagious, and Sharon Tate rapidly learned to share it. Sharon loved Polanski deeply. A simple girl, she gave up her own identity completely in order to keep her husband happy, and she barely winced at his continuing extramarital activities after they were wed. Sharon learned about the cosmos, universal love and voodoo, it has been reported, and gamely played leading roles in the little TV skits her husband created and taped on his portable video tape machine. Sometimes, the rumors had it, she would camp through a taping in the nude, often playing opposite other well-known Hollywood luminaries. The Polanskis also liked to pick up beautiful couples they met at the local discotheques and include them in the home movies, according to the stories. Whenever Sharon and Roman threw a party, the wildest flora and fauna of the new Hollywood were said to turn up—high-octane rock-music groupies, devil worshipers, leather-and-chain lovers, gay stunt men, even stray servicemen fresh from Vietnam whom Sharon and Roman auditioned for parts in Roman's risqué video tapes. The presence of Roman Polanski was clearly having a bigger impact on Hollywood than Roger Vadim's did when he first arrived four years earlier with Jane Fonda. Vadim was not resentful, though. Indeed, he and Jane must have admired the tenacious little Pole's imagination and enterprise.

While Roman, Sharon and their friends were indulging their taste for witchcraft and experimenting with other dark odds and ends of human experience, just a couple of miles away to the north another group of friends was following a similar course. In Hollywood, "letting it all hang out" had become a convenient excuse for certain asocial behavior that would never have been tolerated otherwise. To be a "freak" or to "freak out" in public not only was accepted, but was fast becoming fashionable. It was in such a freewheeling atmosphere that a man named Charles Manson was able to operate without attracting much adverse attention.

Manson was a habitual petty criminal and convict who walked out of a California prison on parole in March, 1967, after serving six years and nine months for his most recent indiscretion. In prison he developed a taste for drug-rock records and had taken to befriending marijuana offenders, who were better educated and softer than the cons he had associated with all his life. After his release he wandered into the Haight-Ashbury section of San Francisco and melded with the hippie dope-and-love community that was then at its zenith there. A beard and a guitar later, the thirty-two-year-old paroled convict was handing out free LSD to people he met on the street. Acid would prove to be Manson's passport back into society, and soon he was surrounded by a following of young runaway girls, dropouts and car thieves. "Charlie is in love with us, and we're all in love with each other," said one of his teen-age devotees. "He writes songs for us and sings them with the voice of an angel." Manson's striking presence, based on, as *Time* magazine later put it, "the eyes of Rasputin and a mystic patter that mixed the Beatles with Scientology," eventually gained access into the fringes of Hippie Hollywood. He struck up a passing acquaintance with several important people in the Los Angeles music business, including Frank Zappa, Dennis Wilson of the Beach Boys rock group and Terry Melcher, a record producer who was the son of Doris Day. By now Manson fancied himself and his "family" as a potential star rock group and hounded Melcher, who had connections with the record companies, for an audition. Melcher, not a little fascinated by Manson, finally arranged for one. After hearing Manson sing, he told him he wanted a few days to think about it. Manson would not be denied; all his life a social outcast, he knew a brushoff when he saw one. He made up an excuse to ride back to Melcher's house in the Hollywood hills, hoping to wring a promise of a recording contract out of Melcher. At the end of the ride Melcher made it clear that he had not been terribly impressed with the singer or the songs and suggested that Manson should devote some time to polishing his musical skills before proceeding further. Manson became angry. Slamming the door of Melcher's car, he departed, but not without first making a note of where Melcher lived. He retreated to the sanctuary of the Spahn Ranch—a little-used movie location he and his family had expropriated in the hills at the northernmost edge of Los Angeles—and turned his and his little army's energies to witchcraft, Jesus freaking, sexual excess, ritualistic bloodletting and mind-rattling paranoia. The Polanski-Tate-Manson destiny had unwittingly begun to take shape late in 1968, although at the time nobody realized it.

By early 1969 the mood in California was a tense, heightened reflection of the mood of the rest of the country. Starting with the North Vietnamese Tet Offensive the year before in South Vietnam, the United States seemed caught in an ascending spiral of frustration that had its loudest expression in the one place that traditionally set the pace for the rest of the country—Hollywood. Robert Kennedy had been killed. The Chicago riots had occurred, uniting all factions of the youth movement, and the stench of national insurrection was in the air. The government was planning to prosecute several leaders of the Chicago demonstrations—grim, militant leftists, happy-go-lucky, drug-sated hippies and gun-toting Black Panthers alike—thus bundling a variety of national disaffections under a single banner and providing them with increased credibility in their appeal to the nation's youth. Richard Nixon had been elected President on a promise to end the war, restore law and order and return the country to its simpler traditional values. Every preinaugural sign indicated that he intended to carry out his promises with a vengeance as he filled his Cabinet and White House staff with rock-ribbed Establishment conservatives.

If the new President believed that his "secret plan" to end the war would cool the antiwar hysteria of the country, he was right—at least for a few months. But the war, out of which the social turmoil of the sixties had grown, was no longer the primary issue. Its relentless, hapless prosecution on the part of preceding administrations had inexorably peeled back the blanket that had covered the basic corruption of the American system for decades: the contradiction between its high-minded, humanist principles and its often not-so-high-minded, dehumanizing practices. Racism, enforced poverty, protectionism of the rich, oppression and disenfranchisement of the poor, bureaucracy, double and triple standards embedded in officialdom, the promulgation of out-of-date values and attitudes, ethnocentrism, benevolent and sometimes malevolent imperialism, ecological rape—all long-standing consequences of the evolution of the American system—were exposed to the consciousness of the new idealists of the United States by the war and the corollary cans of worms opened by its seeming endlessness. With his solidly embedded reputation for speaking out of both sides of his mouth, Richard Nixon, despite his promises, promised little for America's disaffected millions.

Hollywood had always been an escapist milieu, and by early 1969 escapism was at its height. The drug-suffused haze that drifted through the beach houses of Malibu, the mansions of Beverly Hills, the cliff houses above Hollywood and the shacks of the San Fernando Valley was characterized by a growing cynicism that was rapidly transforming itself into a doomsday mania. As the war and its attendant issues continued to eat at America's morale, Hollywood's agitation was perhaps best voiced by starlet Raquel Welch, who still found it necessary to tour the war zone with Bob Hope in order to get publicity. "We would come to some boys who had their legs shot off and were undergoing operations of some kind," she reported on her return. "You say, 'I'm not going to faint, I'm not going to faint,' to yourself, so you stand there and you sway a little. You keep pretending it's not happening, that the wound isn't there."

But the wound was there, and Hollywood, even quicker than the rest of the country, grew more schizophrenic. The innocence and optimism of its earlier, more gentle hippie phase had given way to a wholesale fascination with demonism and violence. Roman Polanski had already revitalized America's taste for sensual horror and was toying with the real thing in his private dealings with some of Los Angeles' more bizarre characters. Now Peter Fonda was on the verge of turning his image into dollars with *Easy Rider*, which told the story of two hippie drug dealers who get killed on their journey "in search of America." In one sense, *Easy Rider* was an unconscious vision of the new Hollywood, drugging its financial troubles away while it searched America for a fresh audience that would lift it out of its filmmaking recession. The film's grim ending, in which the two heroes are shot to death, also reflected the doom and violence of the era, as did Peter himself when he expressed his stylish disillusionment in the film. "I've always thought about suicide," he said. "I've popped pills and drove a car over a hundred miles an hour into a bridge." Fonda's death wish hit much closer to Hollywood's true feelings than did the hippie-love myth, which many continued to cling to—at least visually. It was a myth that would be exploded once and for all, a few months hence, at the home of Roman Polanski and Sharon Tate.

Jane Fonda's role in *They Shoot Horses, Don't They?* was yet another symbol of Hollywood's fascination with youthful violence and despair. To underline that despair, Jane had her long blond mane chopped off and tightly marcelled thirties-style in her natural russet color. "One of the reasons I took the part," she said, "is that I want to play something completely different, something that is not necessarily sympathetic in the conventional sense." She also wanted to get away from the bubble-headed comedy characters she was remembered for in Hollywood. To strengthen herself for the arduous role, she jogged every day for an hour along the beach, swam as much as she could in the chilly Pacific and faithfully followed a high-protein diet. She also read everything she could find on the Depression, even seeking her father out to discuss certain questions. He had created another victim of society twenty-five years before with his portrayal of Tom Joad, and Jane envisioned *They Shoot Horses, Don't They?* as having the potential to be another *Grapes of Wrath*.

After going through her conditioning routine, through weeks of strenuous, exhausting schooling in the flapper-era dances the picture called for, and otherwise preparing herself for her part, Jane started filming early in the spring. Her enthusiasm for the picture mounted. "It's the most beautiful story I've read since I became an actress," she said. "My role is a girl who's really a loser. Men treat her badly, and she can never win. She's embittered and negative toward life. I want to make her a very real character.

"The war we're going through now—well, our country has never gone through such a long, agonizing experience, except maybe for the Depression. The Depression is the closest America ever came before to a national disaster, the kind of thing that unites people and reduces everything to basic questions—eat or not, live or die. Perhaps audiences —especially kids—will be able to come away from seeing *Horses* with the feeling that if we could pull out of the Depression, we can pull out of the mess we're in now. The picture may work on audiences the same way the marathons themselves did, letting people see people who were suffering even more than they are.

"Another thing I like about the film is that it's about people dealing with problems created by society rather than by themselves. They are dealing with them the best they can, yet they are condemned for their solutions."

The filming of *They Shoot Horses, Don't They?* was the first in a series of events during 1969 that would shatter Jane's assumptions about America and, within a year, launch her on a completely new life course. It was a long, arduous picture, and as she delved deeper and deeper into the role of Gloria, the character's despair became her own. Jane had not really had an opportunity to sink her teeth into a dramatic role since *The Game Is Over* three years before. At that time she had lost herself in the part of Renée, and with Vadim orchestrating her performance, she finally gained acclaim as a dramatic actress. She had tried the same thing with her part in *Hurry Sundown*, but between Otto Preminger's insensitive direction and the daily distractions of the Louisiana location work, she had been unable to immerse herself properly in the character of Julie Ann Warren. *Barefoot in the Park*, *Spirits of the Dead* and *Barbarella* had all been walk-throughs. *Horses* represented the first chance to put to use the full range of her acting powers again.

She brought to her part an intrepid determination heightened by an added acting and personal maturity. As shooting progressed and as she identified more and more with the despondent Gloria, she became despondent herself. Eventually, her characterization absorbed her completely—so much so that she finally moved into a dressing room at the studio rather than stay at home in Malibu. "I found I couldn't go to work in the morning as a happy woman and then step into that role. Gloria was such a desperate, negative, depressed person. Gradually I let myself become that way too. How could I go home like that? I'd walk in the door and *auuugh!* So I stayed away. Of course, Vanessa would stay overnight with me every now and then. Still, it took me months to get over it."

Although she did get over it, playing that particular part in that particular movie at that particular time had a lasting effect on Jane. As she looked around at the real world she lived in from the perspective of the fictional but uncannily similar world Gloria inhabited, all distinctions blurred. In the real world it had quickly become apparent that President Nixon did not have a secret plan to end the war after all. He and his official representatives were beginning to mouth the same patriotic platitudes and offer the same empty assurances with which President Johnson's administration had dulled so many American senses for the previous five years. In response, more shrill and violent expressions of anguish and despair were spilling across the country. But now it was not just the continuing war that fired the insurrectionary spirit. It was everything, and everyone was making his voice heard—political radicals, students, blacks, Indians, women, hippies, all stitching their own causes and manifestoes into the broad fabric of the antiwar movement. The country was more hysterical and divided than ever.

Susannah York, who co-starred in *Horses*, recalls that Jane became increasingly moody and disturbed during the shooting of the picture. "Actually, Jane and I had very little communication on the set. Although we were on-screen together a great deal of the time, we probably only exchanged a couple of sentences through the entire film. I just met her socially a few times, as one does, after hours or at lunch or down at the beach. Jane was very much into her role and working very, very hard on it. The few times we talked I could see she was having a problem with her part. I was, too, but she seemed particularly intense about it and upset most of the time."

Another member of the company says, "Jane worked like a demon on that character. I've been connected with a lot of films, and I've never seen anyone go through such agony to produce a performance. It was really frightening, sometimes, the way she'd come off the set after a scene. She'd hold onto that character like it was a priceless possession

. . . no, it was like *she* was possessed, like the character had gotten thoroughly inside her and completely displaced Jane Fonda."

A third observer remembers that Jane became "a fanatic about Gloria. It was like an actress who guzzles a quart of vodka before going on to play a drunk scene, then afterward remains drunk. Jane wore the role on her sleeve. She'd get away from it a little on weekends, but just a little. During the week it was hard to tell the difference between Jane and Gloria. Off the set she walked like her, talked like her, mumbled like her. She had this perennially tired, vacuous expression on her face, and she'd go around with her body slumped over like a sapling. She got thinner and thinner—you could almost see the weight melting away—and before long everybody connected with the picture was worried about whether she was going to make it through."

The grueling shooting schedule lasted into May. Much of the movie was filmed inside an exact replica of the old, well-known Aragon Ballroom on Lick Pier in Ocean Park, an amusement center just south of Santa Monica. During the long, difficult location filming, Jane lived much of the time in a trailer adjacent to the pier.

"God, it was hard doing that part," she said later. "Hard not to become monotonous, yet remain on one line the way the script called for. I'd do something funny, and it wouldn't work. There were so many takes. It was like walking a tightrope over Niagara Falls constantly. . . . When we finished the endurance race sequences, everybody would collapse, weeping hysterically. . . . It was the toughest thing I've had to do—ever.

"I'm opposed to taking your work home with you. That's why the more I got into Gloria, I stayed away from home. . . . I became Gloria. She was uneducated, tough, bitter, cynical. It took me a long time to stop talking like her. Talking bad, using a lotta bad English, et cetera and so forth. And feeling like her. Hard, rough, brittle. . . . I was so miserable. How Vadim stuck with me I don't know. I discovered a black side to my character I didn't know about. . . . Gloria was hopeless, suicidal, and in the end she dies. In my performance there could not be an inkling, a ray of hope. It had to be that way; otherwise, the ending wouldn't work."

When *They Shoot Horses, Don't They?* was released six months later, it was universally praised, with many critics predicting an Oscar for Jane. It was easily the best performance she had ever given. It was muscular and athletic, sensitive and knowing, totally devoid of the sex, nudity and coy naughtiness her reputation was built on. For this she was glad, but she was not particularly happy with the way the picture turned out.

"I wish we could make the movie all over again," she complained to an interviewer. "It could be much better. I'm pleased with the critical response, because everybody connected with the production worked like hell. . . . But it's not what I'd hoped it would be."

Jane believed *Horses* had the potential of being a really great film, a classic, but that something had been lost between its making and its final editing. She disliked the misty opening credit sequence with the galloping black horse; she felt it was a misleadingly romantic softening of the picture's stark impact, a compromise. She had pleaded for the removal of a slow-motion sequence of her falling in a meadow—again, film gimmickry that compromised the film's honesty. And she was especially unhappy about the exclusion of a scene that provided a comprehensible explanation for Gloria's quitting the marathon; Gloria's tragic fate lost some of its credibility as a result.

Jane was right, but try as she did to persuade director Pollack and the producers to make the changes she wanted after she saw the rough print, her feelings had no influence on the final cut. And by the time the picture was released in December, she was no longer emotionally involved with it. She had a myriad of other, more pressing concerns bedeviling her.

20.   Sleazo Inputs

Pop esthetics moved millions of people to do more than rock stars could ever do individually.

—Ellen Sander

WHILE Jane was busy on *They Shoot Horses, Don't They?* early in 1969, Hollywood was aboil with whole new series of "sleazo inputs," as one commentator described the scene. As if taking its cue from Sharon Tate's earlier declaration about Americans' being too inhibited, the film capital had immersed itself in the new pop life-style that encouraged total expression without discrimination. Jane and Vadim were as avid proponents of this philosophy as anyone else, although they remained more amused observers of than participants in it. It was a bitter irony that Sharon Tate, really nothing more than an innocent, exploited bystander, should turn out to be the major human sacrifice to the new philosophy. If Jane Fonda had stopped to think about it later in the year, she would have realized that it might just as easily have been she herself found hacked to death by the drug-crazed minions of Charles Manson.

The Polanskis were regular visitors at the Vadim house in Malibu. Sharon had recently discovered she was pregnant, and she happily looked forward to bearing Polanski a son in late summer. As her concern with her impending motherhood grew, she started to withdraw from the frolics of her friends, and even her husband found his attention drawn to more earthly matters.

Polanski, an aggressive, competitive, cocksure man-child, found his career as a director-writer-producer expanding at a rapid pace. An original screenplay of his, *A Day at the Beach*, was in production in Denmark under the auspices of Cadre Films, the company of which he and his friend Gene Gutowski were principals. He had two more screenplays in preparation—one for Paramount called *The Donner Pass*, a tale of pioneers turned cannibals during the disastrous Sierra Nevada winter of 1846–47; the other for United Artists called *The Day of the Dolphins*, which he expected to direct and co-produce later in the year with Gutowski.

Vadim himself was working on a new movie, which he was writing in the form of a novel. Jane, in the meantime, was talking about making a film based on some stories about women by the Irish writer Edna O'Brien, whom she had come to admire enormously.

Many of the bizarre rumors about the Polanskis' private life were, of course, exaggerations, but there is no doubt that the two, at least through their associations, were at the epicenter of Mondo Hollywood. Because of Vadim's reputation, although it was old-hat now and because of his and Jane's relationship to Roman and Sharon, much of the rumors about the Polanskis spilled over onto them.

In February the Polanskis signed a lease to rent another house in the hills above Beverly Hills—a three-and-a-half-acre property at 10050 Cielo Drive, a cul-de-sac high in Benedict Canyon. The owner of the property was a show business manager named Rudy Altobelli. Altobelli's previous tenant had been Terry Melcher, who once made a halfhearted attempt to interest Altobelli in managing Charles Manson, aspiring rock star. Altobelli declined but had got to know Manson, as had many of Hollywood's leading music and film figures. After Melcher moved out in January to set up housekeeping at his mother's Malibu beach home, Altobelli continued to occupy the property's guest cottage while Roman and Sharon Polanski prepared to move into the main house.

Polanski was educated, intelligent, ambitious. Polish writers, artists, filmmakers and intellectuals who had fled the confining atmosphere of their homeland liked to maintain the old-world tradition of helping one another out. They kept in touch, gossiped extensively about one another, aided one another's careers when they could and even celebrated Polish holidays together. It had been his youthful association with Gene Gutowski that had got Polanski out of Poland and well placed in the Western movie industry.

Polanski encountered another childhood friend in Paris late in 1967—Wociech Frykowski. The two had gone to school together, and Frykowski's father had helped finance Polanski's first Polish film, *Two Men with a Wardrobe*. Frykowski himself had served as an assistant on several of Polanski's early productions in Poland. He had been married twice, once to the well-known writer Agneski Osiecka. He, too, was an educated, intelligent man. He wrote poetry and was part of an energetic circle of Polish artists and intellectuals—some of whom had already left for the West, including Polanski and the distinguished novelist Jerzy Kosinski, another of Polanski's former school chums.

When Polanski met Frykowski in Paris, he did what came naturally—gave him financial help and encouragement—and the two resumed their friendship of earlier days. Soon Frykowski came to the United States to live, and in New York he got more encouragement from Kosinski. Kosinski introduced him to a twenty-six-year-old San Francisco coffee heiress named Abigail Folger who was working at the Gotham Book Mart, a famous old New York bookstore that Kosinski often frequented. Frykowski was used to living from hand to mouth. He was also a man of considerable European charm, and he and Abigail Folger soon paired up. In the fall of 1968 they moved to Los Angeles, where Abigail, in spite of a personal after-taxes income estimated at $130,000 a year, took a job as a social worker for the Los Angeles County Welfare Department. She was deeply interested in the struggle for racial equality and chose as her working area the south-central section of Los Angeles, where she could presumably aid black ghetto children. The section was also a major center of the Los Angeles dope trade.

Frykowski was not long in locating Roman Polanski, and he and Miss Folger were quickly absorbed into the interlocking circles of Los

Angeles' film, music and drug culture. Miss Folger's money, naturally, attracted people. One was Jay Sebring, a hairstyling tycoon who had been Sharon Tate's lover before her marriage to Polanski and who remained a close friend and co-celebrant of the Polanski life-style. Sebring persuaded Miss Folger to invest some of her money in his empire of barbershops and hair-care products.

Sebring's interests were not limited to hair, however. Many of his friends claim he was still hopelessly in love with Sharon Tate and would do anything for her. Even before Sharon married Roman, Sebring became part of the Polanski entourage and himself developed an interest in satanism and masochism. Moreover, he was a charter member of the new Hollywood and was on close terms with many of the people of the music-film-drug set who knew Charles Manson—knew him not only as an eccentric, aspiring musician, but also as a buyer and seller of large quantities of exotic, hard-to-get second-generation hallucinogenic drugs.

Through Sebring, Wociech Frykowski, a poet and dreamer with few employable skills, was introduced to the Los Angeles drug underworld. By spring of 1969 he had become a minor trader in LSD, cocaine, STP, psilocybin, peyote, mescaline and even heroin. Shortly thereafter, according to his and Polanski's friend Witold Kaczanowski—an artist who had also been brought from Europe to Los Angeles through Polanski's generous offices—Frykowski was offered an exclusive dealership to sell the drug methlenedioxylamphetamine in the Los Angeles area. Known more popularly as MDA, this was a euphoric stimulant, said to have certain aphrodisiacal properties, that was coming into vogue throughout drug and sex-sated Filmland. MDA was manufactured in Toronto, Canada, then smuggled into the United States by a Canadian underworld consortium with an umbilical connection to American illicit drug markets. With his exclusive dealership, Frykowski stood to make a great deal of money. But it was a ruthless, cutthroat business, and in order to vindicate the Canadians' faith in him, Frykowski quickly became practiced in the ruthless, cutthroat arts. He had already developed a personal taste for drugs and kinky sex and had renewed his interest in his friend Polanski's fascination with the psychology of terror and the erotic netherworld of the occult.

By early 1969 Hollywood had discovered, among other aberrations, Andy Warhol and his traveling troupe of improvisatory, sex-and-drug-obsessed filmmakers. The jerky, rambling, disconnected Warhol film style had become a minor wonder in the film capital, and screenings of

Warhol movies were a regular part of an evening's at-home entertainment throughout the new Hollywood. Even Jane Fonda and Roger Vadim were amused by Warhol.

"You know," Jane said in an interview in the early spring of 1969, "since I've been with Vadim it doesn't matter what I say to writers. They always imply that we live in some kind of weird, perpetual orgy. Good God, we don't even go to Denise Minelli's, much less to orgies. And we don't go in for that Hollywood jazz. I mean, people drop in here—Peter and his wife, Dennis Hopper, Christian Marquand, Roman Polanski. . . . It's very loose—I mean, casual—down here on the beach. . . . We had Simone Signoret over the other night . . . and we screened [Warhol's] *Nude Restaurant* and *Flesh*. This is an orgy?"

According to other testimony, though, Jane was possibly feigning innocence. One of Warhol's underground performers was a young, well-bred, convent-trained, skinny, attractive and "liberated" girl from Buffalo, New York, named Susan Hoffman. She had come to New York City by way of Paris a few years before to be a model, then was "discovered" by Warhol for his leaden, campy, tongue-in-cheek movies and renamed Viva Superstar. As the movies gained in notoriety, so did Viva, among whose principal talents were her acerbic wit, her exploitability, her deadpan style and her willingness to copulate or masturbate on screen.

Viva wrote a novel about her life. Called *Superstar*, it is for the most part a journal-cum-anthology of childhood memories, family vignettes and verbatim and fantasized conversations (Warholians tend to tape everything that transpires in their life) with various figures in Viva's life. Two of these figures remotely echo some aspects of the personality and alleged life-styles of Jane Fonda, called Jean La Fonce in the novel, and Roger Vadim, who is called Robert. Jean La Fonce is obviously a composite character, but tantalizingly familiar—as a type.

Viva describes a couple of visits by her heroine, Gloria Superstar, to Jean La Fonce's Malibu beach house in early 1969 and also recounts a long, tape-recorded telephone conversation with Jean. Viva tells of Gloria arriving in Hollywood with her French boyfriend (later her husband) to make a movie. She receives a telephone call from Jean La Fonce congratulating her on her performance in a Warhol epic, in which Gloria was on the receiving end of a languorous gang rape, and inviting her and her boyfriend out to Malibu for lunch the following Sunday. Viva describes their arrival at the La Fonce house: Gloria and her boyfriend were taken down the beach to a marijuana party at a neighbor's home. The neighbor had a huge whirlpool bath, and according to Viva's narrative, everyone present waited for Gloria to be the first to take off her clothes and jump in. Afterward, when everyone was sufficiently high, "they picked up some flagpoles and began marching up the beach, chanting and freaking out as they went. Robert filmed the procession with his sixteen millimeter telescopic lens . . ." and Jean La Fonce invited Gloria and her boyfriend for dinner the following Saturday night. At one point in the festivities, Gloria's boyfriend exclaimed, "Zey are really crazy. Zey only smoke pot on ze weekend. It completely freak zem out!"

Saturday's dinner party was, according to Viva's novel, even more illustrative of Jean La Fonce's sense of weekend diversion. She and her boyfriend arrived late to find Jean stoned, wearing a Catholic bishop's robe from the MGM prop department and teasing her crotch with a mechanical vibrator, while Robert, "Gregor Lavitsky," the famous Polish director, and Lavitsky's beautiful blond American movie-star wife, looked on. Lavitsky had passed out, and after eating a large portion of Jean's hashish-laced cake Gloria, who was already high on mescaline, was on the verge of passing out as well. As she recounts it, she later found her boyfriend and Jean La Fonce kissing in the kitchen and was so depressed that she had to lie down. "Do you want to go upstairs and lie on my bed?" Jean asked her.

Gloria, Viva's novel continues, was taken upstairs by her boyfriend. "Jean La Fonce followed and lay down next to me. Jean put her mouth to my left breast. I decided that there was no danger. Suddenly Robert appeared at the top of the stairs. He slowly approached the bed. I pushed Jean away. . . . Jean looked at Robert as if to say, 'Imagine that! She pushed me away!' "

Viva's novel had a two-pronged interest. First, it had appeal for general readers as a chronicle of the shocking psychosexual decadence they were hearing more and more about in America. The readers were suitably shocked, if vicariously warmed. Second, it was an insider's book, and as such its pages were thumbed and riffled by scores of people familiar with the world it described. The insider's judgment was that Viva had told the truth, even if it was just her version of it, and the characters were composites based on several or more individuals out of real life.

Later in the novel, Viva sets down a long telephone conversation between Gloria in New York and Jean La Fonce in Malibu. Gloria's end of the conversation occurs while she and her husband (she had just married her boyfriend in Las Vegas) are in bed trying to copulate under the influence of amphetamines. The conversation ranges over a wide variety of subjects, including techniques of masturbation and sexual intercourse, the virtues of mescaline and speed, the question of whether Jean La Fonce is a lesbian and so on. Gloria promises to send Jean some speed, which the well-known actress claims to have never tried, in exchange for another of Jean's hashish cakes. Jean La Fonce confesses at the end of the conversation, almost sheepishly, that she is "too straight" a person to live up to the reputation that surrounds her.

When questioned about whether the Jean La Fonce of her novel might possibly resemble Jane Fonda, Viva says, "It's all fiction." When the question is put differently, she still insists, "It's all fiction." In fact, she responds to any question about the book with, "It's all fiction."

Viva's editor, William Targ, confirms her contention. He says that the book is based on many incidents out of her life and the Warhol orbit and that no specific individual is intended in any of her characterizations. "It is a work of the imagination," says Targ. "Jean La Fonce could be a composite of half a dozen women in Hollywood known to Viva."

It is possible that in early 1969 Jane was not above indulging in a little licentious weekend sport, but it's hardly likely that she was the perpetual orgiast she claimed all the writers painted her as. The serious dope-and-sex orgiasts of Hollywood were plying their pleasures elsewhere than at Jane's house, and although many of the people she knew were part of that crowd, she remained on the more elderly hip fringe—an amused, nonjudging observer and sometime tentative participant. Her participation, such as it was, was more in the spirit of relaxation and experimentation than of the dark compulsiveness that drove some of those she was acquainted with.

On March 15 Roman and Sharon Polanski gave a catered housewarming party at their new residence at 10050 Cielo Drive in Benedict Canyon. All of hip Hollywood was invited, and a brawl of sorts developed between some uninvited friends of Wociech Frykowski and Abigail Folger and Sharon's agent, which Polanski angrily settled by having the crashers thrown out of the party. According to some witnesses, Polanski wasn't the only one at the party who became angry that day. Nancy Sinatra was among the guests, and she is said to have become incensed over the open dope smoking. She demanded that her escort remove her from the Polanski premises forthwith. As they left, they walked past a white wrought-iron settee on the manicured lawn and noticed Warren Beatty sitting and talking with Jane Fonda and Roger

Vadim. They then encountered a group of scruffy long-haired hippies heading for the house and are said to wonder to this day if the ragged band wasn't Charles Manson and some of his drugged disciples.

The next day Roman Polanski left for Brazil to receive an award for *Rosemary's Baby.* From there he proceeded to England, where he would remain until the end of the summer working on preproduction plans for *The Day of the Dolphins.* Sharon Tate was due to leave a week or so later for Rome, where she would make a movie with Vittorio Gassman before going on to London to join her husband. Polanski arranged for Frykowski and Abigail Folger to live at the house while he and Sharon were in Europe.

On March 23, as Sharon Tate was packing for her trip to Rome the following day, Charles Manson showed up at the front door of the Polanski residence. He is said to have inquired of the whereabouts of Terry Melcher. He was evidently miffed at Melcher for failing to keep an appointment. He was directed to the guest house, where owner Rudy Altobelli lived. Altobelli was also packing to leave; he was traveling to Rome the next day with Sharon Tate. Altobelli testified later in court that when Manson introduced himself, he, Altobelli, said, "I know who you are, Charlie." He claimed that Manson asked him, too, where Melcher was living and that he told Manson he didn't know. He also said that on the plane to Rome the next day he and Sharon Tate discussed Manson.

On April 1, with Polanski and Sharon both in Europe for the next few months, Frykowski and Abigail Folger moved into the house at 10050 Cielo Drive. For the next two months Miss Folger worked in the Los Angeles mayoralty campaign of Tom Bradley, a black man who was challenging incumbent Mayor Sam Yorty.

During this time, she and Frykowski socialized with many of the celebrity friends they had met through Roman and Sharon, both in Hollywood and in Malibu. Frykowski, all the while, was busy building up his dope dealership; he was fast on his way to becoming a main source of supply to many of Hollywood's more fervent users in the film and music industries.

Jane Fonda, in the meantime, said good-bye to Roman Polanski and Sharon Tate and continued to devote most of her energies to filming *They Shoot Horses, Don't They?* She was also having a fling at writing a film script of her own, more as an exercise in screenwriting than out of any expectation that it would be produced. Vadim pressed on with his screenplay-as-novel, and was talking to the producers of *Myra Brecken-*

ridge, a film based on the satirical sex-change novel by Gore Vidal, about the possibility of directing the forthcoming picture.

He and Jane were also talking about a novel they had just read called *The Blue Guitar* by Alex Austin. Published in 1964, *The Blue Guitar* was the story of an incestuous love affair between a beautiful girl and her blind brother in a remote beach setting. Curiously enough, in 1968 Gene Gutowski and Roman Polanski had taken an option on the screen rights. "*Blue Guitar* first came to our attention just after it was published," Gutowski recalls, "when Columbia Pictures suggested that Roman and I make a film of it. They subsequently lost courage because back in 1964 brother-sister incest was potent stuff. Nevertheless, we liked the story, so later on we took an option on it."

Gutowski says that during the spring of 1969 Roger Vadim read the book and approached him and Polanski with an offer to buy the rights from them. "Apparently he and Jane had been contemplating for some time doing a story of incest, using both Jane and Peter, and after looking through various books and stories on that theme had zeroed in on *The Blue Guitar*. Rather than sell, I decided to make it a joint venture between Vadim and us. Vadim had already done *Spirits of the Dead* with Jane and Peter, which was also an incest story, but an awful one, and I guess they liked the idea of doing something more sensational. After an exchange of telephone calls and cables, we all agreed to meet later on in the summer to discuss it." It was the beginning, Gutowski says, of a personally disastrous venture that seriously compromised his standing as a producer in the international film community.

In May, Peter Fonda and Dennis Hopper's low-budget movie *Easy Rider* was released. Not since James Dean in *Rebel Without a Cause* or Marlon Brando in *The Wild One* had a movie actor so captured the imagination and admiration of a generation as did the younger Fonda in his role as Captain America. He projected the polarized mood of America with such forcefulness that the film's many inadequacies were overlooked. *Easy Rider* was an immediate and overwhelming box-office hit. The film became a symbol of the social turmoil of the sixties. Rather than just another movie, it was treated as a piece of contemporary history, an event that required as much analysis as a Presidential election or an assassination, and many commentators saw it as a requiem for the short-lived Aquarian Age and a kind of philosophical preface to a new age of violence, drugs and despair—an age that seemed to have already settled into the hills and canyons of Hollywood.

Easy Rider made Peter Fonda not only an important star, but a man to be reckoned with around the executive offices of the movie industry. Suddenly the studios were falling all over themselves to hand money over to young filmmakers who they hoped would emulate the Fonda phenomenon.

No one was more surprised by *Easy Rider* than Jane Fonda. Shortly after it was released, she said, "When Vadim and I first heard about Peter and Dennis' idea for the movie, we just shrugged. When we first saw it, it was four hours long. Everyone kept falling asleep. Dennis was very possessive about it, but eventually they slowly persuaded him to whittle it down little by little. Now I think it's a great movie."

Jane and Peter continued to grow closer during the spring of 1969, and each fulsomely praised the other in the press. Peter said he had stopped taking LSD and other hallucinogens; he limited himself almost exclusively to marijuana, as did Jane, and he was using his new national stature to become a spokesman for the antiwar movement and ecology. In interview after interview he decried the waste and hypocrisy of American society and thoroughly identified himself with the movement for radical change. After the success of *Easy Rider* was assured, he took his family off to Hawaii to look for a place to resettle and to plan a sailing trip around the world.

As spring drew to a close in Southern California, Jane grew more moody and depressed. Much of her bleakness was the result of her spiritual hangover from playing Gloria in *They Shoot Horses, Don't They?* The emotional investment she put into her characterization lingered in her own spirit long after the filming was finished. She seemed unable to shake the deep feelings of pessimism that haunted her as a result of her total immersion in the character and in the gloomy period in which the film was set. Gloria had been able to find release from her misery only through death. Once filming was over and Gloria was gone from her, Jane was left with all her misery but without the possibility of release.

Researching her part and making the film had raised Jane's political and social consciousness sharply over a relatively brief time. As the months went on, it seemed to her that much of the criticism she had listened to in France about America and the American system was true. Added to this were the continuing escalation of the war in Vietnam and the American government's often brutal suppression of dissent, both of which nagged at Jane's natural rebelliousness and sympathy for the underdog. President Nixon had announced that he would start withdrawing troops in small increments from Vietnam, but he compromised the effects of his announcement by stepping up American bombing of

North and South Vietnam. The antiwar movement reacted with a new outcry. The movement was no longer an isolated whisper of a few radicals; it was a nationwide shout through which the voices of diverse representatives of Establishment respectability were heard. The more vocal and active dissent became, the more assiduously did the Nixon administration appear to be trying to choke it off. Federal trials were being conducted all over the country against activists who were putting their bodies, their careers, their futures and sometimes their lives on the line. "Conspiracies" were being uncovered and announced almost weekly by the government. The FBI, the Army Counterintelligence Corps and other governmental agencies were becoming a massive combined political police force that infiltrated, spied on and sometimes actually engineered the activities of the "subversives who sought to undermine the American way," as one high government official described the militant proponents of peace. Antiwar hysteria was countered by prowar hysteria, and the concepts of patriotism and moral obligation were being fogged by violently contradictory interpretations. Gut emotions ruled the two opposed ideologies, which lay like a sodden blanket over America. As usual, ideological oversimplification was the result and deepening national paranoia the effect.

Jane watched the turmoil grow from the comfortable sanctuary of her Malibu home with an increasing sense of unease. She had been sufficiently disabused of her residual beliefs in the efficacy of the American dream to have grown cynical and disbelieving about the true intentions of flag-waving politicians. As visions of Vietnamese women and children consumed by napalm flashed more frequently in her mind's eye, she grew at once more angry and frustratedly helpless. She realized that she had lived in an ivory tower for her thirty-two years of life and, like many middle-class, liberally reared people, suddenly felt deep pangs of guilt for having clung so long to automatic beliefs that were being contradicted daily by the facts. She had two choices: to withdraw and remain aloof, protecting her own personal turf, which was the common liberal reaction; or somehow to try to do something about changing things, which was the less common but increasingly fashionable one.

Two of Jane's neighbors in Malibu were Donald and Shirley Sutherland. He was the Canadian actor who would soon gain stardom for his role in the satirical antiwar movie *M*A*S*H*. She was his wife; she was also the daughter of a luminary of extreme left-wing Canadian politics. She was an intensely outspoken critic of the war in Vietnam, as well as of other manifestations of, as she saw it, the corruption of the

American system, which included racism and sexism. Although Donald Sutherland was inclined to be politically phlegmatic, Shirley Sutherland had become Malibu's resident radical political and feminist philosopher and an organizer of celebrity support for Indians, antiwar protesters, women's liberationists, Black Panthers and other components of the Third World movement. She proselytized up and down the beach on behalf of her various causes and soon had a more than interested listener in Jane Fonda, whose vision of her own role in life was growing murkier and more unsettled and who, by her own admission, was looking for a way to expiate her guilts and redefine herself.

The pop-rock-hippie-peace culture had become an established way of life for growing numbers of people throughout the country by 1969. It had joined with the radical militant antiwar movement to create, as music critic Ellen Sander implied, an entirely new esthetic and value system in America—a commingling of idealistic liberal activism, serious revolutionism and naughty pranksterism that was loosely designed to overwhelm through mass insult the traditional American pieties and forge a new society in the United States. How many seriously believed in the counterculture's possibilities and how many merely signed on to take advantage of its libertinistic freedoms will never be known, but what is certain is that by 1969 the sense of celebration and merry incongruity that infused this culture had begun to turn ugly and dangerous. As the war went on and oppressive reaction against dissent increased, as drug use proliferated, as senses became more jaded through overexcitation, a distinct and morosely bitter change came over the mood of young America. The change was first noticed in the quality and tone of its prime semaphor—its music. No longer were the Beatles—those irrepressible court jesters of the Third World—and their countless imitators at the forefront of the revolutionary mood. The Rolling Stones, with their frantic, lyrical celebrations of acid violence, sexual brutality and political insurrection, were the new stimulants of the revolutionary imagination. The idea that revolution should be fun, as well as serious, had passed through the crucible of bitter experience and emerged gravely lacking in realism. Those against whom the revolution was directed didn't find it funny at all, and once a few heads were bashed, a few noses broken, the celebratory aspects of the movement—both political and cultural—lost their attraction. Pranking, formerly engaged in as an expression of youthful petulance, became deadly serious; the Molotov cocktail and the dynamite stick replaced the stink bomb and the peace chant in the revolutionary arsenal.

One of the most popular rock hits of 1969 was the Rolling Stones' "Sympathy for the Devil," a throbbing, sardonic celebration of the satanic forces at work in the world—a devil's-eye view of history, so to speak. The devil of the song's title, in the eyes of composer-singer Mick Jagger, is supposed to be responsible for all the violent and cataclysmic events of the past, and sympathy is demanded because all of us are personifications of Satan. "They shouted out/Who killed the Kennedys?" went one of the song's lines. "Well, after all/It was you and me. . . ." It was no small irony that Roman Polanski had been Robert Kennedy's dinner companion the night Kennedy was shot. Like Polanski, Sirhan Sirhan, Kennedy's murderer, had been involved in certain occult and Luciferian pursuits around the Los Angeles area. So had Charles Manson. "Sympathy for the Devil" and other immensely popular rock recordings of its ilk were the leitmotif of the darkening Third World mood; indeed rock music, with its acidic tones and violent rhythms, was no longer a reflection of the times. It was prophecy, and the counterculture became infected by an increasingly obsessive doomsday psychology.

New York, San Francisco, Berkeley, Madison, Cambridge—wherever a major university was situated—were centers of political and social rebellion. And it was not long before unrest began to pop up in such unlikely places as Catonsville, New Haven, Albuquerque, Harrisburg, Milwaukee, Silver Spring, Pasadena, Akron, Midland, Michigan, and Big Lake, Minnesota. Antiwar fervor and activism had metastasized to the most provincial outposts of American society, and with them went all the supplementary crusades of the Third World movement as the hysteria mounted.

Hollywood, despite its scattered cells of political activism, remained the capital of greed, lust, hypocrisy and sense gratification, even though it disguised its natural instincts in the garb and lingo of hippiedom. Filmland, for all its expressions of altruism, was still the center of the haves and have-nots of the creative ego—a hyped-up mirror image of Americana. Money was still king, movies romanticizing youthful alienation to the contrary notwithstanding. A film like *Easy Rider* was nothing unless it made its millions. *They Shoot Horses, Don't They?* had, "bottom-line-wise," as the expression went, not an iota of value unless it won big at the box office. And all the other youth-appeal movies that were in the process of being made would be nothing unless they followed suit. It was exploitation time again in Tinseltown, but as Jane Fonda once said, it is difficult for show business people to separate reality from fiction.

The ecosociopolitical contradiction grew like a malignant tumor in Hollywood's collective brain. Peter Fonda and countless other leading lights decried environmental pollution while they deliberately doused their bodies and systems in biochemical pollutants of the mind-expanding variety. Others railed against American capitalism and its attendant evils while charging $3 a ticket or $20 a kilo. Still others lobbied for social and racial justice, for sexual liberation, for peace and tranquillity—while actively promoting their opposites.

By June Jane Fonda was in a state of intellectual and emotional bewilderment. Heavy with the guilts and contradictions unleashed by her experience in *Horses*, emotionally fatigued and physically exhausted, her personal libertinism in conflict with her expanding maternal instincts, she flew off to Hawaii to spend some time with her brother and recuperate. She read voraciously, had long discussions with Peter on the state of the world and learned the rudiments of playing the 12-string guitar. "It's a whole new form of expression for me," she said.

While Jane was in Hawaii, Vadim learned that he would not get the *Myra Breckenridge* directing assignment. The job went instead to Michael Sarne, a young English filmmaker who had previously directed Donald Sutherland in the movie *Joanna* and was renting a house for the summer near Jane's in Malibu. Jane, Vadim, Sarne, the Sutherlands, others—all were acquainted with Roman Polanski's friend Wociech Frykowski.

After Hawaii, Jane returned with the baby to her farm outside Paris. She was joined later by Vadim, and the two resumed their talk about *The Blue Guitar*. "After a lot of telephone conversations," Gene Gutowski remembers, "Jane, Vadim and I arranged to meet at her farm in St.-Ouen-Marchefroy at the end of June. My agent and I flew to Paris from London. Jane had a car waiting for us at the airport, and we were driven out to the farm. We had a lovely lunch and spent the afternoon discussing the project. Both Vadim and Jane were genuinely excited about doing the film, and among other things we discussed who should write the screenplay. It was Jane's suggestion that we try to get Edna O'Brien."

Nothing had come of Jane's interest in doing a movie of the Edna O'Brien stories she had talked about earlier, but she was still intent on working on something scripted by the Irish writer.

"After the meeting," Gutowski says, "I returned to London and started to draw up a formal agreement based on the deal Vadim and I had worked out—with me producing, Vadim directing and Jane and Peter starring. Jane and Vadim assured me that they could get Peter to join in the venture." The film's budget was to be $1,800,000, with Vadim's directorial fee to be $175,000, Jane's salary $500,000, and Peter's $100,000. All that was left was for Gutowski to find a major American studio to finance and distribute the movie.

During the summer, Frykowski turned the Polanski house into the headquarters of his drug-merchandising operation. Witold Kaczanowski, who was living at Frykowski and Abigail Folger's house while they stayed at Polanski's, later told Los Angeles police that after Frykowski accepted his exclusive MDA dealership, friction developed between him and one of his Canadian suppliers. Stories of violence and bloodletting at the Polanski residence began to circulate throughout the rock-film-dope community during July as more and more cars wended their way up Benedict Canyon Boulevard to Cielo Drive from Sunset Strip, the main street of Hollywood's drug business. John Phillips, one of The Mamas and the Papas rock group, told a reporter that there were people hanging out at the Polanski residence of the type he had been assiduously avoiding for years. Phillips had heard of Charles Manson and his weird family.

Things were tense in the drug underworld that summer. Dope burns—the selling of diluted drugs at high prices—were common. Trust in dealers had vanished, and resentment ran high among the innumerable buyers who got burned. A dope burn, whether large or small, tends to trigger thoughts of vengeance and violence. When a burn involves thousands of dollars, death or death threats often follow. Frykowski, a sophisticated Pole with a highly developed sense of economy, saw in his poor, scraggly hippie clientele a clear opportunity to gain maximum profit for minimum expenditure, and it was not long before he earned a reputation as one of the premier dope burners. Susan Atkins, one of Charles Manson's followers and a defendant at the Manson trial, testified that Linda Kasabian, another Mansonite, came to her once during that summer and complained of being burned at the Polanski residence. " 'You remember the thousand dollars I had?' " Susan Atkins quoted Linda Kasabian as asking her. " 'Well, I went up to some people in Beverly Hills for some MDA'—some new kind of drug . . . MDA. Oh anyway, she went up there to buy some and they burnt her for the bread."

Sharon Tate, heavy with child, returned from London in mid-July and asked Frykowski and Abigail Folger to stay on with her at the house until her husband was able to finish up his work in London, some time in August. They agreed, and with Sharon back in town and Jay Sebring an almost daily visitor, the tempo of the social life at 10050 Cielo Drive picked up considerably. Sometime during the first week of August a friend of Frykowski's arrived from Toronto and was whipped and beaten at the Polanski property. According to the Los Angeles police, the friend was sexually abused, and the whole affair was recorded on the Polanski home video tape machine. Dennis Hopper, who was acquainted with the people at the Polanski house, later told an interviewer for the Los Angeles *Free Press*: "They had fallen into sadism and masochism and bestiality—and they recorded it all on video tape too. The L.A. police told me this. I know that three days before they were killed, 25 people were invited to that house for a mass whipping of a dealer from Sunset Strip who'd given them bad dope." It seems that a few days before, Jay Sebring complained that someone had cheated him out of $2,000 worth of cocaine and he wanted vengeance. After Sebring's death, the police found films at his house which revealed an interest in hoods, whips, studded cuffs and people chained to fireplaces.

Also during the first week of August there was, say some, a party at 10050 Cielo Drive in honor of Roger Vadim and Jane Fonda. They had evidently returned to Hollywood for a while, and the party was probably in the nature of a farewell soiree, for Jane and Vadim were about to return to France.

On August 6, Sharon Tate, Wociech Frykowski and Abigail Folger motored out to Malibu to have dinner at the house of Michael Sarne. According to another of Frykowski's Canadian friends, who saw the Pole on August 6, Frykowski and Jay Sebring were both in the middle of an experimental ten-day mescaline binge. The dealer claims that he had come to see Frykowski about an impending shipment of MDA.

Novelist Jerzy Kosinski and his wife were supposed to arrive in Los Angeles from Europe on Thursday, August 7, to spend some time at the Polanski residence. The Kosinskis' luggage was lost on the way from Europe to New York, however, so instead of traveling directly to Los Angeles, they decided to wait in New York for the luggage to turn up.

On Friday morning, August 8, Sharon Tate spoke to her husband in London over the telephone. He was due to return within the next ten days, and she asked him if he wanted a party for his birthday on August 18. The rest of the day passed uneventfully, although Sharon wasn't feeling up to par. She had invited a group of people over for the evening but later called to say she wasn't feeling well. A delivery boy brought a bicycle to the Polanski residence about 6:30 P.M. that evening. Abigail Folger had purchased it earlier in the day when she'd driven into town to keep her daily appointment with her psychiatrist. Jay Sebring answered the door, wine bottle in hand, and signed for the bike.

According to a woman employed at Sebring's hair shop in Hollywood, her boyfriend delivered a batch of cocaine and mescaline to the Polanski house later that night. She says that Sebring and Frykowski wanted more but that her boyfriend was unable to locate any.

The next day Hollywood and the world woke up to learn that Sharon Tate and her houseguests had been slaughtered during the night. Doomsday had truly arrived.

Compulsively, the film community reconstructed the event: Sharon, Sebring, Frykowski and Abigail Folger were dazed by drugs when burglars broke in. Trying to escape, the victims found the drugs had made them too sluggish. The burglars caught them, beat them, killed them—for kicks, for revenge, out of jealousy. Everyone had a theory. It was Hollywood's recurring nightmare: the movie star devoured by her fans. "Toilets are flushing all over Beverly Hills," one hip Hollywoodite confided. "The entire Los Angeles sewer system is a river of drugs."

The next night the wealthy Leno and Rosemary La Bianca were murdered in similar style at their home in the nearby Los Feliz district of Los Angeles. Leno La Bianca was said to have connections to the drug underworld, and there were those who "knew" that he had sold to Frykowski the diluted drugs the Pole had burned members of the Manson family with.

The day after the La Bianca murders William Lennon, father of the Lennon Sisters, a musical group, was shot dead while playing golf. Everyone agreed that a maniac must be loose in Filmland. Frank Sinatra, ex-husband of Mia Farrow, the original Hollywood flower child and one of Sharon Tate's best friends, hired a professional gunman. Jerry Lewis had round-the-clock bodyguards stationed at his home. Sonny and Cher bought a watchdog, and several mourners at the Tate funeral packed pistols.

Roman Polanski arrived in Los Angeles on Sunday, August 10, and immediately went into seclusion, refusing to face the lights and microphones of the battalion of reporters who awaited his arrival at the airport. Gene Gutowski, who accompanied him from London, read a short statement to the press that decried the sensationalistic rumors of satanic rituals, drug-and-sex orgies, marital rifts and the like that had filled the front pages and airwaves of Europe and America.

Polanski was devastated by the death of his wife and unborn child, but he was also worried about the cans of private films and video tapes that were scattered about the house. His worries were justified. The police, in searching the house for clues, found them before Polanski arrived. Most were in the closet of the master bedroom, and one particular video tape was found in a room off the living-room loft and booked as Item 36 in the police property report. Some of the reels featured members of the elite Hollywood group of actors, actresses and directors that swapped torrid films of one another.

As speculation mounted on the identity of the killers, a blanket of silence fell around practically everyone who had been involved with the Polanskis. To this day, attempts to secure information from those who were close to the scene create tension and uneasiness and resentment. Theories proliferated in the press and around the poolsides of traditional Hollywood, but hip Hollywood was mute. Members of the rock-film-dope culture studiously avoided one another, suddenly found they had pressing business out of town or fled to cabins in the mountains to work on long-neglected songs and scripts.

Nobody mentioned Charles Manson in the newspapers, but Charles Manson's wacky presence hung like full moon over the gloomy soul of the new Hollywood. Rudy Altobelli, for instance, rushed back to Los Angeles from Rome when he heard of the murders at his house in Benedict Canyon. Altobelli said later that he immediately thought of Manson but did not volunteer his suspicions to the police because he was not asked if he had any inkling about who might have been behind the slaughter.

New Hollywood's paranoia was further inflamed when the police began to release information they had originally thought best to withhold. Before they were murdered, said the reports, Sharon and her guests had apparently been tortured. Blood was splattered all over the walls of the house. Footprints in blood trailed randomly across the carpet. Sharon was found with a wound in the form of an X carved across her enlarged stomach, and was minus a breast. Around her neck was a rope, tossed over a living-room beam; at the other end of the rope was the sexually mutilated Jay Sebring. On the front door the word PIG was scrawled in Sharon Tate's blood.

This last detail disturbed new Hollywood the most. "Pig" was the universal hip-slang put-down word, popular among hippies and radicals.

Obviously, rationalized new Hollywood, this was done to draw attention away from the identity of the real murderers. After all, hippies couldn't have done it. They believed in making love, not war. But after Manson was apprehended and the evidence against him mounted, hippie Hollywood was at a loss for words. The official story was that Manson wanted revenge on Terry Melcher, the record producer who had defaulted on his promise to make Manson a rock star, and had sent his marauders to the Melcher home, where they mistakenly slew Sharon Tate and friends. The more likely story is that Manson knew well enough that Melcher no longer lived at 10050 Cielo Drive and that his revenge was directed at Frykowski for the Pole's double dealing in dope transactions with the Manson Family. The actual murderers were two young girls and one boy armed with a gun and sent by Manson. How Wociech Frykowski, a well-built, tough survivor of Hitler, and Jay Sebring, a cool businessman and dealer in drugs, could let two girls and a boy turn the Polanski house into an abattoir, without at least between them injuring one or more of the killers, remained a mystery. What is likely is that they knew who the intruders were and found it difficult to take their threats seriously when the three began lining them up for the slaughter.

Although it could have been argued that Manson and his band were not true hippies, for Hollywood's purpose they were. After all, Hollywood was a town built on the power of the visual, a town where a star eventually became what he looked like or risked losing his career. Thus, if Manson looked like a hippie, he was a hippie. It was as pure and simple as that. As a result, when it was definitely determined that he and his so-called Family were the architects of the bestiality at 10050 Cielo Drive, the cult of hippiedom fell out of favor.

Hip Hollywood had rallied under the banner of drugs, particularly those which induced a stoned passivity. For this reason it was often believed that the drug-oriented stars had been fascinated with self-destruction—the ultimate passivity. Peter Fonda, for instance, had become interchangeable with his souped-up motorcycle, a vehicle traditionally identified with violence and death. Jane Fonda was sex and sensuality personified. In terms of image dramatics, however, no one would be able to top Sharon Tate's tragic, but nevertheless sensational, exit. Thus, the desirability of being identified with drugs and the hippie life-style was finished—at least among the brighter stars.

On the wave of reaction against the cool philosophy of drug passivity, political and social activism became the fresh concern of the new

Hollywood. Most hip stars tried to convert to activism by espousing some cause. Initially it was the rather tame issue of ecology. "What I'm really concerned about now," the formerly easy-riding Peter Fonda is supposed to have said, "is that there are no baby pelicans left on the Eastern coast of America." But whatever Peter—as well as many of the other young stars who took up the cause of the environment—might have lacked in radical thinking, would soon be more than made up for by his sister, Jane.

Part IV

Jane/1969–1973

21. The Seeds of Change

I worry a lot. Right now, I'm worried about Vadim and me.

—JANE FONDA

HER friend Sharon Tate's murder had to have had a profound effect on Jane. When it happened she was already in the grips of a growing spiritual malaise. The things she had learned about herself while acting the role of Gloria had cracked open a door in her sensibilities through which a whole new batch of stimuli poured. Her intensifying interest in motherhood, her growing awareness of the paranoiac violence that was raging throughout the country and, finally, Sharon Tate and Abigail Folger's brutal, senseless murders—all combined to incite in her an agony of indignation, anxiety and fear.

She had already begun to question her involvement with Vadim earlier in the year, and the more deeply committed to the character of Gloria she became, the more she grew dissatisfied with his obsession with sensuality and his pleasant but unserious approach to life. For Vadim, life was merely a series of diversions, and Jane probably began to realize that these diversions were being achieved too frequently at her expense. A basically serious woman, she brooded about the lack of seriousness in their life. Her powerful identification with the fictional Gloria—a woman who had all her life been exploited and abused by men—made Jane wary

257

of her own exploitability. When she began to examine her role in her husband's life, she realized that she was often allowing herself to be used solely for his pleasure. She had spent almost four years trying to be his image of a perfect mate, and although there had been good times, she began to feel deprived of her own identity. Sharon Tate's murder, then, likely became in her mind a symbol of the utter pointlessness of the Vadim-Polanski philosophy of sensationism. In a way, Sharon's slaughter was the result of her cowlike willingness to be exploited by men; Jane was shaken by the realization, yet in it recognized her own vulnerability to the very same kind of exploitation. And when she learned that Charles Manson and his crew of devoted killers had, that summer, been stalking the beach houses of Malibu, she was repulsed. The knowledge was a dramatically chilling insight into the fact that what happened to Sharon might just as easily have happened to her. Sharon's death was nothing more than a throw of the dice.

Jane returned to France and the farm in a highly agitated state of mind. Physically, she was recovered from the exhausting grind of *They Shoot Horses, Don't They?* and was overflowing with energy and ambition. She devoted herself to a variety of self-improvement projects— a speed-reading course so she could race through the many books she was trying to catch up on, self-hypnosis so she could overcome her heavy smoking habit—but nothing seemed to distract her from her deepening and undefined feelings of dissatisfaction.

She went to the huge music festival on the Isle of Wight off the coast of England and was impressed with the way the 250,000 people, mostly young, conducted themselves. The Isle of Wight, along with the Woodstock Festival in the United States, seemed to be harbingers of a new spirit among the youth—a revival of the early flower spirit that had infused the Third World movement back before the years of doomsday —and Jane was optimistic. "It was a whole world of kids, put together by them, witnessed by them," she observed. "And it worked." But the spirit didn't prevail for long, and soon she was reading about more violence taking place in America.

Late in September Jane and Vadim celebrated Vanessa's first birthday. The unalloyed joy of motherhood partially balanced Jane's troubled mood. She often spoke glowingly about the wonders she experienced watching her daughter grow. Thinking back to her own childhood, she was fiercely dedicated to the idea that Vanessa should have a modern upbringing. "I want Vanessa to be educated differently than I was. I want her to learn to think independently. I want her to always feel free and unconfined. Even though she's only a year old, I'm already investigating schools . . . because I remember how long it took me to develop any individuality. When I was in school, I always felt panicked and scared. I will never let her feel that way."

A witness to Vanessa's birthday festivities was Gene Gutowski. "After Sharon Polanski was killed," he says, "everything was in limbo for about six weeks. I was in California for about a month with Roman, helping him sort out his life. When I returned to England in September and learned that Vadim was still anxious to proceed with *The Blue Guitar*, I approached Edna O'Brien. She expressed her delight with both the story and the possibility of working with Vadim and the Fondas. As a result, on September 27 she and I flew to St.-Tropez along with Jane and Vadim's agent, Hugh French, to spend the weekend with them.

"There was a great deal of rapport between all parties. Also, Jane and Vadim's daughter had a birthday party, and everything was very pleasant. We all sort of finalized our deal together, and I was sure I was about to become the producer of the hottest package going. With Vadim directing, Jane and Peter Fonda starring and Edna O'Brien writing the screenplay—well, I was strolling the beach at St.-Tropez contemplating my good fortune and prospective earnings."

Gutowski returned to London and says that on the basis of the arrangement he made with Jane and Vadim he was immediately offered a production and distribution deal by Warner Brothers, subject to the standard completion and performance guarantees on his part. "With the Warner Brothers offer," he recalls, "I really began to work on putting the thing together. I was a little worried, though, because so far I had heard no definite commitment from Peter Fonda, and I received the impression during my weekend in St.-Tropez that all was not well with Jane and Vadim. She was very attentive to her daughter but otherwise seemed uncertain about things."

In spite of her devotion to Vanessa, Jane's uncertainties expanded rather than receded. Sharon Tate's death still hung heavy on her mind. The freewheeling life-style that she and Sharon had shared now seemed shallow and destructive. Vadim, who was more fascinated than repulsed by the events of August, gave her little confidence in the future; he continued to approach life as though nothing had happened, nothing had changed. Jane made a halfhearted effort to conform to his indifference, but deep within her she knew that things had changed irrevocably. It was simply a matter of discovering what the changes were and how she should deal with them.

She had always done things with a passion. Whether it was becoming an actress, trying to make her marriage work, living through pregnancy or restoring the farm—she pursued the activities that were important to her with a compulsiveness that left her both fulfilled and hungry for new dreams to achieve. But now, everything she had been pouring her energies into seemed unimportant. "I needed to go away and put myself in a totally new environment—in order to understand myself and what was going on inside me." She had often listened to her brother talk about the changes he had gone through and the influence the Indian philosopher Krishnamurti had had on him. Meeting Krishnamurti was, to Peter, "like meeting Jesus. He insists that people ask themselves—not him—the questions."

Jane wanted to know more about India and Indian philosophy. Many young Americans had gone to India and come back totally transformed. So had many of the new Hollywoodians—notably Jane's friend Mia Farrow, who had returned shining with a luminescent and mysterious aura of peacefulness. The atmosphere of the multitudes at the Isle of Wight and Woodstock festivals was based on young people's sincere efforts to incorporate Indian principles of love, peace and fellowship into their lives and attitudes, and the demonstrations Jane had seen of this at Wight impressed her. It represented to her a freedom that was several steps beyond the freedom personified by Vadim and his circle. Indeed, Vadim's notions of freedom, based as they were on a sense of rebellion against Christian traditions, hardly seemed important anymore; they were merely another form of repression and selfishness—because they were still gained at the expense of other people.

India was a logical place for Jane to go to seek solace for her vague but high-energy melancholy. "I chose India because I knew nothing about it," she said. "But I knew that by going there I could be completely isolated." Shortly after Vanessa's birthday, she departed for India. The trip would spark a whole new set of impressions and would constitute another deeply felt turning point in her life. Instead of finding solace, she would find anger.

The experience of traveling across the teeming subcontinent overwhelmed her. Until that time, poverty had only been a word to her: "I had never seen people die from starvation or a boy begging with the corpse of his little brother in his arms." The never-ending sights and smells of death and disease filled her with horror and disgust. She couldn't understand her friends who had gone to India and come back singing its praises. "I met a lot of American kids there, hippies from wealthy middle-class families, in search of their individualistic metaphysical trips. They accepted that poverty. They even tried to explain it to me, saying it was because of the religion. But I said, 'To hell with that! Don't you understand that the trouble with these people stems from religion, that it's their religion that's driving them right out of existence?' All these Americans were busy rejecting the materialistic values of life, but they were unable to go one step further and relate the tragedy of the Indian people to the real cause—religion.''

Conditions in India frustrated and maddened Jane the more she journeyed. Not only were her sensibilities offended by her realization of the moral and social slavery that outmoded religious beliefs create, but they were additionally bruised by her first real up-close view of the effects of colonialism—in this case English colonialism. Although India was now an independent nation, two centuries of white English rule and racial exploitation had left it mired in helplessness and despair. Where before Jane had only heard and read about the political and social oppression that existed in other parts of the world as a result of Western colonialism, she now saw it at first hand. Her sense of injustice was further inflamed by a visit to Nepal and Sikkim, where she was entertained by the king and queen. The Queen of Sikkim was the former Hope Cooke, a young American woman who was a contemporary of Jane's. Although Jane was awed by the beauty and remoteness of Sikkim, she found the imperial palace to be symptomatic of the corruption, inequality and injustice of life on the subcontinent. While Hope Cooke, a girl who had come out of educational and social surroundings that were similar to Jane's, was enjoying all the privileges of royalty high in the mountain kingdom of her husband, millions were rotting to death in the coastal lowlands of India. The five-hour jeep trip over the narrow, rutted road between Sikkim and India was for Jane like St. Paul's journey along the road to Damascus. She knew she would never be the same again.

She wanted to stay in India to see more but had promised to return to California by mid-November to do prerelease publicity for *They Shoot Horses, Don't They?* She left for Los Angeles depressed by her travels. But she was also fired by a burning ambition to somehow do something to expiate the guilt she felt for the plight of the miserable masses she had journeyed among. Then she experienced a kind of culture shock that immediately sparked her resolve. Arriving in Los Angeles, she checked into the Beverly Wilshire Hotel, "and when I woke up in the morning I still had in my eyes the crowds of Bombay, in my nose the smell of

Bombay, in my ears the noise of Bombay. My first day back, and I saw those houses of Beverly Hills, those immaculate gardens, those neat, silent streets where the rich drive their big cars and send their children to the psychoanalyst and employ exploited Mexican gardeners and black servants." The contrast was overpowering. "I'd grown up here, but I'd never looked at it in these terms before. India was urine, noise, color, misery, disease, masses of people teeming. Beverly Hills was as silent and empty and antiseptic as a church, and I kept wondering, *Where is everybody?*"

Jane's return to California coincided with two major events—one on each coast—that filled the newspapers and airwaves in November, 1969. One was the Moratorium against the war which drew huge crowds to Washington on the weekend of November 14 and 15. President Nixon responded by declaring that he would be too busy watching football games on television over the weekend to notice the demonstration. Displaying the older generation's characteristic contempt for the antiwar movement and the aspirations of the young and its equally characteristic unwittingness, Nixon played right into the hands of the organizers of the Moratorium, thus closing the circle on the polarization between the Establishment and the forces of dissent. Indeed, many fence-sitting members of the Establishment were repelled by Nixon's insensitivity, and antiwar sympathies mushroomed.

The other event took place in San Francisco Bay when, on November 21, a group of American Indians led by Richard Oakes, a Mohawk, invaded the deserted Alcatraz Island Federal Prison and declared it Indian territory. The Indian community of America had quietly caught the fever of militant activism. The occupation of Alcatraz, for which the government was totally unprepared, was declared a symbolic revolutionary act by the fledgling American Indian Movement to publicize the United States government's long history of duplicity in its dealings with the rights—territorial and otherwise—of the American Indian. During the first few months after Nixon's inauguration, things had been fairly quiet in radical, Third World America. Now things were heating up again. The spirit of Woodstock was dead.

All one had to do late in 1969 was to speak or act out against government oppression or harassment, and one found oneself a hero of the radical movement. Black Panthers, White Panthers, feminists and dozens of other minority activist groups were on the receiving end of government oppression and had become incorporated into the counter-culture. With their occupation of Alcatraz, the American Indians became unwilling but full-fledged members of the movement. And although membership did not always redound to their advantage, one positive effect was the fact that the government, besieged on all sides with increasingly damaging public relations, cooled its heels for the moment on the Indian take-over of the island.

Jane Fonda didn't, though. Fresh from the squalor of India, ensconced in the pristine luxury of Beverly Hills and feeling sour over the contradictions that were bombarding her consciousness, she began to follow the Alcatraz story. She was vaguely aware of her own forebears' role in the social and political disenfranchisement of the Mohawks and other tribes of the colonial Northeast. She was also attuned to the American Indians' struggle for civil rights and self-determination through her association with Marlon Brando and other Hollywood figures who had identified themselves with the Indian cause. When she heard that one of the Alcatraz leaders was a Mohawk, her curiosity was piqued.

Jane happened on a copy of *Ramparts*, a glossy liberal Catholic publication that had been transformed in the mid-sixties into a muckraking, left-wing political magazine. In it she read an article by Peter Collier about the Indians who had invaded Alcatraz. She was astonished by the revelations in the article and immediately wanted to learn more. She decided that instead of returning to France after the opening of *They Shoot Horses, Don't They?*, she would remain in California to see what she could do by way of advocating the Indian cause. The chickens hatched during the making of *The Chase* were coming home to roost.

When *They Shoot Horses, Don't They?* opened in mid-December—just in time to qualify for the Academy Awards—critical reports on the picture varied widely. There were those who found it unbearably depressing, others who quibbled with other aspects. But most of the more perceptive critics hailed it as one of the best pictures of the year, and Jane was lavishly praised for the performance of her career and possibly the best performance of the year by any actress. Pauline Kael, one of the toughest and most uncompromising of New York critics, not only gave Jane's characterization her unqualified praise, but engaged in a bit of prophecy as well. "Fortunately," she wrote, "Gloria, who is the raw nerve of the movie, is played by Jane Fonda. Sharp-tongued Gloria . . . is the strongest role an American actress has had on the screen this year. Jane Fonda goes all the way with it, as screen actresses rarely do once they become stars. . . . And because she has the true star's gift of drawing one to her emotionally, even when the character she plays is repellent, her Gloria is one of those complex creations who live on as part of our shared experience. Jane Fonda stands a good chance of personifying American tensions and dominating our movies in the seventies. . . ."

Vadim had joined Jane at the Beverly Wilshire during November and was growing increasingly impatient with her lingering moodiness over the trip to India and her sudden interest in American Indians. He had thought that her trip would have resolved the discontent he saw in her after Sharon Tate's murder; he was disappointed, then, to find her even more restless and unsettled than before. When she decided that she wanted to stay on in the United States to do more research into the Indians' problems, he reluctantly agreed. They sent for Vanessa, who had been left behind in France, and made arrangements to rent the house in Malibu again.

Vanessa remained the single joy of Jane's life as her mood otherwise darkened during the last weeks of 1969. As an added dividend, having Vanessa with her seemed to cement Jane's improving relationship with her father. "My father and I are very happy with each other now," she said at the time. "He's really proud of Vanessa, and happy that she's so pretty. I feel we really understand each other now. And he and Peter are much closer, too. I think for the first time in his life my father is happy and relaxed."

Fonda spoke publicly of how proud he was of Jane's performance in *They Shoot Horses, Don't They?* But although relations between father and children had improved, Fonda remained aloof from Peter's, and now Jane's, political discontent. Peter hardly ever tried to bring his father around to his viewpoint, but Jane, who found it easier to talk with Fonda, began to. She recalled telling her father about her trip to Russia and how quiet and slow, how human and delightfully inefficient she found the Russians. She then told him how glad she was to think that her daughter was one-quarter Russian. "And my father said, 'How can you say that when you've just explained that the Russians are inefficient?' And I answered: 'But that's beautiful! Dad, you've been so brainwashed with the American idea of efficiency that, for the sake of efficiency, you forget about the human elements!' He did not understand. And this was the first time I realized the incredible gap between myself and the people who brought me up. Not only my father, but the system he represents."

Also joining Jane and Vadim late in November was Gene Gutowski, who flew in from London to attend to some problems that had arisen over the production of *The Blue Guitar*. "Things were getting sticky," he says. "Edna O'Brien had to drop out because she was not able to start working immediately with Vadim on the project. A joint decision was made to use another well-known English writer, Peter Draper. Story conferences were held with Vadim and Draper in London while Jane was in India, and at first everything seemed all right.

"But then the deal began to fall apart. I entered into a contract with Draper to write the screenplay for twenty-five thousand dollars, based on Warner Brothers' assurances to me that they were willing to gamble that amount to get a firm commitment from Jane and Peter, particularly Peter, to star. Of course, Warner's assurances to me were based on Vadim's continued assurances to them that he could persuade Peter to participate, once we had a screenplay. Vadim was especially insistent that Warner's not bug Peter at that moment for a definite commitment, and it was left to him—Vadim—to handle his 'family,' so to speak, once he had a workable screenplay in hand, since obviously no star of any stature would commit to the book alone. Remember, this was after *Easy Rider*, and Peter Fonda could more or less call his own shots."

Gutowski says that the head of Warner Brothers, John Correy, did bug Peter Fonda before the screenplay was finished and received a definite "not interested" from Jane's brother. "Evidently, Peter had not heard a word about it from Vadim, and when he heard about it from Warner's, he was more than a little angry. He said something like not being interested in the brother-sister exploitation Vadim had in mind and insisted that even if the screenplay were Nobel Prize material, he wouldn't change his mind. Well, there went the deal. Warner Brothers pulled out, and after that everything rapidly slid downhill. Vadim and Jane were breaking up and were no longer interested in making pictures together, Peter Fonda was definitely out, Warner's went back on their commitment for the costs of the screenplay, and I was landed high and dry with an obligation to pay Peter Draper twenty-five thousand dollars. Since I refused to pay for the screenplay, taking the position that it was Warner's obligation as a result of their assurances to me, the Screenwriters' Guild, acting on Draper's complaint, put both Cadre Films and me personally on their 'Unfair List,' where to the best of my knowledge I still reside. It has made it almost impossible for me to function as a film producer."

Gutowski tells this story more in irony than anger. He says that his experience indicates one of the hazards of working with Roger Vadim. "It was Vadim, saying that he could easily get Peter Fonda, who got both me and Warner Brothers interested. He strung us out as long as he could, and when he couldn't produce Peter, he quietly disappeared, never once offering to help pay off Peter Draper, no less saying he was sorry. In fact, I never heard from Vadim about it. Nor Jane, for that matter."

On December 30 Jane was given the New York Film Critics' Award for her performance in *They Shoot Horses, Don't They?* She found out about it after stepping off a plane in New York, where she arrived to spend the New Year's holiday with her father. "It's the biggest accolade I've ever been given," she said. "One tries to be blasé about things, but now that it's happened it's very nice." The Film Critics' Award was traditionally a prelude to winning an Oscar. Jane was now anxious to win a coveted Academy Award. "You can't imagine what winning an Oscar does for your career. I'd love to get it. But I'm afraid to think of the Film Critics' Award as an omen. It might jinx me."

On New Year's Eve she gave an interview to Rex Reed for the New York *Times*, and when it was printed three weeks later, Jane again found herself the object of a heated controversy. Reed quoted her as asking, "You don't mind if I turn on, do you?" He then went on to write that "she carefully rolled the tobacco out of a Winston, opened the cap of a dainty snuff-box on her father's coffee table, and replaced the ordinary old stuff that only causes cancer with fine gray pot she had just brought back from—Where? India? Morocco? She couldn't remember—all she knew was that it wasn't that tacky stuff they mix with hay in Tijuana, this was the real thing." Reed studded the interview with descriptions of Jane inhaling lungfuls of marijuana smoke, and the *Times* was blitzed by a storm of angry, denunciatory letters about her behavior.

That New Year's Eve Jane waxed reflexive. She talked about the decade of the sixties and admired the activism of the young. She described herself as being a member of the "sloth generation" of the fifties, "when people had been fed sleeping pills by Eisenhower," and declared her envy for those who were out participating in the life of the country and trying to improve its quality. She implied that she felt that she had wasted much of her life and indicated that she was anxious to do something to make up for it. She praised Vadim, but her words had a hint of the valedictory in them. "Vadim is alive, with all the imperfections that entails. He'll make big mistakes, because he's vulnerable. He has never denied the madness in himself. . . . He's taught me how to live, and if anything happens to our marriage, he'll always be my friend." Something, obviously, was already happening to their marriage.

Jane returned to California. While Vadim worked on another film project, she devoted most of her time to reading about Indian problems and seeking out people who could tell her more about them. She got in touch with Peter Collier, the man who had written the article in *Ramparts*, and asked him to take her to Alcatraz for a firsthand look at the Indian occupation. While she was there, she talked with several of the Indian leaders and was deeply impressed with their uncompromising commitment to their cause and the sad dignity of their frustration. Since the original take-over two months before, which had garnered front-page attention, the occupation of Alcatraz had been for the most part forgotten by the media. The government had reacted with uncharacteristic public indifference, thus avoiding a confrontation, and news of the "symbolic revolutionary act" soon became stale. The Indians remained, but the reporters had long ago left. It was only when word of Jane's visit got out that media interest was again aroused.

Jane came away from her visit filled with outrage and an expanding sense of guilt over the white-imposed plight of the Indians. "I learned about the genocide that had taken place, that is still taking place, the infamies we had done to the Indians in the name of efficiency, in the interest of the white farmers. And I learned that the Senators who are supposed to defend the Indians hadn't done a thing."

Whether "genocide"—an increasingly fashionable term among radicals—was the correct word to use or not with reference to the Indians is a question open to interpretation, but there can be no doubt that the American Indian was the most severely oppressed of all minorities on the continent of North America. The history of white America's treatment of the native Indian has been a long and dishonorable one, made more shameful because it has had the official sanction and cooperation of the United States government. It did not take long before the fever for social and racial justice spread to the long-ignored Indian community. Slogans of ethnic pride such as "Black Power" and "Black Is Beautiful" were soon appropriated by young Indians angry over both the government's oppression of the Indian culture and the collaboration in the oppression on the part of the older Indian tribal establishment. "Indian Power" and "Red Is Beautiful" became the battle cries of the new Indian activists who caught the militant fever of the late sixties. Yet the Indian cause remained ignored in the larger scheme of radical events. It was not until Alcatraz—which the small band of militant invaders vowed to defend to the last man, woman and child—that Indian passions made an impression on white America. Once the novelty of the occupation had worn off, however—mostly because the government was willing to give the Indians their day in the sun—white America forgot about the red men's cause.

When Jane Fonda perceived this, she resolved to do something about it.

Ramparts magazine was the product of a single ego, that of Warren Hinckle III. Hinckle had wrested control of *Ramparts* from its liberal Catholic founder, Edward Keating, and as its editor had turned it into a high-priced radical publication aimed at the Liberal Establishment in America. One of Hinckle's pet ongoing projects dealt with the question of "who really killed President Kennedy." As a result, he was continually involved with New Orleans District Attorney James Garrison, who insists to this day, without revealing how or what he knows, that he is privy to all sorts of dark secrets relating to an assassination conspiracy involving the CIA, the Soviet KGB, Cuban counterrevolutionaries, the French secret service and other representatives of world reactionism. Hinckle was also involved with another prominent advocate of the conspiracy theory, a mercurial left-wing New York lawyer named Mark Lane. Lane had moved into the Kennedy assassination case at its very beginning by appointing himself defense counsel for Lee Harvey Oswald, and when Oswald was killed by Jack Ruby, he became Oswald's posthumous public defender. He was among the spate of authors who wrote postassassination books criticizing the Warren Commission's conclusions and tendering theories on why and how Kennedy was "really killed."

That Hinckle, Garrison and Lane all were and are obsessive publicity hounds with a common nose for the main chance and a shrewd understanding of American gullibility would seem readily apparent from their respective records in the public arena. In addition, Hinckle and Lane were both champions of the left—new and old—and each was journalistically or legalistically involved in all manner of counterculture events, including the interminable trial of the Chicago Seven which had dragged into its fifth month. It takes nothing away from the justice of many of America's radical causes to suggest that when Hinckle, Lane and others learned of Jane Fonda's interest in educating herself about the problems of the American Indians, they were all eager to serve as her tutors.

Lane is a likable bear of a man with a dry, cutting wit and a cornucopia of legal gifts—a man who "thinks well on his feet." He might have made millions as a Wall Street lawyer if such had been his inclination. But his inclinations were diametrically opposed to representing corporate America and advancing the capitalist system. By the late sixties he had grown out of his old-style 1950's New York Socialism and was a full-fledged advocate of Marxist revolution in America. Those who knew Lane and observed the progressive hardening of his political attitudes could never be sure how much of his revolutionary zeal derived from sincere conviction and how much came from his theatrical love for publicly espousing the outrageous. Whatever, in early 1970 he was a tireless campaigner for various revolutionary constituencies, and when the Indians took over Alcatraz, he was among the first white radicals to speak out on their behalf.

As a result of her visit to San Francisco and Alcatraz with *Ramparts* writer Peter Collier, Jane Fonda soon got to know Hinckle, Lane and others in the *Ramparts*-New Left circle. Among the others were Donald Duncan, Fred Gardner and Steve Jaffe. Duncan was a former career soldier and Green Beret who served in Vietnam with the first American forces and wrote, in 1965, a scathing insider's report exposing and condemning the military's methods there. The article was printed by *Ramparts* and later grew into a book called *The New Legions*, which was published in 1966. It was generally ignored by even the liberal Establishment press, which still largely supported the Johnson administration's war policies. Because of Duncan's public repudiation of American policies, he was hounded and harassed by various Army and civilian agencies and was for several years thereafter the object of countless death threats and other anonymous forms of violence. He used his credentials as a Vietnam veteran and writer to become a full-time journalist and editor and returned to Vietnam in 1968 as a reporter for *Ramparts*. He drifted into the antiwar movement more by accident than choice, but by early 1969 he was a full-scale activist speaker and an organizer in the more moderate precincts of radicalism. His principal interests were draft resistance, servicemen's rights and the organizing of Vietnam veterans.

Fred Gardner was, in Duncan's words, "a brilliant, dedicated Communist who could charm the pants off Martha Mitchell." A native of the San Francisco area, Gardner came to Communism early in his life, and although he was intensely active in the antiwar movement from the very beginning, he was a man who marched to the beat of his own drum. He was one of the movement's severest internal critics and was especially outspoken about separating serious revolutionaries from the fun-and-games types who were gaining most of the headlines but contributing little to the Marxist goals of the truly revolutionary arm of the movement. In his late twenties, he was a facile writer, gifted speaker and intrepid, tireless organizer. In 1967, exasperated with the movement's cavalier attitude toward servicemen, many of whom in his tactical view were ripe for radicalization, Gardner began to canvass various move-ment groups for money and aides to help organize GI dissent within the military. Movement leaders berated him for hoping to convert "the enemy," which in their minds every soldier was, and rejected his proposals. Thereupon he made his way with a single co-worker, a girl named Donna Mickleson, to Columbia, South Carolina—the town that served the huge nearby Army post of Fort Jackson—to test his idea. He rented a place on Main Street in Columbia just down the block from the USO, called it the UFO, and opened it as the first "underground GI coffeehouse" in the fall of 1967. By January, 1968, soldiers from Fort Jackson—mostly draftees—were flocking to the UFO, where they got food, beverages, entertainment and clever, low-key political indoctrina-tion. The base had already gained national attention as the site of the court-martial of Captain Howard Levy, an Army doctor from New York who had refused to train Green Berets and was sentenced to Leaven-worth Prison. In February, 1968, it was the first Army post to experience a GI-staged antiwar demonstration, and suddenly Fred Gardner and his GI coffeehouse idea were being hailed by the very same radicals who six months earlier had refused to help him. Gardner quickly became known as the father of the GI movement. He left the UFO in the hands of Donna Mickleson while he traveled to Fort Hood, Texas, Fort Leonard Wood, Missouri, and other Army towns to organize additional off-post coffeehouses.

Steve Jaffe was a young, novice public relations man with strong antiwar sympathies and a seemingly intense interest in the Garrison-Lane-Hinckle assassination-conspiracy theory. He had worked as a volunteer for Garrison's squad of amateur assassination investigators around the time the New Orleans district attorney was prosecuting Clay Shaw for his alleged involvement in the conspiracy and had also spent time with Mark Lane on Lane's assassination theory. In 1969 Jaffe volunteered to travel to France to run down some new sources of conspiracy information that Garrison claimed existed within the French secret service. He returned emptyhanded, but more fascinated than ever with the myriad possibilities of the mystery. Jaffe had worked as a journalist and movie-studio publicist after getting out of college. In 1969, deciding on a career in show business public relations, he got a job with the public relations firm of Allan, Ingersoll & Weber—Jane Fonda's press representatives at the time, as well as Donald Sutherland's. From his position there, he assisted Jane in her early contacts with some of the figures he knew in the radical movement and thereafter became her and Sutherland's personal press agent at the firm.

After her visit to Alcatraz, Jane immediately plunged into a full-scale course of self-education. Usually shy about imposing on other people's time, she overcame her timidity and sought out everyone she could find who might contribute to her knowledge. The fires of reform, which had smoldered quietly for the past few years, suddenly began to rage. She attended meetings, parties and rallies where she met numerous exponents of various left-wing causes and soaked up chilling stories of government oppression and persecution. Once a halfhearted member of the dope culture, within weeks she transferred her allegiance to the peace-and-freedom movement. It was here that her natural sympathies for the downtrodden could really find something to bite into.

22.   Getting the Radical Heat

> *You can do one of two things: just shut up, which is something I don't find easy, or learn an awful lot very fast, which is what I tried to do.*
>
> —JANE FONDA

JANE returned from Alcatraz with a simple passion to do something publicly on behalf of the Indians, but it was only a matter of days before she found herself involved with the Black Panthers. Marlon Brando, the original Hollywood advocate of the Indians back in the early sixties, also identified himself with the black civil rights struggle. He had more recently become a Black Panther sympathizer and was attending Panther rallies and funerals in support of their cause. With Brando as her model, Jane followed suit. She had no choice, really, since the militant Indian movement got much of its inspiration from the various black power groups that had evolved out of the turmoil in the South and were now solidly incorporated in the radical movement.

By 1969, among all the interwoven radical groups, the tiny Black Panther Party was the biggest bête noire of federal and local law enforcement agencies. The Panthers had grown indirectly out of the socialistic Student Nonviolent Coordinating Committee—called SNCC and pronounced "Snick"—three years earlier as a result of impatience and disaffection with SNCC leader Stokely Carmichael's ideas about combating American racism. The Black Panther Party was founded in Oakland, California, by Huey P. Newton, a former law student, and Bobby Seale, an Air Force veteran who had been a member of the Revolutionary Action Movement, a black extremist organization which, according to J. Edgar Hoover, had been providing Stokely Carmichael with much of his Marxist-Leninist Chinese-Communist ideology.

Of the two founders of the party, Newton became the undisputed leader—an arrangement which Seale readily accepted, since he recognized that Newton's gifts as a theoretician and organizer were superior to his own. The philosophy of the Black Panther Party was largely Newton's creation; it differed significantly from the position taken by Carmichael and his followers and initially attracted a handful of young blacks who, like Newton and Cleaver, had lost faith in the leadership and "black power" philosophy of Carmichael.

Although the Panthers did not reject the idea of black power, Newton's program was considerably more radical than Carmichael's. Where Carmichael argued that American blacks were an oppressed colonial minority who, to free themselves, must create a culture and economy of their own, Newton insisted that black revolutionaries should not let their blackness separate them from potential white revolutionary allies. Instead, they should become a vanguard of "revolutionary nationalists" and lead the poor and oppressed of whatever race toward revolutionary socialism. Hence the Black Panther slogan "All Power to the People!" by which the Panthers meant power not simply to black people but to all oppressed people.

The Panthers contended that Carmichael and his followers would probably be content with American society provided that they could purge it of its racism and participate in its benefits as equals. Newton's more extreme view was that the present system was fundamentally rotten, that racism was merely a symptom of its deep corruption and that there could be no peace for anyone until American society and its institutions were not simply "reformed" but fundamentally transformed in accordance with Marxist theory. "Capitalism," Newton declared, "deprives us all of self-determination. Only in the context of Socialism can men practice the kind of self-determination necessary to provide their freedom."

Couched in the inflammatory Newton-Seale oratorical rhetoric and given a boost by white media coverage of Panther street actions, the Black Panther program soon gained national attention. What most readily distinguished the Panthers from other militant groups were their uniforms—black leather jackets, black trousers, jaunty berets, brightly polished shoes and sunglasses—and the fact that they openly carried rifles, shotguns and pistols in the interests of, they said, self-defense. In a confrontation with San Francisco police in 1967, Huey Newton angrily bluffed down a terrified police officer who had ordered him to drop his gun, and the Panthers, then a tiny group of no more than thirty militants, were launched on the national consciousness.

By the fall of 1968 the Black Panther Party had chapters in several Northern cities and more than 2,000 members, all of whom were required to read Mao's *Little Red Book* and acquaint themselves with the use of firearms. They claimed that the circulation of their weekly newspaper exceeded 100,000 copies. Although the party's membership remained marginal, its fame and influence spread quickly.

As a result of this notoriety, the Oakland, Berkeley and San Francisco police became increasingly aggressive. Not only did they follow the Panthers wherever they went, but they began openly to bait and provoke them. Early in the morning of October 28, 1967, several Oakland policemen who had been following Newton's car stopped him. A shoot-out ensued, and an officer named Frey was killed. Newton and another policeman were seriously wounded. Newton was arrested and placed in a prison hospital. Soon thereafter a grand jury charged him with murder and attempted murder. The prosecutor did not, however, produce the murder weapon, a detail that suggested to the Panthers and to other observers that Officer Frey may have been killed not by Newton's gun, but accidentally by the gun of a fellow policeman.

The shooting and subsequent indictment of Newton marked a new level in the continuing program of police harassment which, in the next three years, would result in the arrest and shooting of scores of party members, not only in the San Francisco area but in Los Angeles, Chicago, New York and several other cities. But the indictment further stimulated the growth and enhanced the reputation of the party within the radical movement, especially among white extremist groups. And when, early in 1969, J. Edgar Hoover declared the Black Panthers "the greatest threat to the internal security of this country," their reputation as the foremost domestic heroes of the Third World movement was cemented.

Concurrent with the development of the Black Panthers, the GI movement—a term used by the radical left to refer to that aspect of the antiwar movement aimed at the military—began to grow. On its surface the GI movement, begun almost single-handedly by Fred Gardner with his coffeehouse projects, appeared benign enough—an effort to proselytize active-duty military personnel against the war and to extend to GI's all the privileges of the First Amendment of the Constitution denied them by certain articles of the Uniform Code of Military Justice. One of the favorite punitive methods used by military commanders against GI's who committed infractions of the code or who simply spoke out against the war was immediate assignment to Vietnam combat zones. In addition, the military system of dispensing justice differed in several key aspects from the civilian system, and with more than 3,000,000 Americans in the service, the majority of them involuntarily, the extent to which First Amendment rights available to civilians were not available to soldiers was a new and pressing problem of American social philosophy. Radicals such as Gardner used this as the focus of their public concern for the lowly GI. Below the surface, however, their intentions were far more revolutionary.

By 1969 the GI movement was supported by just about every extremist left-wing organization in the country. Once the revolutionaries moved into the picture, only the most naïve could believe that the GI movement's real concern was with servicemen's rights. Although the various radical groups supporting the GI movement differed on the proper approach to best exploiting the movement, their doctrinal justification for doing so was a unanimous throwback to the Marxist-Leninist past. Soldiers were just another class of worker to be radicalized in accordance with the traditional blueprint for revolution.

Revolutionary parties of every stripe rallied to the GI movement in force during 1968, helping set up coffeehouses, establish movement bookstores and publish GI newspapers. They embarked on intensive programs of political indoctrination aimed mostly at uneducated and often illiterate servicemen. As results began to be seen in the increasing numbers of antiwar demonstrations on military posts and in the almost unbelievable increase in desertions, radical agitation expanded, and more and more organizers turned their attention to fomenting military dissent. But as these activists attached themselves to the GI movement, dissension over the proper political tactics and strategy began to grow, as they always seemed to in revolutionary circles. Fred Gardner, the movement's founder, says, "The opportunists began to take over. As the GI projects came under the auspices of the antiwar movement, they were turned into forums at which long-winded, self-important men and women with a smattering of Marxist phraseology could hold forth. The GI's who were willing to be proselytized were either totally passive or personally ambitious. As the New Lefties came into the movement, it became everybody's personal revolutionary ego trip. And while the career radicals vied for power and influence, the soldiers became forgotten victims."

Gardner had temporarily left GI organizing in mild disgust in early 1969 to cover the court-martial of a group of soldiers who had "mutinied" at the San Francisco Presidio stockade and to write a book about the case as an illustration of the contradictions between the First Amendment and the Uniform Code of Military Justice. Then, because of his fame as founder of the GI movement, he was asked to become president of the newly formed United States Servicemen's Fund (USSF), a money-raising project put together by a group of left-wing business and movement people to provide money for the expansion of the GI movement. He agreed, he says, mainly out of guilt. He was by then ambivalent about the movement he had founded but still didn't want to see it collapse or be destroyed by the "new wave of comrades" or "organizers trying to build their own quick reputations."

In spite of his efforts to combat the dilettantism and divisiveness of the opportunistic New Left elements of the movement, Gardner fought a losing battle. Where, to him, this sort of revolutionary activity was deadly serious business, with no publicity, no rewards and no heroism, to the newer revolutionaries it was romantic gamesmanship full of bravado and romantic, ego-fulfilling satisfactions. The romantic appeal became the dominant factor in the GI movement, and soon such typically romantic figures as the Black Panthers' Huey Newton, Bobby Seale and Eldridge Cleaver became the heroic focus of the movement, rather than the GI's themselves.

Huey Newton, remanded to prison for the maximum "involuntary manslaughter" sentence of fourteen years—despite the inability of the prosecution at his trial to prove conclusively that he shot the late Officer Frey—became the penultimate hero of most white radicals while he languished behind bars. "Free Huey" and "All Power to the People" and "Right On" were now the rallying cries of white as well as black revolutionaries, and informal black-white radical alliances were formed throughout the country. In the meantime, federal and local police forces pressed their campaign against white terrorists and Panthers alike. The whites for the most part went underground, issuing communiqués and building dynamite packs in places the police would least expect to find them. The Panthers, however, had no place to go, and as the police policy of harassment and provocation mounted across the country, they began to drop off like skeet. Panther members and leaders in New York, New Haven, Washington, Detroit, Oakland and Chicago were killed under a hail of police bullets. And in Los Angeles, on December 8, 1969, at dawn, a monumental gun battle took place between an army of police and thirteen Black Panthers at the Panther headquarters in the south-central section of the city.

The incident was a fitting end to the paranoia of Southern and Northern California in 1969. In the hopeful eyes of "respectable" Angelenos, the battle put an end to the small Panther community of Los Angeles. But for radical groups it raised the local Panthers to the status of oppressed martyrs. When word got out that Robert Bryan, a twenty-two-year-old black from Summit, New Jersey, had been at the forefront of the Panthers' counterattack, he was quickly elevated to the status of hero among heroes and became the local symbol of white radical identification with Panther persecution.

Jane Fonda read about the Panther-police battle at about the time she was getting her beginning education on the Indian problem. She had heard a lot about the Panthers through Shirley Sutherland, her Malibu neighbor, and others in Hollywood's growing activist community. Like many whites, she was frightened by the clear-cut violence they seemed to personify. Moreover, she didn't understand their ideology because she had not read Marx, Lenin, Mao, Fanon and the other architects of Communist revolution. Yet she had long been sympathetic to the black civil rights struggle and had been properly horrified at the assassination of Martin Luther King, Jr. But because of her lengthy sojourns in France, she felt almost completely out of touch with the "Black Power" and "All Power to the People" psychology that had surfaced in the black liberation movement. She possessed, however, all the credentials of what the right-wing element in American society liked to call the "bleeding-heart liberal," and like most liberals, she operated much more on emotion than intellect (as, of course, did the right-wing advocates). Thus, when the Los Angeles shoot-out occurred, her natural contempt for the authority represented by the police expanded her sympathies to include the Panthers.

One quality Jane had that most liberals didn't was an insatiable curiosity. She also had the financial means to satisfy it. "Two things I wanted to find out," she said. "One, what was happening with the American Indian. I'd always been aware that they were at the bottom of the barrel. . . . Then, one of the other things I was curious about was the Black Panthers. . . ."

When she became aware of the interlocking tactical connection between the Alcatraz Indians, the Panthers and the rest of the radical movement, her curiosity was piqued even further. "I had understood that it was always the Panthers who took all the harassment, and I asked why. So, after the Indians, I decided to meet the Panthers, and when I did, I was impressed. They were not at all like I imagined. It was the first time I had met black militants with a political ideology, a political discipline, or should I say people who go right to the roots of a problem."

As from the Indians, from the Panthers she heard stories of political and economic oppression, police persecution and provocation that chilled her sense of humanity. She saw pictures of police standing over the bodies of dead Panthers with the same kinds of smiles on their faces that she had seen in pictures of Nazi soldiers standing over the bodies of dead Jews.

Her already-hypertense sensibilities grew more agonized as she read and listened to reports of police brutality directed not just at the Panthers but at all expressions of dissent. The forces of authority were fast becoming the forces of authoritarianism, as far as she could see, and the knowledge worked her into an angry frenzy of frustration and helplessness. Her encounters with the Indians and Panthers jolted her out of her indecision and introspection about herself. She was looking for a cause to which she could devote herself—a new challenge, a new ambition. What could be more fulfilling, and more right, than the cause of social justice?

She might have remained nothing more than an interested observer, however—a petition signer and occasional demonstrator à la Marlon Brando—save for one additional ingredient in her life early in 1970. All her life Jane's personal commitments and convictions had been sparked by the men she had been involved with, from her father to Vadim. It seems unlikely that she'd plunge into a whole new form of commitment without the corresponding emotional support of another mentor. Thus, it hardly seems coincidental that her sudden rush to right the wrongs of the world came at the same time she met a strong new personality. Whether

her rapid transformation to political activism came about as a consequence of her discovery of him or the discovery of him was just an aftereffect of her transformation is anyone's guess. But the evidence of the past suggests the former.

She and Vadim had already grown distant as a result of her loss of interest in his hedonistic and socially irresponsible values. She continued to give him public credit for having "liberated" her, but from her present perspective of dissatisfaction and restlessness it seemed more like a reverse liberation—it had been at the cost of her real freedom and dignity as a woman. Her dependence on Vadim and his life philosophy had ended with the murder of Sharon Tate and with her depressing trip to India, and for four months she had been existing in a limbo of uncertainty. It was as if she were waiting for a new guide to come along and show her the direction she was eager to take.

Among Fred Gardner's many interests was writing for films. He had been hired by the famous director Michelangelo Antonioni to work on the script for Antonioni's Hollywood production of *Zabriskie Point*. Antonioni was an Italian Communist, and *Zabriskie Point* was to be his first American film—a jaded study of the naïve, childish, self-destructive tactics of American youth and an indictment of the vulgarities of the American system that encouraged revolutionary fervor.

While Jane was in the process of learning about the Indians and Black Panthers, she attended a party given in Hollywood for Antonioni. There she met Fred Gardner, the attractive, persuasive, deadly serious Marxist who had started the GI movement, had written a book about the Presidio mutiny and was currently the president of the United States Servicemen's Fund. Out of that meeting came the real beginning of a whole new life for Jane Fonda.

23. A Cross-Country Trip

When I left L.A. I was a liberal. When I arrived in New York I was a radical.

—JANE Fonda

JANE FONDA and Fred Gardner were like two ships that go bump in the night. Jane was journeying into political consciousness and activism; Gardner, who had long been involved in both, seemed to be gradually inching his way out. For Jane, Gardner was her conduit into the mysteries of the radical spirit. For Gardner, she was a charming and totally unexpected relief from the frustrations he was experiencing as a dedicated revolutionary working in a garden of dilettantes.

The meeting came about innocently enough. At the Antonioni party, Gardner overheard Jane say that she was planning on making a cross-country automobile trip—something she had wanted to do for many years—and was hoping to visit some Indian reservations on the way. Gardner, sensing the intensity of her curiosity about the events that were taking place, felt constrained to speak up for his constituency. "He said, 'Why don't you go to some of the coffeehouses?' " Jane remembers. "At the time I didn't even know what a GI coffeehouse was."

Gardner explained the GI movement to her, and she was fascinated— at first more with his style and personality than with the movement itself. She said she wanted to find out more about it, however, and asked what she could do to help. From there began a relationship which, although it was short-lived, brought Jane full force into the revolutionary mainstream of early 1970.

Gardner took Jane in hand, and what started as the political indoctrination of an eager supplicant quickly evolved into a love affair between teacher and student, according to several of their friends. He took her to organizational meetings and introduced her to leftist lawyers involved with military law, from whom she got detailed explanations of the objectives of the GI movement. He introduced her to some of the radicals who were working as organizers on the GI projects. He traveled with her to coffeehouses in Monterey, near Fort Ord and in Tacoma, Washington, near Fort Lewis, where she met the staffs and talked with GI's. Through Gardner and press agent Steve Jaffe she met Mark Lane, the radical lawyer who had lately taken up the GI cause, and Donald Duncan, the ex-Green Beret who was also involved with Gardner in the United States Servicemen's Fund. Although Jane retained her interest in the Indians and the Panthers, under Gardner's tutelage, and later Duncan and Lane's, she focused most of her energies and passions on the GI movement.

By March Jane had pledged herself to the GI cause. She offered her time and services to Gardner and the others in any capacity they wanted to use them. Although she still emotionally identified with the Indians and Panthers, because the GI movement was almost exclusively white she found her most immediate acceptance there. And when her desire to do something became generally known, her offer was seized on with an eagerness that was equal to her own.

Jane was an unexpected bonanza to the GI movement and its sponsoring United States Servicemen's Fund. By 1970 the movement had already begun to splinter and fragment over ideological and tactical differences. At a USSF conference in Lousville, Kentucky, shortly before Jane became involved, the inevitable struggle for control which seemed to affect all the radical branches of the peace movement had taken place. According to Gardner, the newer blood among the movement's leadership was out to take over, using the New Left concept of the collective as their rationale.

The collective was a political idea left over from Marxist philosophy. It had been revived by SDS and other youthful radical groups as the only method of democratic self-government and decision-making. In theory it was the ideal model of democratic interaction. In practice it seldom worked that way. Yet it was an idea that the more impatient of the revolutionary militants clung to and employed to impress their own version of revolutionary activism on the people they sought to proselytize. To people with little sophistication or knowledge about revolutionary history, it was a beguiling notion indeed, and soon the collectivists were springing to the forefront of the radical movement. Theoretically, collectivism provided everyone with an equal and direct role in the political process; there was no intervention of elected representatives as in, say, the American form of democracy. Nevertheless, its theoretical virtues overlooked the frailties of human nature; history had proved that it was simply impossible for humans to operate within such a selfless framework—the lust for power, dominance and personal distinction were simply too strong. The new collectivists understood this. They vowed as part of their revolutionary program, in effect, to alter the conditioned responses of human nature so that mankind would eventually learn to live, work and operate politically within the collectivist framework. To experienced radical organizers like Fred Gardner, this was as realistic as expecting people to give up sex.

In Gardner's view, the collectivists were desperately trying to seize power over the GI and other branches of the antiwar movement in a belated attempt at personal self-aggrandizement. "Their goal was to strengthen the bureaucracy, force out the serious people and make a play for the big money and prestige that had previously accrued to the more moderate elements of the antiwar movement. They called me a loner, idiosyncratic, a male chauvinist . . . later I learned that the strivers are always slandering people on any grounds but that of revolutionary purpose. I heard Don Duncan called 'short-tempered,' others called 'do-gooder' and 'elitist' and 'bourgeois.' I heard Howard Levy accused of being 'unable to work collectively.' According to them, people who talk are 'too verbal' and people who are quiet are 'unwilling to struggle.' It didn't really matter, if they were out to get you they were going to find a way to put you down."

Jane came into the GI movement at the early stages of this internecine struggle. At first her loyalties, romantic and political, were with Gardner, who was still its nominal leader. Soon she would be faced with a choice, however, as the "strivers" began to vie for her allegiance. But first she had more learning to do.

In early March, according to Donald Duncan, Gardner took Jane to Seattle to meet Mark Lane—who was working as a legal adviser and organizer for the GI projects and was touring the country to make a film on the movement—and to observe an Indian demonstration that was planned for Fort Lawton. The demonstration was to be patterned after the Alcatraz invasion as a protest against the federal government's failure to keep its Indian-treaty promises. Fort Lawton was a little-used, sparsely populated Army reserve base; the Indians intended to occupy it, declare it Indian territory and open a native cultural center on the property.

On Sunday, March 8, Jane joined Lane and about 150 Indians as they marched on Fort Lawton. They were met at the main gate by a prewarned force of military police from nearby Fort Lewis. Some of the Indians rushed the gates while others set up diversionary actions, scaled fences and managed to erect a tepee in a small clearing in some woods on the base. One of the Indian leaders read a proclamation: "We, the native Americans, reclaim this land known as Fort Lawton in the name of the American Indians by the right of discovery."

Jane was in the group with Lane at the main gate. In the ensuing struggle, nearly 100 Indians were arrested, along with the ever-visible Lane, and Jane was roughly pushed around. After a few hours under arrest, Lane was released with an expulsion order. He immediately shouted to reporters covering the incident that MP's were beating Indians still in custody. From Fort Lawton, Lane, Gardner, Jane and a few others drove to Fort Lewis to protest the "malicious beatings" that had taken place at the tepee area out of sight of newsmen and had put at least ten of the Indians into the hospital. Lane, a theatrical, calculatingly shrill man who milked every moment of protest for all it was worth, led a small caravan of cars through the gate at Fort Lewis. The caravan was chased down by the MP's, and its members, including Jane, were arrested for violating the Fort Lawton expulsion order and for trespassing. They were detained for a while, questioned, then escorted off the base.

The incident at Fort Lawton was Jane's first close-up exposure to protest-movement violence, and when she saw the burly white MP's clubbing the unarmed Indians, her blood boiled. The Indian invasion attempt, an event that might otherwise have received a few lines of type in the press, was instead splashed across the front pages of the next day's newspapers as a result of Jane's participation and arrest. At a press conference the next day, called primarily to announce the Indians' plans to picket Fort Lawton, Jane was the center of attention, unwittingly upstaging the Indians and causing stirrings of resentment in some of their leaders. Jane announced that she was soon going to take a cross-country trip to visit Indian reservations and Army bases and was joining the movement for the establishment of an Indian and GI Bill of Rights. "I hear from the GI's I've been talking to that we need a GI Bill of Rights," she said, "and from the Indians we need an Indian Bill of Rights. I always thought that the Bill of Rights applied to all people, but I've discovered differently."

Referring bitterly to her arrest at Fort Lewis, she said, "Bob Hope was greeted differently by the local branch of the military-industrial complex. But then, I did not come up here to glamorize war or to urge young men to fight." She went on to say that "I'm campaigning on behalf of human beings, whether they be Indians, GI's or whatever," but concentrated most of her remarks on Gardner and Lane's GI projects. She claimed that GI's were being deprived of their rights to the point where "they're being put on planes at gunpoint and sent to Vietnam if they're caught dissenting." As for the military authorities, she concluded: "If they're getting that uptight about my being on an Army base, it means they're worried about something, as well they should be."

The United States Servicemen's Fund's principal activity in the Seattle-Tacoma area was sponsoring the Shelter Half, an underground GI coffeehouse near Fort Lewis. The Shelter Half was staffed mostly by young revolutionaries affiliated with the Socialist Workers Party, the SDS and the Black Panthers, and its goal was plainly to promote disruption of military activities at Fort Lewis and nearby McCord Air Force Base by plying GI's with how-to-do-it tips on desertion, sabotage, terrorism and other antimilitary acts. This was a step radically beyond Fred Gardner's original concept of the GI movement. Although it was in accordance with the traditional tactics of the Marxist-Leninist revolutionary scenario, Gardner had serious misgivings about the strategy— misgivings based on his fear that the GI's, already victims of the military system, were also being turned into victims of the New Left's impulsive power-hungry and divisive revolutionary style. Nevertheless, he remained at the helm of the Servicemen's Fund and tried to temper the movement's new revolutionary and terrorist fervor with his insistence on maintaining the original concept of the GI projects—the protection of GI rights from the unconstitutional excesses of military law.

Mark Lane, although he was considerably older than Gardner, was a good deal more publicly fractious. Once involved in the GI movement, he exhibited some of the political opportunism and egomania Gardner had begun to criticize. Nevertheless, Lane was a national celebrity of sorts, had a certain amount of clout with the press and was, in his flamboyant way, an effective radical lawyer. As Jane watched Lane operate, she became sold on lending her name, her presence and her money to the movement.

Howard Levy was another national celebrity of sorts and one of the many movement leaders Jane met in the early days of her commitment. He was the young Army doctor who had been sent to prison for more than two years for his refusal to train Green Berets in the healing arts and around whom the GI movement had originally found much of its inspiration when Fred Gardner set up the first coffeehouse at Fort Jackson in 1967. Levy had been released on parole the summer before by order of Supreme Court Justice William O. Douglas and had immediately joined Gardner's USSF, practically running the fund's New York office. "When I first met Jane," he recalls, "I couldn't have been more impressed. She was full of energy, a sense of commitment, and had really been going to school on all the people she'd been talking to. I'd say she was really knowledgeable on many of the objectives of the GI projects."

Jane traveled to New York with Gardner shortly after her Seattle arrest to sit in with him on USSF meetings, to appear on the *Dick Cavett Show* and to meet her French friend Elisabeth Vailland, who was arriving from France at Jane's invitation to accompany her on her cross-country trip.

"I met her at a meeting with Gardner—I think it was at the Essex

House hotel," Levy says. "There were a few others there, some people connected with the fund, a lawyer and so on. Jane questioned me intensively, and we had a really good discussion. She was open, curious, absolutely without any kind of rhetoric—just very nice and very warm. For a while, I was taken aback by being in the presence of this big movie star, but she quickly dispelled any feelings of awe I might have had. She was down-to-earth and completely open, like just one of the guys, and pretty soon I forgot the movie-star business and concentrated on her as a person. And as a person, she was terrific."

Elisabeth Vailland was astonished at the changes she noticed in Jane when Jane picked her up at Kennedy Airport during the second week of March. "It was my first trip to America," she recalls, "but on the ride in from the airport I noticed nothing, so intent was I on the voice of my young friend as she spoke of her commitment, her preoccupation with the political conscience that was in the process of being born."

Jane took Elisabeth Vailland to a meeting with Gardner, Levy and other USSF representatives within hours of her arrival. The next day they met with La Nada Means, a young Indian woman Jane had met at Alcatraz and had brought to New York to appear with her on the *Dick Cavett Show*. That evening, leaving the theater at which the show was taped, Jane, who had passionately but inexpertly spoken about the injustices the Indians had suffered, was spit upon by a man from the audience.

On March 15 she and Elisabeth Vailland flew back to Seattle, where they were met by Mark Lane. Lane had urged Jane to sue the Army for her arrest, and while she was in New York, he had been occupied with a group of young Seattle lawyers drawing up the papers. Jane remained in Seattle for an intensely busy day, visiting the Shelter Half, filing the lawsuit in district court with Lane as her lawyer, picketing and meeting with the Fort Lawton Indians. Among the Indians there was some tension over Jane. At one meeting she was rebuked by one of the leaders for using the Indians for personal publicity. The Indians trusted no white people, not even self-appointed white advocates, and several of them felt that Jane's appearance on the *Dick Cavett Show* would only hurt their cause because they would be identified with a Hollywood publicity seeker. Jane took the rebuke silently, claiming that she was interested only in helping the Indians and had no desire for personal publicity. She found it difficult to understand the Indians' hostile attitude until it was explained to her at a second meeting by one of the more sympathetic leaders. He defined their position and told Jane how she could help them simply by joining with them in demonstrations, not by trying to be a spokeswoman. It was one thing to identify with the Indians, another to represent them in the court of public opinion, and Jane simply did not know enough about the long history of white oppression to be an effective representative. Jane agreed, although reluctantly; such strictures ran against her natural instinct for performance.

The next day Jane and Elisabeth flew to Los Angeles, where Elisabeth met Henry Fonda. Jane had been trying to get her father to share her outrage over the things she had been told by Gardner, Lane and others about American atrocities in Vietnam. "When My Lai broke, it was no surprise to me," she later recalled. "The soldiers I had talked to had already told me too much—about the generals who give transistor radios as awards for the cut genitals or the cut ears of the Vietcong or about the way they throw Vietcong out of helicopters."

Jane said she had been brought up to believe in America's moral perfection and had clung to her beliefs in spite of growing evidence to the contrary, even despite the cynicism of her left-wing friends in France. Now, horrified by the stories she heard and pictures she saw, she found her feelings against the military had hardened. "I told my father all the things I'd learned. He exploded, 'You don't know what you're talking about! We don't do that. We're Americans. And even if the soldiers did it, they wouldn't talk about it.' So I explained to my father that when they start talking, you can't stop them. And he said, 'If you can prove that it's true, I will lead a march to Nixon and confront him.'"

On March 18 Jane invited Donald Duncan, the ex-Green Beret sergeant, and a second Vietnam veteran, a former officer, to her father's luxurious Spanish house in Bel Air to talk to him. "They told him about the massacres, the tortures, everything. My father sat, and he listened very quietly, obviously moved, but he never went to Nixon and confronted him. He said sadly, 'I don't see what I can do besides what I'm already doing—that is, campaigning for the peace candidates.'" Henry Fonda had, like almost every American liberal, finally turned against the war. But like most liberals, he continued to value the American system and instinctively clung to the rationalist belief that the complex issues of world affairs were a many-sided matter beyond the cure of a political point of view based on alien and absolutist theories.

American society has always lived on catchwords and self-righteous rhetoric. But self-righteousness has historically proved to be the enemy of sound analysis. It was such an instinct that brought the United States into the conflict in Southeast Asia to begin with and then, once committed to it, caused us to escalate and re-escalate the war. In justifying the escalations, succeeding administrations in Washington became captives of their own fictions.

The gathering storm against the war also derived from our self-righteous nature. Out of it grew a whole new set of catchwords, and the antiwar movement became captive of *its* own fictions. As fiction warred against fiction, America became infused with a siege mentality. And in the classic reaction to mutual frustration, as in an unhappy marriage, overstatement, accusation and scapegoatism became the order of the day.

Henry Fonda was too rational a man to succumb to the kind of simplistic, undiscriminating thinking that he saw Jane being magnetized by. Yet he probably failed to realize that each time in his life he had rejected Jane's attempts to get him to identify with her feelings, his rejection sent her off on some new tack of rebellion that eventually came back to haunt him. He tried, in his way, to reason with her on this protest business she was getting caught up in, but of course the more they argued, the more they forced each other to strengthen their grips on their respective ideological fictions. Jane soon forgot about trying to convert her father.

During the next week, while she was preparing to embark on her cross-country automobile trip, Jane engaged in a furious round of meetings and rallies on behalf of Black Panthers, Indians and servicemen. On March 20 she attended a meeting with Angela Davis, the French playwright Jean Genet and Panther lawyer Luke McKissick to discuss raising bail money for the Panthers who had been arrested in the shoot-out three months before. Also at the meeting were Shirley and Donald Sutherland and Vadim.

Jane and Vadim were still living together at the Malibu beach house, although Jane was growing progressively more distant from him. When asked about Vadim's attitude toward her new activities, Jane said, "Well, he approves of what I'm doing, though he doesn't agree with it all. It's very difficult for a Frenchman. . . . For example, I'll talk to him about the fact that a Black Panther's bail will be a hundred thousand dollars, and he'll say, 'What are you talking about? In France, nobody has bail.' And I'll talk about a no-knock warrant, and he'll say, 'You never have to knock to come into a home in France.' So it's very hard to explain these things to him. . . . What I'm doing concerns him a great deal, but he knows that he can't stop me from doing it." One can imagine the ironic tableau of Henry Fonda and Roger Vadim commiserating with each other over what they considered to be Jane's folly.

On March 22 Jane visited the Black Panther headquarters in Los Angeles—the scene of the shoot-out—where she talked to some of the Panthers who had been in prison. They told her stories about how, at the Los Angeles County Jail, blacks and especially Panthers were constantly provoked and tortured in the hopes that they would fight back and thus cause their bail to be increased. Then, with Robert Bryan—the hero of the Panther-police battle who had been the first of the prisoners to be released on bail—she traveled to San Diego to visit the Green Machine, another coffeehouse, this one set up mainly for marines stationed at Camp Pendleton. There she sat through more political indoctrination meetings in which the solidarity of oppressed servicemen, blacks and Indians was hailed. She was becoming increasingly impressed with the Panthers and the quiet, cool way they handled themselves. It was a complete reversal of the picture she had had, and she felt happy to be identified with them.

March 23 found her back in Los Angeles, where she spent most of the day touring the movie studios trying to raise Panther bail money, then meeting with Angela Davis, who had just lost her University of California professorship for being a Communist. She also met with Donald Duncan at his house in the San Fernando Valley. They discussed her forthcoming trip, and he gave her an itinerary of Army bases he thought she should stop at.

Two evenings later Jane and Elisabeth Vailland stood in the driveway of her father's house preparing to embark on their trip. Jane had acquired a large Mercury station wagon for the journey, and as she and Elisabeth finished loading it up with their traveling gear, Henry Fonda took pictures, and one-and-a-half-year-old Vanessa scurried around saying, "Bye. . . ." By 6 P.M. they were on their way, with Jane at the wheel.

Their first extended stop was at the Pyramid Lake Indian reservation in northern Nevada. Pyramid Lake had been a long-standing bone of contention between the Indians and the government. Angry groups of Indians were protesting the United States Bureau of Reclamation's diversion of the waters of the Truckee River to a non-Indian irrigation project. The Truckee was the only major source of water for the lake. Pyramid Lake covered practically the entire reservation and, through its fishing industry, was the main supplier of income and livelihood to the local Paiute tribe. Now, with the waters of the lake drying up, the fishing industry was dying. The Indians saw in this a perfect example of how the federal government, serving the interests of white farmers, was indiscriminately abrogating its treaties and further destroying Indian culture.

Pyramid Lake was not the only case of white America's illegal exploitation of Indian resources. Other Indians were inflamed by strip-mining and power-plant developments on the Hopi's sacred Black Mesa in Arizona, on Navaho lands in Arizona and New Mexico and on the Crow and Northern Cheyenne reservations in Montana. Still others were fighting white real estate developments on a number of Southwestern reservations. These and other white incursions of Indian territory were accompanied, moreover, by frictions that made them worse: Indian water rights had been taken away from tribes through fraud and deceit, leases had been signed with grossly unfair terms, and even those terms were not being lived up to and were not enforced.

The method by which leases for Indian-owned resources were approved and signed exposed another, even more serious source of Indian anger. Prior to their military defeat by white America, all tribes had ages-old methods for governing themselves, some by councils of wise and respected elected chiefs, others by hereditary religious or clan leaders. But in 1934 the federal government imposed on almost every tribe a uniform system of tribal councils—styled in the white man's way—that appointed the top tribal officers. Council members were supposed to be elected democratically by the people, but in practice the new system was so alien to large numbers of Indians that majorities of them on many reservations consistently refused to vote in tribal elections and continued to regard the councils as imposed institutions of the white man rather than of their own people.

Many Indians felt that the elite tribal councils were responsible for permitting white exploitation of their resources and in many cases cooperated in it—a charge not far from the truth. Thus, the Indians not only were angry with whites, but were also divided among themselves. The most militant of them had formed the American Indian Movement to reestablish the traditional Indian methods of government, to restore tribal customs and religions and to effect Indian autonomy over their own affairs.

Jane was aware of all this when she stopped at Pyramid Lake, but she was not prepared for what she found. Some of the Indians she had met at Alcatraz arrived at the lake to conduct a demonstration on behalf of the Paiute. According to Elisabeth Vailland, she and Jane were astonished at the difference between the Alcatraz militants and the local Paiute of the reservation—the Alcatraz group was dynamic, fired-up, united, whereas the Paiute were indifferent and melancholy, led by a fat council leader. Jane was depressed by the poverty of the Indian settlement and by the incongruous fact that many of the local Indians were repugnantly obese.

It was the Indians' obesity that remained the dominant image in Jane and Elisabeth's minds as they continued their trip to other reservations. Their next stop was the reservation at Blackfoot, Idaho, where they were to meet La Nada Means, the Alcatraz girl whose brother, Russell Means, was one of the leaders of the radical Indian movement. "On all the reservations we went to," Elisabeth Vailland says, "the Indians were almost without exception grossly fat, the result of all the beer they drank. They drank beer without stop. At first, Jane thought it was due to malnutrition, but she finally agreed that it was the beer." Any illusion Jane might have had, based on her Alcatraz visit, of the Indians as sleek, stealthy warriors was shattered.

Another source or disappointment was the fact that the Indians—especially the Indians of the militant movement—insisted that in order to reunify themselves, they had to revive their ancestral religion. One of their cardinal principles was that white Christianity, to which so many Indians had been converted through the years, had kept them locked into their serfdom; the only way to combat this was to throw off the hold of the white man's religion and reestablish their traditional religious beliefs and rituals. To Jane, an atheist, this was "negative, antiprogressive and antirevolutionary," and she argued heatedly with some of her Indian friends about it.

From Blackfoot, Jane and Elisabeth drove to Salt Lake City. As expected, Jane had been nominated for an Academy Award for *They Shoot Horses, Don't They?* and had to fly back to Los Angeles for the ceremonies. When she arrived, she found that the publicity over her arrest in Seattle and her other activities during the past two months had made her a *cause célèbre* in the film industry. Speculation ran high about whether she had jeopardized her chances for the Oscar, which almost everyone agreed would have been hers without question otherwise. When she showed up at the Santa Monica Auditorium on Oscar night, she was greeted by the usual crowd of movie fans packed in banks of bleachers across from the entrance. When they saw her, many cried out radical slogans, waving their hands in the V sign or raising their fists in the Black Panther salute. Jane stopped for a moment, looked at them, then smiled and raised her fist in return.

She didn't get the Oscar, and although she took her disappointment calmly, many of her friends were incensed. "A pure case of political prejudice," said one. "The whole country knew that Jane should have had it," said another. "It was no contest. They kept it from her because they were afraid she'd get up and make a political speech." Jane shrugged. Three months before, the Oscar had been important. Now it was not so important, except in one sense: It increased her contempt for the rituals of the Establishment.

Jane remained in Los Angeles for a few more days to work on Black Panther fund raising, then flew back to Salt Lake City with Elisabeth to retrieve the car and continue their trip. From Salt Lake City they drove to Denver, where they took part in a thirty-six-hour Fast for Peace organized by various Denver antiwar groups. The small crowd of fasters, which included Dr. Benjamin Spock, Jane and several local Black Panthers, camped out on a small island at a downtown Denver intersection. Jane gave television and press interviews praising the revolutionary spirit in America and expressing solidarity with the peace movement. By the end of the fast she was overflowing with radical ardor.

Her next stop was Colorado Springs, the site of Fort Carson, where she had agreed to participate in an antiwar demonstration organized by the staff of the local coffeehouse, the Home Front. By now everywhere she went in the Denver area she was trailed by reporters, photographers and television crews, and it was not long before it became apparent that Jane Fonda was the biggest thing to hit the radical movement since the Yippies and Crazies of Abbie Hoffman and Jerry Rubin.

Jane took two days off and flew incognito from Denver to New York, where she held strategy sessions with Fred Gardner, Howard Levy and other Servicemen's Fund's representatives. Then she flew back to Los Angeles for meetings with Donald Duncan. During her visit to Fort Carson she had demanded to see the stockade, where three black servicemen with Panther sympathies were under arrest. Now she wanted to return to Carson and mount a demonstration for the prisoners, who she believed were imprisoned primarily because of their Black Panther connections. Duncan advised her on how to go about making an effective protest at the fort and helped her write a speech. Later she went out to Malibu to visit with Vanessa, then went on to a fund-raising party at the Sutherlands'.

Political activism had intensified in Hollywood on the heels of Jane's failure to win the Oscar. So had career opportunism. The journey from the hippie unconsciousness of the late sixties to the political consciousness of the early seventies was complete, and all sorts of young actors, writers, directors, producers and other film people were in the process of making the fashionable switch. With Marlon Brando wrapped up in personal problems, Jane became the focus of the new activism. And once everyone saw that she was in it for real, they flocked to join the bandwagon.

Howard Levy says, "When Jane came to New York and asked about what she could do, she was still confused about her identity. She kept saying, 'I don't just want to be known as Jane Fonda the actress. I want to be something more than that.' She was really champing at the bit to get more heavily into the movement. So we said, 'Now, wait a minute, Jane, you are an actress. I'm a doctor, and one of the things I'm trying to do is organize the medical profession, you know, get doctors to give money and support to the movement. If you were a lawyer, I'd tell you to get out and organize the legal profession. But you're an actress. Organizing is what the movement is all about. So go back to Hollywood and start organizing the film industry.' She agreed, and that's what she started doing. She hated going around asking people for money or calling up strangers on the phone. But she gritted her teeth and did it. She was quite remarkable the way she blasted right in. Of course, she was very close to Freddie Gardner by then. He was a pretty demanding guy, so I suppose a lot of her drive came about as a result of her trying to please him. But she really went at it."

Jane returned to Denver on April 20 loaded with political books for the prisoners at Fort Carson and a strategy for inviting arrest and further publicity. When she was refused reentrance to the base, she went back to the GI coffeehouse and devised a plan to enter illegally with the help of some of the dissident soldiers. Wearing a disguise, she got through the main gate in a soldier's car and drove to an enlisted men's service club. Once inside, Jane removed her disguise and started lecturing the crowd of GI's and passing out the books she had brought from Los Angeles. The astonished GI's flocked around her, and when they realized who she was, pandemonium broke out.

The military police were alerted, and as Jane tried to drive off the post, she was stopped and arrested. After being detained for a short time at the guardhouse, she was released on orders of the commanding general. "He no doubt chose to avoid a scandal," says Elisabeth Vailland, who was detained along with Jane. "The young soldiers who were with us were disillusioned. They dreamed of being arrested."

From Colorado Springs Jane and Elisabeth drove south to visit a

Navaho reservation in New Mexico. They spent the next week traveling through the Southwest visiting other reservations, and arrived in Santa Fe on April 30, a few minutes before President Nixon announced over television that he had ordered the American invasion of Cambodia. To the antiwar movement, the invasion of Cambodia was a gross betrayal of Nixon's promises to end the war. It discredited him forever and marked the beginning of a new wave of mass protest and violence throughout the country. At first, Jane was stunned and dispirited. The leaders of the movement had been saying that their years of sacrifice had finally begun to pay off, that the United States would never dare escalate the war again. When their prophecies proved empty, a momentary pall of despair swept over the movement followed by a new outburst of protest. Right-wing America continued to hail Nixon as a hero who refused to be compromised either by the bad faith of the North Vietnamese enemy or by mounting liberal public opinion against him; left-wing America castigated him as a true representative of the imperialist warmongering mentality of America. Slogans flew back and forth, and the national anger—on both sides—swelled to unprecedented proportions.

Jane met her brother, Peter, in Santa Fe the evening of Nixon's announcement—he was there filming scenes for his new movie, *The Hired Hand*—and they brooded together over the turn of events. On May 1 Jane gave a televised interview to the press. She spoke coldly and cynically of President Nixon and condemned the American invasion of Cambodia as an unforgivable breach of faith on the part of the administration. Even her friend Elisabeth Vailland was surprised by Jane's angry, despairing tone. "I had never seen Jane speak like that before. Her sense of tragedy and outrage was overwhelming. She was crushed by what Nixon had done, she felt betrayed and was very angry, yet her analysis was clear and to the point."

Jane and Elisabeth spent the next two days visiting communes around the Taos area, bringing news of the Cambodian invasion to the isolated hippies. Then they drove to Albuquerque, to the campus of the University of New Mexico, which was in the midst of a student demonstration over Cambodia and the killings of four students at Kent State University in Ohio by the National Guard. Jane was invited to speak at a student rally. It was the first time she had ever addressed a throng of such magnitude. The mood of the crowd was hot with rage and insurrection. Previous speakers had incited it further. When it came her turn to speak, according to Elisabeth Vailland, Jane announced in a cold, hard voice that she was not there as an actress, but as a participant in a political action that was necessary to bring everyone together to join the struggle against the ignominy of America. Jane received a rousing ovation, then joined a march on the residence of the university president, where the massed students demanded the closing of the university as a symbol of protest against Cambodia and the Kent State killings.

She flew back to Los Angeles the next day to attend a press conference announcing plans for mass demonstrations against the Cambodia escalation. She was now completely committed to the movement and offered to use her publicity value, anytime, anywhere, to draw media attention to it. Donald Duncan presided over the press conference. He announced a series of demonstrations for May 16, Armed Forces Day, at military installations across the country and the formation of the Cambodia Crisis Coalition, a group of sixty antiwar organizations. The reporters then laced into Jane with a barrage of questions about her well-published activities in Colorado and New Mexico. "The reporters were sarcastic and aggressive," Elisabeth Vailland says. "They kept trying to make Jane contradict herself, and the atmosphere became very tense. The conference ended up with everyone in a bad mood. It didn't go well."

Jane spent that night at Malibu visiting her daughter and having dinner with the Sutherlands. The next day she was on her way back to Albuquerque and the University of New Mexico, to which she had promised to return to take part in further demonstrations. When she arrived, she found the newspapers full of accusations against her for being a dangerous agitator. In Jane's brief absence there had been riots between radical and conservative students, and the university had been closed. With nothing further to do there, she set off for Killeen, Texas, where she planned to visit the Oleo Strut, the off-base GI coffeehouse that Fred Gardner had organized in 1968.

The Oleo Strut was another of those projects that had been originally designed primarily as an indoctrination center on GI rights but had been transformed by 1970 into a cell of political revolutionaries. It was managed by a young radical named Joshua Gould, and its staff was ridden with dissension over the correct approach to radicalizing GI's. The more tactically moderate Gardnerites sought to keep the focus on legal rights and the avoidance of Vietnam duty, whereas the extreme Trotskyites, as they were called, encouraged Fort Hood personnel to carry out acts of sabotage and terrorism. Gould had been hauled in and out of court on a variety of charges, including marijuana possession, and when Jane got there on May 7, he was hurriedly trying to organize an Armed Forces Day demonstration.

No sooner had Jane arrived than she received a call from Donald Duncan to fly to Washington the next day to give a speech at the huge May 9 protest rally and march on the White House. She immediately left for Washington and found the capital swollen with protesters, police and troops. At the rally Jane opened her speech by crying "Greetings, fellow bums!"—a parody of President Nixon's characterization of protesters a few days before. Then with dozens of other celebrities, including Shirley MacLaine, she joined the head of the march, her fist raised in the Black Panther salute.

She returned to Fort Hood that night and the next day joined the staff of the Oleo Strut in a round of meetings and discussions. At about this time the GI movement was suffering, among other forms of internecine strife, a quarrel over the role of women. Many of the young female radicals resented the ways in which they were used—being assigned mostly the traditional women's roles—and were agitating within the movement for more voice in policy-making and actions. Everywhere Jane stopped on her tour she listened to complaints about how the men in the movement accepted women's inferior status while trying to revolutionize everything else. The complaints of the young women at the Oleo Strut were especially bitter. Jane agreed with them and promised to work on their behalf.

The next day, she went to Fort Hood to distribute leaflets to GI's inviting them to the Armed Forces Day demonstration. The Oleo Strut staff had been barred from the base for engaging in such activities, so Jane went in accompanied only by Elisabeth Vailland. They were immediately stopped by the military police and taken to MP headquarters. There an officer read the military regulations that prohibited the distribution of leaflets and other materials. Jane tried to argue that she was in her rights to be on the base, so the officer placed her under arrest. She was mugged and fingerprinted and then, three hours later, escorted off the post. She returned to the Oleo Strut, where local newspaper and TV crews had gathered, and gave what was by now becoming her customary outraged interview attacking the military establishment for violating the rights of servicemen.

Jane was following the strategy set out for her by Gardner, Duncan and Lane. As Elisabeth Vailland put it, "You must understand that the movement, in Texas especially, needed this kind of press coverage. It was the only way to get across to the people what it was trying to accomplish. For two years the movement had been through a period of lassitude. Everyone was discouraged by the lack of results. People were beginning to doubt the necessity and possibilities of action. The leaders felt it was necessary to reencourage the cadres. I was surprised to find such progress in so short a time. The press and the television, even when they were hostile, were definitely a positive element. The doubters and the timorous were stupefied to find that the movement was getting all that attention—much of it due to the efforts of Jane. They began to think again."

Jane and Elisabeth left Texas on May 12 for Fayetteville, North Carolina, so that they could be there in time to meet Mark Lane and take part in the Armed Forces Day demonstration at Fort Bragg. As they made the long drive during the next two days across Louisiana, Alabama and Georgia, they had time to reflect on Jane's achievements.

Elisabeth Vailland was an experienced, well-read Marxist. Jane was still a novice, as far as her knowledge and theoretical education were concerned, and was anxious to learn as much as she could about the history of Socialism and the achievements of Communism. They discussed the various manifestations of Communism throughout the world and argued its virtues. Elisabeth was a traditionalist; she believed that revolution could be achieved only through the political transformation of the working classes, particularly the blue-collar workers, and it was this to which she had devoted almost her whole life. Jane was less traditional; she had come to abhor nationalism and was much less an admirer of Russian Communism than Elisabeth was. Nevertheless, the Russians had started it all; even if they had failed to achieve the true Marxist ideal, they had at least made it a possibility.

On the drive across the South Jane received a thorough grounding in Marxist theory from her Communist companion and felt in a much better position to discuss it than she had when she'd started the trip two months before. She had set out with a passion to observe at first hand the injustices endemic to the American system. By now she was convinced that her radical friends were correct in their efforts to change America and was more committed than ever to the cause. Jane was not unaware that she was being exploited by the movement. But it was an exploitation she willingly cooperated in, and she felt proud and fulfilled by her ability to bring the attention of America to the radical movement—no matter the risks to her career.

On the way to Fort Bragg Jane and Elisabeth stopped at Columbia,

South Carolina, where they immediately became embroiled in a student demonstration at the University of South Carolina and Jane experienced her first bitter taste of tear gas as police dispersed protesting students. They took refuge at the home of the aging liberal aunt of one of the staff workers at the GI coffeehouse in Jackson. Later, when the aunt learned that her niece had been arrested in the demonstrations, she blamed Jane for encouraging violence and exposing the young girl to danger and asked her to leave her house. Jane coldly and sarcastically thanked her for her hospitality, and she and Elisabeth transferred to a motel. The next day, driving from Jackson to Fayetteville, Jane was contemptuous of the old woman, claiming that such an attitude was typical of the hypocrisy of American liberals. "They talk and talk about supporting progressive causes," Elisabeth Vailland remembers Jane saying, "but when the chips are down, when their tight and comfortable little worlds are threatened, they completely fold up."

Jane and Elisabeth met Mark Lane at the Quaker House in Fayetteville. Lane had come with Rennie Davis, a radical leader and one of the defendants in the Chicago conspiracy trial, and the two planned the day's activities. "Power to the People" was to be the cry of the day. The demonstration began at a local park under a hot noonday sun with speaker after speaker issuing the cry and thousands of demonstrators repeating it. After Davis spoke, he was arrested for using an obscene word. Time was wasted while Lane tried to get him out of jail. Then the demonstration moved to Fort Bragg itself as Jane, Elisabeth, Lane and other activists drove through the gates and started passing out pamphlets on GI rights. They were immediately arrested, and with Lane shouting theatrically about the fact that he was a lawyer and knew his rights, they were driven off to be photographed and fingerprinted. Singing peace songs and clapping their hands to revolutionary chants, each of the arrested group raised a fist when the Army photographer took mug shots. They were then escorted off the base.

Jane made a quick trip back to Los Angeles to appear on a television show about GI rights, then returned to Fayetteville for more meetings with Lane at the Quaker House. On May 19 she, Elisabeth, Lane and Lane's traveling companion, Caroline Muggar, left in Jane's Mercury for Washington, where they planned to call on Congressmen who were sympathetic to the peace movement. Lane knew his way around Capitol Hill, and he and Jane spent most of the next day visiting liberal Senators and Representatives to lobby for GI rights. Jane was the star attraction, and when she called a press conference, dozens of journalists and television crews showed up.

On May 22, after an early morning visit with sympathetic Washington *Post* columnist Nicholas von Hoffman, the foursome drove to the campus of the University of Maryland, just outside Washington, where Jane and Lane were due to speak at a student rally. Waiting for them was a crowd of about 2,000, sitting quietly on the grass in the sun. Jane stood in a tight cluster of people behind the mike while Mark Lane talked about Vietnam. As his speech dragged on, an undercurrent of chatter slowly rose, and students began wandering about or pushing up to gawk at Jane, who was braless under a dark-red linen peasant blouse. People kept trying to talk to her, but her replies were abrupt because she was concentrating on Lane's words. At last she was introduced, and her strong, young, angry voice, strident with passion, stilled the talkers and halted the wanderers.

"Who's getting rich off this war?" she called. "When World War II ended the Defense Department had a hundred and sixty billion dollars' worth of property. It's doubled since then. . . ." This was to be part of Jane's new style as she became a public advocate of the radical movement—statistics. The use of statistics has always been an effective oratorical technique, and Jane was learning to use it like a veteran politician. Occasionally, though, her statistics would backfire on her, causing her embarrassment. But she pressed on.

"Some of you people are just here to get a suntan and have some fun, and this weekend you'll probably go to the beach and lap up beer," she chided. The crowd blinked and grinned at itself. The GI movement—the attempt to turn the soldiers themselves against the war—strikes at the cutting edge of military policy, she told the crowd. "The Army builds a tolerance for violence. I find that intolerable. They think it's normal to throw prisoners out of helicopters because it's the only way they can make them talk. I find that tragic." It was vital, she went on, to get soldiers into the peace movement, and it was vital to support them because it was more of a sacrifice for them to wear a peace button—the risk being court-martial—than for a student to demonstrate. She urged the students to show their support for the GI movement by distributing antiwar leaflets at Army bases, subscribing to GI newspapers, inviting servicemen to speak at rallies and contributing to their legal defense funds.

When she was finished, a group of students pressed around her to ask questions. A young man, a drama student, asked her why she was still acting, still taking part in Establishment activities. "I'm not questioning your motives, of course," he said.

"Well, you are, that's just what you're doing," Jane snapped, and Lane broke in: "You think Jane, as an actress, is any more a part of the Establishment than you are as a student?"

"Tell me," said another man with short hair, not so young. "What are you doing this for? For the publicity? Is this helping your movies?"

"Publicity?" Jane shot back. "What do you mean, I don't get it?"

"Well, you must be getting something out of this."

She glared at him quickly. "You think this is fun? Standing in this heat talking to a bunch of lethargic students? I could be lying by a pool in Beverly Hills getting a suntan. You think this is for kicks?"

The man drifted off, and another appeared to ask what they were going to be doing next. Jane growled: "Doing? What are you doing? Everyone always asks what we're doing. Why don't you stop worrying about us and start doing something yourself?" This was another tactic she had learned lately, primarily from Mark Lane—to turn hostile questions around and throw them back so that they reflect on the people asking them rather than on her. It was an old debater's ploy, and Lane was a skilled debater. For Jane, the tactic came hard, but she was learning.

From the Maryland campus the group, trailed by a caravan of press cars and students, proceeded to nearby Fort Meade to make another test of the Army's regulations against distributing antiwar leaflets and petitions. Once on the post, the reporters got separated from Jane's car, causing a veteran newsman to remark wryly that Martin Luther King would never have lost his entourage like that. As it was, the press entourage arrived at the sprawling Fort Meade PX just in time to see Jane, Lane and Elisabeth Vailland being briskly stuffed into military police jeeps. "We haven't even been able to ask anyone to sign our petitions!" Jane shouted across the parking lot as the jeeps pulled away from the arriving reporters. Expressionless MP's moved swiftly on the dozen students who trickled into the lot.

Jane, Lane and Elisabeth were taken to the Fort Meade provost marshal's office. According to Madame Vailland, "For the first time in our three months of visiting Army bases, we experienced brutality on the part of the military police." They were pushed, shoved and bullied. Mark Lane was recording it all on his tape recorder, and when one of the MP's grabbed it out of his hands and smashed it against the wall, Lane began shouting in protest, identifying himself as Jane's lawyer. Jane and Elisabeth were separated from him; they were locked in a small room and searched by two female MP's. When Jane saw reporters gathered outside the small window, she rushed over and started shouting at them about the treatment the three were receiving.

When they were all finally released, they adjourned to a snack bar on the highway next to the base, where Jane proudly displayed her bruises to news photographers. Fort Meade had been, she reminded the reporters, her fourth arrest "in the cause of peace."

Jane planned to stop in Baltimore before winding up her two-month cross-country trip in New York. Evidently she called her father in Hollywood just after her arrest at Fort Meade to ask him if she and her friends could stay at his house on Seventy-fourth Street. Henry Fonda was just about to sit down for an interview with Guy Flatley of the New York *Times* when he received the call. "Sorry I'm late," he said to Flatley, "but I was on a long-distance call to Washington, talking with my—how should I say it?—with my erstwhile, with my alleged daughter. . . . She asked me if she could go to my house in New York and bring her whole entourage with her—for a *week!* Gee, I would love to have been able to say, 'I'm sorry, but the house is all filled up,' but I just couldn't do it."

How many were in her entourage? Flatley asked.

"Oh, it's not how many," Fonda replied wearily. "It's how unattractive they all are."

24. *Klute*

It's very difficult being married to a Joan of Arc.

—ROGER VADIM

JANE spent the summer of 1970 crisscrossing the country by plane—attending rallies and demonstrations, giving speeches, raising money and donating personal funds to various radical organizations as her affiliations spread. When asked if she knew that several of the groups she was representing were clearly Communist, she shrugged.

"Any organization interested in getting us out of Southeast Asia I'm speaking for," she said.

When questioned about what her father thought of her activities, she said, "It's very hard for me to accept the fact that he doesn't agree with me. He really doesn't. And what saddens me most is that there is no more any possibility for a dialogue. . . . He sincerely worries about me; he sincerely believes that I'm being manipulated by someone. He believes that there is an organization behind me. There's no point in telling him I'm doing this on my own, that nobody ever influenced me politically."

Henry Fonda was well enough acquainted with his daughter to know that she had never done anything exclusively on her own, that the inspiration for every enthusiasm she had been caught up in always derived from the influence of someone else's impact on her. Her social and political awareness had originally been awakened by a complex of factors—her natural liberal sympathy for the oppressed, her disenchantment with the hedonism of her recent years, her revulsion with the increasingly authoritarian responses of the government against dissent over the war, her years of exposure to French left-wing intellectuals and, finally, her never-ending quest for her father's approval. In retrospect it was perhaps this last factor that motivated Jane the most, for it seemed that every time her father had turned his back on her loudest enthusiasms she responded by throwing herself that much more passionately into the very pursuits he belittled.

A psychiatrist might suggest that subconsciously Jane has spent her life punishing her father for the hurts, real and imagined, he had inflicted on her—hurts stemming from her childhood and the death of her mother. She had craved his attention and approval and had invariably been rebuffed or patronized for just about every interest she displayed. To her, these enthusiasms might have been like gifts to him, her way of announcing, "Look, I am a person, and I want you to see me and approve of what you see." But he didn't approve, for he could not accept Jane in any other way than as he conceived her—an extension of himself rather than an individual in her own right. Thus, finding no support for the image she wanted to have of herself, no identity other than what her father imposed on her according to his rules, she was left with little psychic choice but to rebel and seek support and approval elsewhere.

In the end, however, no one else's support could ever replace her father's. No one could ever measure up to her father and the love she had for him. As she grew bored with one form of rebellion, she was compelled to seek another to reaffirm her identity in the face of his continuing indifference—well, not indifference, really, since she managed to repeatedly exasperate him. Perhaps his refusal to recognize and accede to her need to be his equal would be a better way of describing the underlying motivation of her compulsion to leave her mark on the world in some serious way.

When Jane said in an interview, "My father thinks I'm just going through another phase," there was an irony buried in her words that probably not even she was aware of. To Henry Fonda, Jane's flirtations with radical activism were just another of her phases, for that was how he perceived his daughter—a misguided young woman ruled by phases. It was most likely this locked-in perception that was at the root of what was, in his view, her periodically outrageous behavior, yet it's doubtful that he understood that. The irony resided, of course, in Jane's inability to divine the meaning of her father's cryptic dismissal of her, even though she stated his position very well. The subconscious lifelong struggle between them had come full circle, but neither of them seemed to recognize that they were spinning on the same orbital track.

Jane was not being manipulated, except subconsciously by her father. Superficially, at least, her growing commitment to radicalism *was* of her own choice. Nevertheless, her contention that she had never been politically influenced by anyone was not exactly true. She had been and evidently still was being influenced—primarily by Fred Gardner, the highly principled young radical whose political standards were as stiff and uncompromising as her father's personal standards.

The third element in Jane's new form of rebellion was the man she had lived with for six years. She gave him some of the credit for her transformation and at the same time some of the blame. "It's very hard to find a man like Vadim," she was to say later. "He helped me a lot." Nevertheless, she went on, "I don't know why people always saw me as a sex symbol . . . even before Vadim. . . . Then Vadim came and emphasized the whole thing. I say it without rancor, for it was not Vadim who imposed that on me. I allowed it to happen. Vadim does not realize he's exploiting sex, that he's perpetuating the idea of women as sex objects. . . . I was so used to being considered a sex symbol that I began to like it. I didn't expect people to treat me as a person who thinks. But when I went to the Indians and I came in contact with the Panthers, the GI's, my new friends, I realized that they were treating me as a person.

This was so beautiful that I began to feel uncomfortable with people who still considered me a doll. And it completed my own personal revolution, and Vadim was the first victim of it."

Jane announced that she was breaking up with Vadim. As she explained afterward, "Vadim was saying to me: 'The only problem with you is that you don't know what you want. When you do, life will become easier for you.' Well, it happened, and it might seem paradoxical that the moment it happened, I had to leave him."

When she was asked if Vadim understood her leaving him, she said that at first he didn't. "But I think he's beginning to understand now. He's an intelligent man, he respects people, but he wasn't prepared for what happened. He would better understand a woman who leaves him for another man than a woman who leaves him for herself." She claimed that her whole idea of love had changed, that her love for people, especially oppressed people, had made it impossible for her to devote herself to the kind of selfish love that exists between a man and a woman. The only specific love she felt was for her daughter. "I couldn't live without her. I never knew a child could be such a joy."

When Vadim was asked about Jane's activities, he sighed and made his pained reference to Joan of Arc. Then he started being seen in public with a succession of Hollywood starlets. Jane left him at the house in Malibu and rented a $1,000-a-month house for herself and Vanessa in Los Angeles. But since she was traveling almost continually and since she and Vadim remained on friendly terms, Vanessa spent much of her time with her father. "The fear that threatened Vadim the most," Jane said, "was that we would no longer be friends and that I would take Vanessa away from him. But now he knows I would never do that. . . ."

Jane's association with Fred Gardner apparently ripened into a love affair during the summer of 1970 as she threw herself and all her resources into the peace movement. In June she traveled extensively in the West on behalf of the Indians, supporting especially the Pyramid Lake case and another dispute on a Cherokee reservation in Oklahoma.

In July she was busy with Gardner, Donald Duncan and Mark Lane raising money for the Servicemen's Fund. They also made plans to open an office in Washington, to be staffed by Duncan and Marilyn Morehead, the woman he lived with, to gather data on the military persecution of servicemen for their political beliefs and to lobby on Capitol Hill for fairer treatment of GI's.

In August it was the Black Panthers who occupied most of Jane's time. Huey Newton had been released from prison on $50,000 bail pending a new trial, and when Jane encountered him, she was overcome with emotion. "Huey Newton is a great, great, gentle man," she told a reporter. "He's the only man I've ever met who approaches sainthood."

Asked whether she was giving up her acting career, Jane said no but insisted she was only interested in doing films of social and political importance and was not going to play "any more roles that perpetuate the sexist exploitation of women." She had started reading movie scripts again, and in June agreed to star opposite Donald Sutherland in a film to be produced by Alan Pakula for Warner Brothers, called *Klute*. In it she would play a stylish, cynical New York call girl who gets romantically involved with an out-of-town policeman who comes to New York to find a missing man suspected of having employed her services. It was not exactly a film of political or social interest—indeed, it was an ordinary crime thriller—but Jane managed to give it that interpretation when she said, "The movie is about a prostitute. Prostitutes are the inevitable product of a society that places ultimate importance on money, possessions and competition."

Filming of *Klute* was to start in New York late in the summer and last into the fall, so in August Jane rented a furnished East Side penthouse not far from her father's house and immediately turned it into the headquarters of the various groups she was involved with. After returning from Washington in early August, where she, Lane and Duncan held a press conference to announce the opening of the GI Office, she settled in at the penthouse with Vanessa and a nursemaid and began preparing for *Klute*.

The summer had been an apocalyptic one for Jane. She roamed far and wide in the service of the radical movement, and by August she was passionately dedicated to changing America. "Once you've had a vision . . ." she started to say in an interview shortly after moving into the New York penthouse. "People *want* to love, people *want* to be loved. Why not allow people to reap *truly* the benefits of their labors, to *enjoy* themselves, to *expand* as human beings, to *relate* to each other? But in the system we have in this country today it is impossible to be anything but greedy and avaricious and competitive. The system pits people against each other."

What was the solution? A true revolution, she said, indicating that she fully intended to be in its vanguard. "As long as there's exploitation, as long as there's oppression, as long as there's investment, as long as there's efficiency—I will try to change it. Because this is the kind of system we live in! It doesn't respect human life, it makes you a slave, and

it's wrong! Look what it does to women. Just look at the television ads.
. . . It pits women against each other. It's like a disease, a cancer.
Ninety-five percent of the women in this country are totally brainwashed
by this. They truly believe they only exist as a function of how they look,
of how they dress, of the kind of man they're with. The system does
terrible things to women."

Like most people infused with revolutionary fervor, Jane was unwittingly beginning to be infected by the same totalitarian psychology she
professed to despise. It was this that would turn out to be the ultimate
irony of her life. It's a cardinal axiom of history that in any violently
revolutionary situation, the oppressed become the oppressors. Indeed,
the psychological history of revolution seems to indicate that the will to
power is the demiurge of the revolutionary spirit. Jane had acquired a
reasonably good grounding in the defects of the American system, but
her sense of history and her knowledge of the political, social and
economic evolution of man remained shallow and one-sided, buried in
the residue of her incomplete and indifferent formal education. Like
many basically unread idealists, her responses to her perceptions were
almost entirely emotional and without the leavening influence of a
knowledge-refined logic. Of course, emotion and conscience are the
bread and butter of altruism, and they have a logic of their own. But
history shows that these do not, cannot, operate in a vacuum; they are
always tempered, often overly so, by the logic of the mind, which
perceives other factors at work in the historical process—in fact,
perceives history itself as a process rather than a series of radical jumps
from ideal to ideal.

Jane might have keened this from some of her more historically
knowledgeable radical mentors—Fred Gardner, for one, or perhaps
Huey Newton—but evidently she didn't. Even Huey Newton, in spite of
his visceral and inflammatory rhetoric, had gained an understanding of
the historical process. By the time he was released from prison he was a
thoroughgoing self-educated Marxist who believed in dialectical materialism and recognized the contradictory character of history, which
evolves at its own rate through a process of synthesis. Newton, in effect,
had become a synthesisist—a concept which Jane was still too impatient
to contend with except to give lip service to. She had come to her radical
insights and passions relatively late in life compared to her comrades.
And although she was of above-normal intelligence, she constantly
betrayed her lack of understanding of the balance of forces that had
operated throughout history to make her world what it was in 1970.

ane's radicalism, in other words, was an undiscriminating one; it could be nothing more than that, because she did not yet possess the intellectual power to discriminate. Thus, she became, at least spiritually, a slave of her unalloyed emotional logic and an unwitting disciple of the totalitarian point of view that insists there is only one way for the society to exist. One could not quarrel with her assessment of the American system—it was all true, or at least much of it. But the truth is always relative. Therefore, one could quarrel with her impulsive, absolute responses to it.

By the time she was ready to start shooting *Klute* Jane had broadcast her radicalism far and wide through the press. She had earned the rapidly growing enmity of almost everyone in the country who was not committed to her passion. It was not just the American right wing that despised her, however; she also made plenty of enemies within the radical movement itself, especially among the more intellectually sophisticated. She had an unfortunate habit of revealing her own lack of historical perspective and political sophistication in the most public of places, and more than one hardened movement leader blanched when she went onto the *Dick Cavett Show*—her favorite commercial forum—and plainly made a fool of herself.

On this particular show she was caught by an opposing debater on the Vietnam War who asked her if, after all, the American colonies hadn't sought foreign support in their Revolution against the British. "Not that I know of," she answered with high-strung defensiveness. Later, after her opponent had thoroughly embarrassed her, she confessed, "My analogy was beautifully clear in my head, but I completely forgot about Lafayette and the French and all that. I didn't try to cover up, I just said, well, I made a mistake. Of course, everybody jumped on me: *How dare she go on a talk show without*—you know, *She doesn't even know anything about the American Revolution!*

"Plenty of people laughed at me," she admitted. She was envious of "those guys who've thought everything out" and declared, "I've got complexes about my lack of political sophistication." Nevertheless, she pressed on, the gaps in her knowledge becoming more apparent as her diatribes became more impassioned and uncompromising. One suspected, knowing Jane, that her increasingly inflammatory statements were an effort on her part to gain acceptance among those in the movement who doubted her value to it, an overcompensation for her lack of expertise. And as she rushed to fill in the gaps in her education, she took her information unfiltered out of a single reservoir—the reservoir of New Left pamphlet literature. Thus her wisdom, such as it was, became the wisdom of slogan and broad simplistic generalization. Her catchwords became "imperialism," "sexism," "genocide" and the like. And soon she began to lose patience with men like Fred Gardner, who, although he was a devout revolutionary, recognized the folly of trying to build a revolution on romantic sloganeering and reckless, egocentric activism.

Steve Jaffe, professional publicist and amateur assassination investigator, had become Jane and Donald Sutherland's full-time press agent and was responsible for coordinating all of Jane's contacts with the media. Not only that, he was also given a voice in the tactics and strategy of putting across Jane's message. No one who knew Jane well ever doubted the sincerity of her radical commitment or even disliked her for it. She was an easy person to like personally. She had a way of establishing instant, warm, direct contact with people. She treated everyone alike, created an immediate feeling of sincerity, candor and unaffectedness, and projected an energy and selflessness that were awesome. In private, even after her radicalization, she always remained friendly and considerate toward people who did not agree with her. It was only in public, when she would become shrill and hard in her denunciations, that she aroused animosity. Of course, because she was a famous actress, people who observed her were more concerned with her style than with the substance of anything she had to say. And as her ideas became more uncompromising, her style grew more petulant. She might have been much more effective in getting her message across in the early days of her radicalization had she not so assiduously shattered the image people had of her. Had she continued, at least publicly, to be the Jane Fonda everyone was comfortable with and then quietly recited the horrors she had perceived in the American system—its racism, militarism and benign imperialism—the effect would most likely have been that much more stunning. As an experienced actress she should have sensed this. Even if the idea of cloaking her rage behind the mask of performance was intolerable, performance was still her métier.

She chose to follow a different course, however. Because she felt militant, she felt she had to act like a militant. And when she did, using as her models the many rhetoricians she had met in her travels along the radical trail, she lost much of her potential effectiveness. Naturally she had to be true to herself. But in doing so, she paradoxically compromised her impact as a spokeswoman for the movement. And when she was caught in errors of fact or statistic (the more she used the statistics supplied to her, the more she found herself challenged), the less credible her militant posture became.

Many of the people who were involved with Jane in her early days of activism still criticize her for this tactical mistake. There are even those, no matter how much they admired her personally, who insist she did the movement in general—especially the antimilitary phases of it—considerably more harm in terms of public relations than good in terms of fund raising. Perhaps she received wise public relations advice and failed to heed it. Then again, perhaps she received poor advice and accepted it. Some who were involved with Jane suggest the latter.

Howard Levy, who worked closely with Jane and Fred Gardner during the first year of Jane's activism, says, "Jane had all the right instincts, but she was listening to too many people. One of the ones she was listening to was that guy Steve Jaffe, the press agent. Jesus Christ, he was a loser, but he was sure getting a lot of mileage out of his association with Jane and Donald Sutherland."

Jaffe, still with the Los Angeles office of Allan, Ingersoll & Weber, was basically on his own with Jane and Sutherland as his two primary clients. The relationship, at first blush, seemed ideal from all points of view, since Jaffe was apparently in complete accord with Jane's political views. Nevertheless, according to several of Jaffe's professional colleagues, he was a less than competent practitioner of the craft of public relations and press agentry. Bob Zarem, a New York public relations executive who had known Jane from her school days and later worked with Jaffe on several of her movement projects, says, "Steve is a nice guy, but he had no business representing Jane in that very explosive period in her life. He just doesn't know his way around in this business, and he doesn't know how to speak for Jane. After all, she was involved in some pretty complicated ideas, and her commitment was full of complex factors and ramifications. I would have to say that Steve caused her more problems than he solved from a PR point of view."

On August 22 Huey Newton, fresh from San Quentin, flew from California to New York. Jane, Donald Sutherland and Mark Lane went to Kennedy Airport to greet him publicly and bring him back to Jane's apartment for a press conference arranged by Jaffe. Somehow the whole production seemed incongruous, a fact hardly a reporter present did not fail to mention in his coverage. The sight of Huey Newton, the Black Panther desperado (which is how most people thought of him), sitting in the opulent, gilded, baroque East Side apartment that was a tasteless symbol of the racist system he was vowing to overthrow, put a comic cutting edge on the entire affair and made both Jane and Newton seem like playacting revolutionaries. And the shouts of "Right on!" and "Power to the People!" from numerous white and black supporters jammed into the genteel, expensively furnished living room exposed the whole event to radical-chic ridicule.

Jane, dressed in sweater and jeans, took no part in the press conference other than to answer the door, hold television equipment for overburdened camera crews, get newsmen cold drinks and occasionally toss in a "Right on!" Yet long after Newton left, she suffered ugly repercussions from the ill-advised news conference. Not only was the bizarre scene made light of by the press, particularly by some of New York's acerbic local newscasters, but one of the reporters also mentioned the address and telephone number of Jane's apartment. As a result she was harassed by obscene and threatening telephone calls and was inundated by sick anonymous letters. Many of Jane's friends blamed the press' ridicule on Jaffe for arranging the press conference in such a foolish environment, and a few suggested privately that he was inadvertently responsible for the publicizing of Jane's telephone number and address. In any event, as an exercise in press and public relations, the whole affair was a disaster.

The filming of *Klute* spanned September and October. In order to get a good grip of her part as the call girl, Jane accompanied an authentic prostitute on the rounds of pickup bars to observe the action first hand. Rumors around New York's inside film circles had it that she even spent a few nights actually working as a dispenser of sex in one of the city's high-priced brothels in order to lend further realism to her characterization of Bree Daniel.

The shooting of the film somewhat limited the scope of Jane's radical activities, but she still found plenty of time to attend Black Panther rallies and raise money by telephone for the GI Office in Washington. "A year ago, for me to pick up the phone and call practically anyone except the people I was really intimate with was a trauma," she said one day in October. "I hated the telephone. I never answered the phone, Vadim always answered. And if there was any way I could get him to make a telephone call for me, I would do it. Sometimes I would break out in perspiration when I had to make a call to a stranger. Now, I must make forty calls a day to people I don't even know . . . asking them all for favors, for money. I sometimes think: 'What am I doing?' It's impossible that someone has changed this much! When Vadim was here the weekend before last and he saw me making all these calls, he sat there and he said, 'I do not believe it. I do not. I just cannot encompass this change in you!' "

Jane even found a new cause to espouse and publicize—the Young Lords, a Puerto Rican Black Panther-type organization that had taken up arms and seized a church in Spanish Harlem to protest what it claimed was the murder of one of its members by police guards in the Tombs prison. She befriended one of the Young Lords' leaders, a youth who called himself Yoruba, and was amused by the contrasts between the Lords and the Panthers. "It's so different talking to Yoruba compared to the Panthers," she said during this period. "The Panthers are so much more fear-inspiring. When they say good-bye, it's always: 'Power to the People, Sister!' or 'Right on!' Yoruba, he says, 'Nighty night.' "

Much as she did with Gloria in *They Shoot Horses, Don't They?*, Jane managed to infuse the character of Bree Daniel with her own hard-edged sensitivity. She had already proved that she performed best in roles that mirror a troubled world, and because she sincerely believed that *Klute* could make a statement "about the breakdown and decaying of our society," she attacked the part of Bree with slavish dedication. She put Bree right up there on the crest of her own churning emotions and carried her there for two months. By the end of the filming the Bree Daniel that was captured on celluloid had every bit of Jane's alert intelligence, droll sense of humor and appealing vulnerability beneath the character's layer of cynical cool. In exchange, the Jane Fonda of real life grafted some of the tough, hard-bitten Bree Daniel's invulnerability onto her own character and personality. Jane's characterization was not so much a performance as it was an extension and expansion of herself into another person. Afterward she dragged Bree around inside her for months, the way she had Gloria, the marathon dancer.

Once *Klute* was completed, it was back on the speaking and fund-raising road for Jane. There she would unexpectedly undergo an experience which would abruptly complete her radicalization and explode whatever hopes her more moderate friends and family had that her political activism was just another passing phase.

25. Incident in Cleveland

Now they are trying to discredit me by saying I use dope.

—JANE FONDA

WHILE she was filming *Klute*, Jane added the Vietnam Veterans Against the War (VVAW) to the growing number of radical organizations she supported. The VVAW was a coalition of antiwar veterans groups that had surfaced during the late sixties and was organized into a solid political front by radical activists both from within and outside. After the story of the My Lai massacre broke in the newspapers, confirming many of the things Donald Duncan and other dissident veterans had been claiming about the cruel excesses and atrocities of American military policy in Vietnam, the VVAW's stock and credibility rose meteorically. To bring further knowledge of military atrocities home to the American public, the VVAW hit on a plan to put together a series of public hearings at which veterans would testify to the atrocities they had either committed or witnessed. To exploit the hearings' public relations potential, their sponsors called them the Winter Soldier Investigation—an ironic title that derived its inspiration from the famous saying of Thomas Paine during the American Revolution: "These are the times that try men's souls. The summer soldier and the sunshine patriot will in this crisis shrink from the service of his country; but he that stands it now deserves the love and thanks of man and woman." The real patriots of the American Revolution, then, were the winter soldiers; the Vietnam Veterans Against the War chose that designation for themselves in the present crisis.

The public hearings were scheduled for Detroit the following January and February. The reason Detroit was chosen was its proximity to Windsor, Canada, where the VVAW hoped to have American military deserters and Vietnamese civilians testify on closed-circuit television. As always with any major antiwar endeavor, a large sum of money was needed to fund the Winter Soldier Investigation. Jane, who was enthusiastic about the hearings, volunteered to tour the country to help raise it. She started out as soon as she finished *Klute*.

A few minutes after midnight on Tuesday, November 3, 1970—a national election day—an Air Canada jet carrying Jane from a speaking engagement at Fanshaw College in Canada to another at Bowling Green University in Ohio touched down at Cleveland's Hopkins International Airport. Jane, traveling alone, was in a state of deep fatigue from her practically nonstop tour of college campuses. She planned to spend the night at a motel near the airport before flying the next day to Toledo and Bowling Green. She wearily disembarked from the plane and followed the sixteen other passengers to the United States Customs Hall.

Many daytime commercial flights that arrive in the United States from Canadian cities are precleared for customs and immigration by American inspectors at their points of origin; Air Canada Flight 271 from London, Ontario, to Cleveland, because of the lateness of its departure hour, had not been. In the Cleveland Customs Hall was a single Immigration officer, a Customs inspector named Lawrence Troiano and an Air Canada representative.

Jane was stamped through Immigration and directed to the baggage inspection counter at the opposite end of the hall. She placed her suitcase on the counter and waited her turn in line. She says that when her turn came, the Customs inspector—Troiano—immediately ordered her to sit in a chair while he called a superior in Cleveland. It was 12:15 A.M.

Jane says that she was so tired that at first she sat in the chair and paid no particular attention to the strange order. Then she realized that something was up—the inspector had not yet opened her bag. So she rose and asked Troiano why he had ordered her out of line. She claims that he told her to shut up and when he finally opened her bag, he immediately confiscated her address book.

The suitcase was also packed with 102 vials of organic vitamin pills that Jane carried with her for nourishment. She seldom ate regular meals anymore, and most of her intake was in the form of vitamins. The top of each vial was marked with the letter *B*, *L* or *D*, which stood for Breakfast, Lunch and Dinner. When Inspector Troiano saw these, according to Jane, his eyes lit up. She told him what the letters meant—that the pills were vitamins, not LSD-type drugs—but the inspector replied that she would have to remain in detention until his superior arrived from Cleveland. He then called a Cleveland city policeman into the hall and asked him to guard the exit.

Troiano's superior was Special Agent Edward Matuszak. He arrived at the airport Customs hall in response to Troiano's telephone call at 12:45 A.M. It is his contention that when he arrived, he found Jane in a phone booth speaking on the telephone. Jane agrees—she had called Mark Lane, who was in Boston, to tell him what was happening. But when Matuszak arrived, she says he ordered her to hang up and accompany him to the baggage inspection counter.

Jane complied with the order. Then, as she tells it, she was further ordered by Matuszak into the Customs office, where she was told to remain while he consulted by telephone with *his* superior in the Cleveland branch of the Customs Service. She was having her monthly period and was experiencing considerable discomfort as a result of not having had a chance to use a bathroom in several hours. She told Matuszak she had to use the rest room. Matuszak denied the request and told her that she wouldn't be able to use the bathroom until two Cleveland police matrons arrived to search her. This infuriated Jane. She repeated her request. Matuszak again denied it, claiming later that he did so because he suspected that her intent was "to destroy possible evidence of contraband drugs she might possess on her person."

Meanwhile, Mark Lane, having heard from Jane on the phone in Boston that she'd been ordered to hang up, called a lawyer he knew about who lived in Cleveland. He rousted attorney Irwin Barnett out of bed and explained what was happening at the airport. Barnett, who had never met Jane, immediately got on the phone to Cleveland airport.

At about 1:35 A.M. Special Agent Matuszak called the Cleveland policeman guarding the Customs hall's exit over to the office where Jane was being detained. He asked the policeman to keep an eye on her while he went to the adjoining Immigration office to use its telephone. While he was on the phone, he noticed Jane leaving the Customs office with the policeman behind her. He shouted to the officer, "Where's she going?" When he saw that Jane was heading for the bathroom, he rushed out of the Immigration office and blocked her way. Jane pleaded that she desperately needed to go to the bathroom. Matuszak ordered her back to the Customs office, again telling her she would not be permitted to use it until the police matrons arrived to search her. Jane replied, according to Matuszak, by angrily shouting, "What do you want me to do, pee all over your floor?"

They argued for a moment. Then, Matuszak says, Jane tried to throw a punch at him. He blocked the blow and immediately announced that she was "under arrest for striking a federal officer."

"I didn't hit you," Jane said.

Matuszak turned to Inspector Troiano and the policeman and said, "Did you see it?" They nodded in agreement.

Jane started shouting and cursing. By this time two more police officers, having heard that Jane Fonda was being detained, were on the scene. As she struggled to get by Matuszak and reach the rest room door, one of the officers, Robert Peiper, made a grab for her. She spun around and kicked out at him. The combined force of Customs agents and policemen finally subdued Jane and guided her back to the Customs office, where she was shoved in a chair, handcuffed and advised of her rights to legal counsel. She now had an additional charge lodged against her—assaulting Peiper, the Cleveland policeman.

In the meantime, Irwin Barnett had reached the Customs hall by phone, identified himself as Jane's attorney and asked to speak to his client. Matuszak refused to let Barnett talk to Jane until she was searched by the police matrons, who, he said, had just arrived. He was told to hang on for a while, and the open phone was put down on the desk. Jane claims that Matuszak denied her the right to speak to her lawyer. She apparently thought it was Mark Lane waiting on the open phone, so she started to sing the French national anthem to let him know she was being prevented from talking to him. Lane didn't hear her, but Barnett did.

According to Jane, it was another twenty minutes before the police matrons searched her; thus, she was deliberately prevented by Matuszak from speaking to her lawyer. She later said, "A policewoman finally arrived with a sanitary pad. Then she stripped me and searched my handbag and found some tranquilizers, plus an old bottle with a few Dexedrine pills. Dexedrine is not a drug; it's a medicine to help you stay awake when you haven't slept for two nights. I had bought it in the States with a prescription."

If it had truly been Jane's intention, as Special Agent Matuszak suggested, to use the bathroom to flush these capsules down the toilet out of fear that they were incriminatory, her fears would have been without basis. She had purchased the pills in the United States and had prescriptions for them from her Los Angeles doctor, J. D. Walters. Since she had taken them with her to Canada, she was not required to declare them when she returned. The only items Jane was required to list on the Customs declaration she was asked to make were items she might have purchased in Canada amounting to more than $100 or quantities of alcohol or cigarettes in excess of the standard quotas. It is certainly not uncommon for people who travel abroad with prescription drugs purchased in this country to return to the United States and not even think about whether they should declare the drugs. Indeed, the Customs Service does not make a habit of asking the question because it knows that this sort of everyday drug traffic is commonplace. Nevertheless, it is against the law to bring nonprescribed amphetamines into the country.

After Jane was searched and the pills discovered by the policewoman were turned over to Matuszak, he applied to her original arrest an additional federal charge of "fraudulently bringing merchandise into the country contrary to law." Matuszak picked up the phone and told attorney Barnett, who was waiting to talk to Jane, that he was taking her into Cleveland to book her on a warrant charging her with assault and the fraudulent importation of drugs. Although he was obliged to ask Jane whether she had prescriptions for the pills, which were clearly labeled, he failed to do so.

The Cuyahoga County Jail, a tall red-brick building, rises several stories over the adjoining Cleveland Central Police Station in a ramshackle section of the city just east of the business district. Jane was brought to the police station at about 3 A.M. and booked. She was then remanded to the county jail pending a hearing and the granting of bail the next day. Through an agreement with the federal government, the Cuyahoga County Sheriff's Office, which administers the county jail, also looks after federal prisoners. Jane was considered primarily a federal prisoner, although she also faced a hearing on the charge of assaulting Robert Peiper, the Cleveland policeman.

Jane spent a fitful, sleepless night in the women's pen of the county jail. The women's pen is an octagon-shaped area with a series of small, doorless rooms branching off like spokes from a wheel hub. When she was brought in and her handcuffs removed, she found an audience of a dozen or so female prisoners awaiting her. Two of the prisoners were black women who were accused of murdering a black man and distributing various parts of his body around the city, according to Colonel Albert Brockhurst, Cuyahoga County deputy sheriff and administrator of the jail. Another was a young white girl by the name of Barbara Cahn. She called herself a Maoist and had been arrested on several occasions, most recently for assaulting a police officer in a melee between antiwar militants and hard hats. The three prisoners immediately elicited Jane's promise to announce to the world that they had been repeatedly beaten by jail guards.

Irwin Barnett arrived at the jail at seven the next morning, according to Deputy Sheriff Brockhurst. The deputy is a big, gruff cop, a veteran police official who has the air of a man who has seen everything and is surprised by nothing. He is well known around Cleveland for his amiability. "As soon as I was notified that Jane Fonda was a prisoner," he says, "I got over to the jail from my house. I was told that when she was brought in, she was really charged up, cursing and swearing, calling everybody pigs and the like. Now remember, my job was not to judge whether her jailing was right or wrong, it was only to make sure she was secure like any other prisoner and that the jail's routine was kept in order. Anyway, Mr. Barnett showed up around seven. He was a quiet-spoken man, very lawyerlike. He explained the situation to me, that he wasn't able to talk to her at the airport, so I made a deal with him. I told him if he would see to it that his client calmed down and stopped raising such a ruckus, I'd let him go upstairs and see her. I didn't have to do it, I could've kept her up there until regular visiting hours, but Mr. Barnett said he would try to calm her down, so I let him go up."

By now word was out that Jane had been arrested, and reporters and photographers from the Cleveland papers were crowded into the jail's reception room near the ground-floor entrance. Brockhurst recalls that Barnett came back down from his talk with Jane and assured him that Jane would be all right. "He told me that this character Lane would be coming to see Jane Fonda, but he didn't let me know what I was in for."

Mark Lane arrived from Boston later that morning while Jane was still in the women's pen. Heavily bearded, he stormed into the jail with the wrath of Jehovah. He was told that Jane was to appear before U.S. Commissioner Clifford Bruce at 1 P.M. for a preliminary hearing. Lane insisted on seeing Jane, even though he had no license to practice law in Ohio and Barnett was now officially her lawyer of record. Brockhurst says that at Barnett's urging he assented to Lane's demand and arranged for Lane to meet with Jane in his office. "She came in," Brockhurst recalls, "and as soon as she saw Lane there, the two started shouting about brutality and terrorism. She used a lot of filthy language and was going on about how she was going to sue everybody in Cleveland, including myself, for the conditions of the jail and the alleged beatings of the prisoners. If you ask me, this Lane fellow seems to incite Jane Fonda. Anyway, I let them have their say. Then I had her hustled back to the women's area."

Lane immediately went to the reception room and held a press conference. He repeated Jane's charges about the conditions in the jail and the beatings of female prisoners and claimed that Jane's arrest had been illegal, the result of the government's program of harassment of antiwar activists. "Her arrest was an act of terror, pure and simple!" he cried. "An act of violence. . . . This is the Nixon-Agnew terror!" Lane had never been known for understatement, so no one was terribly impressed with his charge. Yet as subsequent events were to show, the charge, at least the essence of it, was correct. Jane's detention and subsequent arrest at the airport appeared indeed to be a form of government intimidation and harassment. The Nixon administration had been accused in many quarters of the political spectrum of encouraging a police-state mentality in the United States and of using federal law enforcement agencies to exercise its political muscle. The Jane Fonda case turned out to be eloquent testimony to the accusation.

Any doubts of whether Jane was indeed singled out by the Nixon administration to be persecuted for her political beliefs have been demolished by some of the revelations produced by the Senate Watergate investigation. America has learned that like many other distinguished Americans, Jane Fonda was considered an "enemy" of the administration and was included in a secret White House list of people to be unconstitutionally harassed and intimidated. Capricious Customs and Immigration Service detention was just one of the methods the administration apparently used to carry out its program of political repression. Among others were phone bugging, personal surveillance, mail interception, entrapment tactics and special tax audits. Jane later claimed to have been a victim of most of these. Knowing what we do today about the administration's "national security" program, there is little reason to doubt her.

Jane was taken in handcuffs before Commissioner Clifford Bruce at Cleveland's United States district court ten hours after being put in jail. He released her in $5,000 bail and scheduled a probable-cause hearing for November 9, the following Monday. A probable-cause hearing is a procedure designed to determine whether there is enough evidence of a crime to send a case on to a grand jury for possible indictment and then to trial. If there's not, the case is dismissed. If there is, it is bound over to a federal grand jury for further investigation and, most likely, prosecution. On the combined federal charges against her, Jane faced, if found guilty, a maximum prison term of more than ten years and more than $10,000 in fines.

After she was released on bail, she and Mark Lane held another press conference. Lane continued to harp on the political character of her arrest. He declared he had discovered that Jane's name was on a special

Customs list requiring that she be stopped, detained and searched every time she entered the country. He also claimed that her personal property—her address book, tapes, lecture notes and pamphlets, which had no bearing on the charges against her—had been confiscated by the federal authorities and were probably at that moment being photographed by the FBI.

Jane gave her version of the incident. "I am not a smuggler," she said. "I am a health-food freak, and the pills they found in my luggage were vitamins you can buy in any health-food store." The tranquilizers, she said, were the same type she had been taking on her travels for the past six years. "I was never hassled until I started talking against the war. . . . It was a political arrest." As for the assault charge, she claimed that she did not strike Matuszak or Peiper. She said she had been held incommunicado at the airport for almost three hours, searched and humiliated and had "pushed" Matuszak only after he blocked her way to a rest room. And about her night in jail, she quipped, "When you think that some of the best people in this country are now in jail, I didn't mind it at all."

The next day's papers headlined her Cleveland adventure: JANE FONDA ARRESTED: ACCUSED OF SMUGGLING DRUGS, KICKING OFFICER. That morning she was brought to the grimy police court at the Central Police Station, where she was arraigned on the charge of assaulting Officer Peiper. With her arrest all over the front pages of the Cleveland press, the courtroom was jammed with curious onlookers. It was the biggest show in recent history, and scores of people had stood all night in the cold, biting wind off Lake Erie to assure themselves a glimpse of the controversial movie star. "I saw her in *Playboy* a couple of years ago," said Fred Jurek, a local lawyer who paused to watch the proceedings. "So last night I took the magazine out again to check what she really looked like. Now she's mixing with all those hippies and she don't look so good anymore."

A furious but controlled Jane pleaded not guilty to the Peiper assault charge and requested a jury trial. Municipal Judge Edward Coleman obliged her by setting a court date for the following January 6. She was intent on vindicating herself and would accept nothing less than the forum of a public trial.

The show then moved to the Cuyahoga County Courthouse, where Jane and Mark Lane filed a formal complaint alleging that Barbara Cahn, the Maoist, had been systematically beaten by guards at the county jail. As Jane left the courthouse, she encountered the battery of reporters that was now part of her Cleveland retinue. She described Miss Cahn's bruises and promised to follow through on the case until the brutality in the county jail was exposed for all to see. A deputy sheriff—not Brockhurst—raised his arm in a mock Panther salute and shouted, "Right on, doll!" Strapped to his wrist, one observer noted, was a Spiro Agnew wristwatch.

Jane left Cleveland that afternoon to give a speech at Central Michigan University for the GI movement and the Winter Soldier Investigation. As she was about to get on a plane at the Cleveland airport, she was served with a summons announcing a $100,000 personal injury suit against her by none other than Policeman Peiper. Irritated and distressed by this additional form of harassment, she would later be immensely glad of it, for it would enable her lawyers to blow the government's entire case against her wide open. After her talk at Central Michigan, she returned to Cleveland and spent the next few days with Barnett and Lane preparing for the probable-cause hearing the following Monday.

Irwin Barnett is a tall, attractive man with a lawyerly mien and an affection for the vocabulary of the courtroom, fond of sprinkling his conversations with terms like "scintilla." He is a model of legal preparedness and is adept at clean, tight, closely reasoned argument. Lane, on the other hand, is a flamboyant pleader who seems to enjoy leaving the impression of a man forever stifled by narrow, unsympathetic judicial interpretations of the procedural rules of the courtroom. With a face that reflects an eternally befuddled look behind thick glasses, he favors sarcasm, wonderment, wit and outraged disbelief as his stylistic tools. As a result, he is an entertaining advocate and makes great points with courtroom spectators. He has considerably less success with judges, however. "Lane's a good lawyer," says one attorney who has worked with him. "But he has a huge ego and sometimes gets carried away with the performances he puts on. His performance at Jane Fonda's hearing got him a lot of local publicity, but I think it also caused the case against her to be dragged out. There were questions that should've been asked that never got asked because of Lane. If they had been asked, my guess is that the judge would have had to dismiss."

Although Barnett was Jane's lawyer of record and did most of the legal research in preparing her defense, Lane was intent on being her lawyer of fact in the courtroom. The hearing started at 10:40 A.M. on November 9. Docket No. 8, Case No. 3684, it was officially entitled "United States of America, Plaintiff, vs. Jane Fonda, Defendant;

Commissioner Clifford E. Bruce, Presiding." Assistant United States Attorney Edward F. Marek represented the government with the help of two other assistant attorneys. Lane and Barnett represented Jane, who sat at the defense table dressed in one of her colorful Bree Daniel call-girl outfits.

The focus of the hearing, as far as the government was concerned, revolved around sustaining its contention that Jane: (1) had indeed fraudulently brought into the United States merchandise contrary to law—namely, "pills and capsules containing amphetamine"; and (2) had indeed "forcibly assaulted a federal officer while engaged in the performance of his official duties." To sustain the two counts, all the U.S. attorney had to do was provide sufficient evidence, within established procedures for the presentation of such evidence, that the government allegations were true. To defeat the counts, the defense had to provide sufficient evidence, again within the rules of presentation, that they were false.

The hearing lasted for more than three hours, with much of its early stage consumed by a heated dispute between the theatrical Lane and the phlegmatic Marek on whether Lane had a right to argue for Jane—in view of the fact that Barnett was her attorney of record and Lane was not admitted to practice law in Ohio. During the protracted debate, Jane heaved an outraged sigh and turned her chair so that her back was to the bench. She remained in that position for some time, she later said, as a protest against the government's attempts, through a technicality, to deny her the right of the lawyer of her choice. Once the argument was settled in Lane's favor—more through the commissioner's exasperation with the bearded New Yorker's disruptiveness than anything else—and Lane had gained the right to cross-examine witnesses, it was the last point the defense won. Barnett moved for immediate dismissal of the charges against Jane on the ground that they did not indicate the commission of crimes. Bruce summarily denied the motions, and from that point on he conducted the hearing within the strictest bounds of courtroom procedure. He allowed Lane, who quickly took over the defense, no leeway in the more subtle aspects of cross-examination. Often he would knock down one of Lane's questions even before prosecutor Marek had a chance to object to it. To Jane and Lane, the hearing was remindful of the Chicago conspiracy trial of the year before, with the presiding judge constantly protecting the government's case and stifling defense efforts to show that the government's charges were politically inspired.

Edward Matuszak, the Customs agent who first arrested Jane, was the government's only witness. After he was led through his testimony by Marek, he was handed to Lane for cross-examination. Lane pounced on Matuszak like a great bushy falcon, using every courtroom tactic he knew to shake the agent's testimony and elicit an admission of government wrongdoing. But each time he ventured onto sensitive turf—sensitive from the government's point of view—Marek objected, and Bruce upheld him on the ground that Lane was wandering beyond questions relating to the government's simple charges. Lane countered that he was trying to show that Jane's detention had been a premeditated act of political intimidation—that the actions leading to her assault arrest were encouraged by the Customs agents' illegal detention, that the pills Jane was supposed to have fraudulently brought into the country had been properly prescribed and were her personal property (which exploded the charge of fraudulence) and that her arrest on the smuggling charge was illegal on its face because Matuszak had failed to ask her if she had the prescriptions for the pills found in her handbag.

As the hearing progressed and Lane got nowhere with the commissioner, Jane grew angrier at what she was sure was Bruce's favoritism. She punctuated his frequent antidefense rulings with muffled cries of disgust, and every time she did she drew an appreciative response from the spectators crowded into the courtroom. The court stenotypist, Dennis Parise, kept his eyes glued to his recording machine as the atmosphere heated up.

Finally, faced with procedural dead ends on every side, the exasperated Lane took a new tack. The commissioner repeatedly forbade him to introduce questions on matters that had not been raised in prosecutor Marek's direct examination of Matuszak. But Lane finally prodded Matuszak into admitting he had made a telephone call to Washington shortly after Jane's arrest. And before the judge had a chance to stop him, he managed to get into the official record the suggestion that the local U.S. Attorney's Office was pressing the case against Jane on orders from someone in the Nixon administration. Marek flew into a flurry of objections. Here is an example from the official transcript:

> LANE (to Matuszak): Did you make any phone calls to Washington on the morning of November 3, 1970?
> MATUSZAK: Yes, sir.
> LANE: Relating to this case?
> MATUSZAK: Yes, sir.
> LANE: Ah, you left that one out [of his previous testimony]. When was that?

MATUSZAK: Sometime around 10:00 in the morning.

LANE: Did you make the phone call?

MATUSZAK: Yes, sir.

LANE: Whom did you call?

MAREK: Objection, your honor.

COMMISSIONER: Sustained.

LANE: He testified about the other phone calls. Why can't we hear about this one?

MAREK: Those were phone calls made at the time he was at the airport.

LANE (to Matuszak): Did you make telephone calls to anyone in the city of Washington, D.C. on November 3, 1970?

MAREK: Objection.

COMMISSIONER: Sustained.

LANE: Now we cannot say. . . .

MAREK: The time period . . . there are 24 hours in November 3.

LANE: Now we cannot say it is before the arrest was made because I haven't asked him the time yet. First I will ask him about the call, then I will ask him the time. Certainly I am permitted to ask him that, your honor.

LANE (to Matuszak): Did you make any phone calls on November 3, 1970, to Washington, D.C.?

MATUSZAK: Yes, sir, I did.

LANE: To whom did you make the phone call?

MAREK: Objection.

COMMISSIONER: Sustained.

LANE: Why?

MAREK: The time.

LANE: We will find that out later.

COMMISSIONER: Well, find out the time first.

MAREK: It is not relevant, Mr. Commissioner, unless these phone calls. . . .

COMMISSIONER: Find out the time first.

LANE (to Matuszak): Was it about this case?

COMMISSIONER: It could have been from the airport. It could have been some other time. You may only ask questions about calls from the airport. Establish the time, Mr. Lane, then we'll see whether it is relevant.

LANE (to Matuszak): Was it about this case, the phone call to Washington?

MAREK: Objection, your honor.

COMMISSIONER: Sustained.

LANE (to Matuszak): Did you talk to someone in Washington?

MAREK: Objection.

COMMISSIONER: Sustained.

LANE (to Matuszak): Did you talk to the Attorney General of the United States?

MAREK: Objection.

COMMISSIONER: Sustained.

LANE (to Matuszak): Did you talk to Martha Mitchell?
MAREK: Objection.
COMMISSIONER: Sustained.

Lane knew he was touching an exposed nerve in the government's case. He was attempting to lead Matuszak into the admission that Jane had been detained in the first place because she was on a secret government harassment list. Such an admission not only might have wrecked the government's case, but would have been a significant public relations coup for Jane in view of its potential for exposing the then little-known fact that the Nixon administration was using its law enforcement powers to harass and intimidate political opponents and dissidents.

Although the ploy failed, the adamancy of Marek's objections provided Barnett and Lane with the key to their later defense. After three hours of Lane's pyrotechnics, Commissioner Bruce, still hewing to his narrow interpretation of evidence procedure, affirmed the two counts against Jane and bound her over to a federal grand jury.

After the hearing, Jane was continued in $5,000 bail. That evening she attended a fund-raising cocktail party at the home of a prominent merchant. The following day she traveled to nearby Case Western Reserve University to give an antiwar speech at a student rally. A local conservative newspaper reported that the speech was received with apathy by a small crowd and that she was jeered and booed by most of the students. A lawyer who was there, however, denies it: "It was a large crowd—maybe six hundred students and teachers. There was a handful of ultraradicals camped up front, and at first they heckled Jane for being too conservative, but I'd say she won them over very quickly. And the crowd was far from apathetic. They were damned enthusiastic."

It was the beginning of an expanding pattern of bad press, though. As Jane stumped the country during the next few months, the drug-smuggling charge remained fresh in the public's mind. Newspapers, especially conservative and even a few liberal ones, distorted reports about her activities and belittled her in editorials. Certain TV newscasters had difficulty concealing smirks of contempt as they reported her latest antiwar or pro-Black Panther utterance. And not a single Establishment media outlet took more than passing note of the fact that both the state and federal assault charges, as well as the drug-smuggling charge, were eventually dismissed.

The dismissals were evidently due mainly to the legal expertise of Irwin Barnett. When Jane was served with the personal-injury summons by Robert Peiper the day she was leaving to speak at Central Michigan, she was profoundly angered and depressed by the police officer's hypocritical attempt to gain personally from the misfortune he had helped create for her. But when U.S. Attorney Marek learned of the suit, he was even more depressed. Barnett, on the other hand, couldn't have been happier, and when he explained his pleasure to the astonished Jane, her mood brightened considerably.

One of the traditional procedural rules of a criminal prosecution is that the defendant does not have a right to learn before trial what the prosecution—in Jane's case the government—possesses in the way of evidence. But what is known in legal circles as "discovery" always operates in a civil action. Thus, a defendant in a civil suit has the right to discover prior to trial all facets of the plaintiff's evidence against him. And when a civil action becomes part of a criminal case, discovery automatically becomes applicable to the evidence in the criminal case. The prosecution is therefore required to disclose its evidence. It was this technical detail upon which the government's case against Jane turned sour. When Peiper filed his civil injury suit, he unwittingly opened up the government's case and, ironically, eventually brought about the downfall of his own lawsuit.

Once Jane possessed discovery, Barnett went to work on the government's position. His intention was to force the government into disclosing its evidence for having originally detained Jane at the airport. To supply this information, the government would have to provide answers as to how and why Jane was on Customs' special automatic-detention list—the reasons why any U.S. citizen was on the list, for that matter. It would also be a public admission on the part of the government that the list existed. Barnett's hunch was that the government would sooner request dismissal of its case—which was at best fragile, anyway—than release such information. He was right. After six months of legal wrangling in which the government kept moving for postponements of the disclosure of its evidence, it finally made a motion to dismiss its case against Jane. The complaint was dismissed on May 28, 1971.

Barnett dealt with the state of Ohio's criminal assault charge with equal dispatch but different legal technique. Through Jane's right of discovery, he soon learned that Policeman Peiper had actually been moonlighting on the morning of November 3. There had been a bomb scare at the Cleveland airport, and Peiper had been hired by one of the airlines to stand private guard duty. So he was not on official police duty when he assisted Customs Agent Matuszak in restraining Jane from using the rest room.

But Barnett didn't really require this information to defeat the state's assault charge. There were innumerable legal precedents on the books to show that Peiper, even if he had been on official duty, lacked the power to arrest Jane under the circumstances. Peiper was an officer of Cleveland's municipal police department, which was responsible for law enforcement at the Cleveland airport. But the Customs Hall at the airport was the property of the U.S. government, therefore federal territory. Thus, by virtue of the applicable precedents in law, Peiper had no authority within the Customs Hall.

Barnett presented a motion to this effect to the Cleveland Police Court. On June 25, 1971, Municipal Judge Edward Feighan ordered the state charge against Jane quashed and dismissed.

More recently, Policeman Robert Peiper's personal injury suit against Jane was dropped.

26. FTA

She may well be the only revolutionary with her own public relations man.

—*Life* Magazine

THE Cleveland arrest left Jane supercharged with equal doses of outrage and happiness. Her outrage came as a result of her firsthand experience with what was surely official government repression. Her happiness derived from the sense of achievement the unexpected arrest gave her. Although she was at first frightened and angry at being detained by the Customs people, once arrested, she quickly saw the positive side of it. It was a perfect opportunity to heighten the level of her acceptance within the radical movement and let everyone know—radical, middle-of-the-roader and reactionary alike—that Jane Fonda wasn't playing games.

Money was becoming a problem for Jane. She had been spending personal funds hand over foot in her travels and support of various organizations—especially the GI Office in Washington, whose operating expenses she had guaranteed for a year. Most of the money she earned from *Klute* had already been spent, and she began to divest herself of possessions and property, including her beloved farm in France, in order to raise more capital. Parting with the farm at any other time would have been heartbreaking, but now she regarded its sale with unsentimental pragmatism. Besides, as she said, "I have no desire to live in France anymore. The fight is here, and this is where I belong."

Jane also gave up the expensive house she was renting and acquired a smaller one in a run-down, low-rent neighborhood hard by the Hollywood Freeway. She furnished it in early Salvation Army style, with mattresses on the floor instead of beds, and turned it into a combination working headquarters-crash pad for radical friends. "As you can see," she told a visitor, "this place is nothing. Everything I have or earn goes to my various causes." The only personal luxury she continued to indulge in was a nursemaid for Vanessa.

Being "poor" didn't seem to bother Jane much; in fact, it gave her a sense of pride. "All I need for my current life is a plane ticket, two pairs of jeans and two sweaters." With her passion fired higher than ever by the events in Cleveland, she was back on the road immediately, jetting from city to city to speak at antiwar rallies, to demonstrate for Indians, Black Panthers, migrant workers and welfare mothers and, most important, to raise money for the Winter Soldier Investigation and the GI Office.

She claimed the pace was necessary because "I still have so much catching up to do, so much guilt to work off. I still need to educate myself. Involving myself in as many causes as I can is a big part of that education. As they say, if you're not part of the solution, you're part of the problem. I'd rather be part of the solution."

And what was the solution? "All I can say is that through the people I've met, the experiences I've had, the reading I've done, I realize the American system must be changed. I see an alternative to the usual way of living and relating to people. And this alternative is a total change of our structures and institutions—through Socialism. Of course I am a Socialist. But without a theory, without an ideology."

If she had no theory or ideology, what did she mean by Socialism? "I mean a way of living where nobody can exploit the others and where the leaders are concerned about people and where there is no competition." Jane admitted that her ideas were utopian but still insisted that radical changes could be made, must be made. When asked if she used the

Russian form of Socialism as her model, she said, "No . . . Russia is just as bad as the United States." But she was impressed with what she had heard about China. "You know, the delegation that just came back from China, they all said to me, 'It's very difficult to talk about because it seems like we're naïve. We were really trying to find the faults. . . .' And then they said, 'We couldn't find any faults. Everyone has enough to eat, everyone has a place to live, everyone has clothes, everyone has a pair of shoes!' They talked about a feeling of everyone being involved, everyone working together. And the most incredible lack of coercion . . . about how everyone dressed alike. Which I think is extraordinary, the leaders wearing the same clothes as the peasants. There are no differences, no class distinctions. . . ."

It was clear that Jane's idealism was racing far ahead of her common sense and that her education and sense of history were growing steadily more overbalanced by the pure heat of the romantic emotional rhetoric she was exposing herself to. Nevertheless, after her Cleveland arrest there was no stopping her. And as she grew more vocal, public criticism and disdain intensified. She expected it from her enemies, who were becoming legion, but she did not expect it from some of the people she thought she was representing.

Her passionate activism on behalf of the Indians had cooled somewhat, especially after she showed up on a television show to talk about their mistreatment and an Indian leader in the audience rose and invited her to "butt out of Indian affairs." Indian folk singer and activist Buffy St. Marie said at the time that Jane was "sincerely trying to tell other people what's going on, but she has unintentionally blown a couple of our most important issues by not really understanding our problems."

In spite of her Cleveland imbroglio, many experienced radical leaders remained unimpressed with Jane's value to the movement, and some thought she was doing it more harm than good through her naïve representations of what the movement was trying to accomplish. "A hitchhiker on the highway of causes," Saul Alinsky, the aging veteran radical activist, called her shortly before he died. "I'm sick unto death of these young revolutionaries who think they've been the first to discover the 'answer.' They talk about revolution the way Billy Graham talks about the Bible. You know, 'Come over to Jesus and you'll all be saved.' It's all bullshit. They're just the new evangelists with a new shaman, hung up on their neurotic-romantic delusions. They know no more about organizing a revolution than I do about making a baked Alaska. They've set real social and political reform in this country back fifty years with their shenanigans and their constant shouting about right-on revolution-ary acts. They wouldn't know a revolutionary act if they tripped over it."

Alinsky's anger reflected the deep divisions that existed within the radical movement by the time Jane came into it. It was not just a case of sour grapes on the part of the older, more experienced activists; there were definite differences of opinion over strategy and tactics. The differences did not exist merely between the young and the old either; they existed basically between the politically sophisticated and the politically naïve, no matter their age. The patient, selfless organizers were pitted against the impatient, egocentric champions of action.

With her lack of political sophistication and her emotional juices racing at full current, Jane began to gravitate toward the latter element of the movement after Cleveland. Originally influenced by Fred Gard-ner, she began to grow impatient with the brand of revolutionism which held that the slow, tedious business of organizing society's economically exploited factions was the only way to effect change. Jane, to reinforce her revolutionary fervor, needed more immediate results. She thus began to fall out with Gardner on this question, and as she did so, the romantic aspects of their relationship gradually died. As she said later, "I was in love, but I had to cut it off because I did not understand him. And having the same political views with a man is now so important to me."

With her need to go where the action was, Jane's militancy became more visible and elicited ever-growing criticism from the public. This she was prepared for; she even welcomed it, because it reinforced her sense of mission and further legitimized the absolute rightness she felt about what she was doing. But if the sniping she received from the Establish-ment counterbalanced the criticism she was getting from within the movement, there was one source of criticism that left her hurt and angry.

She seemed indifferent to the renewal of her father's complaints. "I never got hate mail until Jane took off on this revolutionary kick," Henry Fonda bitterly told a reporter. "She's a bright girl, but she doesn't think for herself. She hears a second- or third-hand opinion about some injustice, and the next thing you know she's screaming revolution. The trouble is that because I'm her father, other people think I agree with her. . . . I get letters calling me a Commie because my name is Fonda."

"I think she makes a lot of mistakes," he said on another occasion. "I think she hurts her causes more than she helps them. She turns people off that she shouldn't turn off. She should turn them on! She is only turning on the people who are already revolutionaries. She doesn't persuade people that *should* be persuaded."

Although they hurt, Jane usually shrugged her father's public remarks off with a wisecrack. But when her brother began releasing sarcastic quotes to the press, her hackles rose. "It hurt when he told a reporter that I get involved in causes without really understanding them," she said. "Why, Peter was the one who really turned me on to thinking about others in the first place. Now he goes around telling everyone that I need to grow up and broaden my outlook."

Although Jane and Gardner had mutually agreed to put an end to their romance, they continued to work together on the Servicemen's Fund. Gardner's replacement in Jane's romantic life was, of all people, Donald Sutherland, her co-star in *Klute* and the husband of Shirley Sutherland, one of the women who had originally got Jane interested in radical politics. Sutherland had already been mildly radicalized by his wife; as a result of his association with Jane, he evidently lost whatever skepticism he had left and became almost as ardent a revolutionary as she was. Only the fact that he was not an American citizen restrained him from the kind of arrest-prone activism Jane was involved in.

Jane's most pressing project immediately after leaving Cleveland was on behalf of the Panthers, and as a result of her activities, she found herself on the receiving end of further criticism within the movement. She went to New Orleans late in November to demonstrate her support for a group of local Panthers who had been occupying a housing project for the previous six weeks while police tried to flush them out. The confrontation had turned into a standoff. In the meantime, the national Black Panther Party had called a "convention to re-write the Constitution of the United States" in Washington, D.C., for November 28. In order to enable the New Orleans Panthers to escape from the housing project and attend the convention, Jane rented four cars in her name and had them taken to the site of the project. On November 25, as the Panthers left the project in the cars—secretly, they thought—they were stopped at a police roadblock and arrested on various charges stemming from the housing-project take-over. New Orleans Police Chief Clarence Giarusso told a news conference the next day that it was "thanks to Jane Fonda that we knew the militants were going to try to make a break." Giarusso said that Jane, by renting the four cars while she was in New Orleans the previous day, had unwittingly supplied the police with the intelligence information they needed to make the capture. "She probably doesn't know yet that she helped us," Giarusso said, "but I want her to know that she has our thanks."

After attending the Panther convention, Jane flew from Washington to

Detroit, then to Atlanta, Chicago, New York, Texas and North Carolina to appear at rallies and meetings—all within a few days. She spent most of December in Southern California, where she gave speeches and raised funds for the forthcoming Winter Soldier Investigation. She also visited with Vanessa, who was staying with her father at Malibu while Jane was on the road. Vadim was living with Hollywood starlet Gwen Welles by this time, and friends of Jane say she was perfectly amenable to the arrangement.

The Winter Soldier Investigation took place during the first week of February, 1971, and passed generally unnoticed except by the radical underground press. Moderated by Donald Duncan and others, the investigation consisted mainly of Vietnam veterans rising to tell of their guilt in participating in atrocities against Vietnamese civilians and prisoners. It was a moving four-day litany of horror stories that brought chilling insights into the officially condoned practices of military leaders in Vietnam. The point of the hearings was to prove that the responsibility for war crimes rested in the highest councils of the government, but these conclusions went largely unnoticed.

America was tired of the war, as well as of the antiwar movement. After the Winter Soldier Investigation, the movement in general went into a state of decline as President Nixon began withdrawing troops from Vietnam in wholesale numbers, thus lulling the American public into an anticipation of impending peace. There was to be no letup for Jane, however. The war was no longer the main issue, as far as she was concerned. "As a revolutionary woman," she announced, "I am ready to support all struggles that are radical."

With Donald Sutherland in almost constant attendance, Jane, who was now thirty-three, began 1971 with her head full of impatient revolutionary plans and a brand new cause—feminism. Her first major announcement was that she intended to organize a troupe of entertainers "to tour military bases and entertain soldiers with something they really want to see."

The idea was originally Howard Levy's, says Fred Gardner. Levy agrees. "I saw Jane in New York. She was feeling at loose ends after the Winter Soldier thing and was complaining that she didn't have enough to do. We were talking about what she could do besides make fund-raising appearances for the USSF, and I suggested something like a Bob Hope type show, you know, touring the bases and giving the troops some really first-class radical entertainment—sort of an alternative Bob Hope show."

Jane was excited by the idea and began work on putting it together.

Soon she had commitments from a few dozen performing friends, foremost of whom were Sutherland, Elliott Gould, Peter Boyle and Dick Gregory, the comedian. On February 17, Steve Jaffe organized a news conference so Jane could announce their plans. "Bob Hope and company seem to have a corner on the market in speaking to soldiers," she declared. "The time has come for entertainers who take a different view on the war to reach our servicemen, too. Antiwar shows are what today's soldiers want." Jane said further that the Servicemen's Fund would sponsor the show, which would be called the FTA show, and that they intended to open it at the 35,000-man Fort Bragg Army base at Fayetteville, North Carolina.

Like "SNAFU" during World War II, "FTA" was a slang acronym used by GI's to mean "Fuck the Army."

As the show rehearsed throughout February and early March, several star attractions dropped out and other lesser-known performers joined. With scripts by Jules Feiffer, Barbara Garson and Fred Gardner, the theme of the show was based on the same sort of irreverence reflected in its title. It was hurriedly put together and consisted basically of a series of skits, many of them bordering on the sophomoric, lampooning the war, the Army, the government and other institutions of the Establishment. The show started in a burst of good intentions, goodwill and enthusiasm among the members of the troupe, but from there on, according to Levy and Gardner, everything went downhill. The tour extended through the spring and summer, and since the Army would not permit the show to be performed on any of its bases, it was forced to play in high school auditoriums or on makeshift stages in GI coffeehouses.

Gardner was also the advance man for the show during the early stages of its tour. Writing in a radical newsletter called the *Second Page*, he says that the reason Jane became so enthusiastic about doing FTA was that she was an actress. She had realized "that the movement might be using her more than she was using the movement," he says. "They had set her up to go on talk shows where she made a fool of herself; they were taking her for enormous sums of money. She figured, correctly, that the only way she could stay in the movement without being ripped off was to function as an actress. As she wrote in the show's publicity kit, 'The most important thing for me is to combine my politics and my profession.'

"Jane did the hiring that made the show happen," Gardner says. "Donald Sutherland came in (by then he was her beau), and Peter Boyle, who was scheduled to appear in her next movie, *Steelyard Blues*. A skilled director, Alan Myerson, and two actors from The Committee [an improvisational political theater group in San Francisco] joined the troupe and were, coincidentally, rewarded with good jobs on *Steelyard Blues.*"

The point Gardner leads to is that although the show started with the best of intentions, it soon became a hornet's nest of political infighting and career opportunism on the part of the cast. In his view, two types were attracted to the show—career radicals and filmland opportunists, both of which felt they could advance their fortunes through their relationship with Jane.

Gardner, already exasperated by the distortions that had been imposed on the movement he started, found it difficult to see anything revolutionary, even radical, about Jane's FTA effort. He says that Jane and the sponsors of the show claimed at the time that "it raised consciousness" and gave dissident GI's a sense of their numbers by bringing them together to see anti-Establishment skits. But it was 1971, after all, not 1967, he says. "The fact that most soldiers hated the war and the brass was well known, and they didn't need their consciousness raised by Hollywood missionaries. The real reason the show was being produced was that it served the interests of a number of movement bureaucrats and opportunists—including the cast."

The FTA show was the last straw for Gardner. After it played at a few Army towns and he realized that most of the performers cared less about GI's than about advancing their own careers, he was ready to quit and turn his advance-man responsibilities over to someone else.

Jane's newest cause—feminism—arose directly out of her involvement in the GI movement. She had long been discussing the oppression of women with various women in the movement, but until putting the FTA show together she had not really made any attempts to deal with her feelings. Touring the Army towns before she organized the FTA show, she had quickly become aware of the constant exploitation of women both in the military and in the movement. One of the reasons she wanted to do the show, she said, was to raise GI's consciousness not only about the war but about women. Bob Hope-type entertainment, she claimed, was the snidest form of sexism with its starlets prancing around onstage in front of sex-starved soldiers and Hope making the appropriately leering jokes. "We're not going to do that kind of chauvinist show with topless dancers and a lot of tits flying," she declared. "If that's the only kind of entertainment soldiers can get, that's what they'll watch. But that's also why American men and soldiers feel women are to be used as sex objects. The violence against Vietnamese women is terrible, and these shows contribute to it."

About her own past role in contributing to the perpetuation of women as sex objects, she admitted, "I have been as guilty as anybody because I did it from ignorance. But no more."

Why her role in *Klute*, then, where she would appear in the nude? "I took *Klute* because in it I expose a great deal of the oppression of women in this country—the system which makes women sell themselves for possessions."

Once Jane latched onto feminism as an issue, it boiled up in her quicker than any of her other radical passions. And according to many of her friends within the movement, Gardner included, her guilt over her former collaboration in sexism became the dominating force and fury of her activism. Soon she was defining male sexist chauvinism in terms of political concepts such as "imperialism" and was having little to do with any man who did not meet her personal standards of masculine liberation.

By late spring, according to Howard Levy, the FTA show had become the bête noire of the GI movement and the single greatest cause of dissension "between the serious revolutionaries and the adventurists who were vying for control behind the scenes." The first show, which played for three performances at the GI coffeehouse in Fayetteville in mid-March, was a resounding success. It attracted full and enthusiastic houses of appreciative Fort Bragg GI's and a sprinkling of government agents at each performance.

The Fort Bragg experience was hard to top. As the troupe continued its tour, it encountered less and less enthusiasm, especially after Fred Gardner quit as advance man. Gardner knew GI's better than anyone connected with the show, and he knew how to get GI audiences out. Once he left, the audiences dwindled; they were limited almost exclusively to the already-committed handfuls of soldiers on each base and the radical staffs of the local coffeehouses.

James Skelley is a former Navy officer who received his commission by way of the Naval ROTC at the University of Minnesota in 1967. Disgusted by the Vietnam War, he became one of the founders of the Concerned Officers Movement, a group of active-duty military officers who banded together in San Diego in 1969 to protest the war. He managed to receive a conscientious objector's discharge but remained in San Diego to help coordinate antiwar activities in the main port of

America's Pacific Fleet. A tall, intelligent, sensitive young man with a healthy streak of skepticism about any and all absolutes, he met Fred Gardner and immediately liked him for his combination of high-minded dedication and discriminating intelligence.

Through Gardner, Skelley met Jane when she went to San Diego State University to speak in April and again in May, when she and Sutherland returned to put on the FTA show—they hoped aboard the aircraft carrier *Constellation*, which was in port preparing to sail for combat duty in Vietnam. When FTA was denied permission to perform aboard the carrier, Skelley persuaded Jane to march in a demonstration against the sailing of the ship. He struck up a friendship with Jane and afterward agreed to succeed the disgruntled Gardner as advance man for the show.

One of his first tasks was "advancing" the troupe's appearance at the Shelter Half coffeehouse outside Fort Lewis in Tacoma. The Shelter Half, really nothing more than a storefront next to a barbershop, was one of the more radical coffeehouse projects and was staffed mostly by members of the local Young Socialist Alliance and the Socialist Workers Party. It received the majority of its money from Gardner's Servicemen's Fund.

"They were not really interested in the GI's up there," Skelley recalls, "and that surprised me because I thought the GI's were what the coffeehouse projects were all about. The place was liberally postered with virulent revolutionary slogans and pictures of revolutionary heroes like Huey Newton and Che Guevara. There was very little attention paid to the question of GI rights; most of the activity was aimed at converting GI's into active revolutionaries and enlisting them into radical cadres.

"Anyway, I was up there for a week or so before the show arrived, but I had trouble getting anyone on the staff to help me organize an audience. It was pretty frustrating, especially when I was led to believe that the coffeehouse staff was there just for that purpose.

"Well, the show came in and did its performance. The audience was so-so, half GI's and half local radicals. But what really pissed me off was afterward. The staff held a party for Jane and the rest of the cast. It was a typical cocktail party, you know, with drinks and canapés. But what was worse was that the GI's were excluded. I mean, the staff locked up the place. It was them getting their kicks rapping with the celebrities, while the GI's were sent on their way. To me, that was the phoniest kind of elitism, and I began to understand why the Fort Lewis GI's were so indifferent to what was happening at the Shelter Half. Apparently this had occurred before. As far as I could see, the staff ran the Shelter Half mainly for the benefit of the staff, and the GI's were just an afterthought. It was this kind of thing that had Freddie Gardner so pissed.

"I also got pretty mad at Jane when I saw her going along with the party. But, then, she wasn't really aware of what was happening. When I told her, she had enough sense to get the hell out of there."

Skelley says that by the time he joined the FTA show it was riddled with dissension. Gardner agrees, and adds that the GI movement in general and its corresponding fund-raising efforts through the Servicemen's Fund were even more seriously strife-ridden. Howard Levy suggests even more strongly that Jane had lost sight of her original goals in the GI movement and was impatient to make it conform to her own vision of it. Since the fund still largely represented Gardner's view, and since she had broken off with Gardner politically, much of the ensuing dispute between Jane and the members of the Servicemen's Fund apparently derived from her disenchantment with Gardner and his more moderate tactical policies. Jane was still working through the fund, Levy says, but a serious rift was developing.

Levy suggests that it was at about this time that Jane decided to pursue the notion he had put in her mind the year before about organizing the Hollywood entertainment industry. In the spring, after the FTA show was launched, she, Sutherland, Steve Jaffe and others put together a group of film celebrities in Hollywood and named the organization the Entertainment Industry for Peace and Justice (EIPJ). Their first meeting took place in April, 1971, at the Continental Hyatt House on Hollywood's Sunset Strip. It was convened primarily as a strategy meeting to work out ways of expanding fund raising for the FTA show and "continuing the entertainment industry's fight to end the war and bring our servicemen home."

By June the EIPJ had, among other sponsors, Burt Lancaster, Sally Kellerman, Richard Basehart, Barbra Streisand, Brenda Vaccaro and Tuesday Weld, plus several well-known producers, writers, directors and musicians. Jane and Sutherland became members of the central steering committee, which coordinated the activities of the several subcommittees representing various occupational specialties in the film industry—actors, directors, writers, technicians and so on.

At a large EIPJ meeting in June at the Musicians Hall in Los Angeles, Jane stated in a speech that what was needed in Vietnam was "a victory for the Vietcong." This not only created a great deal of controversy within the film community, but caused an outpouring of public indignation when it was reported across the country.

One of the EIPJ's main functions was to add to the Servicemen's Fund's money-raising capabilities. According to Fred Gardner, though, the formation of the EIPJ was the straw that broke the USSF's back. Jane's intentions in starting the organization were good, he says, but EIPJ soon turned principally into a means by which ambitious Hollywood opportunists who mistakenly imagined themselves as radicals could meet Jane, Donald Sutherland and other stars and further their careers and standing in the film industry on the pretext of wanting to work for the movement. Two functionaries of the organization, he recalls, were Nina Serrano and Francine Parker, obscure women filmmakers and ardent feminists. He says, "They began convincing Jane (and it didn't take much convincing, given Jane's keen nose for what's fashionable) that the GI show and everything else she appeared in ought to present women in a better light. They let it be known that they were very active in women's liberation and could easily write and direct this pro-woman material."

Later that summer Jane, Sutherland and several members of the FTA cast went to San Jose, California, for location shooting on Jane's new movie, *Steelyard Blues*—described in its prerelease publicity as a wacky, anti-Establishment comedy about a band of social misfits who outwit the law in the merry and sympathetic tradition of Bonnie and Clyde. *Klute* had recently been released to good reviews—especially for Jane—and she felt that *Steelyard Blues* should be another installment in her crusade to make films of social and political significance. The picture was to be directed by Alan Myerson, the director of the FTA show. It was his first feature film, and Jane again played a prostitute.

Francine Parker and Nina Serrano, according to Gardner, criticized the character Jane was playing and fed her more favorable lines to insert in the script—thereby fueling a feud between Jane and director Myerson, who, Gardner claims, the two women wanted to replace.

They didn't replace him in *Steelyard Blues* but soon took over as directors of the FTA show. According to other observers, they created so much dissension on the set of the film that Jane was ready to quit. Jim Skelley, who was there for part of the filming, suggests that the only reason Jane didn't quit was that Donald Sutherland was the film's producer. Nevertheless, he says, the atmosphere on the set was thick with tension and argument. "Jane was in one camp with Francine Parker and some of the other women. Myerson was in the other with some of the actors. Donald was sort of caught in the middle, and he almost broke up with Jane right then and there. I haven't seen the picture, so I don't know how it came out, but I do know that the filming of *Steelyard Blues* caused the whole character of the FTA show to change."

Skelley recalls attending a long and bitter meeting at The Committee's theater in San Francisco shortly afterward. "Jane had insisted that Francine Parker take over the FTA show. They had this meeting, and some of the performers in the FTA cast were summarily dismissed from the show by Jane and Francine for being 'sexist.' Then some of the others quit in protest. One actress was fired in a particularly humiliating way, and I was really surprised at Jane for her lack of sensitivity in going along with Francine the way she did. By this time, she was really uptight about male chauvinism and was growing, I think, a bit unreasonable on the subject."

Francine Parker is a swarthy, mannish, tough-talking New Yorker in her early forties who today lives and works in Hollywood as a free-lance filmmaker. When asked about her version of the events surrounding *Steelyard Blues* and the FTA show, she refuses to discuss them except to say that the film eventually made of the show, for which she received credit as director, "is damned good." When asked what kinds of films she is interested in making, she responds, "I'll make anything I get paid for."

Howard Levy is bitter about the role he says Francine Parker played in the disintegrating relationship between Jane and the Servicemen's Fund. He tells of a meeting he and Paul Lauter, a founder of the fund, had with Jane, Donald Sutherland and Francine Parker in Jane and Donald's suite at the Chelsea Hotel in New York after the completion of *Steelyard Blues*. "I remember that meeting vividly because it was such a fiasco. It made it almost impossible for those of us in the Servicemen's Fund who were still interested in supporting the FTA show to continue working with Jane. She had surrounded herself with people like Francine, Steve Jaffe, all these hot little opportunists who didn't know beans about what was going on in the movement.

"There were two issues at the meeting. One was to discuss some fund-raising tactics they were using on the West Coast; the other was to negotiate about how much money we would be able to provide to send the show overseas.

"By this time Jane was feuding with Paul Lauter and Bob Zevin, two of the original organizers of the fund. With Freddie Gardner more or less out of her life, Jane had started her own fund-raising campaign through the EIPJ, and it was effectively compromising the things we were doing and creating confusion among a lot of the people we depended on for money. It was almost as if Jane was intentionally counter-fund raising. Not only that, it seemed she was out to destroy the Servicemen's Fund's credibility by writing letters that cast us in a bad light.

"We wanted to use the film that had been made of the show's first performance at Fort Bragg for fund-raising purposes. We had a deal in the works to sell it for showing on Eastern European television—a deal that might have got us about twenty-five thousand dollars. These were the two things Lauter and I met with Jane at the Chelsea to discuss.

"Well—Francine was doing most of the talking for Jane, and she was abusive and irrational. What was worse, Jane went along with it. Francine accused us of all sorts of evils, like exploiting women and trying to ruin Jane's career. Sutherland chimed in with threats against Lauter, and they almost had a fistfight. When Lauter stood up to Donald's challenge, Sutherland very discreetly backed off. The meeting went on and on in this vein, with shouting, recriminations, accusations, most of them from Francine. She claims to hate men, but has the worst masculine qualities of anyone I know, including men.

"Francine and Jane didn't want the film to be used, first, because it was a mediocre film and they thought it might hurt Jane's standing as an actress and, second, because Francine didn't have anything to do with it and wanted to make a film of her own. But when I suggested that they put the question to a cast vote, they said they couldn't do that. I said why not, it seemed the most democratic way of settling the issue. She said it was Trotskyite. I said, what does Trotsky have to do with it? She said it would be a vote that appealed to the lowest common denominator— meaning, I suppose, to the feeble intelligence of the members of the cast. So we argued over that. It seemed all decisions about FTA were now being made by this tight little triumvirate of Jane, Francine and Donald, while at the same time they were always talking about how important it was that everything be done 'collectively.' Well, I didn't see anything very collective in their way of doing things. It just didn't make any sense—everything they did was a contradiction of what they said. They now had their own little antiwar movement going, and since they owned the bat and ball, they were going to make the rules.

"Whatever respect I'd had for Sutherland I lost that day. He's not the smartest guy around, but the way he was pandering to Francine blew my mind. He acted like a man who had been brainwashed. My biggest disappointment, though, was Jane. We worked well together when she was first getting into the movement, and she really followed up on some of my ideas. But now, I don't know—in a way I felt sorry for her. She had started listening to some bad people, some incredibly bad people, and had lost sight of what the GI movement was all about. At one point in the meeting she took me off to the side and said, 'Howard, we've always worked together so well, and we've always got along and I like you very much. But I can't understand how you can continue to work with these people.' I said, 'Jane, come on, what do you mean by *these people?*' She meant Lauter and Zevin and some of the others in the fund. I just looked at her and shrugged. There was no use trying to talk to her anymore. And with Francine Parker going on the way she was, I finally just threw up my hands and walked out. The three of them were just too irrational to try to come to terms about anything with."

27. They Called Her Hanoi Jane

What Jane Fonda has done is treason!

—Representative Fletcher Thompson,
Republican-Georgia

JANE'S feud with the Servicemen's Fund eventually led to a complete break. Levy says that she and Sutherland turned FTA into their own personal antiwar effort with the help of Francine Parker and Steve Jaffe. Jane, Donald and Francine incorporated the show under the FTA acronym and called the new organization Free Theatre Associates. With money from the Servicemen's Fund drying up, they made plans to take the show on a tour of the Pacific with funds raised by themselves.

In October, Jane published an article in the *New York Times Sunday Magazine* in which she declared herself a full-fledged feminist. She said she had received her final inspiration while filming *Steelyard Blues*. The article was a deeply felt plea for women's liberation, and Jane made a special point of declaring that her feminist passion did not come out of any personal psychological problems but was the result of her recognition that the oppression of women—both blatant and subtle—was a social problem which all women shared.

Concurrently, she appeared on television in a series of skits produced by Nina Serrano and directed by Francine Parker in which she played the roles of six different women—housewife, teacher, Playboy bunny, secretary, nurse and hippie. The program was designed to show "each of these types as they are oppressed by today's society."

About her relationship with Donald Sutherland, she would only say she could no longer conceive of having a relationship with a man and doing for a man what she had done for Vadim. "It will never happen again. I will never be a wife again." Nevertheless, she said, she still believed in the old-fashioned kind of love she had had with Vadim— "your heart speeding up when you hear his voice over the telephone, your fit of dizziness when you see him, your feeling of loneliness when he's away. I still believe in that kind of love because it's the most beautiful in the world. . . . Still, I do not have that kind of love right now. But I'm not unhappy about this. I am very serene with the man I'm having a relationship with right now. We are friends. We think the same things. When we're together, it's delightful; when we are apart, we remain friends. I mean, he is not indispensable to me, I am not indispensable to him. He doesn't feel as if he possesses me, and I certainly don't feel that I possess him. Our attraction involves learning and respect, and we don't expect our relationship to continue forever. . . . We don't even feel the need to be physically faithful, because we know that sleeping with another person does not diminish what we feel for each other."

The first public sign of dissension in the FTA show came just before Jane and the rest of the troupe prepared to leave for their Pacific tour. Country Joe McDonald, a popular rock star who had been appearing with the show on its domestic tour, called a press conference and announced that he was quitting because of Jane. He called Jane "simple-minded," "totalitarian" and "unable to work truly collectively." He said he had been active in the peace movement from its earliest days, whereas Jane and Donald Sutherland had only been involved for the past two years. "The press has catered to them, but the movement has been duped by them," he charged. "Their place in the hierarchy is much lower than they think it is . . . they've assumed a position of authority they don't have, and I'm not going to be any part of their ego trip.

"I want to demystify Jane Fonda and Donald Sutherland," McDonald went on. "They're novices. I think she's had a bad effect on the movement. She has created dissension. People are starting to look at her as a leader of the movement, which she is not. Nor is Sutherland. . . . Jane insists on being the producer and on raising all the money, and her secretary and her press agent are the secretary and press agent for the FTA show. No one else has any say."

The secretary McDonald referred to was a young radical woman named Ellen Ruby who had changed her name to Ruby Ellyn and was hired by Jane to look after her personal affairs. The press agent was, of course, Steve Jaffe, whom Howard Levy holds responsible for the fact that the Pacific tour received practically nothing but sarcastic notice in the nation's media.

"The FTA show should be a true collective," McDonald went on to say, "and it should be up to the collective to decide what they want to do. The FTA show projects a very liberal attitude, but all the real radicals have been pushed out. If it's not going to be a radical collective, they should say so. I would have stayed with the show if it were possible to work out the conflicts collectively. But it's just one or two people making the decisions, and they wield complete control." He concluded by saying that Jane was "not even a radical feminist, she's just a novice feminist."

Jane remained silent in the face of McDonald's public attack. Instead, she continued to raise money for the Pacific tour and to rehearse the recast show. They were planning to leave at the beginning of December, but their first stop was scheduled for New York—to play a final fund-raising performance at Philharmonic Hall.

Bob Zarem recalls that Steve Jaffe had come to work with Zarem's firm—Rogers, Cowan & Brenner—bringing Jane and Sutherland with him as clients. Jane asked Zarem to handle press relations for the Philharmonic Hall performance. "She was really interested in keeping attention away from herself by this time," Zarem says. "She came into New York expecting a lot of press publicity for the show but wanted none for herself. Of course, the press was really only interested in her, not the show, and I had a hell of a time convincing her that the only way we'd get press coverage was if she would cooperate in interviews. At first she refused. I understood her position—she'd been getting a lot of criticism about dominating the show and wanted to keep a low profile.

But there it was—no interviews with Jane, no effective press coverage. Eventually she gave in and gave a few interviews, and it helped the show at the Philharmonic enormously."

Holly Near, a pleasant, red-haired young singer-actress-songwriter and pacifist, had just joined the cast. She remembers hearing about the dissension during the past summer but claims that by the time she joined the show, just before it left for the Pacific, everyone was on good terms. "We played Philharmonic Hall," she says, "and the show was very well received. Then, on the tour, everyone was united behind Jane and Don and Francine."

The night after the Philharmonic Hall performance Jane, Sutherland, Francine Parker and others in the cast taped a David Susskind television show in which Susskind questioned them about their aims. In the course of the discussion, Sutherland attempted to use statistics to prove a point about GI disenchantment over the war. He claimed that in the previous year, the Army had experienced 176,000 desertions. When Susskind asked him where he got the figure, Jane interjected: "From the Pentagon—not a very reliable source." Actually it was they who were not very reliable sources.

No matter how one felt about the antiwar movement, one could be sure that the statistics constantly tossed off by peace activists were erroneous, either by design or through emotional exaggeration. In Jane and Sutherland's case, it was most likely the latter. It happened that the number of desertions in the U.S. Army during the previous year was 65,643, a disquieting number indeed, but not the 176,000 claimed by Jane and Sutherland. It was a small point, but it illustrated how prone inexperienced radicals were to using exaggerated statistics to make their points. Of course, they could easily have argued that such exaggerations were justified in view of the government's lies about its successes and failures and purposes in Vietnam. But such an argument reflects unfavorably on the integrity of radicals and revolutionaries who pledge allegiance to telling the truth about America. Doubtless, there is much truth to be told. But one loses confidence in the radical portion of our society to tell it when its representatives resort to the same techniques used by those they accuse of fogging the truth. And it lends credence to the charges of radicals like Fred Gardner and Saul Alinsky, who were as critical of uninformed instant revolutionaries as they are of those who would preserve the corrupt status quo.

As the FTA show prepared to leave for the Pacific, Gardner published his aforequoted article in the *Second Page*, the radical San Francisco newsletter, which was scathingly critical of the turn the GI movement had taken. He was especially disdainful of FTA. "The show," he said, "does not fight imperialism. It does nothing but advertise organizations and projects that have utter contempt for soldiers. . . . The movement this show speaks for is not much of a threat to the men running America. It's full of missionaries and fakers. It's a movement that has never done—that scorns and vilifies—the slow hard work of building an organization that will take power and reorganize this society."

The article was Gardner's valedictory to the GI projects, the Servicemen's Fund and Jane Fonda—all of which he had been instrumental in bringing into the mainstream of the antiwar movement. By the fall of 1971 the movement had no mainstream anymore; it was as rent by ideological factionism as its GI branch was. Serious revolutionaries like Gardner were withdrawing into reflection and contemplation to let flag-defiling novice radicals and flag-waving ordinary citizens wage a war of name-calling and mutual self-righteousness.

FTA left for the Far East at the beginning of December, with a stop in Hawaii. As an alternative to Bob Hope's annual Christmas tour, it offered plenty of contrasts. Where Hope's show had glossy production numbers, a big band and a succession of scantily clad starlets, FTA had makeshift props and a small combo, and the performers determinedly hid their physical charms most of the time under jeans and baggy sweaters. Where the Hope show clipped along on brisk, risqué one-liners spiced with patriotic flourishes, FTA loosely mixed readings, songs and satirical skits to underline such assertions as Jane's: "We must oppose with everything we have those blue-eyed murderers—Nixon, Laird and all the rest of those ethnocentric white American male chauvinists!"

But where Hope and his troupe were whisked from base to base like VIP's, Jane and company encountered red tape and visa problems virtually everywhere they traveled. Judging from the mixed success of the performances, the authorities may have overestimated FTA's appeal. At one show in Japan a group of hecklers rushed the stage and were warded off only at the last moment. At another show, in a large gymnasium in Iwakuni, Japan, roughly one-third of the audience walked out before the show was over. Most of the people who attended the performances, according to cast member Holly Near, were there to see Jane. "That was the big disappointment," she says. "I thought we'd have a much greater effect than we did. Oh, don't get me wrong, I think the show was a success to a certain degree, but I'd guess that the majority of the audiences came to see Jane. In other words, if she hadn't been connected with it, I'm sure our audiences would have been nonexistent."

Once they saw Jane, many were disappointed. One fan who had been hoping to see Barbarella on stage lamented: "She looked too plain and sounded too shrill."

Yet there were many who appreciated the show's naughty irreverence, and Jane felt that she and the troupe had really accomplished something positive. "This is definitely going to be a part of my life," she said on her return to the States at the end of December. "I'm sure the remembrance of the evenings, and of how many of their fellow GI's were there, will come back to many servicemen at their moment of decision in the future."

Jane returned to a renewed barrage of public outcries as she continued to call for a Vietcong and North Vietnamese victory. Howard Levy makes a cogent analysis of what drove Jane on. "She's very alert and perceptive. I don't doubt, I've never doubted her sincerity. But sincerity is a funny thing with Jane. For some strange reason her sincerity drives her into obsessive-compulsive behavior. As a revolutionary she has one flaw. She is unable to put things into any larger perspective. She came into the movement late, not only in her life but in its life as well, when it had already been torn apart by tactical quarrels and ideological infighting. She never really learned the nature of the movement, the nature of radicalism for that matter, and she just didn't have the ability, or patience, whatever you want to call it, to work within the rules. Revolution has rules like everything else, rules that have evolved through years and years of trial and error. In effect, she tried to start her own version of the movement, which is what a lot of people did, mostly young and not-too-well-educated people. Now this is something only someone who doesn't really understand the nature of revolution would do. She just couldn't work within the logical perspective of the revolutionary idea in America. In a really oppressed country, where ninety-nine percent of the population are serfs and one percent the economically elite, it's possible for a rapid revolution to take place, and when I say rapid I mean even then something that takes time—years and years. But to expect that to happen in the United States is the most immature kind of wishful thinking. To think you can make something like that happen means you are stuck with a bad case of egograndiosity. I'm afraid to say it, but I think Jane caught a bad case of egograndiosity. From then on, when she started thinking she could do something which, if she looked at it in some kind of historical perspective, couldn't be done, it was all downhill for her. She not only hurt herself with the general public, she hurt herself with the movement, too, or what was left of it. I really hated to see that, because I think Jane could've been a real positive force in things. Basically, she lost the ability to discuss, to negotiate. I'm not sure she ever had it, mind you, but if she did, she lost it to this sense of moral superiority she has. That's why it's so damaging to have personalities in the movement. In the public's mind, they become the movement itself, and Jane certainly wasn't the movement."

Jane went to Paris in January, 1972, to make a long-postponed film for French director Jean Luc Godard, who was lately devoting his talents to producing long, tedious Maoist pictures like *La Chinoise*. The new picture, which was to co-star Yves Montand, was called *Tout Va Bien* (*Everything's O.K.* in English), and would prove to be another of Godard's tiresome exercises in revolutionary propaganda. At least Jane was being consistent in her desire to restrict herself to making movies of political and social significance.

While in Paris, she stayed with Vanessa in a large, plain apartment on the Left Bank which she shared with five other women and which was organized along the lines of a feminist commune. "Godard," she told a reporter, "is the only person I've ever met who's truly revolutionary." What she meant was that Godard was living a revolutionary life—he produced his films through a film cooperative he had formed with several other film-industry friends and spent every waking moment of his life in pursuit of his revolutionary dream. She added that she was undeterred by the criticisms and downright expressions of hate she had been the target of and intended to expand the FTA show into several touring companies under the auspices of the EIPJ. "These days, a lot of people hate me," she said. "They say, 'Where's her sense of humor?' I haven't lost my humor at all. But it's hard to feel any humor when our bombs are killing innocent Vietnamese!"

While in Paris, Jane made her first contact with representatives of North Vietnam and expressed a wish to visit their country.

She returned to Hollywood in early April to be on hand for the Academy Awards, for which she had been nominated for her role in *Klute*. At first, she planned to refuse the Oscar as a protest against the system if she won. "But a woman who is much wiser than I am said to me, 'You're a frigging subjective individual, an elite individual, it's really typical of the bourgeois middle-class family girl to want to refuse the Oscar.'" She was persuaded that accepting the award would be a positive political tactic, because "the Oscar is what the working class relates to when it thinks of people in movies. That's what the masses of people in America, who think I'm a freak and who think that people who speak out in support of the Panthers and against the war are all some kind of monsters, relate to. It's important for those of us who speak out for social change to get that kind of acclaim."

There was a great deal of pressure on Jane from her movement friends to make a political speech if she won, but after a long talk with her father she decided not to. Although he disagreed thoroughly with her politics, he convinced her that her already well-known feelings would be infinitely more eloquent if left unspoken. "I said, 'I implore you not to,'" Henry Fonda claimed afterward.

Win she did, and when she followed her father's advice and saw its effects, a gradual change came over her. Not in the intensity of her emotions about the war and the American system, but in the way she expressed them.

Henry Jaglom, a movie director and friend of Jane's, says her silence at the Oscar ceremonies was a "pure political act in itself. Sure, a lot of people were unhappy that she didn't take advantage of the moment to let loose. But Jane showed what she was made of. Everybody in Hollywood was waiting to come down on her. It was a beautiful piece of political theater, what she did, and the next day she could call all those slob producers and movie moguls up and raise more money than she'd raised in the past two years just because they'd be so grateful she didn't fuck up their happy little gathering."

Jaglom is an unabashed admirer of Jane's. A member of the EIPJ who has worked with her closely on several projects, he insists that in spite of her early mistakes, Jane was a positive factor in the movement. "Sure, when she first got interested she made some goofs, most of which came about because she had a lot to learn. But once she learned what she had to, she was magnificent. I've never known anyone who can translate a conviction into action the way she has. She's had to put up with an incredible amount of shit in the past three years, and a lesser person would have gotten discouraged a long time ago and crawled back into her shell. That says something for Jane right there. While a lot of people were wrapped up in arguments and quarrels about how to get things done, she was out getting things done."

After the Oscar Jane remained in California for a while, planning new projects and giving speeches. She spoke at an antiwar rally in San Francisco's Golden Gate Park on May 1 and declared, "All over the world America is regarded as an enemy." She described the fighting in Vietnam as "an uprising of the people of the South." Whether her assessment was an unintentional slip or her real belief, again she was taken to task for her lack of knowledge about the history of the Vietnam conflict.

Jaglom defends her: "So what if she made an occasional factual error? The woman was talking to the real issue, which was the fact that the United States was clobbering the hell out of the Vietnamese people. I mean how could anyone quibble over minor factual errors when so much more was at stake? What was at stake was that we were destroying Vietnam, number one, and number two, our people weren't being told the truth about what we were doing. Those were the issues that were really important, and it makes me laugh when I hear people arguing about whether Jane's figures on the number of tons of bombs being dropped every day were right or Laird's figures were right. The fact is, an awful lot of tons were being dropped, and an awful lot of Vietnamese civilians were being wiped out while we argued the figures. That's what Jane was really saying. She was trying to get attention away from these silly diversionary games and onto the real problem."

Jane had met Tom Hayden a short time before her Oscar. Hayden, one of the country's original and still most respected young radicals, had matured into an experienced revolutionary. Not only did he have a long and distinguished record of selfless organizing, he possessed a sharp, incisive intelligence and a talent for logical theorizing. He was a thoroughgoing revolutionary, but more of the Gardner-Alinsky than the romantic overnight-change school. With a battered face that was a cross between a young Jimmy Durante and a worn nickel, Hayden was a cool, forceful activist without any of the martyr's zeal of many of his colleagues. He was one of the few radical leaders who was taken seriously by Establishment politicians. Most of the optimistic idealism of his early days as a leader of the SDS had been seared out of him by beatings and cold jail cells in the South, the misery he saw in Newark's black ghetto and the firsthand evidence of the venal quality of American militarism he picked up on his two trips to North Vietnam. He had been sentenced, as a defendant in the Chicago conspiracy trial, to five years in prison and was free on bail pending the outcome of his appeal (which would eventually prove successful). He couldn't leave the country, but when Jane told him she would like to visit North Vietnam, he told her he would see what he could arrange through his contacts with the government there.

Jane went to New York at the end of June to give a press conference for the opening of Francine Parker's film of the FTA Pacific tour. Peter Knobler, editor of the rock music magazine *Crawdaddy*, was on hand at the Drake Hotel. "It was a largely sympathetic crowd," he recalls, "and Jane handled the few baiting questions that were asked beautifully. I had never seen her before, and I was really impressed with the way she handled herself. This one writer from *Cosmopolitan* magazine got up and asked her how it felt to be the most misunderstood woman in the world—a really inane question. Jane fielded it like a pro, turned it right around on the lady from *Cosmopolitan* and got her to apologize for asking it.

"Afterward I went up to Jane and introduced myself. She was very friendly and invited me to sit and talk. I asked her a question I was very curious about, and also curious to see how she'd answer. I asked her if she was a Communist. She answered it very well and made me feel a little guilty for asking it. She said, 'That's not something I bandy about, Peter.' Of course, she was right. I mean, it's like asking someone how much money they make."

Bob Zarem set up the press conference. "Shortly afterward I left for France on my vacation. I picked up a Paris *Herald Tribune* one day and was astonished to learn that Jane was in Hanoi. She hadn't told me or anyone else a thing about it."

Jane traveled to Hanoi incognito in mid-July at the invitation of the North Vietnamese. While she was there, the news media at home reported almost daily that she had urged American servicemen to desert during broadcasts over Radio Hanoi and was also making other pro-Hanoi statements. When she returned, it was to face the wrath of a fuming nation. The people of the United States could tolerate her previous forays into radicalism, but actually to go to Hanoi and "consort with the enemy"—this was too much!

"Hanoi Jane!" "Red pinko!" "Commie slut!" Such epithets, mixed with a handful of cheers, greeted her when she landed in New York. Branded a traitor by two Republican Congressmen, who demanded an investigation, Jane brushed the charges aside. "What is a traitor?" she asked at a news conference hastily put together by Zarem's secretary. "I cried every day I was in Vietnam. I cried for America. The bombs are falling on Vietnam, but it is an American tragedy."

Jane was profoundly affected by her trip. As she related the details of her stay in Hanoi, her anguish was plainly visible. She defended her loyalty by saying that the things she had done were done for the sake of

America. "The bombing is all the more awful when you can see the little faces, see the women say, 'Thank you, American people, for speaking out against the war.' I believe that the people in this country who are speaking out are the real patriots."

When asked if she might only be seeing one side of the issue, she responded, "There *are* no both sides in this question." She contended that the United States was completely wrong and North Vietnam was blameless for the war and angrily referred to President Nixon as a "cynic, liar, murderer and war criminal."

Asked if she thought she wasn't being used by the North Vietnamese for propaganda purposes, she replied, "Do you think the Vietnamese blow up their own hospitals? Are they bombing their own dikes? Are they mutilating their own women and children in order to impress me? Anyone who speaks out against this war is carrying on propaganda—propaganda for peace, propaganda against death, propaganda for life!"

The news conference was a mobbed, tumultuous affair. Everyone there could sense they were facing a changed Jane Fonda. She wasn't giving a performance—she was deadly serious and deadly convinced of everything she said. Where once her antiwar sentiments seemed to many an exercise in image-making, now those sentiments came from the very core of her being. She was distraught and flushed as she talked to the newsmen. Gone was the calculatedly cold responses of previous news conferences. Her voice trembled with the agony of her emotions and the frustration of trying to talk to people who remained skeptics.

Many Americans were won over by Jane's throbbing anguish—she was like a mother who had just lost her child. Others were not, and indifferent doubts about her sincerity were transformed into furious doubts about her sanity. With the new wave of criticism, it became clear that the government no longer thought of her merely as a nettlesome nuisance but as a tool of the Communists. Suddenly America realized that it was going to have to live with Jane Fonda for a long time.

Her millions of critics were sure she was in for it now, and those who weren't sure prayed she was. The government had been growing more and more interested in Jane's activities during the past two years. The arrest in Cleveland was the first indication of this. Following that, she had been the subject of FBI and military surveillance, her movements quickly filling up dossiers in Washington (Henry Jaglom, her EIPJ colleague, says that he has undergone the same type of harassment and at one point received a telephone call from a man who identified himself as an FBI agent and who offered to sell him his dossier for $25,000).

Then she had been investigated by the House Internal Security Committee—the successor to the House Un-American Activities Committee—for her involvement in the FTA show. Now she was being recommended for prosecution on charges of treason by Congressmen Fletcher Thompson and Richard Ichord.

Jane accused Thompson of trying to make political hay with his Southern conservative constituency in an election year (he was running for the Senate) and said she looked forward to an investigation, even a prosecution. "I welcome the opportunity to tell Congress what I have seen in Vietnam," she announced. "But I have done nothing against the law. Furthermore, the Nuremberg Laws define President Nixon's actions in Vietnam as war crimes and give every American citizen a legal basis and moral right to resist what is being done in our names."

As it turned out, the Justice Department decided that Jane was right—she had not broken any law. But Ichord and Thompson pressed on. They sponsored a bill in the House of Representatives that would make it a felony in the future for any citizen to visit a country at war with the United States. The measure, called unofficially the Fonda Amendment to the 1950 Internal Security Act, failed to pass—no doubt because the entire question of whether North Vietnam was really at war with the United States or the United States was at war with North Vietnam had never been resolved by Congress. It's no small irony that the outcry against Jane was led by men who, by their failure to exercise their duty under the Constitution to make a determination about this question, gave the antiwar movement much of its impetus and justification. The question of the constitutionality of three successive Presidents waging war without the formal approval of Congress seemed a clear-cut one, but Congress never answered it. The fact that Jane was above prosecution for treason or sedition would appear—though no one took note of it—to prove the unconstitutionality of the war, therefore its illegality, not only under international law but American law as well. If the war were constitutional—if the Congress had officially declared war on North Vietnam—then Jane would undoubtedly be in federal prison today.

The public outcry against Jane was a sad commentary on the intelligence of the majority of the American people, especially those who imagined themselves vigorous defenders of America's honor and integrity. Their rage was laden with contradictions. No matter how ill people thought of Jane, and no matter how naïve she indeed might have been, she was not the issue. Nor was the issue other individuals who represented the antiwar outlook. Nor, for that case, were anti-Communism, or the fulfillment of treaty obligations, or any other geopolitical considerations the issues. The issue was the "patriots" themselves—the vast American public which permits violations and distortions of the law at the highest level, then defends the violators out of an equally distorted sense of patriotism. It is a patriotism born of ignorance and nourished on political pieties and myths like "Peace with Honor" and "Keep America Strong." It is a patriotism that thrives on the fervor of mindless absolutes, as mindless as the revolutionary absolutes it inevitably spawned and became threatened by. The outcry against Jane proved once again that self-righteousness is still mankind's primary operative trait and that the concern for plain, objective righteousness is still far beyond our reach, no matter how much lip service we pay to the concept.

Jane received the ultimate accolade when, early in August, she was taken to task by none other than Mrs. Richard Nixon in a news conference at the White House. "I think Jane Fonda should have been in Hanoi begging them to stop their aggression," the usually bland and silent First Lady said with uncharacteristic public indignation. "Then there wouldn't be any conflict for her to be protesting about."

Somehow, Pat Nixon's comment put the whole tempest over Jane's trip in perspective. The question of whether the United States' prosecution of the war was right or wrong—morally, legally or in any other way—however long it was debated, would never be resolved. Rather, we would go on meeting simplification with simplification. We would continue to leave the substantive question of whether Jane was right or wrong in going to Hanoi and doing what she did, regardless of her motives, unanswered in the storm of accusation and counteraccusation.

But the question can and should be answered. Since we are a nation devoted to simplistic pieties, it's answerable, very simply, this way: If the public believes, as it seems to, that there is a right and a wrong and no middle ground when it comes to the national honor, and if the public believes, as it claims to, in the efficacy of the law, then the public must believe that a person who engages in an activity that breaks the law is wrong. Conversely, the public must accept the fact that a person who engages in an activity that does not break the law is right. Therefore, if that which is not wrong is right, then Jane's trip to Hanoi was as right as any other lawful activity. Anyone who would dispute that would then admit that life and its judgments aren't so simple after all, thereby loosening the chain of absolutism we bind ourselves in. When we can all admit to that—radical and reactionary, "traitor" and "patriot" alike—we might then begin to solve some of the more troublesome, seemingly insoluble problems that beset us. Until then we will all remain, ideologically and emotionally, slaves of our contradictory altruistic and fascist natures.

28. Someday

I've grown to know Mr. Hayden and I admire him very much.

—HENRY FONDA

"FASCISTS!" came the cry. "Are we going to let these fascist pigs have four more years in Washington?"

"No!" came the collective response of hundreds of young demonstrators gathered in Miami for the 1972 Republican Convention. The date was August 21. Jane had traveled to Miami, upon her return from Hanoi, to join radical counterdelegates protesting the war and to speak at a rally honoring George Jackson, the black convict killed at San Quentin during the summer.

Her trip to Hanoi had put her in a more determinedly militant mood than ever. But with the Nixon administration promising that "peace was at hand" and the military draft on its last legs, the radical movement itself had shrunk to a shadow of its former size and passion. To be sure, there were loud and harried demonstrations at both 1972 Presidential conventions. But they lacked the numbers and spontaneous fire of four summers before. What was left at Miami was the hard-core, never-say-die revolutionary cadre of a radical movement on the verge of expiring for want of an issue.

Jane was not about to let it die, though. After tearfully describing on the *Dick Cavett Show* the horrors of what she had seen in North Vietnam as a result of American bombing, she announced that she and Tom Hayden were going to tour the country right up until election day to "counter the lies of the Nixon administration and tell the truth about what the United States is doing in Vietnam."

Calling themselves the Indochina Peace Campaign, she and Hayden set out in September on a nine-week, ninety-city tour of the country while Nixon and McGovern conducted their own more conventional campaigns. Holly Near, the young California singer and pacifist who had been a member of the FTA cast, accompanied them. "It was a grueling trip," she remembers, "but we found a lot more people eager to hear what we had to say than we thought. Jane and Tom would speak; I would sing a song or two; then we'd show slides Jane took in Vietnam and answer questions. It was all pretty low-key; there was very little harassment and no heckling to speak of. It sort of restored my faith in the American people, and let me tell you, we really hit some isolated places. Jane was fantastic; I've never seen anyone so dedicated. Even if people didn't agree with her politics, they listened to her with respect and consideration. It was an altogether exhilarating experience."

The tour received very little press coverage nationally, considering Jane's political notoriety. Steve Jaffe had resigned his brief association with Bob Zarem in Rogers, Cowan & Brenner to strike out on his own, with Jane and Donald Sutherland still his chief clients. Whether the minimal press coverage was due to his inexperience, as is suggested by Zarem, or to Jane's design, is uncertain, but it would certainly seem that Jane would want as much press attention as possible.

Zarem attributes the lack of coverage to Jaffe. He recalls that "at about that time, Jane asked me as a favor to set up a meeting between her and some journalists and writers around the New York area to discuss her Hanoi trip and the peace campaign. There was some thought that one or two of the writers might want to cover the campaign for one of the magazines like *Harper's* or *Atlantic Monthly*. I got ten or eleven well-known writers together at the Blackstone Hotel—David Halberstam, Pete Hamill, Larry King, people like that. Anyway, Halberstam helped me organize the meeting. Then Steve tried to move in, as usual, and only managed to succeed in getting everybody mad at him when he started laying out ground rules for the meeting. Halberstam, in particular, really laid into him. He just didn't seem to know how to handle press people, and I'm convinced a lot of Jane's problems with the press for the past three years stem from this."

But then, the lack of press coverage on the countercampaign may have stemmed from Tom Hayden. Hayden, a practiced organizer, believed in keeping a low profile. Certainly on the basis of his record in the movement he could not be accused of being a publicity hound. He was a crafty and uncompromising radical who believed that revolution was made in the streets, not in the newspapers.

In any event, the tour proceeded quietly and without any particular newsworthiness. Except for one thing: Jane fell in love with Tom Hayden. And became pregnant by him.

If Fred Gardner had been the Andreas Voutsinas of Jane's later career as a radical, Tom Hayden was the Roger Vadim. Where Gardner gave her the impetus and tutelage to become an activist in the face of her initial uncertainties, Hayden gave her the confidence, security and acceptance she had been seeking to confirm her radical legitimacy. Ever since she met him eight months before, she sensed he was everything a revolutionary man should be—brilliant, selfless and largely liberated from the male chauvinism that other radical leaders had not been able to overcome. Besides that, he was an established star, so to speak, of the movement—the perfect mentor to help her refine her radical ideology and commitment.

Once the elections were over—with McGovern wiped out by the Nixon landslide and the antiwar movement dissipating fast—Jane flew to Norway to begin filming the role of Nora in the screen version of *A Doll's House*, Henrik Ibsen's classic play about a turn-of-the-century woman who fights to liberate herself from the domination of men. Hayden joined her there. Joseph Losey, the director—a gloomy American expatriate who had left the United States for political reasons during the McCarthy era and settled in England—has few pleasant things to say about working with Jane on *A Doll's House*, despite the fact that they both had similar sentiments about the United States. "I have directed the most temperamental stars of all time," he says, "but I have never encountered the likes of Jane Fonda."

Losey had wanted Jane for the movie. He was sympathetic to the women's liberation movement and thought *A Doll's House* would be an ideal vehicle through which to make a filmic statement of his feelings. Knowing how Jane felt, he concluded that she was the perfect actress to play Nora. He quickly changed his mind, however. "After my experiences with her in Røros, Norway, where we shot the picture, I have decided she's confused; she wastes time and energy on too many causes."

According to Losey, Jane was arrogant, imperious, thoughtless and unprofessional. "She was spending most of her time working on her political speeches, instead of learning her lines, and making innumerable phone calls about her political activities." Losey finally had to threaten Jane that unless she agreed to work with the rest of the company, he would stop shooting. They finally reached an agreement, he says, but even then things didn't improve much. "Her problem, I think, is her family, her uptight background and her marriage to Roger Vadim."

Losey adds that in his view, Jane has encased herself to avoid being hurt by men. "And for a woman to encase herself like that is not an easy way to live. . . . She shrinks from any man touching her, with the exception of Tom Hayden. . . . The problem with Jane is that she has little sense of humor. Working with her is not an experience I would particularly like to go through again."

Filming of *A Doll's House* lasted through the middle of December, 1972. Although it was well known among her friends that Jane was by now completely and unabashedly bisexual in her private life, no one had really taken seriously her claims that she would never marry again, for she was never the model of consistency. Therefore, no one was surprised when she announced from Norway that she and Tom Hayden were in love and were planning to marry "as soon as I am able to."

Michael Maslansky, the film's publicist, said, "There is real feeling and affection between them. They are very much in love and spend as much time together as they can, most of it planning antiwar activities. But it's strange, I have never seen them hold hands or kiss. . . . They spend most of their time trying to convert people to their point of view."

Explained Hayden: "We have agreed not to talk in public about our engagement. What we want to talk about is the peace movement."

Jane agreed. "We are campaigning for peace together. That is what we are interested in. Our relationship is a very private thing, and we don't intend to let it interfere with our activities in the movement."

Tom Hayden admired North Vietnam immensely. He once suggested that "the future of the world comes from Hanoi." By this he appeared to mean that unlike other nations, North Vietnamese society was unique because it was indistinguishable from its government; that North Vietnam had found the perfect expression of Socialism. And that the nation had been forced into this happy accident by decades of war and resistance. To him, North Vietnam was the finest model in history of a revolutionary society. He theorized that perhaps it was not completely an accident, however, but a case of history reshaping itself through the unwitting collaboration of foreign nations seeking to impose their will on North Vietnam. Philosophically, it's a shaky but interesting theory. So thoroughly does Hayden believe in it, evidently, that he is adamant that North Vietnam survive in order to remain the example for future society as history reshapes other nations.

Jane, of course, repeatedly exclaiming her love for the Vietnamese people, was surely seduced by the theory. With Hayden's intellectual affection for Vietnam and her emotional love, they discovered a bond between themselves that was infinitely more magnetic than mere conventional attraction; it gave their relationship a dimension they believed few people ever achieved. They would soon attempt to turn their love into a revolutionary relationship modeled on the family relationships they both had observed in North Vietnam. Compared to the nobility of North Vietnamese nationalism, where everyone is an integral component of the society and therefore of the government, all other forms of nationalism paled into insignificance. Whether the theory is valid or not, Jane and Tom Hayden are apparently committed to it and have vowed to spend the rest of their lives fighting for the survival of North Vietnamese society.

When President Nixon instituted a massive saturation bombing of the Hanoi area late in December, allegedly to force the North Vietnamese government's hand in the peace negotiations, Jane and Hayden reacted with horror and despair. Jane, in Stockholm after finishing *A Doll's House*, took part in a demonstration against the bombing at the U.S. embassy and was promptly splattered with a can of red paint by an unsympathetic observer. The can of paint was symbolic of what might happen at any time, for Jane has lived since Hanoi with almost daily threats on her life.

From Stockholm, she and Hayden flew to Paris to consult with Xuan Thuy, chief North Vietnamese negotiator at the Paris peace talks. He told them, Jane said, that the renewed bombing "would be futile, that Hanoi would not be bombed into compromise of its fundamental national rights."

She and Hayden returned to the States just after her thirty-fifth birthday in late December. Shortly thereafter, Jane flew to the Dominican Republic, where she obtained an overnight divorce from Roger Vadim. On January 21, 1973, in her modest, sparsely furnished house off Laurel Canyon Boulevard on the San Fernando Valley side of the Hollywood Hills, she and Tom Hayden were married. The free-form ceremony was conducted by the Reverend Richard York, an Episcopal priest. The festivities, which included the singing of Vietnamese songs and the dancing of Irish jigs, was attended by more than 100 well-wishers, including a group of Vietnamese students, Jane's father and her brother.

Jane, wearing a pair of scuffed pants and a proletarian shirt over her protruding abdomen (by now she was four months pregnant), introduced everyone to everyone else and made a little speech. She described her travels throughout Vietnam and admiringly explained how the family ties there were the closest she had seen in any country of the world. She told how children were the most important people in Vietnam because they meant home and love and togetherness—qualities that had escaped her throughout her life but which she now felt she was on the verge of finding. She announced that she was expecting Hayden's child and that she wanted to marry Hayden so as to start a truly revolutionary family—one based on home, love and togetherness.

Two days later the Reverend Mr. York received a "Letter of Godly Admonition" from the Episcopal bishop of California suspending him from further priestly duties for marrying a divorced woman without permission from the bishop.

With her second marriage, Jane's life has settled into a style that will probably sustain her for some time to come. Before leaving for Norway to make *A Doll's House*, she had agreed to write her memoirs for a New York publishing house. But after her marriage to Hayden she dropped the project, at least temporarily, and rededicated herself to continuing her work in the revolutionary movement. Soon after their marriage she and Hayden moved to the shabby seaside community of Venice, just west of Los Angeles, and embarked on an even more austere life than before. On July 7, 1973, Jane gave birth to a son who she and Hayden named, for reasons that remain obscure, Troy O'Donovan Garity.

Jane launched a new wave of antagonism in March when she disputed stories of returning prisoners of war that told of systematic, widespread torture in the North Vietnamese prison camps. Her reaction was that of a mother whose child has been accused of wrongdoing—reflexive, angry-hysterical, blindly disbelieving. She in turn accused the returning prisoners of being nothing less than "liars and hypocrites," and said she could not conceive of the gentle North Vietnamese resorting to such barbaric practices. But as more and more returning prisoners confirmed the original stories, she modified her reaction. She admitted there "might have been some torture, but if so, they were isolated incidents, and what do you expect when these fliers are the very men who have been raining bombs on you for so many years?" When two of the prisoners she interviewed when she was in Hanoi returned and said that they had been tortured into talking to her, Jane was silent.

Her reactions shouldn't surprise anyone, nor should they infuriate. They were the reactions of someone consumed by a faith and loyalty